KEY OF SEA
MARY STELLA

"Ms. Stella has done it again! She has created another story, full of life like characters that jump off the page and pull the reader into her world. This time around she tackles some important issues but does so with style and a flair that is her own. The end result is a treasure for the romance reader."
— K. Ahlers, Independent Reviewer

Silver Imprint
ISBN 1-932815-08-2
$9.95 US

Jewel Imprint: Ruby
Medallion Press, Inc.
Florida, USA

DEDICATION:

To my dear friend Marilyn Staron who loves the Keys and
was here for the tarpon inspiration.

Published 2005 by Medallion Press, Inc.
225 Seabreeze Ave.
Palm Beach, FL 33480

The MEDALLION PRESS LOGO
is a registered tradmark of Medallion Press, Inc.

Printed in the United States of America

Library of Congress Cataloging-in-Publication Data

Stella, Mary.
 Key of sea / Mary Stella.
   p. cm.
 ISBN 1-932815-40-6
 1. First loves--Fiction. 2. Fishing guides--Fiction. 3. Divorced women--
Fiction. 4. Florida Keys (Fla.)--Fiction. I. Title.
 PS3619.T47646K49 2005
 813'.6--dc22

                              2005009436

ACKNOWLEDGEMENTS:

Neverending thanks to:

Beth Ciotta, Jen Wagner and Lyn Wagner for critiquing my manuscript, rooting me on to completion and patiently listening when I whine.

My entire family — brother, sister-in-law, nephews, aunts, uncles, cousins. Years ago, you dubbed me the family writer. I guess it stuck.

Deb, Jenn, Lo, Melissa, Mo, Nipps, Tiffany and the squirewriters loop. I look forward to the day when we celebrate your first sales. Dean and Julio, thanks for the extra male insight.

CHAPTER 1

DORA LEE MORRISON finally realized her marriage was over the day she experienced a true bonding moment with the dead tarpon mounted on her husband's wall. She and that fish had a lot in common. Both of them had been caught by J. Walter Morrison III, scion of the department store conglomerate created and expanded on by JWMs senior and junior. Both, for many years, had been proudly displayed — the trophy fish that hung as no-longer-living proof of his skill for reeling in the big ones. She, the trophy wife that confirmed his skill for reeling in the younger ones. Now after fourteen years, J. Walter was throwing her back.

The tarpon gaped as if astonished to be in this predicament. *Right back at you, fella,* Dora thought. She hadn't seen the divorce demand looming on the horizon. When J. Walter informed her that he wanted to "dissolve their union", she'd stared, every bit as pop-eyed and frozen while her heart shook and her brain struggled with the words. He'd droned on about their "satisfying partnership having run its course" and "the need to investigate new ventures". He graciously assured her that their pre-nuptial agreement would "tide her over" while she explored her options. Then he packed his overnight case and left their Treasure Coast mansion for a four-day fishing trip in the islands. Like the acquiescent wife he expected, she'd quietly followed him to the door and watched him drive away in his late-model black Porsche. Then, pure terror punched her in the chest and she'd sunk, gasping, to the floor.

A few months later she still wrestled with the new reality. She struggled to sit upright in a deep arm chair in his British Indies-colonial inspired-office. Leather-bound first edition Hemingway novels sat on the shelves of his credenza. More trophies displayed to impress, she realized, since J. Walter would never dream of taking a reading break in the middle of a work day. Where had he put the picture of the two of them, the one that used to sit on his desk positioned so that guests would naturally see it when they first sat down?

Quality leather and expensive cologne scented the air. Hopefully they covered the rank odor of fear surely seeping like garlic from her pores. Her lawyer argued that after more than a dozen years of devoted marriage, she was entitled to a larger amount than the money agreed upon before they'd wed. She forced herself to breathe evenly when J. Walter's lawyer firmly countered that the financial settlement was more than generous. After all, she'd moved into homes he already owned and, in terms of holdings or income, she'd brought nothing substantial to the marriage.

He couldn't have portrayed her as more of a gold digger

if he'd handed her a miner's hard hat and pick axe.

"Nothing? I brought myself." Dora squashed a shriek. "I'm a good wife, Walter. A helpmate, you said. Who's at home every night to hear about your day?" She thought back on years of entertaining business associates and friends. "Think of the charity functions I worked on because you said it was important for your wife to be involved. How many events did we attend so that Morrison's Stores were properly represented?" How many cool looks, barely-polite smiles and snide whispers had she endured that never let her forget she'd begun her association with him as a lingerie model for his family's stores?

"Work days and business deals that you barely understood. How many of those charity meetings and events have you attended since we separated?" J. Walter cut her off with a condescending smile. "Calm yourself, Dora. There's no need to make this transaction ugly."

"Transaction? This is our marriage. We aren't talking about a business deal!"

"Aren't we?"

His coldness froze the air in her lungs. What happened to the witty, sexy charmer who'd so dazzled her when they first met at a Morrison's-hosted fashion show? The man who'd swept her off her ostrich-plume mules almost from the minute he'd invited her to join him for champagne after the fashion show, smiling into her eyes and ignoring the fact that she was wearing scraps of satin and lace under a transparent silk baby-doll nighty.

Now, the expression in his eyes scorned her as if she wore bargain-basement rags instead of a custom-tailored, cool linen suit.

"Dora, you had nothing when we met. You got what you wanted when we first married and are now leaving with far more than even you could have dreamed. Be a good girl. Don't be greedy."

Be a good girl. How many times had she heard that over the years? *Dora, you won't have time to volunteer for the animal shelter. Be a good girl. You need to join the hospital ball fundraising committee.* He made it sound so essential that, of course, she understood. *You want your grandfather to stay with us over Christmas? Dora, the old man would be no more comfortable here than I'd be staying at his little marina. You know my family expects us in Aspen. Be a good girl and visit him another time.* It was important to Walter that she got along with his family. She'd choked down the slight to her beloved Grampa Willie and had gone to see him in the Keys the week before the holiday instead.

Dora, I'm almost 50, he'd said a few years into their marriage. *My sons are grown men. I don't want any more children. Be a good girl and don't make this an issue.*

That edict hurt worst of all, but again she'd agreed. The day she became Mrs. J. Walter Morrison III, she'd left behind Dora Lee Hanson of the Florida Keys. In the process she'd worked her butt off to be the woman he wanted, the wife he expected, and she'd succeeded from the top of her trendy hairstyle to the tip of her uncomfortable but gorgeous Jimmy

Choo slings. Memories bounced around in her brain so fast, she couldn't concentrate. Apparently taking her silence for agreement, Walter nodded his approval.

"Sign the papers, Dora. I'll write you the first check."

He made it sound like severance pay for an employee he'd fired. Or worse. If he thought their marriage all came down to money, then . . .

"I wasn't a gold digger. I was in love with you."

All four of the room's other occupants stared. Walter arched a single brow, his fallback expression when anyone dared to disagree with him. His attorney looked smug. Her lawyer's face twitched with the effort to stay neutral. Only the tarpon appeared sympathetic. At that moment, she understood fighting the divorce was useless. Although they'd lived separately for months, in her heart of hearts she'd still cared for him and nurtured the hope that they'd work things out. Now she knew the truth. Her marriage couldn't be saved.

She'd never known that it was possible for love to die in an instant, but Walter had killed it as surely as he'd bludgeoned the tarpon to death. Whatever emotion or affection might have lingered evaporated in the rising heat of anger. There in the tasteful, "old money" office, something snapped. He wanted out of this marriage? He'd get his wish, but she wouldn't completely surrender her pride.

She narrowed her eyes and leaned forward, gripping the edge of the desk to keep her hands from trembling. "Fine. If this is a business deal, let's negotiate. You can have the divorce, but these are my terms. Increase the amount of the pre-nup by fifty percent."

He opened his mouth to protest and she ran right over him, adrenaline propelling her like a racer to the finish line. "You can afford that amount if you divorce twenty wives, Walter, and that's my fee for making this convenient."

"I'm prepared to be generous, but only to a point. We'll adjust it, say, ten percent."

"You pay more to your tailor. Forty percent."

Walter's lawyer broke in. "Mrs. Morrison, you signed the original agreement in good faith. He doesn't have to raise it at all."

Obviously feeling in control and willing to be magnanimous, Walter beamed. "I'll go as high as an additional fifteen percent."

Magnanimous her ass. She was fighting for her life. "You'll go to thirty percent. If you don't agree, I'll drag this out as long as possible and then . . ." She aimed and fired a shot in the dark. ". . . you'll have to wait that much longer to go public with your new girlfriend."

That at least wiped the smile from his face. He abruptly sat back and nodded at his attorney. *Score!* Dora snorted. "Does this one at least break thirty? Does she know you carry an AARP card?" She shook her head, disgusted at both of them, having long ago realized that her comparatively youthful twenty-five had been a big part of the attraction when he'd culled her out of the crowd.

"Next, I keep the jewelry you bought me." At the moment, she loathed the idea of wearing any of it, but gemstones could always be sold.

"And my Mercedes."

Judging by the furious look in his crows-feet framed, Lasik-corrected eyes, she'd reached his limit. "Agreed, but that's as far as I'll go, Dora. It's more than enough and much more than you deserve."

Bullshit. Her entire settlement didn't match what he paid in clubhouse fees every year. He was getting off light and both of them knew it. A dull buzz filled her head and drowned out the fear. She needed something else. A symbol. Not money. He could afford that without breaking a sweat. No, she needed something he prized. Something he would really hate to lose.

Got it! Coolly, she sat back in her chair and smugly smiled. "There's one more thing and this is absolutely non-negotiable." She pointed at the wall behind his head at her new-found comrade.

"I'm taking your fish."

The purple splotches that quickly mottled his tanned skin told her she'd chosen well. He tried to refuse, but she waved him off and glared at her silent attorney.

"Earn the fee my soon-to-be-ex-husband has to pay you. You've all heard my terms. Write it up, or whatever you law-yers do, and we'll settle."

As soon as the man opened his mouth, Walter and the other attorney jumped in. They could fight about it for the next two billable hours if they chose. She was leaving as soon as she claimed her prize. The fish was mounted on a polished wood board that was bolted into the wall. Her Prada bag didn't hold any power tools, but damned if she'd let that interfere. She picked up Walter's silver letter opener and attacked the first bolt.

"Stop that immediately."

She ignored him.

"Dora!"

"I'm busy, Walter." The letter opener slid out of the bolt and ripped a four inch gash in the expensive wall paper. "Whoops. That's what you get for distracting me."

"Damn you, I said stop. If you don't, I'll call Security."

"Go ahead. I'm sure the society editors will love the story of J. Walter Morrison throwing out his low-rent wife over a plastic-coated dead fish."

"You wouldn't dare make fools out of the two of us."

Fourteen years of complacency and acquiescence dissolved like sugar in the rain. She whipped around, waving the letter opener. "I couldn't possibly make a bigger fool out of myself than you have already, but I'll be more than happy to even the score. Face it. You now have much, much, MUCH more to lose than I ever will."

Returning to the fish, she again attacked the bolt. "Go ahead and call Security, but you'd be better off contacting Building Maintenance. Tell them to hurry up here with a real screwdriver. The sooner they help me get *my* tarpon off the wall, the sooner I'll get out of your life."

🐾 🐾 🐾

MAYBE IT WAS the surprising resolve in her voice or her novel don't-mess-with-me attitude. It could have been whatever his attorney whispered to him or, more likely, the way she brandished the letter opener like a dagger. Whatever the case, he finally caved and in minutes two uniformed maintenance men arrived to liberate the tarpon and tote it out of his office down to her car.

Mercedes sedans were not designed to carry one hundred-and-twenty pound fish as passengers. The men almost gleefully set about finding some sturdy cord to secure her booty to the roof. After tipping them generously, she drove out of the store's parking garage. With a two-fingered wave, she saluted the attendant as if there were nothing the least bit unusual about her roof ornament.

Two blocks away, the fear returned in a swelling, choking wave, forcing air from her lungs. Nausea roiled in her stomach. A cold sweat broke out on her skin and the shakes set in. She pulled over into the first open parking space, turned off the car and rested her head on the steering wheel.

Divorced? *Oh my God!* She'd promised to vacate the house within a week. In seven days she'd not only be husbandless, but also homeless. Her settlement, while it would support her for awhile, wouldn't fund a home in this exclusive area. Not when she now also had to pay for basic necessities and all the extras. She might have been living the good life for the last dozen plus years, but she'd never forgotten the early days when every dollar was allotted even before it was earned. Her hands trembled, drawing her attention to her long elegant fingers enhanced by a perfect French manicure. How quickly priorities changed. Forget weekly pampering. She needed a place to live.

She needed a job, but she hadn't worked in years and demand was non-existent for thirty-nine year old former underwear mannequins.

What in the world was she going to do now that she was no longer the glossy, polished wife of J. Walter Morrison III? One swipe of her signature on a legal decree and it was almost like the last fourteen years had never existed. All of a sudden she was back to being that nobody Dora Lee Hanson from Nowhereville in the Florida Keys.

She fumbled for her cell phone and pressed the buttons for her grandfather's marina. Years ago, she couldn't wait to leave her hometown behind. Right now, at this quaking, nauseating, mind-numbing moment of truth, home was the only place she could think of to go.

🐾 🐾 🐾

THE DAY WAS winding down to dusk when she finally pulled into the marina complex parking lot, exhausted. After several days of packing, hauling what she didn't immediately need to storage, and the long drive down, her body was so stiff that when she got out of her car, her bones crunched like the pea rock underneath her tires.

Hanson's Marina and Mall read the entrance sign. The

mall part was optimistic at best. This small row of weather-beaten stores was as far away from being a mall as it was from being a space colony on Mars, but Gramps had his own brand of humor.

"Gotta make the tourists feel at home, Dora Lee," he'd told her with a wink. "I reckon any place that holds more than one shop counts as a mall in the Keys."

Considering the only department store within fifty miles was a Big K, he had a point.

She'd hoped to get here earlier, but a boat-hauler with a flat had backed up the Eighteen Mile Stretch between Florida City and Key Largo and put her behind schedule. Now the shop owners were no longer busy with customers. Instead, some of them were already seated in a cluster of resin chairs and ramshackle rockers on the creaky porch. For as long as she could remember they'd gathered like this, with their pop-top beers or iced teas, to watch the sunset and swap stories about the day. The nightly ritual continued, even though faces had changed over the years. Right now every one of them watched her instead.

She tugged at the knotted waist of her linen blouse and smoothed the front of her walking shorts. Why were they staring? She glanced back at her Mercedes. For its own protection, she'd wrapped and tied a plastic tarp around her prize, but the ends had flapped free on the drive. Even in the Keys, the bundle made a pretty strange sight. That must be it. She smiled and strode forward, only to wobble in her high-heeled sandals. Damn! She'd forgotten that heels and pea rock went together like sand and silk. She should have worn flats instead. Gamely, she slowed her steps to avoid tripping and smiled again.

"Good evening, everyone. Nice night for sunset. Is Willie here?"

"Who wants ta know?" barked a bald man with a grizzled beard and leather vest open across his barrel chest.

He was new. Judging from the fire-breathing dragon running the length of his arm and the spider web pattern across his skull, he must be Leo of Leo's Tattoo and Piercing Palace. That store had been a boat canvas shop during her last visit.

"Willie ain't come up front yet," said the skinny woman beside him. Good Lord, she sported at least a dozen earrings in each ear and a stud in her nose for good measure. A miniature barbell glinted in her tongue when she asked, "Kin we help ya?" Wariness shaded the words and her eyes, with their matching brow rings, were narrowed.

The munchkins hadn't acted this suspicious when Dorothy's house crash-landed at the entrance ramp of the yellow brick road.

Dora stopped short of the steps, suddenly cautious about entering their territory. "I came to see Willie. I'm . . ."

A door creaked open. "Dora Lee? That you?"

Finally, someone she recognized. Mack Ricks had owned the bait and tackle shop since Jimmy Carter was in the White House — and had the snapshot of himself with the President after a fishing trip to prove it. He dispensed advice as easily as he did live shrimp and ballyhoo. If fish were biting within twenty nautical miles on either side of the island, he'd know where and could tell you what bait you needed to catch them.

He was a little older now, his wiry terrier hair a little grayer, but the gap-toothed grin was genuine. He was also her grandfather's oldest friend which made it easier to smile in return. "Yes, Mack. It's me." On steadier footing, she hurried up the steps and gave him a quick hug. "I've come for a visit with Gramps." A breather and a chance to regroup was more like it, but she kept that news to herself.

"He'll be glad to see you. Been awhile," he scolded lightly.

"Yes. I know." She resisted brushing her shoe in the gravel like a chastised teen. Nobody scuffed two-hundred dollar shoes.

Tattoo-man knocked back a swig of beer, and then gestured at her with the can. "This the fancy-pants grand-daughter he always talks about? Didn't think she came 'round here much."

"Hush, Leo," admonished his companion.

He swigged again and belched in reply.

Mack swung around and placed a broad hand on Dora's back. "Leo and Tilda biked down to the Keys and opened up the tattoo place mid-summer last year."

She nodded and smiled. "Nice to meet you."

Before she could ask again about her grandfather, a newcomer bustled out the door of another unfamiliar store. Island Aromatics Emporium read the lettering on the broad pane window. Candles, bottles, and jars were displayed on draped scarves in all the vibrant colors of a tropical sunset.

"Rosa, say hello to Willie's granddaughter. Dora Lee, Rosa Sanchez."

The woman was maybe five-feet-tall with long chestnut hair, liberally streaked with gray, all gathered in a long braid down her back. A loose lavender gauze top layered over a purple and aqua flowered broomstick skirt that hung down almost to her sandaled feet. When she came forward to shake hands, the delicate fragrance of jasmine scented the air.

Her hand and her face were surprisingly smooth given her obvious age. "*Hola*." Nut-brown eyes appraised. "You know, I make a botanical cream that will take care of that crease in your forehead. *Sí*. It is better than Botox for smoothing worry lines."

A forehead crease and worry lines? Dora's hand shot up to her face. No way could the stress of the last week have already wiped out years of skin-pampering facials and expensive lotions. Since when had insults replaced salesmanship? "Thank you, but I have my usual skin care regimen with me."

The woman's eyes cooled and the porch crowd *harrumphed*. Okay, maybe that had been a little harsh. Dora winced and softened her words. "But any cream that can do what you say is certainly worth trying."

Satisfied, Rosa nodded like a doctor confirming a diagnosis. "Woman your age better see to her skin properly. I'll fetch a sample of my Key lime exfoliator, too. My products are all natural. Worked wonders for Tilda here." She slapped the pierced lady affectionately on the shoulder in passing. "When she first came here, her face was rough as the bark on a palm tree. Now look." With that she re-entered her store.

Dora glanced around. "Mack, do Bitsy and Vince still run the Marina Mart?"

"Yes, ma'am. But they've got some good help, so they're up in Ocala for a week. Little Ginny had another baby girl. So, they went on up to help out and spoil the rest of the kids."

"That's sweet." If she remembered right, their daughter Ginny had been several years behind her in school.

The sun sank lower in the sky and with it, her energy level. Her whole body wanted to sag inside her clothes. "You know, I think I'll go find Gramps."

"He oughta be around about now." Mack cocked his head and listened. "In fact . . ."

A cheerful, slightly off-key whistling reached them right before her grandfather came around the corner, carrying a fishing pole like Andy Griffith strolling through Mayberry.

When he caught sight of her, the whistling stopped, re-placed by a happy shout. "There's my baby girl!"

Seeing that grin split his face lifted her spirits like nothing else could. As if she really was still a girl, she ran down the steps. His arms wrapped around her and squeezed. Nobody on earth hugged like her grandfather. Held snugly to his chest, she breathed in the smell of clean soap, mingled with a trace of machine oil and a splash of Old Spice.

"Hi, Gramps." For the first time in days, the cold dread clogging her lungs eased. "You look great!"

He did, from his battered dock shoes and work shorts up to the brown, craggy face and full head of silver hair. Eyes the deep yellow-gold of polished amber crinkled at the corners as he stepped back and studied her in return. "As beautiful as the day you were born. But. . ." He stroked his thumb down the side of her mouth and lifted her chin. "You look tired, darlin'. Rough drive?"

She glanced away and nodded. "Rough couple of days."

"You didn't say much, but I could tell something was troubling you when you called to ask if you could visit." Keeping an arm around her shoulders, he turned her toward the porch. "Like you had to ask." He shook his head, chiding her softly. "Tell your grandpa what's wrong."

If she started talking now, she'd blubber like a baby in a minute flat. Right now, all she wanted was to hide inside his hug and forget everything else.

She sighed, the sound like air escaping from a balloon. "I will, Gramps, but tomorrow, okay? Let's just enjoy the sunset."

"Okay, baby girl. You've met everybody, right?"

At her nod, he sat them both down on the top step, leaned against a column, and pulled her against his shoulder. "We'll watch the show, and then get your things indoors. I opened up the cottage for you. After that, Ruby's coming over for dinner. Bet it's been awhile since you had stone crabs fresh from the ocean."

They were one of her favorites, but her appetite had disappeared along with her wedding ring. Still, she wouldn't disappoint him. "More like forever. I never order them in restaurants."

"Not the same as your own catch." He chuckled. "As long as the season's still on, I'll take you out pulling traps one day and . . ." He straightened and peered at her car. "Dora Lee, is that a fish tied on your roof?"

If her laugh was a little weak, nobody commented. "All part of the story."

"This'll be something to hear." He rubbed her back and whispered so nobody else would hear. "Whatever the problem is, we'll take care of it. Don't you worry."

She nodded automatically, but fear snuck in another jab to her stomach. This wasn't something anybody could easily fix. In any event, it could wait another day.

Wide strokes of rose, peach and mauve painted the sky and shimmered on the water. The sun turned a glowing gold. A soft breeze kissed her face and the quiet calmed her skipping nerves. With a last flaming glow, almost as if it was taking a bow, the sun slipped below the horizon. The small audience applauded and Dora clapped along with them, just as she had hundreds, no maybe thousands, of nights before.

"*Eso luse tan bonito,*" Rosa said.

"Pretty enough," was Leo's comment. His chair groaned as he boosted upright and pitched the empty beer can into a recycling bin. He reached for his wife's hand when she rose. "Come on, woman."

"See y'all tomorrow," she said as they left, heading for the full chrome Harley parked on the side of the building.

"I'll drop you off home, Rosa, and save you the bike

ride," Mack said. He rolled her bicycle toward a battered, but still-sturdy pickup, hoisting it easily into the truck bed.

They were pulling out onto the Overseas Highway when a truck towing a flats boat turned in. The driver waved out his window and Mack honked the horn in answer.

"This guy must not know everyone's already closed down for the night, Gramps."

"Oh, he knows all right. He's just getting home a little later than usual." Willie stood, pulling her up with him. "Get ready to say hello to another old friend of yours, darlin'."

"A friend of mine?" Mindful of the newly discovered forehead crease, Dora forced away a frown.

The truck stopped in front of the porch. As the occupant got out on the far side, she glimpsed a baseball cap and mile-wide shoulders but the vehicle's roof obscured the man's face. He rounded the hood and she caught her breath.

"Bobby Daulton? Is that you?"

It sure was, in a living, breathing, grown-up version. Deep-water tanned skin stretched over high cheekbones. Eyes she knew were sea-green gleamed in the remaining light. Lines fanned at their corners, accenting their shape. Straight nose, full lips bracketed by slashing dimples. A square jaw with a small cleft.

Good Lord. He'd always been a cute kid. Now hand-some didn't even come close to an adequate description.

It was more correct to say that Bobby was the brother of her oldest, dearest friend. Dora smiled thinking of Jo Jo. As children and teens, they'd spent more time with each other than with anyone else. Years ago, Bobby had teased, bothered and annoyed them, as only younger brothers could. Then, just before she'd left town, he'd shifted from boy to man, at least in his mind. He'd taken to giving her long looks when she came over and even flirted a time or two. At twenty-five years old, she'd been flattered by his puppy crush, but he was Jo Jo's kid brother. Was he even eighteen the last time they'd seen each other? Even though he had the makings of a world-class charmer, she'd nipped his little experiments in the bud.

The warm memory of an old friendship brought a smile to her face and propelled her off the porch toward him for a hug. "Bobby, what a nice surprise! Proverbial long time no see."

Before she reached him, he stepped back, leaned against his truck and crossed forearms roped with muscle across his broad chest. Beneath his cap's brim, he regarded her steadily. A jerk of his chin acknowledged her greeting.

"Dora Lee."

His voice was deeper than she remembered, and colder than ice in a bait box. For some reason he was anything but glad to see her, and wasn't that awkward as hell? Stung, she dropped her arms to her sides and struggled not to show her disappointment. "So, um, how've you been?"

"Well enough."

Who are you? she wanted to ask. *What have you done with friendly, enthusiastic, talk-a-mile-a-minute Bobby?*

Maybe a crowbar would pry more words out of him. She sure wasn't having any luck.

Thankfully, her grandfather joined them. His warm

hand on her back was as comforting as a blanket in winter.

"Evening, Bob," he said. "Good day?"

Shrug. "First-timers."

Gramps laughed. "More cash than experience, huh?"

She'd forgotten her grandfather's knack for saying a lot with very few words. Maybe it was some kind of guy-code because Bobby didn't waste one more syllable than necessary either.

"Yeah, but they boated some."

"Taking 'em out again tomorrow?"

He shook his head and rolled his eyes. "They'd rather play golf. Probably spend the whole day talkin' about their big day on the water."

Wow. Two whole sentences. Encouraged, she jumped into the conversation. "I can't wait to see Jo Jo. How is she?"

"Good."

Bam! Mr. Freeze returned. Darned if she knew why, and right then she was too tired to care. She gave him an overly bright smile. "Please tell her I was asking for her and I'll call soon."

"Yeah, she'll be glad to hear you'll find time to see her while you're slumming."

CHAPTER 2

LUCKY FOR HIM that Willie kept an arm tight around his granddaughter and turned her away quick. Even in the failing light, he'd seen her golden eyes fire up at the slumming crack, ready to fry him on the spot.

The woman had always been easy to rile, but that'd been a low thing to slam her with. Dora Lee might hate most of her conch roots, but she loved his sister. Even though she didn't come around often, he knew that they kept in touch and Jo Jo had visited Dora Lee and that rich-ass husband of hers regular enough over the years. Thinking of his sister, he winced. If that comment got back to her, she'd blast him with both barrels.

He lifted off his cap and swiped an arm across his forehead. Hell, if he were smart, he'd apologize, but then he'd have to go and see her. That was the whole damn problem. When he'd pulled in to the lot tonight, the last person he'd expected to find was the star of all his teenage wet dreams.

Hadn't even recognized her at first; seen only a looker with great breasts and a mass of brown hair piled on top of her head. He'd wondered who in the hell would look so comfortable leaning on Willie. When he'd come around the car and she jumped up off the steps, surprise had sucked the air right out of his lungs.

Mile long legs stretched from her shorts to those stupid, sexy little sandals. She'd called his name in her husky voice and he'd known her right away. The blood buzzed in his brain as the past delivered a roundhouse punch. He could barely breathe, let alone talk so he'd covered it under a cold mask and a nasty crack.

He slammed back into his truck and drove around to the slips where he docked his cruiser. Thankfully, the boat slips were on the opposite side of the compound, away from the little group of guest cottages where he guessed she'd be staying. On her infrequent visits, she'd never stuck around long, according to his sister. He'd never had to plan to avoid her over the years, but a few months ago, he'd moved his boat to Willie's marina.

"Might not have been the smartest move."

Jesus. Five minutes of Dora Lee and he was talking to himself. Better to remember that he wasn't still a teen with hyperactive glands. With luck and timing, he'd steer clear of her for the rest of her little jaunt to the old stomping grounds.

The dock creaked under his feet as he walked to his boat. Automatically, he checked the lines before stepping aboard. Ducking his head, he walked through the door into the main salon of the cruiser and pitched his keys onto the counter of the lower helm station. A couple quick steps down to the galley and he nabbed a beer from the small fridge. Twisting off the cap, he gulped down half.

Damn, she'd looked good. Most women didn't get more beautiful when they got older. Leave it to Dora Lee to drop-kick that theory on its ass. No wonder he'd been caught off guard. How was a man supposed to think straight when, without warning, he came face to face with the only woman to break his heart?

"I CAN'T BELIEVE Jo Jo's brother grew up to be a jerk." Dora seethed as she yanked one of her suitcases along the path to the cottages. Luggage wheels didn't roll smoothly over pea rock.

"Bobby's a good man, darlin'. Don't judge him too badly from one meeting." Willie ambled beside her as if he weren't carrying an overstuffed garment bag in one hand and also had a tote slung over his shoulder.

"Accusing me of slumming wasn't harsh?"

"It's just a word. Maybe a poor choice of one, but he didn't mean anything by it." He stopped before a little cottage and pulled a key out of his pocket. "Dora Lee, I didn't get a chance to repaint the place like I'd hoped."

"Don't worry about it, Gramps, since apparently I'm only *slumming*," she huffed.

"Don't get in a sulk on me, young lady."

A quick swat on the behind when she passed him and

entered the cottage took her back. No matter what youthful trauma she'd experienced, she could cry on his shoulder until she exhausted her tears and talk his ears off about her problems, but he never could tolerate whining or pouting.

Unlike most of the rest of her life, that hadn't changed. Like she had as a teen, she wrinkled her nose at him over her shoulder. "Yes, sir!"

He flicked a switch and soft light filled the sitting area. The furniture was more worn than she remembered; the rag rugs scattered on wide-plank floors more faded. Washed-out Keys seascapes behind cloudy glass hung on butter cream walls. Graying lace sheers decorated the windows. In the past, the little cottage had always looked cozy, homey, but time had marched on here, too, leaving it shabby without the chic.

The place was clean at least, and dust-free. And there, on the breakfast counter that separated the space from the tiny kitchenette sat a chubby blue glass vase filled with a cluster of bright native flowers.

"Aww, Gramps. They're beautiful." She stuck her nose in the blooms and sniffed.

"Ruby picked them right out of her yard."

A note propped against the vase read *Welcome Home* in big bold print. It had been so long since anyone had welcomed her anywhere, the simple greeting brought tears to her eyes. Whirling, she threw her arms around Willie's waist and hugged him tight. "Thank you," she snuffled against his chest.

His big hand settled on the back of her head, smoothing her hair as if she were still a teenager and not a grown woman.

"You're welcome, darlin'." He hugged her in return, and then stood her back from him a bit. "Dora Lee, whatever's troublin' you, it'll be easier if you talk about it."

"I know. It's just. . ." She looked away. How could she tell him that her dreams had crashed like burned-out stars? Years ago, she'd left the Keys with her head high and her eyes locked on the future. She hadn't known exactly where the road would lead back then, but she knew it was brighter and bigger than the world she left behind. Stubbornly determined, Dora Lee Hanson had kicked the coral dust off her sandals and high-stepped her way over the rainbow.

Now she was back and, instead of a nice temporary visit, she felt like she'd started a prison sentence. The rest of her life with no parole. She looked down at the broad stripes of her blouse. DK does prison wear.

She glanced at the note again. *Welcome Home.*

"Dora Lee?" Eyes filled with concern, Gramps waited for her to finish her explanation.

Buck up, she told herself. Misery might love her company, but her grandfather loved it more. He was always thrilled to see her and damned if she'd let her mood spoil the moment for him. Seeing as how she had no immediate plans for her future, she'd have plenty of time later to be miserable. For now, she'd give him an answer that would probably anger him more, but worry him less.

"Walter's divorcing me." She slumped against the counter and waited.

Not for long. Gramps smacked his thigh. "Rat bastard."

Bet nobody had called her husband that name before and from the look on Gramps' face, he was just getting started. "That stuck-up sonova . . ." He caught himself. "Why didn't you tell me your marriage was breaking up?"

"I didn't know." It pained her to admit she'd been totally duped. "I thought that things were fine."

"So what happened?"

"I'm not sure if it was what, who or a combination of both."

"He cheated on you? That ass . . . ah, damnit, darlin', I'm sorry." He caught her up in a rib-squeezing hug. "No wonder you're wiped out. But don't you worry. You're home now and we'll get you back on your feet in no time."

If only it were that easy. "Right now, I can't think past my bed in the other room. Gramps, I know you promised stone crabs, but I'm not really hungry. Would you mind very much if I skipped dinner?"

"You bet I would. Going without food will only make you feel worse and I sure as hell ain't leavin' you here when you're this blue." He grabbed her bags and took them into the bedroom while she tagged behind.

Like the living area, this room hadn't changed, except for also getting older and more dingy. The same painted iron bed was covered with a simple white quilt and crocheted pillows made for her by her grandmother. A wicker rocker, its paint chipped and cushions worn, sat in the corner. A yard of lace, yellowed with age, draped across the distressed top of the old wooden dresser. Her parents, so young when they'd died in a car accident, Gramps and Nana smiled at her from photographs in simple metal frames.

A set of figurines — the main characters from her favorite childhood movie, *The Wizard of Oz*, sat on a porcelain rendition of the yellow brick road. Her fingers traced the little statues of Dorothy, Toto and their new friends Scarecrow, Tin Man, and the Cowardly Lion. A collector's edition, her grandparents had purchased them when she was a young teen and she'd treasured them ever since.

Glancing at Gramps, she smiled. "Remember these?"

"'Course I do. Birthday and Christmas presents over two years. Lord, how your pretty little face lit up when you opened those boxes. Sort of like you're doing now." He squeezed her shoulder. "C'mon, baby girl. A good meal'll do you a world of good. Besides, Ruby's looking forward to seeing you."

She tried once more to beg off. "I'm really not up for company."

Gramps would have none of it. "Ruby ain't company. She's family and you know she's got a way of looking at things that makes 'em all seem better than you expected."

That was the truth in spades.

"Come on with you now." He took her arm.

It would take more energy to argue than to go along. She stifled another sigh and then picked up her handbag and walked toward the door. "Gramps, I don't know where to start."

"I do. I want to hear about that new roof ornament." He pulled the door shut behind them. "It's his, ain't it?"

In spite of her tiredness, she grinned. "Not anymore."

🦀 🦀 🦀

"YOU TOOK IT right off the wall of his office? With him sitting there?" Ruby Maguire rocked back in her chair, laughing. "What a hoot!"

She plopped another scoop of cole slaw on Dora's plate without asking. "I woulda paid good money to see that, girl! He musta swallowed his tongue."

Dora snorted. "He was too busy threatening me with Security." She cracked open a stone crab claw and sucked out the meat.

"Sounds like you got him around to your way of thinkin' right quick."

"He didn't have a choice."

"There's always a choice, darlin'."

"Not when he wanted me gone as quickly as possible." He hadn't left her any options either, not even a ghost of a chance at reconciliation. Unexpectedly, she'd become as welcome in J. Walter's life as a tax audit.

Her grandfather snorted. "A man's got no business chasing skirt when he's got himself as fine a wife as you. Especially at his age."

"Willie, age never figures into it when a man's glands take hold."

"You got a point there, Ruby."

"I usually do."

Dora continued to eat while listening to their banter. They'd been easy with each other, just like this, for as long as she could remember. When she was a kid, both her grandmother and Ruby's husband Gus had still been living and the four of them had been the closest of friends. Ruby and Gus had helped both her and her grandfather cope when her grandma died. Eight or so years ago when Gus succumbed to cancer, Willie had returned the support. A few years later, he and Ruby had slid from friendship into something more.

Something she didn't need to know the details about. She heard enough kidding and joking between the two of them to know that passion didn't die when the Social Security benefits kicked in.

Even without being married, they were a solid couple. As solid as she'd envisioned she and Walter would be when they, too, were older.

"So, Dora Lee, what are you going to do now?"

Good question. If she ever figured it out, she'd be glad to tell him. Right now, she didn't have a clue. She was too old to return to lingerie modeling. Too unqualified to do much of anything else.

Stuck for an answer, but not wanting to sound as useless as she felt, she forked in some cole slaw. She chewed thoughtfully and swallowed. "Guess I'll take it easy for a little while. Regroup."

"Keys are the right place to do that, for sure. I know your gramps here'll be glad to have you around for longer than a weekend. We all will."

"Got that right." Gramps grabbed a roll from the basket and offered her the rest.

White flour products hadn't passed her lips in at least five years, not since the day J. Walter said her slacks were snug. Over the years she'd slid up the scale to a size twelve, but with her height and excellent tailoring, she hadn't thought she looked that bad. But one comment from Walter and she'd seen a porker in her mirror and begun dieting like a woman possessed.

She put up her hand to refuse the basket, but the warm, yeasty aroma triggered a full-fledged carb craving. Snatching a roll, she slathered it with butter. It was already established that her modeling career was over. Nobody cared if she grew as big as Fat Albert, the weather-slash-spy blimp that floated in the sky above the Lower Keys and kept tabs on Cuba.

"Eventually, I need to get a job."

"It's good to keep occupied. I know how all fire busy you were with all your fancy galas and those other . . . well, whatever it was that took up all your time," Gramps continued. "There's plenty you can do around here to keep from getting bored." He nodded. "Heck, Jo Jo's got a full plate running things at the theater. She'd be tickled to have your help."

"You liked playing with my dolphins when you were a kid," Ruby added. "Now that Jack's busy getting his Internet security-whatever business going and showing his wife how much he loves being married to her, he's got less time to help around Dolphin Land." Her blue eyes glowed with pride. "Victoria and I have plenty to do, what with her research and our presentations. Come on over whenever you want and see what we've done with the place."

Like there was anything that she, with her high school diploma, could contribute to the work of a world-famous Ph.D. Dora shoved the roll in her mouth and chewed slowly while they continued their helpful suggestions. Bitsy and Vince always needed reliable staff for the deli. She'd never run a meat slicer and would probably lose a finger in the olive loaf. Rosa had been thinking of supplying her products to local gift shops. Too bad Dora only knew about using lotions and skin creams and nothing about making or marketing them.

At least Gramps stopped short of suggesting she lend a hand with boat repair or at the fueling docks. With her luck, she'd upset an oil tank or break a gas pump and cause an environmental disaster. Her depression increased with every job possibility that she wasn't qualified to do until finally she was shoveling food into her mouth to quell the rising tide of panic. Even Leo the tattoo king had more marketable skills, and wasn't that just a joyful thought?

Willie and Ruby were both so comfortable with themselves, acting like none of this was any big deal. To them, she supposed, it wasn't. They'd been doing their jobs all their lives, and doing them well. Nothing fazed them. Nothing ever had. Not even last year when Dolphin Land suffered dire straits had Ruby caved. She'd hooked up with Dr. Victoria Sheffield and now her little dolphin facility was a respected research and education center.

Dora suppressed a belch from the extra helping of cole

slaw and thought longingly of her tennis club and charity balls. She could organize the hell out of a five-hundred-dollar-a-plate dinner, right down to the room décor and the centerpieces. She knew how to consult an interior designer and implement his suggestions to decorate a room. For sure, she knew how to handle a taste test with a caterer and select a meal that left guests oohing, ahhing, and delicately wiping their perfect mouths on monogrammed linen napkins.

In short, she was supremely qualified for a life that was no longer hers to live. Ex-trophy wife was hardly something to list on a resumé. Her fork fell from nerveless fingers and clattered on the plate.

"Dora Lee?" Concern ripe in his voice, Gramps reached for her arm. "You okay?"

"Uh huh!" She pasted a big smile on her face. "That was some meal. I couldn't eat another bite." Hopefully, the load of food she'd piled into her stomach would stay put. Just in case, she'd head back to the cottage and avoid a public hurling of crab meat and despair.

She pushed back from the table and stood. "I hope you don't mind, but I'm going to leave."

"Darlin', we ain't had near enough time to catch up. Do you have to run off?" Ruby protested.

"I'm going to be around for awhile. We'll have plenty of time." Quickly she hugged each of them. "Besides." She winked hugely, knowing it would make them laugh. "I'm sure you two can find something to occupy your time."

Her grandfather studied her for a moment, then leaned

back in his chair and slanted a look toward Ruby. "There's always pinochle, I guess."

Ruby hooted and smacked him lightly on the arm. "Or not."

While the two of them laughed, Dora grabbed her handbag, blew them a kiss and slipped out the door.

The night was warm, but not uncomfortably so. Clouds blocked the moon, but periodic lights helped her make her way across the complex past long rows of slips. The docked boats rose and fell with the gentle lift of the water beneath them. Most were dark, but the shadowed lights and drift of sound from occasional cruisers indicated that they were occupied. Living aboard a boat was one of the most affordable kinds of housing available in the Keys.

She breathed deep and relished the coolness of the light breeze wafting in from the south. Breathe and release. Breathe and release. The bleak thoughts from dinner receded. She might not know what she was going to do with the rest of her life, but she didn't have to decide right at the moment. Breathe and release.

Surprisingly, the queasy feeling faded and her panicked mood lifted. Her money would tide her over for awhile. Shabby though it might be, she had a place to live for as long as she needed. Gramps and Ruby loved her and would be in her corner always. She looked forward to hanging out with her best friend. There was plenty of time to figure out her future. For the moment, all she had to do was relax and recover from the emotional trauma of the last few days.

The breeze gusted and she glanced up. Dark clouds had

thickened overhead. Storms could blow up in a matter of minutes in the Keys and, from the scent of rain, one was definitely on its way. She'd picked up her pace to get indoors before the rain started when she remembered that the fish was still on her car.

She hadn't transported that thing hundreds of miles to have it ruined on her first night home. Although she couldn't drag it to her cottage and didn't want to bug Gramps again, she could at least secure the plastic cover. Veering off course, she hurried past the boat repair bays toward the parking lot, rounded the corner, and ran right into a solid chest.

She bounced from the impact. "Ack!"

Hands like iron grasped her upper arms and pulled her upright. "What the hell?"

"Bobby?" She looked up. Oh yes, it was him all right.

"Dora Lee, what are you doing?"

The impact left her breathless. At least she thought that was the reason and not the realization that he was holding her close to his rather broad chest. The sensation was a lot more pleasant than she expected.

"Running into you, apparently."

That obviously didn't thrill him, because he released her like her skin had turned poisonous. "It's late and weather's coming. You shouldn't be out here."

Either his voice had deepened over the years, or growling came naturally.

A very sexy growl, at that.

"I'm on my way hom . . . to my cottage, but there's something I need to do first. Night, Bobby." With an airy little wave, she slipped past.

He surprised her by falling into step. "What's so important that it can't wait until morning?"

Interesting. Their collision must have shaken loose his communication skills. This ranked as a real conversation.

"I need to wrap my fish."

"Your what?"

They reached the parking lot. Most of the plastic covering had pulled free and snapped in the increasing wind. "Holy hell!" Bobby said. "That's a trophy-sized tarpon."

"It's going to be a ruined trophy-size tarpon if I don't cover it again."

"How much does it weigh?"

"One twenty or so, not counting the mounting board." She grabbed for flapping plastic and tried shoving it through the ropes securing the fish to her car.

"That isn't going to work." He shouldered her aside and tugged at the knots. "I'll haul it indoors."

From deep freeze to an offer of help? She'd ponder the switch in attitude later. Instead, she gathered in the tarpaulin as he released the ropes. "I can help."

He shot her a look like he didn't think she could lift anything heavier than a champagne flute.

"I can!"

That got her a snort and a shrug. "Lift when I tell you and we'll try not to scratch the shit out of this pretty paint job."

She gripped the tail end. On his three-count they hoisted

together, but she knew darn well he took the brunt of the weight with his thickly-muscled arms.

"I got it, Dora Lee."

"You can't possibly tote that all the way to the cottage. It's too heavy."

J. Walter would have paid someone else and not even made the attempt.

Bobby shot her a look like she'd insulted his masculinity. "I've carried heavier women."

"This fish isn't going to wrap its fins around you and blow in your ear while you do it." But she bet he had a list of women a mile long who would do so gladly.

In the sparse light a dimple flashed as his lips quirked. "All right then, let's go."

She tried not to resent that he took on more of the weight and still managed to do it one handed. In the years since high school, her friend's *little* brother had certainly filled out and muscled up.

Carrying the fish between them like a bridge, they headed toward the cottages. Hers was the only one occupied at the moment. When she was younger, they'd been filled year round, mostly with fishing enthusiasts. Back then, all the guests cared about was hitting the water as early as possible, fishing all day and crashing into bed at night before getting up the next day to do it all again. The little buildings suited them fine. Then, over the years, consumption grew more conspicuous and even the ardent fishing crowd had gravitated toward the bigger hotels with more amenities, or weekly vacation rentals. It became more troublesome than profitable for Willie to operate this part of his business. So, he'd closed most of the buildings and used others for storage, but always kept one available for her infrequent visits.

Despite years of tennis, her arms and back protested by the time they reached the first cottage. "I need a second here," she gasped and lowered her end of the board to the ground when he stopped. "Sorry."

A typical guy-shrug said it all. He crossed his forearms and leaned on top of the board. "Have Willie take you out on the boat to pull traps regular and you'll build up that arm strength."

"That must be your workout routine."

Like she wanted him to realize she'd noticed. *She* didn't even like realizing it. Suddenly anxious to be out of his company, she picked up her end again. She took a step and promptly stumbled as her foot sank into a hole. Her heel caught and threw her off balance. She dropped the board and crashed to her hands and knees.

"Shit!"

"You okay?" He easily pulled her to her feet like she didn't weigh significantly more than the tarpon.

More startled than hurt, she dusted her hands together. The outside light from her cottage illuminated a crater in the ground.

"A land crab hole." Loathing dripped from her voice. For as long as she could remember, she'd hated those things as mean, destructive pests.

"Dora Lee, are you sure you're all right?" Bobby took her hands and turned them over to inspect the palms. Calloused thumbs stroked her skin, but she was too annoyed to enjoy the sensation.

"I'm okay. Thanks." When he released her hands, she planted them on her hips and scowled. "Leave it to the Keys to have crabs that don't like living in water."

"By the size of that pit, this one's a big sucker. Look." He pointed out another, smaller hole. "There's its escape hatch."

Most people accepted land crabs. They shrugged and went about their business, but Dora had hated them from the time she was a pre-teen and they infiltrated the flower beds she and her grandmother had lovingly planted around their home. Sneaky bastards, they burrowed in the ground and mostly kept out of sight except in the spring when they often scuttled from one side of the highway to the other to breed. Locals swerved to avoid them rather than risk a punctured tire on the crabs' huge, sharp front claws.

"It'll need that escape hatch if I see it," she groused, knowing it was an empty threat. Even the ruthlessness of trapping and killing them was only a temporary fix. Like monsters in an old B-movie, more kept coming back.

Bobby laughed and she snapped her head up to glare.

"C'mon, killer. That storm's coming closer." With both arms under the heavy tarpon, he hoisted it up. "I got it," he said when she tried to reclaim an end. "Go on. Get your door open."

The heel on her sandal was broken, forcing her to hobble.

Land crab one, two-hundred dollar sandals zip. Back less than a day, and her old nemeses already had the upper hand. Well, that damn thing had better stay on the lawn next door and steer clear of her cottage. She had enough things bugging her at the moment to put up with any crap from a crab.

She pushed open the door and he hauled in her prize.

"Where do you want it?"

Good question. It looked even bigger in her tiny living room. Then again, so did Bobby.

"Behind the couch for now," she decided, and dragged an end away from the wall.

He slid the tarpon into the space and stood. "A beauty like that and this is how it ends up." Scorn etched lines around his mouth. "Didn't your husband ever hear of 'catch and release'?"

"Only when it came to me," slipped out before she could stop herself.

"What do you mean?"

"He . . . we're divorced." She dropped her handbag on the chair.

"So that's the reason for the visit."

That he didn't make it a question rankled. And here, they'd actually been getting along. "I don't need a reason to see Gramps."

"When we were kids, you never did anything without knowing what for."

He'd grouped them together like she wasn't seven years older. Maybe he'd still been a kid, but back then, she'd been a woman with a dream to accomplish. So sue her.

"There's nothing wrong with having a plan, and right now, I plan to enjoy my visit with Gramps, Ruby, and your sister." She lifted her head and walked to the door, a queen dismissing her subject. "Thank you for your help, Bobby. Have a good rest of the night."

Speculation lit his sea-green eyes and his mouth quirked again. "I'll be seeing you around, Dora Lee," he said, and left.

Now, why did that sound like more than just a friendly goodbye? Damned if she cared enough to figure it out tonight. She shut the door with more force than necessary and hobbled off to the bedroom. Slipping off the sandals, she dumped them into the trash can. The old fashioned bed covered in a soft, faded quilt called to her. Suddenly, she was fed up with crying, fussing, and worrying about the future. At this point, she was tired of simply thinking. Until tomorrow, the rest of the world could sink like Atlantis under the ocean and she wouldn't care. Stripping off her wilted clothes, she flung them over the wicker rocker and marched into the adjoining bathroom. Right now, the only thing she needed to manage was a hot shower and a good night's sleep.

CHAPTER 3

Dirt, tree limbs, and J. Walter on a bicycle whirled around her in a wind tunnel. Bent at the waist, she pushed against the swirling wind, fighting her way through the storm while land crabs clawed at her feet and all of the Hanson's Marina and Mall shop keepers sat on the porch, staring and pointing to mock her lack of progress. From a distance, a woman's voice called her name.

"I'm coming. I'm co . . ." Wrestling the bedclothes like they were kudzu vines, she sat up and blinked at butter cream walls. Dust motes danced in the morning light. Cripes, what a weird dream, brought on no doubt by tiredness, stress, and the big meal.

"Dora Lee? Come on, girl, I know you're in there."

That voice wasn't a dream! She scrambled from the bed, knocked her shin on the chair and swore, but kept moving. Yanking open the front door, she had a second to brace herself before Jo Jo flung her arms around her and knocked her back a step.

"You're home! Hot damn, Dora Lee. I about screamed

Bobby deaf when he said you were in town. Why didn't you tell me you were coming? How come you didn't call me instead of making me find out from my brother two days after the fact? How the hell are you?"

For a pint-sized woman, her best friend hugged like a python. Dora squeezed back. "I got here the other night in time for sunset and dinner with Gramps and Ruby. I should have called, but I was beat and needed a couple of days to catch up."

Cat-like green eyes shimmered joyfully from her friend's gamin face. "No worries. I'm just glad to see you! It's about time you came home for a visit. It's been too long." Jo Jo's strawberry-blond curls bounced when she nodded. "Way too long." Twin slender braids of auburn framed her face. With the contrast between the darker braids and the rest of her curls, she looked like she was styling her hair after ancient Celt warriors. The braids swung when she looked around. "Why don't I smell coffee? You were still sleeping? It's almost ten!" She bustled past her into the kitchenette. "Never mind. I'll get a pot brewing while you work on waking up. I stopped by Marielena's Bakery for *Pan de Gloria*."

As familiar with the cottage as Dora herself, she quickly located an unopened can of coffee and the filters for the automatic machine. "So, how long are you staying? We're in rehearsals for the summer fundraiser — wait 'til you hear what we're doing this year — but we'll catch up, don't you worry." She poured water into the machine and switched it on. "You got cream, right?" She stuck her head in the refrigerator.

"Yep, should've guessed that Willie wouldn't forget. I swear, girl, I just love your grampa, but you already know that."

Lightning-force energy in a five-two frame. That was Jo Jo. From the tornado in her dream to the whirlwind in her kitchen, Dora could barely catch her breath. She staggered to a stool and burst out laughing.

"What's so funny?" Not that her friend needed a reason; she joined in for the sheer joy of laughing.

"Jo Jo, you're better than a hundred cups of coffee," Dora said when she could finally speak. "If we could bottle your spirit and sell it, the world would never need another anti-depressant."

"If everybody laughed more and worried less, they wouldn't need drugs in the first place." The multi-colored scarf points of her skirt spun outward and gypsy hoops swung from her ears when she whirled back to the counter and stroked the petals of a bloom. "Gorgeous. They sure brighten the place. So, come on, girl, catch me up." She grabbed Dora's arm and pulled her into the sitting area. "Love the fish! Can I use it for a prop in the show?"

"Of course." As if there were any doubt. Nobody said no to her friend, no matter what she asked or wanted. If they didn't agree to something right off, she'd charm them into it. Between her engaging smile, sunshine personality, and the fact that ninety-nine-point-nine percent of the time she asked for a good cause, almost everyone was willing to be charmed.

On the rare times that didn't work, she'd pull out all stops. One memorable evening, when a city councilman resisted taking part in a celebrity waiter fundraiser, Jo Jo had serenaded him with bawdy song parodies at a packed local eatery until he laughingly gave in.

Now she plopped down cross-legged on the couch. "Bobby told me about the divorce. Why didn't you tell me your marriage was in trouble? You doing okay with it? What happened?"

Although most of the time her friend managed multiple trains of thought with Amtrak efficiency, when it came time to listen, she devoted all her concentration. Intensity darkened her green eyes, making it seem like she didn't just hear the explanations, she absorbed them.

Once Dora finished the tale, Jo Jo popped up to fix their coffee in chipped earthenware mugs and returned to the couch. Taking a sip, she put her mug on the table and leaned forward, her expression fierce.

"Tell me straight. Do we have to go up and publicly humiliate that jerk?"

Oh, my God. "You'd do it, too."

"Damn skippy, I would. There's no end to the misery we could cause." She gazed across the room like she was plotting the scene and setting the stage for one of her play productions. "Do you know the chippy he's hooked up with now?"

"No. I don't think I want to, either."

"Too bad. We could go undercover at the country club and stage a fake conversation to make her think he's also boffing someone else." She tapped her finger on the coffee mug. "Oh! Morrison's is a publicly-traded company, isn't it? Let's buy a couple shares of stock, show up at the next board meeting and wreak havoc. He'll crap a cow when we walk in."

The mental image was priceless. "He'd crap the whole herd, but those things follow an agenda and protocol to the letter. They'd toss us before we caused any real fuss."

"You're right, but it's too bad. I have the perfect outfit. Vintage Jackie O, right down to the pillbox hat."

Shakespeare had declared the whole world a stage, so Jo Jo owned a costume for every occasion. She'd once arrived at a high school dance in a vest, mini-skirt and slouch hat, all made out of faux Dalmatian. Any other girl would have looked ridiculous. Jo Jo carried it off like a Paris runway supermodel. For their high school prom, she'd donned a 1960s Grecian sleeveless gown layered in apricot and cream chiffon and shone like a goddess.

Right now that goddess had other things on her mind. "So, if you aren't going to plot revenge on your lousy ex, what's next on your agenda?"

Why did everyone ask that, as if she actually had an agenda? "I'm thinking about having a *pan de Gloria*. Maybe two. Or three."

"Coping with carbohydrates. Always a good choice."

Dora got up, walked back to the kitchenette and opened the bakery bag like it was a treasure chest. She pulled out sweet, soft, powdered-sugar covered "glory bread". "Want one?"

"Of course." Jo Jo brought the mugs for a refill, then picked a rich pastry from the bag, tore off a piece and bit into it. "Ahh. All the taste with none of the nutritional value and worth every single bite." She licked powdered sugar from her lips. "After you've finished with calorie therapy, then what, a shopping spree? A vacation! You took him for some dough, right? We can spend a long weekend in the Bahamas, just us and some cabana boys bringing us tropical drinks. No? What about a wild weekend in the Big Apple? We'll take in some plays. I'm dying to see *Moving' Out* or *Wicked* or even *Avenue Q.* Too bad *The Boy from Oz* closed. I don't care that Peter Allen was gay. Hugh Jackman is so fine that my hormones heat up when I think about him. I rented *X-Men 2* again just for his naked scene."

The thought of Hugh Jackman in the buff didn't generate so much as a flicker of interest for Dora. *How depressing.* She shrugged. "I haven't really thought about it. I guess I'll hang around awhile and, uh, consider my options."

"Hey, just having options is a plus. What'cha got in mind?"

Nothing. Reality whopped her upside the head again. The soft confection stuck in her throat like cardboard and she coughed out a cloud of powdered sugar. Grabbing her mug, she gulped coffee and gasped. Her eyes teared from the hot liquid.

"Dora Lee!" Jo Jo snatched a glass from the drain board, filled it with water and shoved it into her hand. "Cripes, girl, are you okay?"

Now that they'd begun, the tears refused to stop. Instead, they spilled over her eyelids, running through the powdered sugar coating her face. She swallowed water down the wrong pipe and coughed again. "No! I'm not . . ."

Cough. "Not okay. I don't have options." Coughing caused more tears to flood and her nose filled with snot. "No options. No plans. Not even one, damn . . ." She wheezed in a breath. "CLUE!"

Her friend dumped the remaining pastries onto the counter and turned the paper bag inside out, sending up a small mushroom cloud of sugar. She smacked the bag over Dora's mouth. "Breathe."

Her esophagus spasmed and her lungs jerked in her chest, but she managed an unsteady breath, then another. All the while she tried not to think about the pitiful picture she made, standing in this shabby cottage, coated with powdered sugar and tears, hyperventilating into a bakery bag.

If this was her future, she wanted to go back to bed, cover up her head and sleep for a hundred years like the Florida version of Rip Van Winkle. Unfortunately, her pint-sized friend had a grip like a truck driver and held her firmly with one hand on the back of her head while the other clamped the bag over her mouth until her breathing evened out.

"You okay now?"

When she nodded, Jo Jo took away the bag and put it on the counter within easy reach. She dampened a dish towel and gently wiped Dora's face. "Whew. Don't freak out like that again, okay? I'm not used to it from you."

"Sorry. Getting kicked out by my husband is a new experience."

"That'll set you back a few steps, for sure, but it isn't the end of the world."

"But it is in a way." Dora heard the whine in her voice and sucked in another breath before continuing. "All I've done for the last fourteen years is been J. Walter's wife. That's who I was and now all of a sudden, I'm not anymore. I don't know who I'm supposed to be instead." She got off the stool and paced the small cottage. "I'm too old to model. Too young for Social Security. Even with the divorce settlement, I can't afford to not work. That settlement may be all I have to see me through retirement."

"You make it sound like you're one step away from assisted living. You're not even forty years old."

"Forty with no job skills and no experience." She held up a hand to stave off any rebuttal. "You should have heard Gramps and Ruby last night going down the list of jobs available around here. Do you have any idea how depressing it is to realize that I'm not qualified to do a single one of them?"

"Dora Lee Hanson, I cannot believe I'm hearing this junk come out of your mouth."

"Junk?" Shock nearly set off another bout of hyperventilating.

"Junk." Emphatic nodding set blondish curls and red braids bouncing. "Yeah, it sucks that your stick-up-his-ass husband cheated on you and demanded a divorce and I still think we should go up there and make him miserable, just for the satisfaction of it. It bites that after all those years of planning or going to parties, shopping and traveling around, you now have to work for a living. J. Walter might have given up on you, but, and this is a bigger butt than old Mrs. Comisky's ass back in ninth grade, you never have been a woman to give up on yourself."

Dora sat down suddenly on the arm of the overstuffed chair. Jo Jo was right. Her friend might flit around with the energy of a souped-up hummingbird, but at her core she was rock solid smart. Her brows drew together. "I don't want to give up," she whispered.

"Of course you don't, and you won't. The odds are a lot more in your favor now than they were when you first left town. Hell, back then, we only thought we knew it all. Probably a good thing, too, or we might have been too scared to even try to make our dreams come true."

"Back then, I knew what I wanted. We both did. You were going to be a Broadway star."

"And you were going to be a famous model, then learn all you could about the business so you could run your own agency."

Dora snorted, the sound somehow more plaintive than scornful. "I only got as far as parading my boobs and ass around in expensive underwear. If I'd stayed with it instead of marrying Walter, I would have learned the business somehow. Then I'd at least have some training to fall back on and I wouldn't be in this position."

"But you would have missed out on the good years of your marriage. As sour as it tastes right now, I saw you in the early days. You were happy, Dora Lee."

"You're right. I was." She'd loved Walter, plain and simple. Although he'd dazzled her with the lifestyle he offered,

she'd never have married him without love. That made his betrayal that much more painful. He might have killed her love
as quickly as a speeding car flattened a possum in the road,
but she still mourned the loss. "It's all gone." The admission
zapped an ulcer-like pain in her stomach.

"Except for the money settlement." Jo Jo pursed her lips.
"I don't mean to reduce this to dollars and cents, but at least
he didn't leave you broke. You've got enough to start over.
All you need to do is figure out the where, what, and when."

"Is that all?" Right now, she could barely figure out if
she wanted to chance another pastry or simply stick to coffee.
"I hope nobody expects me to decide that today."

"Nope. Not today. Probably not tomorrow even. But
if you don't have everything mapped out by the end of the
week, you're in trouble."

"What?!" To her way of thinking, she was entitled to a
couple of weeks of depressed confusion. Anybody who got
uprooted from the life they were used to would feel the same.
"You aren't . . ."

Jo Jo's face was dead pan solemn, but her eyes twinkled.

"Oh. You aren't serious."

"Gotcha."

"Very funny," she groused.

"Why, thank you." Her friend curtsied. "My goal is
to not be serious today. In fact, my entire *raison d'etre* is to
have a great time spending the day with my bestest friend in
the whole wide world. You brought a swim suit home with
you, right?"

"It's stuffed into one of my bags somewhere."

"Well, pull it out, girl, and let's head for the beach. My stuff's in the car." She rinsed their coffee mugs and upended them in the sink, then took Dora by the arm and tugged her upright, laughing. "We'll pretend we're basking in the Bahamas. Then we'll move on to the Trade Winds — it's a great new outside bar and restaurant on the ocean side — for afternoon drinks and flirt with all the men down here on fishing trips."

"I haven't flirted in, well, in forever."

"It'll come back to you." She gave her a playful shove down the short hallway. "The day Dora Lee Hanson forgets how to flirt is the day I plan your memorial service."

Jo Jo entered the compact bedroom and spotted her luggage. A smile like sunshine spread over her face. "From the number of bags, I guess you're staying a while. Way cool." She looked around. "Wow, this room hasn't changed. Between the droopy curtains, that old coverlet and the chipped furniture, I could use it as a set design in a Tennessee Williams revival. You know, since you're gonna stick around for an extended visit, why don't we spruce up the cottage? A little paint, some new curtains. We'll make it more like home. There's no place like home, right?"

The last thing she wanted was to think of the Keys as her home again. "Maybe. I'll think about it." She rummaged in her tote bag and pulled out a one-piece maillot in a vibrant royal blue, complete with a ruffle-edged skirt that she pretended covered her thighs. Gone were her bikini days.

Slipping into the miniscule bathroom, she quickly washed her face, brushed her teeth and exchanged her nightclothes for the swimsuit. She drew on a cover-up that hung to her knees and found the sandals she used to wear around her pool. A towel and her sunscreen went into a canvas bag and she was ready. "Jo, do me a favor for today, please? Let's just have fun. No talking about my future or what you think I should do for the rest of my life, okay?"

"Deal. Instead we'll debate truly important subjects, like who has the best ass — the aforementioned Hugh Jackman, Antonio Banderas, or my brother."

CHAPTER 4

"YOUR BROTHER?" DORA half shrieked, half laughed on their way out the door.

"Hey, you saw him last night. Tell me you don't think my baby brother grew up into one fine man?"

"That's not the point. I don't care how good looking he is, I'm not discussing your brother's ass with you. You're his sister."

"It's just an observation, for cripe's sake. It's not like I want to jump him." Jo Jo walked briskly, her sandals making little flop-flop noises when they hit her heels. "'Course, I'm probably the only single woman in a three-mile radius who doesn't. There're a fair number of married ones, too, but Bobby's got standards."

"A man with standards. Imagine that."

"Hey, he always thought you were prime."

Dora stopped so suddenly, her sunglasses slipped half-way down her nose. "To a teen-aged boy, anybody with breasts is prime."

Jo Jo snickered. "That's pretty much true, but more so

when it came to you. Tell you right now, if situations were reversed, he'd sure look at *your* ass and talk about it."

"About how it's gone south and has more dimples than a golf ball? Don't ever feel you have to share the details of that conversation with me, okay?"

"Dora Lee Hanson, knock that off right this minute. You're as pretty as you were twenty years ago, when just about every boy in town, including my brother, was half in love with you."

"That's just plain ridiculous." Suddenly Dora laughed, remembering those long ago days. "Bobby was a walking mass of out-of-control hormones and a kid to boot."

"From what I've heard over the years, he's learned to put those hormones to good use. He's no kid anymore."

Oh, she'd noticed last night, not that it mattered. The same rules applied. "He's still your brother. Besides, he's seven years younger."

"So what? If you really thought age mattered, you wouldn't have married J. Walter."

"That's different."

They reached the parking lot and Jo Jo fake-staggered against her old convertible. "Is that a double standard I see before me?"

"No!" Dora thought about it. "Well, yes, I guess. Okay, I'll give you that, but I still have a good point."

"Like?"

"Like my fifty-nine year old husband booted me for a younger woman, not an older one."

"Your *ex*-husband is a horse's ass. Besides, this isn't about him, it's about Bobby."

"That's my other point. Why are we discussing your brother and me anyway?"

"Hey, why not? You're here. He's here." A speculative glint appeared in Jo Jo's cat-green eyes. She looked over in the general direction of the boat slips. "You know, I don't think he's got a charter today, maybe we could . . ."

"No, we could not." Dora slung her bag into the back seat. "No matter what it is that you're thinking, Josephine Joan, forget it." The last thing she needed was her friend to plot some sort of grand matchmaking scheme. "My marriage just broke up, remember? With the exception of Gramps, men are not high on my hit list right now. I'd sooner skewer a guy on a barbeque spit and slow roast him over hot coals than date him."

"But . . ."

"No buts. No maybes. I mean it. I don't care that Bobby is better looking than Antonio Banderas, Hugh Jackman, AND Pierce Brosnan combined. I wouldn't care if he WAS Hugh Jackman at this point and plopped himself down on a towel right next to me at the beach." She yanked open the car door. "Pierce Brosnan himself in full James Bond mode could show up at this Trade Winds place and offer to shake more than my martini and I still wouldn't care." She plopped into the seat and slammed the door shut for emphasis. "I am *not* interested!"

⁋ ⁋ ⁋

SO DORA LEE thought he was better looking than Zorro, Wolverine, and James Bond combined. Ordinarily, stacking up against a comparison like that would give a man something to strut about, Bobby thought as he leaned against the side of the marina building. Too bad she'd followed it up with her declaration of non-interest. Dora Lee sure knew how to puff up a guy's ego and then shoot it down in the next breath.

He waited until he heard his sister's car pull away before pushing off the wall and walking around the corner. Eavesdropping hadn't been his original plan, but when he realized he was their topic of conversation, the last thing he wanted to do was interrupt.

They'd delivered an earful for sure. At least Dora Lee admitted she liked his looks. On the other hand, that crack about skewering men for the barbeque pit made his ass muscles clench in protest. He wasn't sure whether to thank or spank his sister for bringing him up. If he ever put a move on Dora Lee, he'd do it without her help. Or her interference. And he was a long way from deciding whether he wanted to turn that "if" into a "when".

A man didn't rush back into the fire that had already burned him once. At least, not until after he thought long and hard about it.

In the process of going up the steps to the deli and convenience store, he stopped and looked at Dora Lee's car. Classy wheels. Good lines, juice in the engine, built like a brick house. Sort of like Dora Lee. Had she picked it out for herself, or was it her husband's choice as another one of his status symbols?

Her *ex*-husband.

Almost as soon as he'd realized she was divorced, that this wasn't one of her infrequent visits, heat had flickered through him, like charcoal embers poked back to life. Damn, but he'd thought the torch he'd once carried had long been buried under the ashes of his poor rejected adolescent heart.

Geezus, but he'd been a teenage sap. The sun didn't just rise and set on Dora Lee. As far as he was concerned, it shone all day long just to make her smile. Back then, he'd been a kid whose dick led his heart around in a puppy-love crush. A lot of years had passed since and now there was nothing puppy-ish about the rekindled burn inside him. Nope, he had a case of full, howling-at-the-moon lust.

If Dora Lee could be believed, his timing still sucked. She wasn't any more interested in him now than she had been before. At eighteen, riding on liquid courage, he'd put a sloppy move on the woman of his dreams and been shot down faster than a clay target in a shooting match. Not that she'd been a bitch or cruel about it. Worse, she'd been kind, patting him on his arm while she explained that as Jo Jo's kid brother, he was like her brother, too.

All he could do afterward was crawl off with his pride in shreds and watch while she took her dreams on the road. Three weeks later, he'd joined the Navy. Times had changed.

He wasn't a wet-behind-the-ears kid anymore. He'd learned more than a thing or two about being a man and a whole helluva lot more about women.

He'd heard enough of the conversation to realize that getting dumped for a younger model had hit Dora Lee in more than her heart. She'd always been the prettiest girl in the Keys and while she'd never bragged on her looks, she'd never questioned them either.

Bobby snorted. From the look he'd gotten of her ass last night, he knew it still rated high on the squeezable scale. He wiped his palms down the sides of his shorts. Hearing her doubt anything about her own attractiveness was an insecurity she'd never shown before. That didn't sit right with him. Not one bit.

Dora Lee might not be interested in anything hotter than the sunny day, but what woman didn't respond to the offer of a strong shoulder from an old friend? He could do friendship while he figured out if he wanted to act on his interest.

Jo Jo was right that he didn't have a charter for the day. He rubbed his knuckles over his jaw and ran through his options. Since he never spent his days off lazing around in the sun, his sharp-minded sister would know he'd overheard them if he suddenly showed up at the beach.

Dropping by Trade Winds later on was a different matter. They'd be at least a couple of hours at the beach, he figured. Jo Jo's house was on the way to the bar, so they'd more than likely stop there first for a quick rinse or whatever it was women did to freshen up without looking like they'd spent a lot of time doing it. Yeah, he had plenty of time to meet up with Willie and go over some business before heading out to offer his shoulder to Dora Lee.

🦀 🦀 🦀

SEPARATING THE TOURISTS from the locals at the outdoor bar was simple. Bright sunburns perfectly outlined patterns of white skin left by angular sunglasses on the faces of the men who'd come to the Keys to fish during the day and troll for female companionship in the late afternoon.

"Like red and white reverse raccoons, aren't they?" whispered Jo Jo when they walked up to the bar.

Dora Lee nodded and eased onto a high stool. "That has to hurt."

Jo Jo leaned across the bar and delivered an enthusiastic smacking kiss on the twenty-something bartender. "Hi ya, handsome. We need tall, cold, and tropical. Make mine with rum. Vodka base for her, right, Dora Lee?" She boosted herself up onto her seat. "Told you this place was cool."

Dora looked around and agreed. Casual, but nice. A rectangular wood bar, coated in polyurethane, protected by a tiki hut roof. The bartenders moved easily inside the space, mixing drinks and serving them with smiles. A long pier jutted out over the ocean. Some people fished from it, others sat talking, drinks in hand. A cool breeze blew, keeping humidity and bugs away from the patrons.

"Just look at that view," said Jo Jo.

"Funny how we could grow up here and never get tired of looking at the ocean, isn't it?"

"It'd be like getting tired of looking at fine art, but I didn't mean the ocean." Jo tilted her head slightly toward the end of the bar. "I was talking about *that* view."

Dora sampled the fruity drink the bartender slid in front of her and glanced to her left. Her friend had quicker radar than the military. In less than a minute she'd zeroed in a quartet of men, all dressed in polo shirts and pressed shorts.

"Well?" Jo Jo prodded.

"At least they're missing that boiled-lobster look." They weren't "oh-wow" handsome, but not ugly either. Still, if good sunscreen usage was their best attribute . . . She sucked in a good long slurp of her cocktail, savoring the kick the vodka lent to the fruit juice. Maybe she really was past the point of being bowled over by anyone.

"I think they're cute in a vacationing-preppy sort of way." Jo Jo sipped some of her drink, her lips lingering on the straw while she made eye contact with the last guy on the left.

"Aww, geez. Do you have to jump right into it?"

"Relax, girl. It's not like you're on the hunt for husband number two. It's only flirting."

"But . . ." Any hope of stalling evaporated when the man locked his gaze on Jo Jo like a bird dog on point. He nudged the man to his right which set off a chain reaction to the other two. Almost perfectly synchronized, the four picked up their drinks and approached.

"Here they come." Jo Jo looked as delighted as if the

whole thing were a surprise party planned in her honor. "Smile now and, remember, it's only . . ."

"Flirting. Right. Got it." Simple social interaction at a casual bar, not a royal presentation. Dora gulped some more of her drink, welcoming the alcohol-induced glow blooming inside her, and smiled at the foursome homing in on their location. She could handle this, handle them. Her friend was right. It was long past time she had a little fun.

A couple of more hours and as many potent drinks later, she still waited for that fun to begin. The two men on either side of her had started out polite and pleasant enough, but the scotch they'd slammed back like over-aged frat boys had washed away the classy veneer and left behind a pair of horny dogs. Dora Lee polished off the most recent drink bought for her by Frank, or was it Ed? Hell, it might have been Tim or Dick. She'd given up on remembering their individual names and dubbed them the Fradtick Four in her mind.

"Hey, baby, want another?" Fradtick One all but drooled on her shoulder while he pretended he wasn't staring at her breasts.

It wasn't easy to force another "Aren't you the nicest guy" smile while pretending just as hard that he wasn't a complete ass and sliding his roaming hand away from her upper thigh. "Not yet."

"Anytime you're ready, I'm your man," he slurred, pressing a wet kiss to her cheek.

There wasn't enough vodka in the world to wash down that hunk of cheese. He was as transparent and sticky as cellophane wrap and, *eww*, was he tonguing her ear? She shifted away, which put her in eye contact with his buddy.

Fradtick Two barely matched her in height. His prominent Adam's apple bobbed when he talked and she had to concentrate on not nodding in sync.

He grinned at her sloppily. "You are one gorgeous thing, Sara Lee." A sly look in his bleary eyes, he picked up her other hand and stroked her palm with a finger. That same finger sported a neat white circlet of skin. He'd probably slid the wedding ring off right before entering the bar.

She jerked her hand away. "That's *Dora* Lee."

F One guffawed and shot scotch fumes into the air. "Yeah, idiot. Sara Lee's the baking company. Cakes and stuff."

Undaunted, Two winked. "Nobody doesn't like Dora Lee. Bet you're every bit as sweet and . . ." Her stomach curdled when he slowly licked his lower lip. ". . . tasty."

Seduction by ad slogan? Lord save her. "You know what. I changed my mind." She turned back to the first Fradtick. "I'll take another drink. Right now. Make it a shot." Maybe the buzz in her brain would block their repulsive come-ons and leers.

"Now you're talking!"

While he waved over the bartender, Dora looked at Jo Jo to see how she fared. Either the other pair had a lot more style or her friend was doing a world class acting job, because from all appearances she was having a great time. Her gamin face alive with laughter, she patted the arm of the one on her left who was leaning with both hands on the bar instead of pawing at her thighs. Meanwhile, Fradtick Four on the right said something and Jo Jo turned and beamed like he was the wittiest man alive. She whispered something in his ear and he flushed like a schoolboy. Emboldened, he leaned closer, but she gave him a friendly nudge with her shoulder and he moved away.

Her friend slid off the stool and picked up her bag. "Back in a second. Keep an eye on these boys while I'm gone." She tossed them a wink over her shoulder as she walked toward the restrooms and the men smiled like she'd thrown them gold coins. Now, *that* was flirting the way it should be. Fun, light-hearted, sexy.

At one point, she'd been a pro, but marriage must have sapped the flirting talent right out of her. Or sucked the fun from it. Hanging out with these yahoos was no more enjoyable than gum surgery without Novocain. Dora knocked back the vodka shot, hoping for a quick numbing. A sweaty hand slipped down her back, and she grabbed it quickly, digging in with her fingernails before it reached her butt. Enough was enough. She'd rather be the blood buffet to a swarm of hungry mosquitoes than endure another grope.

Catching the bartender's eye, her arm flopping a little like an under-stuffed scarecrow, she pantomimed a scribbling motion in the air to signal for their tab, even though most of the drinks had been purchased by the not-fab-four. Elbowing Fradtick One out of her way, she fumbled for the bag at her feet. Her head swirled when she straightened. Maybe that last shot hadn't been the best idea. Still, if the bartender moved fast enough, she could shanghai Jo Jo at the Ladies' Room door. The preppy Romeos had other ideas.

"Hey, baby, you aren't deserting us now. Night's still young."

"Yeah, sweet cakes, we're just getting started."

The other pair protested, too. "I didn't hear your friend say she planned to go," growled one, belligerent.

"We're just about ready for dinner," added his pal.

Bet I know who you want for dessert, she thought. "Sorry, fellas, we forgot to mention a prior engash . . . engagement." Her lips felt like putty, but she stretched them into a smile. "We'll cash . . . catch you around." She slipped off the stool and then grabbed the bar for support. Weak-kneed from the cocktails, she knocked into the man on her right.

Taking full advantage, he hoisted his arm around her shoulder like a heavy sandbag. "See, I knew you didn't really want to leave. Whatever else you're doing, I got something better planned." His hand slid over the top of her breast and he licked her neck.

Vodka, fruit juice, and disgust roiled in her stomach. She shoved away from him and almost toppled over. A big, calloused hand settled warmly on the nape of her neck, steadying her balance and drawing her close when she tried to yank free. Damn, those drinks screwed with her perception. The pretending-to-be-single moron's chest hadn't looked anywhere near as broad and hard as it now felt against her back.

"Hope those plans are flexible, buddy."

That wasn't his voice either. She tilted her head back and

looked up. Blond tousled hair and cool green eyes swam into her field of vision. "Bobby?"

"Sorry I'm late, babe." He bent his head and slowly brushed his mouth over hers.

Oh, my.

"Who the hell are you?" Neck-licker scowled. "We've been buying her and her girlfriend drinks all afternoon."

Muscles bunched when Bobby shrugged. "Right generous of you to help my lady kill some time." He grinned down at her like a man who knew a woman would forgive him anything. "Tried to call, but you know our cell service."

Playing her part, she nestled her head against his shoulder and lifted her hand to brush his tanned, wind-roughened cheek. No overly-smooth, exfoliated skin there and, oh, he smelled good from whatever manly-man soap he used. Somehow, she kept her eyes from crossing and smiled crookedly. "I knew you'd get here when you could."

That earned her a wink and another light kiss. Oh, yes, she'd definitely had too much to drink if a brotherly smooch buzzed through her like another vodka shooter.

The other sot who'd been shouldered aside spoke up, his Adam's apple quivering indignantly. "She never mentioned you at all!"

"Like you didn't mention being married?"

That shut them both up, and Bobby directed his attention to the remaining pair. They just turned away and focused on their drinks. Game over and all the points went to Bobby.

He slipped his hand from the back of her neck and

around the front of her shoulders, hugging her easily. Bet he could hoist shipping containers with the corded muscles in that forearm.

"Hey, Sammy. What's the tab for the ladies?" When he heard the amount, he fished a roll of cash out of his pocket, thumbed some bills out one-handed, and gave them to the bartender. "Keep the rest."

"Thanks, man."

"Babe, where's my sister?"

Darling? Babe? She blinked. That was laying it on a little thick. She should probably tell him to back off a little, but he was propping up most of her weight and if he took her literally, she'd hit the ground like a sack of cement. Besides, the full-body hug made her feel cozy and warm — not skeevy like old Nick-Lecker.

Luckily, said sister answered before she had to make a decision. "I'm right here, little brother." Never let it be said that Jo Jo couldn't jump into a scene and improvise. "About time y'all got here." Her accent dripped magnolias and honeysuckle. "Women could die of hunger waiting for you to show up and buy dinner. Why, if these gentlemen hadn't been kind enough to keep us company, I swear we would have perished from total boredom."

A devilish glint in her eyes, she sashayed over to the bar like she was channeling Scarlett O'Hara. She kissed her way down the row of Fradticks, leaving a trail of vamp red lipstick imprints on their cheeks. "Y'all enjoy the rest of your evening." Turning her back on them, she winked broadly.

"Where to now, my darlings?"

Bobby's chuckle vibrated against Dora's back before he stepped to her side, keeping an arm around her waist when she wobbled from the sudden shift. Grinning like she was a cute little beach bunny, he cheerfully slipped her sunglasses from atop her head into position on her nose. He offered his other arm to his sister and escorted them from the outdoor bar like Ashley Wilkes at a cotillion. "Ladies, what's your preference?"

"Anywhere that you pick up the tab," Jo Jo answered. "Dora Lee, got a place in mind?"

At this point, she wasn't sure she had a mind — period. She shook her head, surprised when alcohol didn't slosh from one side of her brain to the other.

"Sis, I vote we hit the first place on the road home. The sooner we get some food into her, the better."

"Not hungry."

"You gotta eat something anyway. Sammy's drinks are tall on booze, short on mixer."

"I ate!" she protested. "Fruit."

"Cherries, pineapple, and orange slices on a toothpick." Bobby snorted. "If that's all you put in your stomach since lunch, no wonder you're plastered." They reached his truck. "Come on, you two. Jo Jo, we'll come back for your car."

"Bro, I'm okay to drive. Honest. Dora Lee had quite a few more drinks than me."

"She did?"

"I did?" Not that she'd been counting.

"Heck, yeah, girl, and I think that last shot pretty much put you over the edge."

That explained a lot, although specifics faded fast in her ninety proof haze.

"All right, follow us along," Bobby said.

"Dora Lee can ride with me."

"Nah, I've already got her this far. I'll tote her for the rest of the way."

"Okay, bro!" Jo Jo toddled off.

"Huh? Wait!" Even snockered, she didn't like decisions being made without her input. Men had done that to her a lot lately. Beginning with J. Walter not giving her a choice in the divorce. Unfortunately, she didn't speak up fast enough, because Jo Jo was already in her car. "I thought women won the right to vote last century," she groused.

He unlocked the car and opened the door. "We gave you the choice of restaurant, but you didn't want it. Up you go."

She stayed put and glared, although the sunglasses probably blocked the impact, wagging her finger at him. "I don't remember you being this bossy."

"The Navy brings out the 'take charge' in a man. Get in."

Her foot missed the running board and she fell back against him in full-body contact. The back of her head to that squared-off chin. His chest to her back. Her ass against his — oh, my! Her best friend's little brother's not-little-at-all hard-on pressed firmly against her rear end.

"Whoops," she squeaked out.

His arm came around her waist and his other hand

grasped one of her hips. Laughter rumbled against her from her shoulders to her butt. "If you'd fallen for me like that years ago, I'd have followed up on the invitation. But not now."

"Invitation shminvishason. I lost my balance."

He snickered and boosted her up into the seat.

"Why not now?" What, was she nuts? She didn't *want* him attracted to her. Definitely *not*. But, damnit, first J. Walter, and now Bobby?

"Not my kind of action." Pulling the seat harness, he reached across her chest, his prime face very close to hers.

She grabbed his shirt before he could pull back. What was wrong with her that men who used to want her no longer did? "What the hell does *that* mean?"

Firmly, he snapped her buckle closed, disengaged the stranglehold on his shirt, and stepped out of her reach. "It means you're too drunk to think straight." He slammed her door and walked around to his side of the truck. Climbing into his seat, no running board needed, he pulled his door closed and jammed the key into the ignition, turning over the powerful engine.

Drunk as she was, she realized he'd dodged the question. He must really not want to explain, which only confirmed her suspicions. Besotted, clammy-handed tourists aside, she'd lost her appeal to red-blooded males.

Maybe it was shallow to worry about losing her attractiveness when her whole life had turned upside down, but this was one additional lousy blow to her quickly dwindling self-esteem. She closed her eyes against an abrupt swell of tears and rested her head back against the seat. Before the sedation effects of too much alcohol overcame her, she took one last stab at salvaging some of her pride. "That wasn't a fishing pole in your pants."

CHAPTER 5

WHAT SOUNDED LIKE a live rehearsal by the trashcan lid-slamming cast of *Stomp* finally roused Dora from her alcohol-induced coma. Rapid-fire taps, clashing aluminum, and the rumble of what was surely an impending earthquake shook the very walls. Inch by painful inch, she rose up on her elbows. Since when were the Middle Keys a tour stop for hip performance troops? Grabbing onto the iron headboard for support, she quelled the acid roil in her stomach and prepared to beg the cast to go far, far away. She lifted an eyelid half a millimeter and a shaft of sunlight speared into her brain. A machete halving her skull like a coconut would hurt less.

Peering through gummy eyelashes, she braved the window. There was nobody there. No dancers. No musicians. "Ohhhh," she groaned, and fell back across the mattress. That distant rumble and screech of shearing metal must be the garbage company collecting trash from the Dumpster at the marina.

Temples throbbing, she gingerly pushed herself upright again. Untangling her legs from the sheets, she swung them over the side of the bed, hoping to anchor her spinning brain. Whoever claimed that vodka didn't cause hangovers was a devious bastard.

She shuffled to the bathroom. A look in the mirror and she gasped, which sent another lightning bolt through her brain. Red veins criss-crossed the whites of her eyes like routes on a road map. She could tote groceries in the bags under her eyes. Her hair looked like it had been styled at the house of Einstein.

After three glasses of cold water to wash down a fistful of aspirin, she forged forward into the shower. So much for conservation, always so important in the Keys where fresh water was piped down from the mainland. Leaning against the ancient tile, she waited in the steam for the aspirin to work its medicinal magic before she even attempted to wash her hair. Even then each hair follicle jerked painfully at her scalp.

After the long shower, she pulled on clothes with only slightly less difficulty than performing a gymnastics routine, and stumbled to the kitchen. Making coffee was a struggle, but she managed. While it brewed, she ate a day-old Cuban pastry a few crumbs at a time, hoping to soak up whatever remained of the previous evening's excess.

They'd never made it to dinner. From the way she slumped against the door of his truck, Bobby had obviously realized that she couldn't sit upright in a restaurant, let alone handle utensils. Besides, from what she remembered of their last words, neither one of them wanted to spend any additional time together. He'd half-carried, half-dragged her to the cottage, opened the door when she couldn't get the key in the lock, and offered to help her to bed. She'd snootily assured him that she wouldn't make him suffer another minute in her obviously unappealing company, but it came out sounding more like, "Muffer a stint in oh Beevis an apple dumpling."

Far from intimidated by her grandness, he'd snickered. "You're not a very happy drunk, Dora Lee."

"Bite me," she'd slurred, which made him laugh louder.

"Pick the spot, darling, and I'll take a rain check." With that he'd turned her around, squeezed her shoulder as he pointed her through her door, and left.

Alone, she'd stumbled down the hall, fallen face forward on the bed and known no more.

Until this morning, when all the misery crashed back. She swigged more coffee, wishing that she'd imagined the whole incident and that the past week had been one long, bad soap opera-type dream sequence. That she was still the adored wife of J. Walter Morrison, instead of his cast-aside ex. That she was back in her beautifully decorated, perfectly-appointed Treasure Coast home rehashing the positives and negatives of an elegant dinner party, and preparing to play tennis at the club.

Instead, she sat in this faded, drab cottage, nursing a killer headache and feeling every bit as old, out-dated, and insignificant as the building. A little spider scurried across the floor and she couldn't muster enough "eek" factor to stomp it flat. She had a sudden image of herself thirty years down the road, sitting in this same spot while spiders encased her in cobwebs. Her old-lady skin parchment-thin and pied with liver spots, and dark hair turned the dingy gray of wet newspaper.

Acid churned in her stomach while she absorbed those images. Despair built in her lungs like hot air inflating a balloon, the pressure pushing, stretching, distending her internal organs until finally it was either burst or . . .

"AHHHHHHHHHHHHHHHHHHHHHHHH-HHHHHHHHHHHHHHH!" The scream exploded and catapulted her out of the chair back down the hallway. The hell with her aching head, she thought, as she searched for a pair, any pair, of matching sandals. She couldn't sit in that desperate reality one second longer. Heedless of pedicured toes, she jammed her feet into the shoes and ran from both the vision and the cottage like Ebenezer Scrooge fleeing the ghost of Jacob Marley.

🦀 🦀 🦀

"I'M WORRIED 'BOUT my girl, Ruby," Willie said, pacing around his small kitchen. "I never seen her sunk this low before."

"Only been a little while, darlin'. She's taken a pretty hard hit and even a woman strong like Dora Lee needs a little bounce-back time." Ruby drank down some coffee and smiled. "Don't worry so much."

"But she ain't bouncing. Not a bit. She's sinking. You'd think that Jo Jo dragging her off for some fun yesterday would've helped, but to hear Bobby talk about it this morning. . ." He dragged a hand through his hair. "Hell, he said she was three sheets to the wind and as miserable as a person could be when he caught up to them at Trade Winds."

Ruby crinkled her brow. "You ask, or did Bobby track you down to tell you?"

"He was on his way out to pick up his clients and . . ." He stopped when she shot him a sharp look out of her bright blue eyes. "What's going on in that head of yours, woman?"

"Just thinking it's mighty interesting that he gave you a full report. What was he doing tracking them down anyway? His sister and Dora are long past the age when they need a chaperone."

"Not according to him. Said some preppy tourists were working some heavy octopus moves on her, but he bailed her out before they got too far."

"Never known either one of those girls to not be able to take care of themselves, no matter what the situation — drunk tourists or otherwise."

"Me neither, but . . ."

"But maybe Bobby didn't give 'em a chance to handle it, seeing as how he showed up all convenient like." She pursed her lips and nodded. "Mighty good timing, if you ask me."

"We're supposed to be worrying about Dora Lee. Why are you wondering so much about Bobby Daulton?"

She brought her empty mug to the sink and rinsed it. "I just think that it's plain interesting that he's involving himself so much in your granddaughter's activities right off the bat."

She leaned against the counter and gave him that mischievous grin that always lit up his insides and ask, "You think he's still—"

"After all this time?"

"Why not?"

"Because he . . . because she . . ." As much as his brain scrambled for reasons, he couldn't think of one. "Damn, Ruby. You think?"

She shrugged, but her eyes twinkled.

"Damn." He wasn't at all sure how he felt about his friend and partner having a thing for his granddaughter. Not when her husband had sucked the wind clear out of her sails. "No. No way. Not now. She's got enough problems."

Ruby slid her arms around his waist. The top of her sun-bleached head barely came up to his chest and her frame was so tiny in his arms, it felt like she'd blow over in a good gust of wind. But he knew she was as sturdy as a banyan tree. Not once in her life, even back when her husband Gus had died, or her nephew Jack had been injured so bad awhile ago had she come anywhere close to toppling.

She tilted her head back, looking up at him. "Dora Lee is gonna be just fine. You'll see."

"I don't know how you can be so sure. I still say the last thing she needs is anybody dogging her!"

"Listen to you, Grampa. Your girl's had men on her tail since she grew out of her training bra. Un uh uh." She shook her head when he protested. "I ain't saying the divorce didn't knock her off her game, but she'll get on track in no time. In the meantime, nothing puts a woman back on her feet faster than having a good looking son-of-a-gun like Bobby Daulton sniffing around."

Maybe she had a point, but he'd seen too much confusion and sadness in his granddaughter's eyes to give up the worry. He frowned. "I don't think she's ready."

"Bobby's smart. If he's interested, he'll figure out how and when to cast his line."

"I don't know. From the time she was a kid, Dora Lee always knew exactly what she wanted and how to go after it."

"Heck, yeah. She sure knew how to get around you!"

"That she did." His arms tightened. "But now, I don't see that gleam in her eyes. It's like the divorce knocked out all the dreams."

"Aww, darlin'. Don't fret so." Ruby leaned her head against his chest. "Maybe it's just that she's not sure what she should dream for now. Have a little faith. She'll figure it out and when she does . . ."

A pounding on the door interrupted them.

"Gramps? You in there?"

They untangled themselves while he answered. "Yeah, come on in."

Dora Lee rushed in like scorpions were stinging her heels.

"Jesus, Mary and all the saints, what's wrong?"

"Hi, you two." Striding through the room, she gave them each a quick kiss. "Good, there's coffee."

Willie gaped at Ruby while Dora Lee grabbed a mug and poured. His granddaughter looked like hell. No wonder, considering the night she'd had. She practically chugged the brew, not bothering with cream.

He winced, thinking of all that heat pouring down her throat. "Uh, baby girl, is there something going on?"

"No. There isn't." She slammed the now empty mug on the counter. "That's the problem. I have nothing going on. Nothing to do and I am damned if I'm going to spend the day decaying in that cottage with cobwebs hanging out of my hair."

How much had she drunk last night that she was hallucinating things this morning? Whatever the amount, it hadn't clamped a leash on her tongue.

"It's Sunday, right? You aren't working are you, Gramps? Great. Let's do something. Anything. Go fishing. Crabbing. Hell, you can teach me how to change the oil on a 150 horse power outboard engine. I don't care. Just don't leave me alone doing nothing." Her voice cracked on a plaintive wail. "Please?"

He thought he was worried before? The desperation on her face scared the crap out of him. "Sure. We can . . . we were . . ." Geezus, he'd never seen her like this, and damned if he knew how to handle it. He pulled a bandanna out of his pocket and wiped his forehead.

"Your timing's perfect, Dora Lee."

Bless Ruby for whatever she was about to suggest.

His granddaughter whipped around. "Perfect for what?"

"Why, we were just going to stop by your place and drag you on over to Dolphin Land. You know how I'm just dying to show you everything we've done with the place. Jack'll be glad to see you and even gladder to introduce you to Victoria. She's got a presentation to finish up today — wait until you see her in action. I told you the other night that she just got the *Delphinid Prize* for the research she did right here." Ruby elbowed him in the side, jolting him out of his shock.

"Yeah, baby girl. I promised Jack some help with the fish house cooler. Ruby and Victoria can show you around while we work."

"Go get your things. It's been awhile since you saw the gang." Ruby physically turned her around and urged her out the door. "Put a move on. We'll meet you out by the truck."

When she jogged off toward her cottage, the couple looked at each other, wide-eyed.

"Thank the Lord for your quick thinking. I don't know what just happened, but I sure as hell don't like it." Willie shoved the bandanna back in his pocket.

"Maybe there's something more to what Bobby said than I thought," Ruby admitted. She reached for his hand and squeezed. "Don't worry too much, darling. I'll find out what fired up the flare in her butt, just you see if I don't. Besides, a day around the dolphins will do her good. Can't beat the gang as a cure for whatever ails a person."

CHAPTER 6

THE DIFFERENCE IN Dolphin Land as Dora remembered it and the facility she walked into today was astounding. Like expecting a grass hut and finding a mansion.

She said as much to Ruby, who immediately pooh-poohed the comparison.

"Now, we ain't as grand as all that. We sure as heck don't worry anymore about paying our fish bills every month. We cleaned up nice, got the buildings fixed. See that kind of bluey-green trim on the doors and shutters and all? Jack thought it was too girly, but Victoria insisted and said the color matches his eyes." She snickered. "He grumbled the whole time, but kept painting."

Oh, she downplayed the change, but her scrawny chest puffed out with pride and a toothy grin stretched so wide across her face that her eyes squinted. "We get a fair amount of tourists coming through, enough that we've hired on some folks to help out. Got some young trainers on staff and a couple of guys to handle the maintenance. Jack still super-vises the work and lends a hand, but that Internet security stuff keeps him pretty busy."

The older woman pointed out more improvements while they walked toward the front lagoon. For the moment, the two of them were alone. Needing some supplies, Willie had opted to take his own truck and stop by the home improvement store on his way from the marina. It had given Ruby the chance, she crowed, "To ride in style in that fancy set of wheels you got yourself, girl." Dora had gladly driven them over in her Mercedes. Soon enough the car might be more valuable as an asset to sell, but for the drive up the highway, she did her best to share the older woman's enthusiasm for the luxury automobile.

"We even got ourselves a website," Ruby continued. "Most of our visitors are school groups and research students who wanna attend the presentations. There's a whole crop of college kids applying for internships with Victoria. Can you beat that?"

Since Dr. Victoria Sheffield had published her paper and won the *Delphinid Prize* for marine mammal research a few months before, according to Ruby, she'd become even more of a draw. The grant money that came with the honor funded additional studies. The whole field was as alien to Dora as brain surgery, but she understood that it was a huge deal. This Dr. Sheffield must have a 200 point I.Q. to have accomplished so much. Lord knows, her skin must be thicker than a shark's for her to have stood up to Jack Benton. Dora had known him over twenty-five years and he was no easy mark. To hear Ruby tell it, the woman scientist had concealed big parts of her story to finagle her way into Dolphin Land at a time when Jack had his own plans in place for saving the facility.

"Our Victoria had her heart set on proving herself as a dolphin researcher and she wasn't about to fail. Sure, she hit a couple of roadblocks, but she wouldn't let them stop her. Not even Jack and, I'm here to tell you, he was the biggest road block of all."

Ruby's whole body vibrated when she laughed. Dora shook her head in disbelief. The former DEA undercover agent was easily one of the smartest, most intimidating men she'd ever met — and that included the captains of industry who were her ex-husband's cronies. To have challenged him, this Victoria must possess a backbone of iron and eighteen karat gold nerve.

Dora envisioned a studious, no-nonsense woman in a white lab coat, with her hair pulled back in a severe bun, a clipboard in her hand, and a pen behind her ear.

But that image didn't fit with Jack. Loving and intensely loyal to family, he was breath-stealing gorgeous and, when he chose to be, more charming than any three other men put together. He'd dated beautiful girls all through school and had they not been raised as almost-family, they might have taken up together themselves for a time. A nerdy, bespectacled, serious scientist just didn't seem his type.

A gorgeous blonde like the one across the lagoon with long legs and a body to die for was exactly his type — which might explain why he'd strode onto the boardwalk and hoisted her into his arms.

Wow. Even from a distance they made a great couple, fitting easily into each other's arms as they walked off the boardwalk together. His arm looped over her shoulder, hers around his waist, with her hand tucked into the back pocket of his shorts. Their body language, the way they leaned into each other, the look they shared when she laughed up at him and he smiled down — everything proclaimed them a couple richly, deeply in love.

Dora swallowed hard. She couldn't remember the last time she and Walter had fit so well together. If ever. She blinked back wetness behind her sunglasses and summoned a smile. "I gather that's Dr. Sheffield?"

"If it wasn't, then Jack wouldn't have just been melting her lips under his. Yep, that's our Victoria."

Brainy, beautiful, brave, and successful. As if those attributes weren't enough, she had a fair amount of family money, too. Dora's spirits sank lower, already intimidated by this paragon of perfection.

Suck it up, she told herself as they approached. Paragon or not, this woman was now Ruby's niece, which made her family. She summoned up a warm smile, ready to politely shake hands.

Jack tossed formality away with a hug that lifted her clear off the ground. "Dora Lee! Heard you were back in town. Hot damn, sugar, it's good to see you."

His eyes *did* match the tropical color on the buildings. Right now they were lit with welcome. Maybe too much welcome. Few wives would be happy to see their husband greet another woman with that much warmth and enthusiasm.

"It's, um, good to see you, too, Jack. How are you?" Wriggling out of his hug, she stepped back, glancing at Victoria.

"Better than a man has a right to be, Dora Lee. Meet the reason." Jack draped his arm around his wife's shoulder, drawing her close for the introduction.

"It's a pleasure to meet you, Dr. Sheffield."

Expecting daggers, she found instead a genuine friendliness in the other woman's deep brown eyes.

"Dr. Sheffield comes out for presentations and interviews. I'm Victoria, or Vic, to family." She clasped Dora's hand in both of hers. "Willie and Ruby have told me so much about you. I'm thrilled to finally meet you."

From all appearances the woman actually meant it, radiating sincerity from the top of her blond braided ponytail to the glinting gold toe rings on her sandaled feet. Obviously, she wasn't the least bit threatened or territorial about her gorgeous husband.

Of course, said husband was looking at his wife like she was the wellspring of his happiness and personally responsible for sunlight. What woman wouldn't be secure in that kind of love?

They were technically beyond the newlywed stage, but judging from their body language and the intimacy in their shared looks, this honeymoon wasn't ending anytime soon. This reminded her of something else.

"I'm sorry I wasn't able to attend your wedding. We . . . my husband . . . ex-husband . . . Walter and I were . . ." Walter had flat out refused to travel to the Keys for the wedding of people he didn't know, and she'd been too embarrassed to come alone.

Victoria covered over her stuttered pause. "Well, now we can thank you in person for the beautiful frame set. It's exquisite."

And completely inappropriate. Who needed antique-style, scrolled silver picture frames in the Keys? She should have taken the time to find out the couple's tastes and needs, rather than dropping into Morrison's and selecting something so impersonal.

Her smile wobbled, but she shored it up. "You're welcome. Anyway, I heard your ceremony was lovely."

Victoria beamed. "We were married on the beach at Sombrero. I don't think there's ever been a more beautiful sunset."

"My wife's partial to sunsets, aren't you, sugar?" Jack winked.

She laughed. "Let's just say that some are more memorable than others."

Their by-play spoke volumes of the rich, secret meanings and intimate references tightly-bonded couples shared.

Dora had known Jack for most of his life — through the hell-raising high school period and the very infrequent times when their paths crossed in the Keys in the ensuing years. An undercover DEA agent, even when home for a visit, he'd walked with the leashed energy and graceful power of a jungle cat who could strike whenever necessary. He'd devoted himself to the agency, but nearly died during a mission.

A mission that left him with a shattered knee that ended his undercover service.

He'd lived and breathed his career busting illegal drug manufacturers and importers, and been forced against his will to give it up. That couldn't possibly have been easy to accept. A man like Jack would have fought that fate with everything he could muster. So how on earth could that same, supremely-alpha male appear so completely happy, relaxed and, damnit, even content?

Okay, she had to know, but she'd find a sensitive way to ask. "Jack, it's amazing what you've all done here at Dolphin Land. It's, uh, quite a change."

"You got that right. For awhile it was touch and go whether we'd survive, but then Victoria finagled her way in and gave us a jump-start."

"But we wouldn't have made it without us all working together!"

"That's right," his aunt added. "Victoria, you, me. Willie did his part. It took teamwork."

That wasn't the answer she'd hoped for and she tried again. "The teamwork paid off, that's obvious for everyone to see. But . . ." Oh, hell, now all three looked at her. She took a breath. "Jack, I don't mean to be nosey, but was it difficult making the adjustment? Leaving the DEA?"

"That? Nah. Not so much."

His aunt nearly snorted out her sinuses. His wife gave him a *yeah, right* look.

Surrendering, he lifted his hands and laughed. "Okay,

okay, stand down, ladies. Truth is, when I finally realized that I couldn't go back to the DEA, I was a world-class pain in the ass and mostly took it out on Victoria." As if he couldn't stop himself, he cupped his wife's chin in his hand and kissed her warmly. "Thank God, and this woman, I came to my senses in time and accepted the situation."

"Just like that? That was your dream job!" How did someone switch gears so easily?

The corner of his mouth quirked and he shrugged. "I found someone that mattered more. Victoria got me started in the right direction."

Did he mean his successful transition had hinged on finding the right person? As far as solutions went, that was the furthest one out of her grasp. She'd built her last dream on her first marriage. Damned if she'd wager her happiness on someone else again.

"But honey, there's a lot more to it than that." Victoria protested. "Yes, we had our relationship and you focused on helping me make *my* dream come true, but that isn't all you've accomplished and you know it." She turned to Dora. "Once Jack accepted all the facts, he explored his options and redefined himself."

Tropical blue eyes rolled. "Redefined. Oh, yeah, I live to *explore* that pop-psych stuff. Goes down real easy with a couple of beers on a hot day."

"Hush." She squeezed his arm. "Although he saved me and my project from my ex-fiancé, we all knew in the long run that he doesn't have the patience for research observation and repetitive trials. There was no way for him to be completely happy until he discovered work that he himself truly enjoyed."

"Exactly!" Ruby nodded. "Once he knew that Dolphin Land was out of trouble, he got working on his new business."

"But how did he decide? I mean, it's not like you stroll on the beach, turn over a shell, and *bingo*, there's your new goal in life." If it were that easy, Dora vowed she'd walk every beach in sight from dusk until dawn.

"He inventoried his skills."

"Jack's always been real good with computers and that online stuff."

"It's so damn fascinating to have three gorgeous women talking about me like I'm not here."

He sounded so disgruntled they all laughed, but Dora made sure she directed her next question to him. "Internet security? What exactly does that mean?"

"I work with law enforcement agencies investigating Internet fraud, scams. Do some online undercover work searching out pedophiles. That kind of stuff. I have plenty of contacts from my agency days and, since it's all online, I can do the work from here." He shrugged it off like it wasn't any big deal, but she recognized the pride in his eyes.

In short, he'd reinvented his own dreams, developed an entire new career, fallen in love, and still found a way to help his aunt with her facility. At the same time, he probably leapt tall buildings in a single bound.

Dora resisted the urge to scuff her sandal on the pea rock

like a disgruntled teen. Jack was beyond impressive, but then, he'd always been larger-than-life. Unfortunately, she didn't have his wealth of skills and experience to draw from to solve her own dilemma.

The conversation transitioned to Victoria's research and, from the comprehensible, but compelling explanations of her theories and methods, Dora immediately understood why her presentations were so popular. Small wonder that scientists and students alike clamored to visit the facility to learn more about her work.

"She's getting more and more invitations to give lectures at schools all over the country," Ruby proudly added. "All expenses paid and speaking fees to boot, but so far she's turned down most of the offers."

"I have work here."

"That's what she always says."

"Not always. I'm going to that conference of marine science teachers next month."

"Oh yeah. All the way up in Jacksonville. But you turned down the trip to Hawaii."

Willie joined them before Victoria could answer. "Darlin', are you on that argument again? Mornin', Victoria." He leaned down and gave her a tight hug, and then clapped Jack on the shoulder. "Son, when it comes to not being able to keep your aunt from speaking her mind, your track record's still unbroken."

"I have about as much luck at it as you. Since the fish house drain won't fix itself, I vote you and I go do something we have a chance of accomplishing."

He gently squeezed Dora's shoulder. "Good to have you back., Don't be a stranger. Aunt Ruby, please quit pestering Victoria to leave home. I like having her around." Proving his words, he pressed another lingering kiss to his wife's mouth, bringing a warm flush to her honey-tanned skin.

"If you liked it any more, your house would rock off its foundations."

He roared with laughter, affectionately bussed his aunt on the cheek, and then sauntered off with Willie.

Victoria had a difficult time looking stern with her face blushing deep red. "Ruby, I can go to Hawaii next time. Rhett and Ashley are so close to making the next connection in the cooperative communication project. I don't want to leave right now."

"You always say that. Next time you'll figure out another reason not to go."

"No, it's just that I have better reasons to stay." The blonde's smile encompassed her departing husband, her aunt-by-marriage and the entire facility — including the gray marine mammals swimming around the nearby lagoon.

Shielded behind her sunglasses, Dora stared at the brilliant woman, amazed that she had myriad opportunities to travel everywhere and yet chose to stick herself in the Keys. But, it was clearly her preference. Then again, she obviously loved her work and the trio's combined efforts had created the perfect place for her to pursue her goals.

Dolphin Land was clearly thriving. The pod of dolphins

had also increased in the last year, including one mini-tor-pedo-shaped baby. "Look at that little tyke of Marian's zooming along." Ruby chortled. "We ain't got a good look at the underside yet, so we don't know if it's a boy or a girl, but it's every bit as smart and curious as a baby dolphin can be — and it's only a couple months old. Mama's got her flippers full for sure, but the other girls help. Melly in particular likes playing auntie."

In addition to the new arrival, they'd imported two teenagers, now named Peter Pan and Wendy, from a facility that had closed in Mexico. "We're pretty sure that Wendy's pregnant, too. Another blood test ought to confirm it. The family's definitely growing — at least on that side of the lagoon." She glanced at Victoria. "Probably won't be too long before it grows on this side of the lagoon, too."

"Ruby!"

An impish grin negated the guileless look in the older woman's blue eyes. "Look at it this way, when you turn up with a positive test, with that new equipment, we can ultra-sound you right along with the dolphins."

"Knowing you, you'll want to do the test with me lying right down on the dock."

They laughed at the image and Dora joined them, even though the thought of babies closed a fist around her heart. The quiet glow on Victoria's face confirmed that this would be yet another dream come true.

"Oh, speaking of tests reminds me that I promised to email my father the data reports from last week's trials," the lovely researcher said. "Although his stroke made it difficult for him to read, he doesn't have any trouble understanding when his caregiver relates the information to him. Would you both excuse me?"

"Sure thing, darlin'. Can't keep the great man waiting. You go on ahead," Ruby answered for both of them, then turned to Dora. "I gotta remind our men to check the temperature gauge in the cooler. I think it's acting up again. You all just hang out right here and keep the gang company, you hear? Go on down on the dock if you want to play. I'll be right back."

The older woman bustled off with a lot more energy than Dora could lay claim to herself, at least today. Although the hangover had mercifully left, a discontented malaise had settled over her spirit.

She stifled a sigh. Everybody was so damned happy and content. Even the dolphins. They dove and surfaced in rhythmic patterns, their bodies sleek and graceful as they glided around in the sparkling water. Off in the distance, two of them suddenly leaped high in perfect synchrony, then re-entered the water with barely a splash. Dora caught sight of the baby's little fin zipping around. The water swelled in its wake, a sign, she guessed, that Marian was chasing the youngster, probably to keep it out of trouble. Dolphin mothers knew their jobs.

They probably never had identity crises or relationship woes. Dolphins didn't mate for life. Well, they mated for *all* their lives, but didn't limit themselves to only one partner. Dora very much doubted that female dolphins ever worried about being dumped for younger, prettier models. Maybe dolphins didn't worry about much of anything at all. Wouldn't that be a welcome relief?

There was something very relaxing about watching the dolphins swim. They seemed to time their circuits, rising to the surface right in front of her to breathe and make eye contact.

To the casual observer, they looked so similar with their gray, counter-shaded bodies, bottle-nose rostrums, and dark eyes. If Dora hadn't practically grown up around them and visited over the years, she'd have a hard time telling them apart. Luckily, she'd never forgotten the differences that identified them as individuals. Robin's white markings on his dorsal fin. Melly's pink patch under her pectoral fin. Rhett's more robust girth. Scarlett's rostrum, grown pinkish and scarred as she aged. All so beautiful, no matter how old — or how young, she amended, as the unbelievably cute calf sped by once again.

A slender female popped up and released a soft breath from the blowhole on top of her head. She rolled to the side and watched Dora. This one was Wendy. When Ruby had first pointed her out, Dora had noticed the newcomer's incredibly lovely eyes. Every bit as dark a brown as those of her lagoon-mates, the clearly defined whites in the corners set them off, making them appear even more soulful. Naturally buoyant, she floated in the water, almost as if waiting for an acknowledgement.

Ruby had always insisted that the dolphins liked attention and reaction. "Hey, pretty girl," Dora ventured, deciding that ignoring her presence would be, well, rude.

Wendy whistled a three-note tone, and then sank out of sight, deep below the water's surface. So much for wanting attention. It was time to head back to the cottage anyway, Dora decided. As nice as it had been to see Jack and Victoria and admire the new and improved Dolphin Land, everyone had more important things to do than keep her company. Even the dolphins.

When she turned away to find the others and say goodbye, a loud, piercing shriek made her jump. She looked back. Wendy had returned, carrying a bright green toy plastic ring on her rostrum. "What is it, girl?"

Apparently that was all the encouragement the dolphin needed. She flipped up her head and sent the ring flying through the air.

"Whoa!" Dora snared it. "Nice toss."

The dolphin screamed again, almost like she agreed, and then opened her mouth.

Did she want to play? "Okay, but I'm not throwing it right at you." With their eyes situated on either side of their heads, dolphins couldn't see directly to the front. The ring was hard and she didn't want to risk bonking the animal on the melon, so instead she tossed it several feet to the side. Immediately, Wendy gave chase, moving her head slightly from side to side, using her echolocation. The underwater sonar was such an effective sense that the dolphin could find almost anything, even in murky water or with her eyes closed.

Sure enough, she quickly returned with the ring and tossed it again.

"With your aim, you'd make a heck of a ballplayer." Dora grabbed the toy and let it fly further out into the lagoon.

The game continued back and forth between dolphin and woman. After a few minutes, Dora was certain her pal had grown bored when she swam to the front of the nearest floating dock without the ring.

"Thanks for the fun." She smiled and waved, ready to leave, but the dolphin again had different plans, sending another scream-like sound from her blowhole. "What now?"

The animal stayed at the end of the dock, emitting an astonishing range of sounds from squeaks to squeals, piercing whistles to rude-sounding raspberries. Concerned, Dora looked around, but there wasn't another human in sight. She stared. "I don't know what you want."

The communication gap was about as wide as the one she'd experienced in the last months of her marriage. At least she and J. Walter had spoken the same basic language. How was she supposed to figure out the demands of another species?

There were plenty of people who believed that dolphins possessed psychic powers, but even Ruby, who claimed the dolphins understood her ninety-nine-percent of the time, believed it had more to do with innate intuitiveness and interpretation of body language than any mystical reason.

In the meantime, if those screams rose any higher up the

octave scale, they'd shatter glass windows, but apparently the rest of the people at Dolphin Land either couldn't hear her or they were used to it and chose to ignore the noise.

It was clearly up to Dora. "Well, if psychic divination is out, let's go with trial and error," she muttered, not quite believing she was about to problem solve with a marine mammal. Maybe the dolphin had tired of the ring, but still wanted to play. Dora spotted a large sea grape leaf, picked it up and flung it into the lagoon.

Pffthhhhwwwffftttt.

"Judging from the razz, you don't like leaves, huh?" A hula hoop was hooked over the stair railing. Maybe that would do the trick. Dora approached the dock and Wendy whistled. "Well, that's better." Encouraged, she continued. The animal responded with a remarkably human-sounding giggle. "Yeah, you *are* funny." She grabbed the hoop and walked down on the dock. Damned if the animal didn't flip to her back and wiggle her pectoral flippers as if applauding.

"Thank you so much for your approval. After this past week, I'll take any positive reinforcement I can get." She tossed the hoop out into the lagoon. Wendy sped away, jumped gracefully over it, and then came up through the middle and swam back, cheering herself with a melody of whistles. "Beautiful!" Dora applauded, and then knelt at the edge of the dock and reached out to lift the hoop over the dolphin's head.

Wendy had other ideas, and instead rose vertically until she was almost eye to eye. Then, she used her pec fins and splashed the water with all her energy.

"Hey, wait a minute. Quit it!" No use. Within seconds, Dora was drenched. The salt water might ruin her linen shorts and blouse, but for the life of her, she couldn't get upset. Not when the dolphin's antics were the most fun she'd had in longer than she could pinpoint. Certainly more enjoyable than getting drunk the previous evening.

"Just remember. You started it!" She dunked her hands, gold rings and all, and shoved handfuls of water at the dolphin.

The battle continued until Dora was sopping wet and her stomach hurt from laughing. "Okay, okay!" She drew in a breath and then burst out with another peal of laughter when the dolphin got in another well-timed splash. "You win, okay? I give up." She lifted her hands in surrender.

To all appearances, the dolphin understood because she turned to her side and offered a flipper. Dora tapped it with enthusiasm, like a "high-five." Still kneeling, she opened her arms wide with a flourish, acknowledging her with a bow. "Thank you, my friend."

Maybe it was a coincidence. Maybe without realizing it, she'd delivered a signal, but the dolphin gracefully rose further up out of the water, leaning in close and resting her head against her shoulder. Instinctively, Dora wrapped her arms around the animal's body. Closing her eyes, she hugged her for a few sweet seconds, tenderness filling her heart. She kissed the dolphin gently on the rostrum. When she let go and sat back the dolphin sank just as gracefully into the water. "Pretty girl, you're the best."

"Baby girl, you're a mess. Guess we know who lost the water fight."

Dora stood and looked at Willie and Ruby, who had been standing there for God only knew how long. "No losers here, Gramps." She grinned. "Except maybe my clothes, but it was definitely worth it."

"The gang has a way of bringing the sunshine out for everybody, that's for sure. I've been telling people that for years."

"And years and years."

Laughing, Dora ran up the steps from the dock and gently elbowed her grandfather. "She's right, so why shouldn't she let other people know. Isn't that the whole point?"

He quizzed her with a glance. "The point of what?"

"Of Dolphin Land. Of Victoria's work." She waved her hand in a wide arc. "Of everything here that they've worked so hard to accomplish. They're showing and telling people all about these amazing animals." Mindless of her wet clothes, she threw her arms around Ruby for a giant hug. "Thank you."

There was nothing frail about the old woman's returning squeeze. "You're always welcome here."

"I know, but that isn't what I meant. Everything and everybody at Dolphin Land reminds me that, no matter how bad it seems things are, it's always possible to make a comeback." She reclaimed her handbag from a nearby bench and kissed both of the older people good bye. "I'm going to take off now. See you back at the marina."

"But we were gonna ask you if you wanted to grab lunch

and go out on Jack's boat for a little while!" he protested.

"Tell him thanks, but I'll take a rain check."

"What are you gonna do back there all by yourself? Too nice a day to mope around."

A few days ago she'd have disagreed. In fact, she'd have defended her right to mope for the next month. "Don't worry, Gramps. I'll be fine. I have thinking to do. A comeback of my own to plan."

"That's terrific. What'd you decide to do?" Ruby's grin was almost as broad as the smile on one of her beautiful dolphins.

Dora winked hugely. "I still don't have one damn idea, but at least now I'm ready to start thinking about it!"

CHAPTER 1

DORA LEE MARCHED up to the cottage, shoulders squared and eyes narrowed, taking in every detail. Weeds poked through the pea rock path and stuck up in clumps amid the St. Augustine's grass. Hibiscus trees and bougainvillea bushes grew over the windows of some of the buildings, their flowers brilliant against faded, peeling paint. Aluminum awnings, chipped and crooked, shaded dusty glass windows.

Looking further down the path that ran through the twin rows of buildings, she saw the sparkle of water. The property even had its own small beach, which had always made a private, restful spot for guests. Back when she'd been growing up, this area had been so pretty. No wonder people had paid to come and stay in the cottages. She crossed the lawn next door, avoiding the treacherous crater she'd stumbled into a few nights before. Now a land crab was her only neighbor and that lousy crustacean didn't pay squat.

Thanks to Willie, her cottage was in much better shape than most, but even this one had long passed its prime. She opened the door, tossed her bag on the chair and kicked off her sandals. They'd grown older together, the property and her. Right by the door was a mirror set inside a metal mermaid sculpture with hooks beneath it for jackets. She glanced at her reflection, noting fresh color on her skin from the visit to Dolphin Land, but then focused on the shallow lines fanning out from each eye and the puckering around her mouth. She frowned and the puckers turned to grooves. On the other hand, her lips themselves plumped out nicely and her eyes were still as big and gold as they'd been all her life. Her hair barely had more than a handful of gray strands mingled in with the rich, still glossy brown, but even if it turned white overnight, chemists had developed a gazillion coloring products.

"So I got older. Sue me," she said, and winced, remembering that, technically, that's exactly what J. Walter had done when he filed for the divorce. Just like she'd dieted her heart out, she'd probably have undergone Botox injections or scheduled a nip and tuck if doing so would have made him happy. Forget her objection to pumping weird chemicals into her skin or a fear of ending up with an inflexible rictus instead of a natural smile. In a desperate step to hold on to her marriage, she'd have done whatever he asked. But he hadn't asked. He'd just moved on.

Well, screw him. With any luck, whoever was doing just that was lousy in bed. Colder and stiffer than a frozen board. Better yet, maybe he'd already discovered that the "performance problems" he'd experienced the last few times he'd tried to make love with her weren't, as he'd accused, because she'd let her body go soft. No, if there were true justice, he'd found out it was his own advancing age that kept his penis from getting hard — no matter how gorgeous the body underneath him happened to be at the time. To really complete the justice, he'd try every single one of the new erectile dysfunction — what a great name for chronic inability to get it up — pills and have them all fail miserably.

The delicious thought cheered her. After all, why should she be the only one suffering after the divorce? Hey, why should she suffer at all?

"Enough!" She glared at her own reflection and paced the little room.

When Dolphin Land was on the skids, had Ruby collapsed? Jack lost his whole career, but that didn't grind him into the dirt. Victoria, from what she'd heard, had decided on a goal and gone after it.

The revelations she'd begun to recognize at the facility bloomed in her brain. She wasn't the first woman dumped by her husband and she sure as hell wouldn't be the last. How she dealt with it made the difference. The pain was unavoidable, but she could decide whether to dwell in misery. Right now, she'd had enough to last until the next decade.

She stalked over to the window, kicking over a small footstool. "I need a goal. A plan." Hell, she needed something constructive. Not one of those dozen or so jobs her darling grandfather and Ruby had suggested. More of a project toward which she could channel her attention while she figured out the rest of her life. Somewhere there had to be something that would suit. She smacked the heel of her hand on the small wrought-iron table by the window. The magazines stacked on top promptly slid off and hit the floor.

Crouching, she grabbed them and plopped them on her lap while she sat on the lumpy, overstuffed chair. *Coastal Living*, May 2001. *Cosmopolitan*, October 2002. Even Oprah's magazine, with its emphasis on celebrating spirit, didn't do the trick. She needed concrete suggestions, not trendy pop-psychology.

The great and powerful *O* was no help at all. "Damn it!" She flung the magazine across the room like a Frisbee. It caught the corner of a faded picture and knocked it off the wall. The frame cracked and the glass shattered on impact. "Crap. At least it wasn't the mirror." She didn't need a second's more bad luck, yet alone the requisite seven years. Jumping up, she stormed into the kitchenette and rummaged under the sink for the dustpan. She swept up the mess and stood ready to toss it into the trash, when the perfect yellow rectangle on the wall grabbed her attention.

"What a pretty color." Such a cheerful contrast to the surrounding faded butter cream. She looked around the room, taking in the muted stripes of the couch and the scuffed, dull wood planks of the floor. Turning slowly in a circle, she compared the washed-out dinginess of the room with the warm, bright hominess she remembered when she and her grandmother first decorated it all those years ago. They hadn't had much money to work with, but together they'd created an atmosphere that was both comfortable and happy. Perfect for a stranger staying the weekend, but nothing that anyone would want to call home.

"Well, I'll be damned." Botox and face lifts — no way. But a rehab for this room? *That* she could do something about.

She dumped the broken glass in the kitchen trash can, and grabbed a big plastic bag from under the sink. The dingy gray curtains were so old that they shredded when she ripped them from the windows. The faded pillows so dust-laden they sent up a cloud when she shoved them in the bag along with the curtains. Magazines, more generic pictures, an afghan sieved with holes. Cheap candy dish. A plain vase with dirt-streaked silk blossoms and an old, flaking conch shell. Before long, she'd filled two huge bags and started on a third, plowing through the cottage's bedroom like a madwoman. Items shattered when they smashed together in the bags, but the sound didn't faze her. The bedding was limp and faded and most of the towels in the bathroom were threadbare and unraveling at the hems. She kept only what she immediately needed but, Martha Stewart as her witness, as soon as possible she'd replace them even if her closest option was the homemaking guru's own collection at Big K.

Each time she hauled out a stuffed bag, she ran back inside and continued her rampage. Dust swirled everywhere, speckling her clothes when she gathered up the oval area rugs and dragged them out the door, adding them to the growing discard pile. Finally, the rooms were as empty of unnecessary junk as she could make them and she took a break to reassess.

Bent over from the waist, she blew out her breath like a racehorse after a sprint. Her clothes, which had never fully dried from the water play with the dolphin, now stuck in wrinkles to her skin. She shoved sweat-streaked hair off her face with a grimy hand and looked around the sitting area. She'd stripped the room down to bare walls and now zeroed in on the furniture.

When she bounced on the chair and springs poked her ass, she bounced right back up on her feet and grabbed it like a wrestling opponent, wrangling it out the door. The couch's cushions were in slightly better shape, but that faded upholstery had to be redone. She could probably salvage the little wrought iron table with a bottle of glass cleaner for the top and a coat of fresh white paint on the base and legs.

Paint. That's what the whole room needed now. New color from the walls to the window frames. Dora stripped off her filthy clothes while she ran to the bedroom. Fifteen minutes later, freshly showered and dressed in denim sailing shorts and a navy cotton tee, she dashed out the door heading for her car and the home improvement store down the highway.

🦀 🦀 🦀

BOBBY STEPPED OFF his cruiser and walked down the dock, a man supremely content with a day well spent. The day's charter had been the best kind with a pair of experienced anglers who loved the sport. He rolled and flexed his shoulders.

Out on the water by eight a.m., he'd poled that boat from Staron Spit to Granny's Hump, looking for tarpon, bonefish, or permit. The fish did their part, being where he expected to find them given the day's weather, water temps and wind conditions. The fish hit lures all day long and gave the men all the fight they could handle, testing their skill with fly rod and reel. More than half the strikes shook free early, but a foursome of tarpon, some nice-size bonefish and one big ass permit stayed hooked and battled all the way to the boat. At forty-plus pounds, that permit rated a picture before Bobby released it like all the others.

The client would grin every time he showed that picture and told the story. Hell, when Bobby had dropped the pair off at their hotel, the man had still been grinning and he shoved an extra hundred buck tip into Bobby's hand.

Hot damn, he loved his work. There hadn't been a time he could remember in his entire life that he hadn't wanted to work on the water. He'd started early helping his father set and pull traps, filled with Florida lobster or stone crabs, depending on the season. His old man had taught him the way of the water, the tides and the winds. Countless days they'd gone out fishing as a family, too, chumming out at the reef for yellowtail snapper or bottom-rigging for grouper. In high school, he'd signed on as a deck hand on some of the big sport fishing charters. Those captains had, for sure, shown him how to find fish, but they'd also educated him on how to deal with clients — the anglers and tourists who paid hundreds of dollars for a day on the ocean with an experienced captain.

The father of a good buddy introduced him to fishing the flats, that fine art of poling a light boat across shallow water, while you scanned for the fish. He'd fallen hard for the special techniques needed to fly fish, casting line with precision to tempt the fish into snatching the hook hidden in the lure.

On his way to the marina stores, he ran his hand down the sleek line of his flats boat. Some businessmen relied on computers and spreadsheets. A carpenter needed saws and drills. A doctor used x-rays, scalpels and, nowadays, lasers to operate. All he needed was his storehouse of fishing knowledge, rods, tackle, and this seventeen-foot sleek beauty with her one-hundred fifteen horsepower outboard. Rarely was there a day that he couldn't earn his living.

During his hitch in the Navy, he'd dreamed of getting out and taking his place on the water as a flats fishing guide. He allocated part of every paycheck to his boat fund, determined to afford the best vessel possible. Small wonder he cleaned her up and rubbed her down every night, and used a special polish every couple of weeks. The engine was tuned to the tightest precision. The chrome gleamed.

A lady, on her way out of his door and his life, once accused him of treating his boat better than his girlfriends. She had a point. This boat had lasted longer in his life than any of his relationships, helped him earn a good living, and gave him a lot less grief than any woman he'd ever dated.

On the other hand, there were some things no boat could do for him, beginning with simple sex and ending with even better sex. Yeah, women as a species were definitely irreplaceable in that area, bless their warm bodies and big . . . smiles. Even if he'd never hooked up with an irreplaceable girlfriend, he'd liked enough women over his life to hang with them for weeks, months sometimes.

Not one had lasted longer than a year through no fault of theirs. Nah, he liked them a lot. Cared enough about some of them to settle in for a short term thing and damn sure found a lot more that got his dick hard and his blood humming. But after awhile, the whole relationship thing tightened around him like a shirt shrunk in the dryer and he needed a way out before the set-up suffocated the life out of him.

So, yeah, he'd take the blame for torpedoing his past relationships, even though he sometimes wished he could assign responsibility to someone else. Rounding the corner of the mall stores, he shot a look in the general direction of the cottages. A particular someone else named Dora Lee Hanson. In fairness, he couldn't fault her. She'd never cast her line his way, hoping he'd hit her lure so she could play him for awhile before she cut him loose. Nah, all those years ago, he'd been the angler and she the prize. The big one that got away.

He never figured she'd swim anywhere near these waters again, but now that she had, he'd be smart to haul ass in the opposite direction. So it made no sense at all that, instead of taking a seat with the other marina residents already gathered on the communal porch, he waved and veered off on a due course for the path that led to her cottage.

If he hadn't spent a sun-drenched day on calm water cooled by a light breeze, he'd swear a hurricane had blown through the cottage area. Or that a tornado had touched down and left a pile of debris right outside Dora Lee's little place. Trash bags stuffed to capacity were heaped in a black plastic mountain. A glass-topped table and the kitchenette stools lay on their sides on the lawn.

Knowing how much vodka she'd soaked into her system the day before, he'd expected to find her nursing a hangover, or at least lazing around like the Lady of the Manor. Something or someone had lit a fire under her ass. He navigated an obstacle course of cardboard boxes overflowing with magazines and God knows what other crap and rapped on the door.

"Come in."

That voice of hers always hit him like neat whiskey. He swallowed over the punch. "You planning a yard sale?" he asked, pushing open the door. "Holy hell."

CHAPTER 8

ALL THE LIVING room furniture was shoved in the middle of the room and covered with paint-spattered sheets. Pale gray shoe prints trailed across the plastic protecting the wood floor. Three of the walls were primed and Dora Lee gripped a long-handled roller, attacking the remaining wall with a nice shade of aqua paint.

Gone was the Treasure Coast lady wardrobe. A white Hanson's Marina T-shirt was tucked into denim shorts that hugged the curves of her excellent ass. She'd pulled her thick hair through the back of a ball cap and stuck her feet into old sneakers.

As far as views went, this one awed him as much anything else he'd seen in his life, including a 35-foot-whale shark, the coral formations of the Great Barrier Reef, and a typhoon off the coast of Malaysia. He indulged himself with a good long look before speaking. "What are you doing?"

"Indulging my passion for art. What's it look like?"

Even a hangover couldn't knock the smart-ass out of her. Good thing, because he'd rather deal with that attitude than the vulnerability he'd seen lurking the day before. "Like you lost at paint ball." It was true. Primer and paint splattered her from the cap to the kicks. She even had some on her skin.

"I haven't begun to fight."

"You aren't kidding." Somehow by herself, she'd boosted that stuffed tarpon on top of the kitchen counter and covered it in bags. Its tail stuck out a little, so behind her back he stretched the plastic over the fins to shield them from flying paint drops. If he'd been the angler that fish would still be swimming in the ocean, but he figured it meant something for her to have wrestled it from her ex's possession, so the least he could do was help her protect it.

He doubted she'd ever painted anything bigger than the nail on her big toe and her technique sucked. She compensated for uneven, random strokes by loading on extra paint and rolling it up, down and sideways. With that amount of paint, those walls might need a week to dry, but they'd be completely covered.

Give the woman credit. Between ransacking the place, hauling out the junk, and smearing primer on most of the room, she'd done a boatload of work. He surreptitiously touched his little finger to one of the primer-coated walls and discovered it was only a little tacky. She must have started hours ago. If he'd had to bet on her condition, he'd have put money on her spending the day lying on a beach chair, half dead to the world. He sure wouldn't have figured she'd take on this ambitious a project. Hell. He wouldn't have guessed she had any idea where to start, let alone make this much progress. Now he was dying to know why.

Finishing the wall, she rested the end of the handle on the floor and studied her handiwork. "What do you think?"

Standing beside her, he tucked his hands into the back pockets of his shorts and rocked on his heels. "Not bad." But she looked better, even with aqua speckles on her arms. Underneath that cap, her beautiful gold eyes gleamed. "You know, there's a way of rolling in sort of a 'W' that'll give you the coverage you want with a lot less paint."

"I think it looks great. It's fresh. Bright."

"Well, yeah. Sure." What red-blooded man wasted his time staring at a wall when she was around? He cocked his head and inhaled. Underneath the paint fumes, he smelled her perfume. Exotic, rich. Definitely not the cheap scents she and Jo Jo used to buy at the drugstore when they were teens. Even back then, one good whiff of Dora Lee made his tongue loll out of his mouth, so why expect anything different?

She looked damned pretty in her paint-spattered work clothes, but he'd think the same whether she wore a sack, a gown or, his libido voted, nothing at all. Between the body hugging T and shorts and that perfume, a man would have to be missing parts not to get turned on. He'd better think of something else fast before she caught a look at the tent in his cargo shorts.

He stared at the walls, the furniture, the fish. Anything to get his eyes and mind off of her. "So, what brought all this on? Or do you always wake up and redecorate after tying one on?"

That netted him a quick scowl. "I didn't wake up and do it." She balanced the roller in the paint tray. "I went to Dolphin Land first."

That explained nothing. Positive there was more to the story, he waited. Not only didn't she elaborate, she didn't even look at him. Instead, she tapped the lid on the paint can with the handle of a screwdriver, checking that it was closed tight. "Everybody over there doing okay?" he prompted. "It's the first you've met Vic, right? She's something special, isn't she?"

The screwdriver smacked down on the lid. "Yes. Very special."

Uh oh. Trouble lurked up ahead if Victoria Benton and Dora Lee disliked each other. "You two got along, right? You'll give Ruby and Willie simultaneous heart attacks if you didn't."

"Of course we got along." Finally she glanced at him instead of everywhere else in the room, her expression testy. "I just agreed that she's special. She's great. Nice. Friendly." Picking up a roll of blue mark-off tape, she walked to the window and began ripping off strips, haphazardly sticking them to the frame and sill. "Victoria's also smart, successful, and beautiful. On top of it all, Jack's so in love with her, he's not only sure she hung the moon, he probably thinks she created the entire solar system."

"She's in love with him, too, you probably noticed."

"Of course I noticed. I might not have a happy marriage

anymore, but I recognize one when I run smack dab into it."
Her tone was so sharp, it could cut bait.

"Easy, woman. I was just making a point that they've got a good thing together."

"Yes. You're right. They do."

Geezus, was she protecting the wood or patching it up from major surgery? "Dora Lee, all you need is a strip or two to keep paint away from the wood. You don't have to pile on that much tape. Of course, you should have taped it off before you started with the primer, but it doesn't look like you did much damage." She kept working as if he hadn't just told her the right way to do the job. "Here. Let me show you." He reached for the tape roll, but she snatched it back, snarling like an angry cat.

"It's finished." She tossed the tape roll in the corner and stalked over to a stack of supplies. Ripping open a bag of rags, she wiped her hands.

Shit. She'd gone from testy to pissed off in less time than it took a pelican to flap its wings. From the pinched look on her face, he bet that hangover had caught up to her again or she'd have realized he was only helping. He rewound back to a safer topic. "They've all done wonders at Dolphin Land. Amazing what a few coats of paint can do."

She stopped rubbing her arm and spoke slowly, her voice so frosty he half-expected her breath to give off vapors. "Yes. *Amazing* what wonders a person can create with fresh paint."

Bingo. He looked around the rest of the room and his earlier "Not bad" echoed in his head. *Double shit.* No wonder she was pissed. She'd fished for a compliment and he'd thrown her a clunker. Definitely time for some damage control. "Makes a world of difference. Like you've done here." He slowly turned in a circle. So what if the paint was thicker than mangrove sludge. It still looked pretty and she was right. It brightened up the room. "Yeah. This is a great color."

That ought to make her feel better. Maybe she'd loosen up and tell him what he really wanted to know. "So, did seeing Dolphin Land set you off?"

"Set me off?"

Crap. The Lady of the Manor returned in full-fledged snoot. "Did it start you on the idea to do all this work?"

"In a manner of speaking. I simply decided that if I'm going to stay here for any length of time, I may as well be comfortable. This was a logical beginning."

The action might be logical, but the timing wasn't. The way she continued to avoid the real question told him there was a whole lot more going on here than a new room color. "You've stayed here plenty of times. Why take on something this big today?"

"Why not?" She shrugged and turned away.

Oh, yeah. The Dora Lee he knew never danced around a subject. Definitely there was more to the story. He didn't stop to think why it was so important to him to know. Hell, since she was already angry, he had nothing to lose by pushing. "Because you've had a rough week? Because you drank enough vodka to sink a Russian sailor? Because . . ."

"Would you shut up already about my bout of drunkenness? It's not like *you've* never had a few too many."

"No argument there, but we're talking about you. Hell, Dora Lee. Even I'd have had trouble settling my head on my shoulders. I sure couldn't have tackled all this work and put in a full day. Especially when there wasn't any reason to do all this right now. You could have put it off until tomorrow or the next day. It's not like you've got a set schedule."

"No. You're right. I didn't have to do this today, or tomorrow, or the next day or even the next hundred days. I have nothing important going on, do I? But guess what? I *chose* to do it today. I wanted to start making a difference in my . . ." She threw down the paint rag. "I just felt like it, okay?" Crouching, she picked up the roller and the tray. "And now I feel like I've done enough. So, thanks for dropping by, Bobby. See you around."

He ignored the dismissal. "What did you want to make a difference in, Dora Lee?"

"My living environment," she snapped.

"Un uh. If that's what you meant, you'd have said so."

"Would you get out of my way so I can take these outside?" Her eyes reminded him of sun flares — blazing hot.

"Why can't you just tell me?"

"Because it's none of your damn business."

"But there is something else."

She hoisted the roller like a club. "Bobby Dalton, I swear if you don't move, you'll be wearing aqua."

"Like I'd let you." But he'd sure enjoy the tussle. Heat was heat and that tent in his shorts wasn't going down because they were arguing. In fact, the opposite was true.

"I am sick to death of you not taking me seriously." She swung the roller one-handed and he barely managed to avoid the head and grab the handle before she smeared him in paint.

"I take you plenty seriously." He clutched the end of the paint tray before she could fling it at him. "What else is bothering you?"

"Nothing that getting you out of my house won't cure. I am so damn tired of men not listening."

They fought a brief tug-of-war over the tray, sending some its contents sloshing over the sides to the plastic sheeting on the floor, before he seized possession. "I'm listening. You're just not saying anything serious. I'll quit poking if you tell me what put a bug up your ass."

"A bug up my ass? A *bug* up my *ass*?"

She yanked at the roller, but he held on tight.

It made her even angrier. "What is the big deal, Bobby? I wanted to redecorate the cottage. Make some positive changes. Why? Because I *could*. If there isn't one other constructive thing in my life at the moment, at least this is something I can accomplish. Something I can control."

She dropped her end of the handle, letting it swing into his shin. "There's your answer," she said, and stalked out the door.

That he understood. He went after her, still carrying the roller and tray until he could put them down on the gravel outside. "Hell, Dora Lee, why didn't you say so in the first place?"

She dropped the trash bags she'd picked up and planted her hands on her hips. "Why should I have to? What business is it of yours what I decide to do?"

"It isn't my business. I asked because I wondered." Because everything about her fascinated him. Even after so many years.

"You criticized first."

"Okay. You got me there." Behind the anger, he saw the hurt in her eyes. Hurt that was so not like the woman he'd known years before. That bastard ex of hers had done more of a number on her than he realized. Too bad *he* wasn't the one stuffed and mounted on that board.

He'd never been good at dealing with women and their feelings except for his sister, and like Jo Jo, Dora Lee brought out his protective streak. No man got away with hurting the women he cared about, not even himself. He gently took hold of her arm and turned her around to face him.

"Honey, I'm sorry."

"You're sorry?" She couldn't look more surprised if he'd sprouted feathers and Fantasy Fest beads.

Lord, he hoped she wasn't one of those women who made a man grovel. The pole in his pants reminded him that he only went on his knees to a woman for one reason, and begging forgiveness wasn't it.

Down, boy. This was the wrong time to think about sex. He cleared his throat. "Yeah, it doesn't matter if your way of doing it is. . . different." God forbid he say "wrong". "You're getting the job done and the results are good."

She narrowed her eyes, suspicious, and scraped her teeth over her full bottom lip. "You really mean it?"

"Definitely."

Her tentative smile made him feel like he'd struck gold and he forged ahead. "I totally get that thing about being in control. Hell, it's half the reason I'm my own boss. I call the shots."

Have mercy. Her pink tongue quickly washed over those lips while she considered his words. "Your clients pay, so aren't you really working for them?"

"Not the way I see it. They can't find fish on their own and what they can't find, they can't catch. If they aren't willing to listen to me, they may as well hang a line over a bridge and hope a fish swims by."

She laughed and, suddenly he'd not only found gold, he'd located an entire treasure ship.

"But, Bobby, I know men like your clients. Surely there are some who think they know better and try to tell you your job."

Scratching his head, he screwed up his face, exaggerating the expression as if he were thinking hard about the comment. Like he'd intended, she laughed again and he chuckled. "Some, but they only try it once."

"Then what?"

"They listen to me or find another guide."

"But if you lose them, you also lose their repeat business and their referrals. That doesn't make your future secure."

"Dora Lee, I've got iron clad security. Turning away a

couple of pain-in-the-ass clients can't hurt my rep. I'm one of the best guides in the Keys."

"Obviously one of the most modest, too." Her eyes twinkled when she teased.

He winked. "It ain't bragging when I can back it up."

Throwing up her hands, she laughed harder. "Please, if that ego inflates any bigger, it'll suck up all the oxygen." She picked up some of the trash bags crowding her lawn. "I do get your point, Bobby. Thanks."

"For?" He swung a bag over his shoulder and grabbed a couple more.

"For apologizing. And for agreeing that it's okay to want to call my own shots."

They started off together. "You don't need anyone's agreement," he said as they cut across the lawn.

"I know, but still it's good to have positive feedback. Oh, crap." She stopped in her tracks, dropped the trash bags and stared at the ground. "Damn it!"

"What's wrong now?"

"Look!"

Clumps of clay-like material and shiny pellets lined the opening of the land crab hole. "What the — that looks like cat litter."

"Of course it's cat litter."

"Of course?" Guess painting wasn't the only project she'd started this afternoon, and this one looked like a conversational land-mine waiting to explode. In the last half hour, he'd learned enough to warn him to step carefully.

"Uh, honey, why did you pour it into a land crab hole?"

"You know how I feel about these creatures. I want that crab gone, so when I went to buy the paint and supplies, I asked some of the men what to do. They had a lot of suggestions, but this seemed the least . . . drastic."

"You really hate these suckers, don't you?"

"Absolutely. The thing has no respect for personal property, but I couldn't bring myself to gas it to death."

He choked. "Gas?"

"I know. It sounds awful. A teen who works there said I should get chlorine tablets used for swimming pools and toss them down the hole. Then rain or morning humidity will release gas vapors that will kill the crab. I don't think that's very good for the environment, do you? Besides. . ." She shuddered. "I don't want to be a crab Nazi."

His chest constricted as he struggled to hold back his laughter and he nearly strangled when he asked, "Someone else suggested cat litter?"

"Right. He said they hate it." She leaned over the hole. "But it's still in there."

"Yeah. Probably dug itself out as soon as you plugged the entrance."

"Maybe I bought the wrong kind of litter? I thought about getting some of that pine-scented stuff, but I don't know if crabs have a sense of smell."

Oh, yeah. Step real careful now. He rubbed his hand over his face, wiping away the smile that threatened to break free. "I don't think it matters what kind you use. That guy at the store was pulling your leg."

"But he swore that he'd tried it."

"Maybe he did it once and got lucky."

"Well, it certainly didn't work for me." She looked so disappointed, he wanted to hug her, but she'd probably elbow him in the gut and the laughter would escape.

He inhaled deeply through his nose and carefully chose his words. "I swear I'm not criticizing, but pretty much everyone around here accepts land crabs as a fact of life. You could just let it be."

"Bobby Daulton, do you see the size of this hole? There's another one by the next cottage over." She waved her hand in a wide arc. "If I don't stop them now, they'll build a whole underground crab condominium complex."

Clearly perplexed, she narrowed her eyes and twisted her gorgeous mouth into a scowl. He tried not to stare and imagine the taste of those lips.

"Well, I tried to play fair." She shifted her weight from side to side. "But I guess I don't have any choice."

"Turning your lawn into crab Auschwitz isn't going to work either. That kid's crazy if he thinks so."

"You know, he was sort of spooky looking, like he really enjoyed telling me to gas the crab. Cruelty to animals is supposed to be one of the signs of a potential serial-killer. Maybe his parents should be worried."

He was almost afraid to ask. "Did those men have any other suggestions?"

She gravely nodded. "Boiling water."

"Boiling water?!" That did it. Laughter burst from him like a water spout. "Geezus, Dora Lee. I'm sorry, but it's just too much to think of you creeping out of the cottage with a pot full of hot water to cook them in the ground." Even while he guffawed, bent over with his hands grasping his knees, he kept an eye on her out of self-preservation, ready to ward off blows if she attacked.

Her lips clamped so tightly together that they trembled and her shoulders shook. Aw, sweet Jesus, he didn't mean to hurt her feelings. *She's been through so much the last couple of days. Don't let her break down.* He'd die if she . . .

Laughed.

Some women giggled. Others chuckled, but not Dora Lee. Hilarity started low in her belly and, when she threw back her head, out poured great swelling and ebbing waves of sound.

She laughed and all the years she'd been gone from his life disappeared. The over-elegant society wife with her designer clothes and let's-do-lunch attitude bit the dust. In her ball cap and shorts and that paint-blotched shirt, with her thick dark hair pulled back in a ponytail, she looked exactly like the girl he'd tagged after from the time he could walk. The teen who'd ruffled his hair like a second older sister. Her golden eyes shone like treasure coins and she was every bit as beautiful — no, more beautiful — than that fascinating twenty-something-year-old woman who'd taken his heart and never given it back.

Rocking back and forth, she sputtered, "Can't you . . .

just imagine? Me! Sn-sneaking . . . up on the . . . c-crab. You're right. Too, too fu-funny!" She shoved him on the shoulder and worked to control her breathing.

God *damn* she was gorgeous and now, since she'd started, he was free to grin and laugh as much as he wanted. "Hey, try it anyway. If it gets the job done, who cares if it's primitive?"

"Primitive!" That sparked another hoot. "I bet the Calusa tribe used containers — even if they had to weave them out of palm fronds!"

"With an ocean full of seafood, do you think they even bothered?" He paused and made a big show of rubbing his chin, like he was really thinking about the problem. "Maybe we should try a batch. Could be a delicacy we've overlooked."

"Bobby, stop!" she shrieked. "Next you'll suggest we ask Bitsy and Vince if they want them for salad at the deli."

"To hear you talk, they'd have a never ending supply. Anytime you want me to set up some traps, let me know."

"We'll team up. I'll drive them out of the hole and you catch them."

Teaming up to do anything was a fine idea. The best he'd heard. That ear-to-ear smile took his breath away, even more than the laughter.

Any plan he'd had to take his time, to think about all the pros and cons involved in making another play for her, evaporated on the spot like a single drop of rain under an August sun. The idea that he even had a choice was useless, like setting a course for Cuba without charts or a compass. He was every bit as in love with her now as he'd been from the beginning. Maybe more. All he had to figure out was the when and how.

She was right about one thing; back then he *had* been a kid. The timing hadn't been right, so no wonder she'd slipped the line and swam away. Lucky for him, he'd learned a lot since then — about life, about women and about setting a goal and making it reality. Nowadays, around these islands, when Bobby Daulton set a hook, the target didn't wriggle free.

CHAPTER 9

"I DON'T LIKE her."

"Who, Leo?"

"That fancy-pants granddaughter." The biker tattoo artist tilted his chair and gestured toward Dora Lee and Bobby walking down the cottage path.

"She don't look so fancy now," Tilda said quietly. "She's dressed purty much normal."

Her husband snorted. "Don't you be fooled. Dressing like folks don't mean she acts like one of us."

"She is not so friendly as Willie. That is true." Rosa rocked slowly back and forth. "She has not been in once to my store."

"Well, she sure as hell ain't giving me any business. Her kind don't appreciate good ink." Leo hoisted his beer, emphasizing his point. "That woman's trouble. We been here how many months and this is the first she's been around to visit her grandpa? Now she ain't been in town more than a coupla days and already she's changin' things. You shoulda seen that load of paint and stuff."

The screen door opened behind them and Mack joined the group. "It's been awhile since that cottage had any work done. I don't blame her for sprucing it up, since I think she'll be staying awhile."

"Dora Lee's not a bad girl at the heart," commented Bitsy, back from her grandbaby-spoiling trip. "She's just fancier, like you said, than we're used to."

"I never got why she thought she was such a big deal. Seems like any woman can catch a husband when she parades around in underwear, showing off her . . ." Her husband Vince caught himself and washed away the rest of his comment with a swig of tea. "Anyhow, that husband of hers was a piece of work, too. Bits, remember that one time he come down with her to visit? Whole time he looked like a tourist that done stepped on a fire ant nest. Like it hurt him to stand still long enough to chat."

Bitsy glumly nodded.

Mack shook his head. "Y'all ain't being fair. I'm betting she grows on you."

"Like a boil." Leo gulped beer and wiped his flame decorated forearm across his mouth. "Bobby better watch his ass. Look at him dogging around. That ain't good. Bet the first time she gets a better offer, she's out of here."

"Maybe, maybe not, but Bobby's a big boy. If he wants to point in that direction, I reckon he can take care of himself." Mack propped his arm on a bent knee. "As for Dora Lee, whether she stays a week or a year, it's up to her and she's welcome. She's family and Willie's over the rainbow to have her around."

"Me, I hope she is here a long time for Willie's sake and if not so long, then at least until I can show her all my products." Rosa's hoop earrings danced when she nodded. "Her kind spends much to save their skin."

Leo grumbled. "All I'm sayin' is . . ."

"Hush now," warned his wife. "They're coming this way."

"Evening, folks." Bobby's greeting encompassed everyone as he and Dora Lee reached the group. "Got room for a couple of more porch-sitters?"

"We'll make room." Mack got up from the step and leaned his hip on the railing instead.

"Bitsy! Vince! You're back. How are Ginny and the kids?" Dora Lee hugged the two of them — who barely managed to cover their surprise — and nodded at the others. "Hello, everyone."

With the exception of Mack, the store owners might have been acknowledging a total stranger, responding mostly with cautious nods and, in Leo's case, a jerk of his bald, spider-webbed head. The guy'd never been the warmest of the group, but that was cold, even for him. Bobby sat on the porch well away from the tattoo king and pulled Dora Lee down beside him. If she was aware of the overall drop in temperature, she didn't show it.

Always one to sniff for business, Rosa got her attention. "Dora Lee, have you tried my skin lotion, yet?"

"Oh, I did, Rosa. You were right. It's a great product. I love the scent!"

The aromatherapist nodded as if the answer was no less than she expected.

"Do you have some hand cream, too? I think I'm going to need it after all this painting!"

That warmed the temperature up some. Pretty soon they were chatting about face masks, eye balms and a bunch of other stuff he'd never heard of.

Tilda ventured an opinion. "My face gits mighty dry riding on the bike, but that face cream softened it right up. Y'oughta try it, right . . . " She stopped and flushed when her husband scowled.

Dora Lee caught that exchange. Her eyes darted from man to woman and she opened her mouth to make God knew what comment. Bobby squeezed her hand and shook his head. For all the good it did.

She raised a brow at him, before giving Tilda a warm smile. "Your skin is lovely. Thank you for the recommendation. Rosa, may I try some?"

"*Sí.* I will get you that and the hand cream." The woman rose and bustled into her store.

More than some rough skin got smoothed over in the exchange. Leo continued glaring, but at least his wife was no longer embarrassed. Bobby squeezed Dora Lee's hand again, this time in acknowledgement, and winked. Rewarded by her wide, breath-nabbing smile, he broke eye contact before his tongue rolled out of his mouth like a pleased hound.

Whoo. Down, boy. He looked around. "No Willie tonight?"

"Nah, my guess is he's staying over at Ruby's. You'll

see him in the morning if you need him for anything," answered Mack.

That meant Dora Lee was on her own for dinner. Well, hell, he couldn't have that now, could he? She could barely move around in her cottage, let alone cook and sit down for a meal. Left to herself, she'd probably call his sister, unless he thought up something quick. Not that he didn't love Jo Jo's company, but he'd a far sight rather have Dora Lee alone for awhile and dinner on his cruiser was a fine opportunity.

The group fell silent to watch the sun complete the evening descent. Almost immediately after the final blast of vibrant color, the store owners stirred from their chairs and bid each other goodnight.

Bobby stood, bringing Dora Lee to her feet alongside him and kept her there with his hand folded around hers as the others sorted themselves out and left for their various homes. When they were the only ones left, he turned to make his dinner invitation and saw her watching Leo and Tilda's motorcycle pull out onto the Overseas Highway.

"Did I do something specifically to put him off?" she asked.

"Don't take it personal. Leo got the short end of the friendly stick somewhere along the line."

"Maybe so, but there's something more. Something with most of them, in fact. I definitely wasn't a welcome guest at this little party."

Not as far as he was concerned. To him, she *was* the whole party and he damned sure didn't want her feeling like she wasn't welcome around the complex. Especially when she was showing signs of tapping back into her roots.

"Honey, by sunset they've all downshifted into chill mode. No place does mellow like the Keys."

"Now I know I'm right." She shot him a look. "Or you wouldn't have tried to feed me a line of bull."

Hell. She'd always been sharp about reading people. How her husband had managed to run around on her without her knowing was beyond him. "I wasn't bullshitting you."

Her eyes turned cool in the dim light and he caved rather than put a rise to her temper. "All right, maybe a little." He lifted his hands in surrender. "Give 'em time to get used to you being around again. They'll warm up."

"Except for Leo."

"Since he doesn't like most people, you really shouldn't mind."

She was silent and then sighed. "Well, at least he's honest about it. I can respect him for not pretending otherwise to my face."

"Folks down here pretty much let you know where you stand right from the get-go."

"A lot of people in other places could take a lesson."

Ouch. How he'd love to punch out the lights of whomever had made her feel bad. Since he couldn't, he opted to make her smile instead. He whipped off his baseball cap and slapped it against his chest. "Dora Lee Hanson, I solemnly swear to always let you know right where you stand." Rewarded with a quick laugh, he grabbed her hand and started walking toward the marina. "I'll even give you advance notice. In another minute, you're going to be standing on board my cruiser while I fix us both dinner."

"Bobby, I'm not dressed for dinner." She stopped in the parking lot and gestured at her paint-spattered clothes. "Look at me. I'm a mess."

Letting loose a whistle, he grinned and tugged to get her moving. "New meaning to 'pretty as a picture', if you ask me."

"That was *so* bad," she groaned, but smiled widely.

"Better than if I said that the aqua on your clothes brings out the blue on your skin."

"Bobby! That settles it. At least let me go clean up." She reversed direction, but he spun her back.

"You can wash up on the boat." He slung his arm around her shoulders, blocking another turnaround. "Quit arguing. I've got fresh-caught yellowtail snapper waiting for the fry pan."

She bumped her hip against his. "This more of that 'take charge' Navy stuff you told me about?"

"Aye, aye, woman."

Finally, he got the laugh he'd wanted and, bonus, felt her relax. Despite her fussing about her appearance, he thought she looked better than fine. Dressed down and splotched with paint, maybe, but she'd burn him dressed in burlap. With her softness brushing against him, his brain went south.

Love and lust packed a wallop, but getting punch drunk before the first date was no way to impress a lady — even when said lady had no idea that this dinner-for-two was a date. He sucked in a deep draught of night air, restored the flow of oxygen to his brain and distracted them both by talking about the boats they passed on the way to his slip. When they reached his cruiser, he led her onto the dock, pulled the boat in as close as the lines and tide allowed, and handed her aboard his home.

🦀 🦀 🦀

SHE'D BEEN HELPED into limousines with less finesse. He grasped her hand, steadying her as she stepped across the gap between dock and boat deck, and then swung himself aboard with confident power and fluid grace. She walked in the door of the main salon and wondered how he squeezed those broad shoulders through what looked like a too-narrow opening. But he managed, his movements smooth and easy like everything else.

No matter how hard she looked, she couldn't find the gangly boy that she remembered in the muscular frame of the man now removing his cap and shaking up the wavy mop of tawny sun-streaked hair.

You shouldn't be looking at all, she reminded herself. What did it matter that he'd grown into a hot bod? First of all, this was Bobby, her younger almost-brother, so she was immune. Secondly, even if he'd been a stranger on the street with this body-to-gawk-over, she was barely divorced and not interested. That tight little tickle in her belly didn't mean anything more than hunger for that fresh yellowtail. Thirdly, she was . . .

Staring.

He'd caught her, too. While she'd been arguing with herself, he'd taken up position against the far wall of the salon, which, in the small space wasn't that far away at all. To escape embarrassment, she turned in a slow circle, checking out the surroundings. The space wasn't even that small, but his six-foot-something body took up so much room. What area remained was paneled in glossy teak with shiny brass accents. A leather recliner, too big for the area but designed for a man-sized body, took up one corner. A padded bench ran along the other side. An oval woven rug in deep blue and burgundy lay over the wood plank floor. A couple of brass and glass ships' lanterns, some compact electronics, a few small watercolor seascapes and family photos completed the décor.

Very tidy. Except for a couple personal items and some sort of sportsman magazine on the table by the recliner, there wasn't a bit of clutter. Whatever else he owned must be neatly stowed in the bank of teak cabinets built into the wall. She completed the circle, discovered him still looking at her, and covered the swift hum in her veins with a smile. "This is what's meant by ship-shape."

"Close enough." He pushed off the wall and eased past her down a small flight of steps to a miniscule galley. "Would you like wine or beer?"

"Wine, please, but first . . ." She looked down at her hands and clothes.

Understanding, he jerked a thumb toward another series of steps. "Forward head and cabin are below."

"All right, then. I'll, um, freshen up a bit."

The cabin was bigger than she expected and mostly taken up by a king size bed neatly covered in a sea-green spread. No cramped bunks for Bobby. Same thing with the bathroom, although how they'd maneuvered in a full-size shower stall was either a marvel of engineering or a miracle.

The air smelled like soap and Bobby's aftershave. She washed her hands, looked in the mirror and burst out laughing.

"What's so funny?" he called from above.

"You weren't kidding about the paint!" Blue spots freckled her face. "I need a washcloth."

"Middle drawer on the right."

A place for everything and everything in its place. Scrubbing away, she removed the paint splatter, neatly folded the washcloth and left it on the sink. It was a little too intimate to use his hairbrush, so she settled for redoing her ponytail by hand and left off her cap. Another look in the mirror and she wished for lipstick. Not that she was primping. No way. She *always* wore lipstick, so the fact that she wanted it now was no different.

Oh, hell. She *was* primping. Enough of that, she told herself as she switched off the lights and went above.

He handed her a glass of white wine and slowly looked her over head to toe, toasting her with his beer. "Nice."

"Flatterer."

"Nah." He grinned, teeth even and ultra white, contrasting

with his deeply-tanned skin. "If I wanted to flatter, I'd say that your eyes are the color of the gold coins Mel Fisher brought up from *The Atocha*."

The compliment warmed her more than she deemed safe. Smarter to deflect it. "Hopefully, after they cleaned off almost four-hundred years of ocean mud."

"You know what I meant. Smart-ass."

But she didn't know how to respond, so she rolled her eyes and turned her attention to the food he was preparing. Neatly shaped fish filets were lined up on paper towels, waiting to be dredged in batter and laid in the frying pan. The scent of red pepper and saffron rose from a steaming pot he'd set to boiling on the little range.

"Mmm. I love Spanish rice."

"Nothing fancy."

Behind him on the opposite counter sat fresh broccoli in a steamer pot, ready to take its place on the stove.

"Looks good to me. What can I do?"

"Have a seat at the table and talk to me while I fry up the fish."

She slid onto the bench and tasted the chilled, pale wine. "I like your boat. It's beautiful."

"Thanks. She wasn't always, but she's come around."

"How long have you lived aboard?"

"Only a couple of months. I've been working on her for awhile. She'd been neglected for years. When I claimed her, she was listing badly and nearly derelict."

"Claimed her?"

He explained passing the boat in the harbor week after week and determining that she'd been abandoned. A request to the proper agency set in motion the procedure to confirm that she'd been left by her owners who'd probably decided she wasn't worth the trouble or expense to haul her out of the water.

"That sounds like a lot of work for a derelict boat." Dora sipped her wine and thought it over. "I mean, why invest so much up front when you couldn't be sure of the outcome?"

"I knew." One by one he coated the filets and gently laid them in sizzling butter. Reaching behind him for the broccoli pot, he switched it out with the rice.

"How?"

"Even at her worst, she had good bones." He topped off her glass from the bottle, and then splashed some wine into the pan. "I dove to check her hull and went aboard for a look at the engine. Between your grandpa and me, there isn't much on a boat that we can't fix."

"I know." Up and down the entire Keys, when it came to boat repair, Gramps was practically a legend.

"So I took ownership, hauled her out. Took weeks just to get her clean. I did most of the work myself."

The expression on his face spoke more than words of the satisfaction he'd derived. While he cooked, he told her about replacing rotted wood with new lathes, stripping the decks and bringing them back to high gloss. With her grandfather's help he'd overhauled the engine, fixed pumps and rewired the electronics. It had taken a staggering amount of work just to make the boat seaworthy.

"My goodness. You must have used every free minute!" Wine slid crisply, easily down her throat. "It would have been easier to buy something in better condition."

He shrugged. "Maybe for some. But this lady's special." A knowing smile creased his face, lit his sea-green eyes. "She was worth every dollar, tired muscle, and scraped knuckle."

A man who put that much sweat equity and care into his home earned the right to pride in the accomplishment. Dora looked around with new appreciation of the gleaming wood and polished brass. "You brought her back to life."

"In return, she's given me a home. Not a bad deal. Here. Grab these." He handed her plates and silverware. "Napkins are in the cabinet behind you. Dinner's ready."

They transferred the platter of food to the dinette and dug in, the fish so tender that it flaked on her fork. "This is so good," she said, savoring the saffron-flavored rice. Even the crisp broccoli, never her favorite vegetable, tasted terrific. "I didn't realize I was so hungry."

Bobby laughed and served her another snapper filet. "Look at all you accomplished today. You worked up an appetite."

She thought about it for a second. "You know what? You're right. I did work hard, more than I have in, well, in a very long time. It feels good."

He'd switched to wine for the meal and now raised his glass in a toast. "Here's to good effort and great results."

"Here, here!" She clinked her glass against his, and then drained it.

"Want some more?"

"Wine or food?"

"Either."

Her full stomach decided the answer. "It was delicious, but no more, thanks. I can't afford to grow out of my clothes."

"Dora Lee." Bobby snorted. "You're a long way from fat."

She carried their plates to the sink and automatically began washing. "Not as far away as I used to be."

"From where I'm looking, you're a knock-out. Always have been."

"I'd accuse you of flattery again but . . ."

"But you know I'm right." He took the wet sponge from her hand. "Leave the rest. I'll do them later. It's too nice a night outside to waste doing dishes. Snagging the wine bottle and their empty glasses, he led her through the salon and up the next set of steps to the open deck.

A cool breeze blew in from the north. A three-quarter moon rose above the mangroves. Overhead, a thousand stars glinted, sharp and amazingly clear in the night sky.

"Ohh, they're *so* beautiful. I'd forgotten that down here the stars shine so much brighter." Smiling, she turned to him. "Why is that?"

He lit a citronella candle on a small table. "Less competition. We don't have all the buildings and street lights diluting the darkness."

"Brilliant," she breathed, awestruck.

"Thanks."

"Not you, goof." She elbowed him in his very hard ribs.

He laughed and pulled her down beside him on a long bench seat. She hadn't thought she wanted more wine, but since he'd already poured, she took it from him and sat quietly turning the glass in her hands.

The citronella candle might have been a protection against mosquitoes, but that didn't diminish the flame's golden glow. There was just enough light for them to see each other. The night around them was soft and silent. Water gently slapped against the docks, wood creaked, and from here and there came low snatches of television programs or music from one of the other boats. Overall the marina was quiet. When a trio of pelicans flew past she heard their wings beat against the air.

Like in the cabin, here, too, there was a place for everything and everything in its place. People settled in aboard their well-cared for boats. The boats themselves docked in straight lines of slips. Native birds bedded down for the night in mangrove trees across the channel. Countless stars twinkled in their eternal constellations. Bobby leaned back, relaxing on the cruiser that he'd restored from the edge of ruin.

Then there was she . . . a visitor in this place that so many others called home. Born and raised here in the Keys. A true conch, as the natives called themselves, but not at all sure that she belonged.

Maybe she did. Maybe she didn't. Maybe she simply didn't know the right answer. Her gaze roamed the deck, but her thoughts turned inward.

"Bobby?"

"Yeah, babe?"

"You really like what you do in life, don't you?"

"I wouldn't do it otherwise."

"It's enough for you? Being a guide?"

"More than enough. It's everything I ever wanted to do for a living." He played with her ponytail, rubbed his knuckles over the nape of her neck. "I don't think I was even ten the first time Mack and my pop took me out on the flats. I tangled the line more often than I threw a clean cast." A chuckle rumbled in his chest. "I wouldn't have caught a damn thing if Pop hadn't handed me his pole once he had a permit on the line."

When he slid his arm around her, she probably should have pulled away, but it felt good to sit beside him so companionably in the lovely, quiet evening and listen to him tell the story.

"By the end of the day, I was hooked as solid as any fish," he continued. "Told Pop then and there that I was born to be a fishing guide."

Lost in his tale, he probably wasn't even aware that he flexed his fingers and caressed her shoulder. Absorbed in listening, Dora still felt every light touch of his fingers and the solid press of his thigh against her leg. Felt them, and did her best to ignore the warmth the contact created.

She shifted lightly and he stopped, but resumed the gentle massage when she settled. "In all the years since you never wanted anything more? Never wanted to be anywhere else?" The concept was difficult to accept. "All my years growing up, I wanted to be any place *but* the Keys."

"You sure did." He shrugged. "Don't get me wrong. I wanted to see some of the world and I got my chance in the Navy. Hawaii. The Persian Gulf. Japan. Every place is different and interesting, and I got a kick out of the traveling, but the Keys are home."

"You could make your home anywhere."

"True. Here's where I choose."

"But why? How did you know? Did you feel it?"

He drank from his wine, tilted his head back and looked up at the sky. "Maybe it's more that I trusted my gut. When I got out of the Navy, I'd saved some money. I knew what I wanted to do, so I put the plans into action, a step at a time."

"No looking back?"

"You don't make progress if you're always looking back and second-guessing yourself. Instead, I kept my mind on the goal and everything I did from that point revolved around achieving it. Now, every time I launch my boat in the water and take out a charter, I know I'm doing what I'm meant to." His grin flashed white, bringing out that slash of dimple. "Doing it better than just about anyone else, too."

"There's that amazing modesty," she snickered.

He retaliated with a tug on her ponytail.

"Hey!" Laughter spoiled the protest. "Can I ask you something else?"

"Is it about my feelings? Guys hate that, you know?"

"Buck up, sailor. You can take it."

"Go easy on me, woman."

His mock groan brought out another smile. "Seriously. If this is everything you ever wanted to do with your life, what if you couldn't do it anymore?"

"Ah, hell, I've never had to think about that, Dora Lee. Thank God. But, I guess . . ." He tilted his head, looking out over the stern of his boat to the dark water of the cove. "It's like anything in life. You do what you have to, make adjustments where you need to and get on with your business."

"You make it sound so easy." Too easy, she thought, finishing the last of her wine and putting the glass on the table.

"If I woke up tomorrow and couldn't be a fishing guide anymore, I'd still have to make a living. So, yeah, to that extent it _is_ easy. Do anything, but do something."

Do something — for the rest of her life. Yes, she'd get right on it as soon as she figured out what "it" was. It must be nice to be Bobby with his totally defined sense of self and secure future. Over the years, he'd developed more than his body. Lord, how she envied him his unshakeable self-confidence. Sure, she'd had the same attitude back in that distant world known as her twenties and early thirties. Funny, how J. Walter changing her carefully planned life without her consent had knocked that confidence to an all-time low. A sigh escaped.

Bobby resumed the soft massage, his touch soothing to her tired muscles. "You don't have to decide this minute. In the meantime, you've got your cottage redecoration to keep you busy."

"True. And when I'm done, it's going to be the prettiest

little place you've ever seen. Inside and out."

"There, now that's a positive plan. Too bad it's sitting smack dab in the middle of all the other run-down buildings."

"Maybe I'll just keep going until I run out of cottages," she joked. "I can put off a decision for months."

"That's one way to give yourself time to figure out things."

"But not knowing makes me nervous!"

He picked up the bottle. "Have some more wine. Smooth the edge off those nerves."

"No." She shook her head. "I better not. The last thing I need is a repeat of last night's drunken spell."

"I don't know. You were cute falling all over me."

She whipped around and shot him a glare. "You just had to remind me."

Grinning lazily, he traced behind her ear to the curve of her jaw with his forefinger. "It's not something I'm likely to forget. Why should you?"

"Then, let's remember that we aren't standing right outside your truck. This time, if I lost my balance, you'd have to carry me all the way back to my cottage."

"If I had to I could."

"In a fireman's li . . ."

A finger against her mouth stopped her retort. "Don't you dare make another crack about your weight. Geezus, where do you women get these notions?"

She could argue the point, or take a nip out of the finger gently rubbing her lips. Nipping might lead somewhere she wasn't sure she wanted to go. Instead, she turned her face away, avoiding a choice all together.

"Not going to answer me, huh?" He angled his body toward her, bending his knee on the bench seat.

She glanced sideways, caught his lazy, amused, and damned sexy grin. "What's to answer?" Amused was he? Tilting her chin, she airily waved her hand. "You know us women and our silly notions."

Snagging the hand, he kissed her palm. She jerked back like she'd touched flame, but he held on and pressed it against his thigh. "I don't think you're silly, but I sure as hell don't get why you think you're fat."

"Not fat, exactly but . . ." Embarrassed about her physical flaws, her cheeks warmed. "You probably don't remember, but once upon a time, this was a terrific body."

"It's still terrific. And you're wrong if you think I've forgotten what you were like before." Eyes glittering in the scant candlelight, he looked her up and down, and then locked his gaze directly into her eyes. His voice deepened. "I remember everything."

CHAPTER 10

Ohh, Lord. Where had the oxygen suddenly gone?
"Bobby, I . . ."

"Shhh." Leaning forward, he cupped his free hand around the back of her neck and brought her forward to meet his mouth.

His very warm, firm, and "where did he learn to kiss like this" mouth.

His lips gently rubbed at first, teasing before he slanted his head and sealed them over hers. He took his time with the kiss, holding her steady and drawing her in deeper. Shock or surprise unbalanced her and she swayed. She felt him smile before he wrapped his arm around her, leaned back and shifted her onto his lap.

It felt . . . amazing. Muscled arms surrounded her, full, wind-rough lips moved over hers in a leisurely kiss that spun out forever. She inhaled a trace of his aftershave, mingled with salt air while he held her as if there were nothing else in the world that he'd rather do than kiss her until her brain fogged and her eyes fluttered shut.

Then he kissed her some more, slicked his tongue once against her lips and slipped it inside her mouth as confidently as he did everything else. She jolted once, tasting the wine and heat of his mouth. He settled her more surely in his arms, and then skimmed his hand down her cheek. Lightly grasping her chin, he tilted it up to deepen the kiss and she melted like the wax in the candle.

Her fingers closed against his soft shirt and roped muscles while she gave herself up to myriad sensations. Lights flickered behind her eye lids and pulse points throbbed to life. Still, he kissed her like she hadn't been kissed in — damned if she could remember how long — and what did it matter anyway? She only knew that it had been far too long since she'd felt so good, so wanted, so beautiful.

So, what in the hell did she think she was doing? This was Bobby, for God's sake!

Immediately she stiffened and yanked her mouth from underneath his.

"Take it easy, sweetheart," he crooned, stroking her shoulders and pulling her back into position for another kiss.

She squirmed, pushing against his chest. "Stop."

"Why?"

"Because I . . . we . . . Bobby, you're . . ."

"Not hearing a reason in there, Dora Lee."

He swooped in for another kiss and she turned her head. She had to make him understand. "You're Jo Jo's brother."

"So what?"

"Younger brother." It hurt to admit it, but she did. "I'm

too old."

"I don't think so," he snorted. "Neither did you a minute ago." He smiled, a teasing light entering his eyes as he drew her body up against his chest. "Come back here and I'll refresh your memory."

If she let him get his mouth on hers again, he might succeed. She'd nearly succumbed already, seduced not only by his kisses, but also by the sheer pleasure of being wanted again by someone, anyone. It didn't matter that he wanted it, too. Damned if she'd take advantage. Instead, she squirmed, shoving so hard against his chest she nearly toppled from his lap.

He caught her before she hit the deck. "Careful."

"Let me up."

"All right, all right. Take it easy, woman." Holding her securely, he stood and set her on her feet in one easy motion. He didn't completely let go, but instead gently ran his hands up and down her upper arms while he searched her face with curious eyes. "What is it really, babe?"

"I told you."

"No. You said you're too old. That isn't true."

Admitting that the age difference bothered her had already shot a dart into her pride. No way would she confess how desperately she craved a balm to her ego. "You're Jo Jo's . . ."

"Younger brother. I heard you before, but that doesn't float as an excuse. My sister would shake pom-poms and lead cheers if she knew we were together."

"How did . . . ? Regardless. You're off-limits."

"Geezus, Dora Lee. Why? I'm thirty-two, not a kid anymore."

Why couldn't he accept it without pinning her to the wall? What was she supposed to say? *I can't be with you because I feel like an aging, out-of-shape, cliché of a dumped trophy wife and you're handsome, built, and pulse-rocking sexy.* Oh, yes. That was a confession she was just *dying* to make. She spun out of reach, facing the railing. "My reasons aren't important."

He followed, bracing his hands on either side of her and nuzzling the nape of her neck. Tightening her muscles barely prevented a delicious shiver from running the length of her spine. "That tells me you don't *have* a good enough reason."

Trapped, she faced him, placing a shaky hand against his cheek. Triumph lit his eyes and her spirit wobbled. God, how good it would be to jettison her objections and dive in — the hell with consequences. Those seven years separating their ages meant zip to her glands. On top of her physical response, she *liked* this man. And because she did, she refused to put stroking her pride above salvaging his well-being.

He turned his head to kiss her palm, a sweet gesture that squeezed her heart.

"Bobby, I can't do this. It's wrong."

This time it was her turn to stop a protest with a finger pressed to warm lips. "Let me finish. You're right about the age difference. It doesn't matter that I'm older, but it *does* matter that you're Jo Jo's brother, yet for a different reason than you think.

"Because you're her brother *and* my friend, I can't use

you like this." Her voice sounded wistful and she struggled to smile.

"Use me how?"

"To make myself feel good," she whispered.

"Oh, sweet Christ."

His arms locked her so tightly to his body that she felt every solid muscle from his chest to his . . . *Every* solid muscle.

"I *want* to make you feel good. Hell, I want to rock your world."

Oh, boy. "That's not the kind of good I meant." Could she screw up the explanation any *more* thoroughly? "In some ways it would be easier if this were only about sex."

"Sex *is* easy. As long as we don't complicate it." He slid his hands down over her butt.

She reached around and slid them up again. "It's already complicated."

"How? Geezus, I feel like I'm navigating without a chart here, babe. You're gonna have to make it clearer."

Clearer, right. She could do that, if he moved off a couple of feet so she could reorganize thoughts scattered by the slow strokes of his big hands up and down her back. Wiggling her hands between them up to his chest, she pushed lightly. "Give me some room, Bobby. Please."

When he complied, she drew in a deep breath. He was right. Dancing around the truth was only sailing them further into murky waters. "Okay. Here's the deal. My husband — my ex-husband — hadn't touched me in months. On top of everything else, he cheated on me. Probably with a woman younger than you. That's his m.o." Now that she'd started, the words tumbled out. "I know I've let myself go. No . . ." She put up a hand to stop his instant objection. "You disagree, and bless you for it, but I'm not the woman he married. That woman was a size four with flesh that didn't sag and jiggle when she strutted around in her underwear."

"Like at his age J. Walter's ass isn't sagging in the hammock when *he* struts around?"

He had a point. Even with regular workouts, her ex's muscles were no longer as pumped and toned as they had been when he was younger, and he sure as hell measured nowhere near Bobby-sized buff. "Maybe so," she conceded. "That might be part of the reason he strayed."

"Damn straight. A man trolls for young tail to prove he can still catch it."

"Exactly! But it isn't just men. Look at me. At us."

"Don't you dare compare yourself to him. Not the same thing at all. I'm the one doing the fishing here." He narrowed the space between them, reached for her again, but she blocked the move. "You've been hit hard." The timbre of his voice dropped to a low, sexy hum. "I can make it better. Let me."

"No." She shook her head. "No matter how good being with you makes me feel, I won't use you to fix my self-esteem." She stepped out of range. "That's why instead of staying, I'm going home. I like you too much to use you as a Band-Aid."

"A what?" Geezus! Where did she get her ideas? Before she could scoot down the stairs, he snared her hand. "Hold it right there. There're two of us in this conversation and I want my say."

"What's the point? You heard my reasons."

"Heard them. Don't accept them." The flat refusal put her back up, he could see it in the stiffening of her spine. Fine. Sometimes the target swam toward the boat and other times it fought the set of the lure. He could handle either scenario so she didn't slip away.

"Damn it, Bob . . ."

Hauling her close, he cut off her words by crushing her mouth with a kiss. Before he'd been content to tempt her slowly, but now he had a stronger point to make. *Band-Aid my ass,* he thought, nipping her plump lower lip and then swiping it with his tongue before he took full possession of her mouth. Heat and anger spiced the kiss, but he kept on, backing her against the railing. Her lush body squirming against his damn near sent him over the edge before suddenly her lips softened, opened and, with a stroke of her tongue, she yielded.

He treated himself to a long taste, hot enough to set his pulse throbbing before reluctantly letting go. Both of them panted like wrestlers in a match and her eyes widened like great golden moons. She opened, her mouth but no words came out.

Good. Let her stay quiet until he said his piece.

Grasping her chin, he tilted her head. "Dora Lee, take a good look and really see me. For the last time, I'm not a green kid anymore, so forget who I was — who we both were back then." He brushed his thumb across her lips, pleased when they trembled. "Much as I appreciate the consideration, I gotta tell you, babe, even if you wanted to, you couldn't use me for a bandage or anything else."

God, he loved her taste, so he went back for more. A gentler kiss this time that drew out a sweeter response. He all but smacked his lips afterward.

"You can pretend that you'd only be using me if we got involved. Maybe you even believe it, but I know different." A grin slowly spread across his face. "Now that I do, you bet your gorgeous ass that I'm going to prove it to you."

Letting go of her soft chin, he took her hand. "Come on. I'll walk you home."

He counted off beats, reaching four before Dora Lee snatched back her hand.

"I'll see myself back to the cottage. No need to trouble yourself." She sailed past him down the steps.

"No trouble." He got to the main deck in time to grab the lines and pull the boat closer to the dock. The tide had dropped some, so he gave her a boost. With her long legs, she didn't need the help, but he liked palming her butt. Since she was already annoyed, he couldn't do more harm, so why not please himself?

Yeah, right then he was happier about the whole situation than he'd been since she landed back at her home port. They'd made some progress, even if she didn't agree. 'Course, other than announcing her departure, she hadn't said anything else.

Took something to knock her speechless. Judging from the set of her jaw and race-walk stride, he figured she was building up to a fine reaction.

He was right.

Planting her hands on her hips, she stopped in the parking lot. "Whatever you think you accomplished with your little demonstration, you're wrong."

"Well, shucks, Dora Lee. All I wanted was to kiss a beautiful woman. Accomplished that just fine." Her eyes flared. If he smiled, she'd probably fry him, but what the hell. The more charged up she got, the more beautiful she looked — all fiery spirit and gleaming eyes.

He cocked his head and shot her a grin. "Be happy to demonstrate again if you need reminding."

She growled low in her throat like a ticked-off she-cat. "You're the one with the memory lapse. Not ten minutes ago I told you no. Not 'maybe' or 'I'll think about it' but no. It's for both of our goods and I'm not changing my mind so that you can indulge some adolescent fantasy." Whirling, she stalked toward the cottage path.

"Never was one for settling." The darkness slowed her down some and he easily kept pace. "Now, taking action once my mind's made up, that's a different matter."

"You can take your action and toss it off the Seven Mile Bridge."

"Good one," he laughed. "But you aren't warning me off."

"I don't have to warn you off. All you need to know is that I'm not putting us in the position of . . . where . . . to. . . "

She started over. "You needed to prove something by kissing me. Fine. We kissed. We liked it. We're adults. It happens. End of game. No repeat."

"Don't call it a game. I'm not playing."

"Neither am I."

The light outside her cottage glowed up ahead like a little beacon. Given the chance, she'd probably sprint to the door to avoid continuing the discussion. To stall her, he playfully bumped hips. "Cool. We agree we're both serious."

"You're annoying." She grabbed the door knob like it was a docking cleat. "Go ahead and pretend to misunderstand, but from now on, I'm not letting you get your hands on me."

Oh, yeah? "Honey, as a strategy for getting rid of me, that's way off course." Before she could retreat indoors, he leaned in and planted one last good kiss. "You all but double-dog dared me. I'm gonna enjoy proving you wrong."

Ignoring her scowl, he smiled broadly. "Sleep good. You'll need your energy tomorrow."

"Only for my redecorating project!"

"That, too." With a deliberate wink, he strolled away, laughing aloud when he heard the door slam shut.

CHAPTER 11

"OF ALL THE pig-headed, macho, alpha . . ." Dora stormed through the living area back to the bedroom. "I try to do the right thing and *not* take advantage of him, but does he get it? No!" She sailed the ball cap into a corner and toed off her paint-spattered sneakers. "No. Of course not. *He*, being a man, decides it's a challenge." Her decision made perfect sense. Bobby's refusal to agree was no more than male pattern arrogance.

In the midst of yanking the T-shirt over her head, she caught sight of herself in the mirror. Her swollen mouth was rosy without a slick of lipstick. She lightly touched her lips, positive they still vibrated from that final lip lock.

That man knew how to kiss. Potent to the extreme.

She flopped back on the bed, staring at the cracks in the ceiling paint. The sooner she put tonight out of her mind, the better. Forget how he made her head reel and jazzed her nerve endings in ways she hadn't experienced since . . .

Since months and months ago before J. Walter took up with some other woman who still wore a single digit dress size.

So what if Bobby might be the only man she knew who actually found her attractive and had a hot, thorough way of making her feel good? She couldn't allow the sensual buzz to override her common sense. It would be all too easy to give in. If she didn't love his sister and think so highly of Bobby, she'd take what he offered and revel in the sweet sensations. If she thought less of herself, she'd cave to the challenge, but she wasn't a prize to be won.

She'd already been one man's trophy and had no desire to repeat the performance. Anymore than she could turn into a female version of her ex, disregard Bobby's well-being, and bag him as a trophy of her own.

No way. There were other, more important things to do. Like figure out a plan for the rest of her life. She needed to get organized. Make a list. Do something other than obsess over her suddenly humming hormones and stare at the cracks in the ceiling. She looked at her Oz figurine collection. Had Dorothy crumpled in a heap at the beginning of the Yellow Brick Road? Of course not! The little Kansas cutie survived a tornado and took off for the Emerald City, in red-sequined pumps no less.

Dora Lee bounced up off the bed and out of the room. She paused in the hallway and studied the living area with its jumble of protected furniture and drop cloths on the floor. Even though the place looked a mess with only some of the wall space covered in blue, the entire room already appeared fresher. A wide smile broke over her face. Amateur skill level aside, she was well on the way to transforming old and dreary into bright and beautiful. And that was just with paint. Wait until she changed out the furniture, added accessories, and brought in all those warm touches that gave a place life and character.

It might not be a five-hundred-dollar-a-plate charity dinner, but she was in the process of accomplishing something concrete. On a small scale perhaps, but that made her no less proud. Not at all sleepy, she grabbed a screwdriver and pried open a can. After carefully stirring the paint, she poured some into the tray and wiped away drips with a rag. She picked up a roller and, mindful of Bobby's comments, coated it with far less paint than before. He was right! The paint spread more evenly but still covered the wall with brilliant blue.

She got into a rhythm of rolling, up and down in a W, dipping into the tray for more paint and then rolling some more. The darned walls looked so pretty, they made her smile and think about the rest of the décor. Seascapes and beach scenes would enhance the shore cottage look. Or, she considered carefully, she could go for contrast with bolder, more modern slashes of color. Furniture choices would come first and set the theme. Maybe she wouldn't salvage the couch, but replace it and the armchair with something overstuffed and supremely comfortable. Choices that would invite someone to snuggle in with a good book, a cup of tea, and a plate of cookies, warm from the oven.

That meant she'd have to renovate the kitchenette, too, and actually add an oven. She tilted her head and considered the space. In her mind's eye, white-painted wood cabinets with seed-glass in the doors replaced the current faux-grain veneer style. Gleaming white tile with maybe some cheerful floral accents for the backsplash and warm stone-look counters. What would look better — stainless appliances or ceramic? She'd have to browse the big home improvement store again and compare. Re-dipping her paint roller, she returned to the task at hand. With the plans filling her head, she was about to become a regular customer.

She hadn't been kidding when she'd told Bobby that she'd transform this little dwelling from run-down to spectacular. Although she'd always worked with interior designers on her Treasure Coast home and never implemented anything without J. Walter's approval, she'd learned a lot about color pallets, furniture placement, and accessorizing. On this, at least, she was confident she could succeed with stunning results.

Only the rest of her life was up for debate. She could keep busy for awhile revamping her cottage inside and out, but after that . . . The roller shot up the wall, excess pressure funneling out little streams of paint. Easy, she told herself, bringing her technique back under control. She'd think of something down the line. Her mouth quirked in a wry smile. At least she was developing new skills. Maybe Gramps would let her practice her new-found painting talents on other buildings around the marina.

Earlier, she'd joked as much to Bobby. An image of herself, dressed in a succession of pressed linen outfits dripping with paint, made her laugh out loud. Oh, that would be the day.

Wait a minute. Slowly, she lowered the roller head into the paint tray. This cottage didn't have to be the only pretty one sitting among all the others, like a single lovely rose in a thicket of weeds. Her mind flashed back to her childhood, growing up at the complex with Gramps and Nana, when all the cottages were in use — mostly by vacationing fishermen, older couples and, occasionally, small families who were satisfied with the small private beach instead of a pool.

Over the years, Gramps had lacked the capital to make the renovations that might have kept the property viable for guests and he'd been reluctant to risk the rest of the marina as collateral. Rightly so. The marina and boatyard were all he had to support himself and secure his retirement.

Not that Gramps ever planned to retire. "I already go fishing whenever I want, Dora Lee," he often said. "I don't need to give up work I like doing to sit on my ass and get old."

Instead, after Nana's death, he'd slowly given up on the hospitality business. Dora peered out of her taped window through the darkness at the cottage next door. Some of the buildings were used for storage, but the others . . . For all she knew they were still filled with their furnishings, gathering dust and cobwebs.

She put down her paint roller, wove her way around the piled up furniture and slipped out the front door. That nearly-full moon sat higher in the sky, illuminating the path and the buildings in soft, silvery light. Dora picked her way to the intersection of four paths, stood in the middle and slowly turned around. Night hid some of the cottages' flaws, but not all. Metal awnings, although bolted down over windows to shield against hurricanes, showed their age in loose fittings and flaked paint. Roofs sagged and rain gutters were missing. A bird's nest poked through a light. Spindly old hibiscus and bougainvillea trees crowded the outer walls. Gramps must come through regularly with a chain saw to prune back the limbs and a weed whacker to tame the ground cover, but that was the extent of the landscape maintenance.

"What a mess," she whispered. But still . . . What if?

A few years back, she and J. Walter had vacationed in Bermuda. While he fished for blue marlin, she'd shopped the towns, charmed by the vivid colors of the buildings. Down in Key West, rainbow pastels brightened many of the Victorian-style cottages. She circled again, this time not seeing the dilapidation in the gray and black shadows. Instead, she imagined tidy paths leading up to cheerful buildings dressed in bon-bon shades of pink, blue, lavender, and yellow, offset by cool white Bahaman shutters. Lush, green, sculpted tropical trees and shrubbery hugging the buildings. Stately palm trees providing shade from the hot, golden sun.

Bright white doors would open to luxury accommodations. Plush, comfortable seating, tiled floors. Beds to sink into with four-hundred count cotton bedding and half a dozen pillows. Polished granite bathrooms with gleaming accents and baskets of signature lotions and creams to pamper. She could practically smell their scents and feel the smoothness on her skin.

The vision played through her head like a movie, and like any good movie, drew her in until she not only saw the images, she experienced them.

What if?

Could she? Dare she? Dora whirled, heading for her cottage as fast as she could navigate the path. Inside, she grabbed a pen from her handbag and then rummaged for paper — finally settling for ripping a bag in two pieces and pressing them flat on the kitchenette counter. Ideas shot out like bullets from her brain. She jotted them down as fast as she could as if the words on paper made them real. What to do first? Hire a contractor. Someone to inspect each building and make a list of structural repairs. No! Maybe an architect should see the cottages first to study the basic room layouts and design luxury accommodations. Then they'd know how much structural work had to be done from top to bottom.

Color schemes. Fabric pallets. Furnishings. Accessories. They would all come later, but she wrote the words *Highest Quality* and underscored them twice. By the time she was finished, she'd transform this rundown bunch of buildings into a beautiful, totally charming, elegant and exclusive . . . what? Resort? No, too lofty.

Luxury guest cottages. Simple concept, but she'd come up with the perfect name later. For now, she needed to focus on the designing, the rebuilding, and the decorating.

The cost.

She sank down on a stool. Her heartbeat thundered in her head and nausea roiled in her stomach, worse than that morning hangover. All the ideas that had blossomed in her imagination quickly withered. Granted, her divorce settlement wasn't chump change, but it wasn't a Midas treasure. A mixture of equities, bonds and cash, right now the total amount safely sat in a brokerage account, hopefully building for her future. That was the familiar kind of investment.

Investing in herself was alien territory. She stared at her freshly painted wall, feeling even more like Dorothy gazing at a distant Emerald City. She envisioned her little gathering of guest cottages as clearly as if they already existed, but to get to that goal, she'd have to cross a treacherous path. Those glorious red poppy fields had drugged Dorothy and her friends before they reached the Wizard's home.

Here in Dora's world, if she screwed this up, no good witch could wave a magic wand to save her ass and her money. Could she take the risk? J. Walter would no doubt scoff at the very thought that she could be an entrepreneur. For that matter, she was only a few beats away from scoffing at herself. It wasn't like she had hotelier experience.

On the other hand, she knew how to hostess. How to create a gracious atmosphere and make guests feel comfortable. Surely, that counted as valuable life experience.

Do anything, but do something. Bobby's motto replayed in her mind. Somehow she didn't think he'd meant, "Risk your entire financial security on a half-baked plan, launched on the basis of painting one small room."

Once sparkling spirits flattened and the day's exertions with its emotional and physical ups and downs, sapped the remains of her energy. She pushed herself to her feet and trudged to the bedroom. Sleep. That's what she needed. A chance to shut down the worries, the insecurities, and, if she could, the electricity still lingering from Bobby's big time kiss demonstration.

A hot shower relaxed her muscles to jelly. Maybe tomorrow when she wasn't bone-deep exhausted, she'd rejuvenate her confidence. Hell, that nap in the poppy field had revitalized Dorothy before she marched on to meet the Wizard. A good night's sleep couldn't hurt. She crawled into the old iron bed, killed the light and dropped into welcome oblivion.

🐰 🐰 🐰

MORNING STREAMED GOLDEN light through the lace curtains of the window. The first thing she saw when she opened her eyes was her set of Oz characters, colorful and cheerful in a sunbeam. She stretched, aware of muscles that twinged and ached from their previous day's labor.

She'd slept, but not solidly. Every few hours, she'd woken up from dreams of candy-colored buildings and lain there in the darkness while ideas and insecurities ran through her tired brain. The wild desire to put her new plan into action battled with the woeful fear of financial ruin. Twenty years earlier, nothing had seemed impossible. Why, she'd have already been on the phone setting up appointments. Of course, back then she didn't have the means, but that hadn't stopped her from pursuing her modeling dream. Now when she had money, the risk of failure loomed large, like a black cloud blocking the sun. Apparently, she'd lost her gumption along with her perky boobs.

Everything looked clearer in the morning, her Nana had always said, but right now the only clear things she needed were a fresh perspective and an objective opinion.

In other words, she needed Jo Jo. If ever there was a woman who accomplished pie-in-the-sky schemes with rock solid practicality, it was her best friend.

She rolled out of bed and hurried through her morning routine. First thing on a Monday morning, Jo Jo was bound to be at the theater seeing to one of a thousand details. She'd wanted her to drop by and see the plans for the theater group's summer fundraiser, so a morning visit would accomplish two things. Three, provided Dora hit that Cuban deli and bakery for breakfast and coffee.

🦀 🦀 🦀

"No, DARLIN', YELLOW gingham won't do for Myrtle's costume." Jo Jo spoke into a cell phone headset while she paced the stage. "She's a dance hall singer, not a western school marm." While listening to the response, she simultaneously jotted notes on her clipboard. "Yes. Uh huh. Flashy satin and fishnets. Blazing red would be good. Purple, too."

A natural multi-tasker, Jo Jo juggled projects like a Key West street performer tossed bowling pins. She was never still, Dora thought as she stood just inside the door of the little theater. Whirling one way, she adjusted the position of a stool, made more notes then crossed the stage again to a box of props, sorting through them while she continued her conversation. The whole time, she tucked her clipboard under her arm and kept the phone clipped to her silver-studded black leather belt. She'd gone for biker chick chic in her outfit this morning. A black jersey knit halter topped off curve-hugging jeans over black boots. Tanned, toned arms sported a dozen silver bangle bracelets. Silver hoops swung from her ears and she'd pulled her strawberry blond hair back in an onyx clip.

On her next turnaround, Dora rattled the bakery bag and caught her eye.

A wide grin crossed her friend's face and she held up an index finger to signal "one minute" while she wrapped up the phone call. "Now, you're talking! That's gonna look great for the Can-Can number. Good going. See you at rehearsal. Oh, that reminds me. I need Tommy guns for the singing gangsters." She pressed a button on the cell and jumped off the stage. "I smell coffee. Hallelujah, sister! Gimme a hug, first."

Dora laughed, hugged, and handed over a to-go cup. "Saloon girls, Can-Can and singing mobsters? Should I ask?"

Jo Jo boosted her butt onto the stage and sat, bouncing her heels. "We're doing musical highlights of shows from different times and places in history. *Pirates of Penzance, Annie Get Your Gun, Guys and Dolls.*"

"Sounds like fun. Lots of dancing and very colorful, too."

"You have no idea." She snickered. "I talked some of the guys into doing *We Are what We Are* from *La Cage Aux Folles*."

"And it isn't even Fantasy Fest." Dora took a seat in the front row. "Only you."

"It's gonna be a blast. You'll come, right?"

"Of course. Can I do anything to help?"

"Silly question. Do you want to serve wine, usher, or help with the silent auction? Yowsa, this is great coffee. What's in the bag?"

Dora handed over the goodies. "Put me wherever you need me most. Tell me more about the show. How did you come up with this idea?" While her friend expounded on the staging, music, and performers, Dora listened and studied the stage, set like a Wild West saloon. The whole event came alive in her mind with Jo Jo's explanation.

"I can see it. Right down to the feathers on the drag queens' costumes. You're amazing!" She laughed, somewhat ruefully. "I don't know where you get the energy, or how you go about making it all happen."

Jo Jo swallowed the last bite of a honey-dipped pastry. "It's a lot of work, that's true." She licked her fingers with an appreciative *yum*. "But like with any play, we work from a script. That's our master plan and we go from there. Who does what. We budget for each aspect. Setting up a timeline is important. It's all in the organization."

Dora considered that while chasing a bite of croissant with some rich coffee. Some people wrote Jo Jo off as being as flaky as the pastry, but her work ethic was as solid as any

CEO's. "At the beginning it must be overwhelming. All those things to consider and everything you have to accomplish to put on a performance. I can't imagine."

"That's only because you've never done it, but think about those fancy charity events you used to plan. They're another kind of show." Jo Jo ticked off points on her fingers. "Find a place. Set a date. Decide a budget. Even though it's a charity event, you have budgets. Pick a theme. Plan a menu. Design the invitations. See. Not so different. Just in your case, you work with a committee while I have a cast and crew."

"Don't you ever worry that you won't be successful?"

"Hell, yes! Long about three hours before the curtain goes up, I get a bad case of flop sweat. It ebbs the first time the audience laughs out loud, or applauds a scene. By the end of the first act, I'm ready to celebrate. What about you?"

"With a charity ball?" Dora thought about all the different dinners and events she'd helped organize. "I can't relax during the event. I'm always watching to see that the meal is being served on time, that the food is good. I look to see if the guests are enjoying themselves. If they're dancing."

"So, you never kick back and enjoy the results of all your hard work?" Her friend looked appalled. "What fun is that?"

"Well, they were important, not just for the organizations they benefited. If they didn't go well and I was involved . . ." She spread her hands. "J. Walter always felt that the events reflected on his reputation." And she'd always been too worried that she'd overlooked something vital to the evening's success.

"Oh, hell. I was right. That couldn't be much fun. Leave it to old 'stick up his ass' to make it all about him."

Her bluntness jolted a laugh out of Dora. "It cracks me up when you call him that."

"That's the mildest nickname." Jo Jo reached into the bag for another goody. "These are terrific."

"It's so not fair that you can eat two of those. I'd kill for your metabolism." A fair share of curves in her hips and bust packed her friend's five-feet-two frame, but she never looked fat, only sexy. When Jo Jo sashayed past, men's eyes rolled back in their heads.

"I work it off keeping busy."

As usual, she was always busy. The two of them discussed the rest of the upcoming show while they finished their treats and sipped coffee. After a few moments, Jo Jo tilted her head and fixed her sea-green eyes — copies of her brother's — on Dora.

"So, girlfriend, what's going on with you?"

Dora ran a finger over the plastic top of her coffee cup. Away from the marina complex, in this theater that her talented friend had rejuvenated practically from the ground up, her idea of renovating the guest cottages seemed more far-fetched than planning vacations to Mars. But she'd come here for an objective opinion and, at least, she knew that Jo Jo wouldn't laugh in her face. She cleared her throat. "Well, yesterday I got it in my head to redecorate my cottage."

"Cool! I've seen what you did with that mausoleum — I mean mansion — up on the Treasure Coast. You'll work wonders with this little place."

The rapid enthusiasm made it easier to continue. "After dinner with Bobby . . ."

Jo Jo's eyebrows shot up to her hairline.

Dora raised her hand, forestalling the questions. "I made a joke about not stopping with repainting my own place, but making all the others look just as pretty. Later, after . . ." No, she wasn't going into details about the challenge! "I sort of got this idea that maybe I *could* renovate the whole area and open up a business for guests again, but this time, make them more upscale. Luxury guest cottages." Suddenly, the words poured out and she revealed her entire wish list of plans, from marble vanities to the hot tub.

"So, anyway, that's some of what I thought." Rubbing the back of her neck, she laughed nervously. "It probably sounds ridiculous and I'm a fool for even considering it."

"Ridiculous? Hell, no!" Jo Jo jumped off the stage, grabbed her up out of her seat and danced her around in a circle. "It's a terrific idea."

Laughing, they fell back against the stage. "Hot damn, girlfriend. I'm impressed. You went from thinking you didn't have a clue, to hatching a champion idea in less than a day."

Jo Jo lifted her coffee cup. "I propose a toast to the beginning of a beautiful life plan. Come on. Raise that cup and we'll make it official."

The positive reaction eased some of fear's chokehold on Dora's chest, but she was still a long way from secure. She hesitated too long and her friend's cat-like eyes narrowed.

"Okay. If you weren't excited about the idea, you wouldn't have brought it to me, so what else is going on?"

"It's just . . . you know, I've never done anything like this before! It's huge and I'll risk everything I have for the future on what could be a total bomb." She threw up her arms and paced. "Sure, it's easy enough to dream about color schemes and furniture, but what do I know about taking a fantasy and making it real?" A wide sweep of her arm encompassed the stage, the lights, and the entire theater. "It's not like I'm staging a play. At least you have a script as a starting point." All of a sudden, the obstacles loomed like boulders in her mind.

Jo Jo snorted, reducing those obstacles to pebbles. "If you can dream it, you can do it, Dora Lee. Remember what I said about organization and a plan." She hooked her arm through Dora's. "Bring those pastries and step into my office. You need a script. We'll open up a spreadsheet. By the time we're finished, we'll have a list of needs and budget line items. Then you can call around and get people working on figures so you know what you're working with."

"Spreadsheet? Um, well . . ."

Jo Jo glanced her way. "You know how to run a computer?"

"Sort of. I can web surf, check email and do a letter."

"There you go. We'll have you running formulas in no time. Oh, and hey, I got people you can talk to for your designs and such. Best architect in town has the lead in the play we're staging this fall."

Slowly, like a seed pod breaking open, Dora's hope blossomed. Maybe when they put it all into black and white, her idea wouldn't seem like so much of a pipe dream. "That would be great. I don't know anybody in town. I've been away for too long."

"You'll get to know people again right quick, sweetie. Especially now that it looks like you're sticking around." An ear-to-ear grin broke across her gamin face. "My best friend's staying. That's the best news of all!" She pushed open the backstage door and they navigated around various boxes, furnishings, and props to the small staircase leading upstairs to the office. "That's gonna make my brother a happy man, too."

"This doesn't have anything to do with him!" she protested. Her decision definitely was *not* based on Bobby.

"Not yet maybe, but c'mon. You two had dinner together last night." Jo Jo snickered and squeezed her arm. "I don't need the details now. We have plans to make, but that doesn't mean I won't pump you unmercifully for them later."

Terrific. According to Bobby, Jo Jo would fully support the two of them embarking on a full-fledged, no-holds-barred, no-clothes-necessary relationship. Dora would have to make it perfectly clear to both of them that she wasn't interested. Knowing her friend, Jo Jo would accept the decision a lot more easily than her brother.

Whatever the case, she couldn't worry about it now. Putting together a workable plan definitely took priority over a runaway case of raging hormones.

Three hours later, if not set in stone, the project had definitely taken more concrete shape. On a neat and tidy spreadsheet, which Jo Jo had taught Dora how to format, was a list of tasks with a column for plugging in price quotes. They'd visited the websites of at least a dozen establishments from Aruba to Key West that had the look and amenities she thought she could offer, and printed out photographs and rate sheets. Jo Jo had also made up a list of contractors and architects for Dora to call for estimates.

Then they'd keyed in the website of a computer company and her friend had explained what features and programs to look for in a high-powered notebook and printer.

They'd even given her project a name — Key of Sea Cottages.

"It's catchy, Dora Lee, to stick in people's minds," Jo Jo assured her. "Just think of the advertising slogans." She tilted back in her desk chair and waved her arm in an arc as if picturing the words on a billboard. "Key of Sea Cottages — in harmony with paradise."

"Or, Key of Sea Cottages — Relax the rhythm of your life," Dora suggested.

"Get in tune with a great vacation."

"Jo Jo!"

"Yeah, I know. Too corny." She stood and handed Dora the folders with all the documents. "You've got time before you have to think about your advertising anyway, and you'll need to hire an agency to design a campaign. I'm good, but international advertising is beyond my range of experience."

"Mine, too." A little jolt of mixed fear and excitement zapped her solar plexus. "What am I talking about? This whole thing is beyond my experience."

"Challenge is a good thing, Dora Lee. Remember, it's like you're staging a play. You've got your script." She tapped the folders. "You're planning the set. Next, you'll get the cast and crew lined up. First, you've gotta talk to your grampa about the whole deal. Get him on board. Not that it's gonna be a problem."

"I hope not, but still, if he hates the idea, I'll understand. It's his place."

"And you're his granddaughter and only blood family. Willie's gonna be so over the moon to have you around."

"I hope so."

"I know so." They left the office and headed down the steps. "All that brain power's made me hungry. C'mon. Let's hit the grill." Shooting Dora a glance, she smirked. "I think I've held back my curiosity long enough."

Uh oh. From the sound of it, she was in for some Jo Jo-style interrogation. "There's not much to tell."

"Oh, bull crap. You think I don't know my own brother better than that?" Outside, she locked the doors of the theater behind them and they climbed into Dora's Mercedes. "If that boy got you alone on his boat, for sure he didn't stop with dinner."

Dora opened the car windows and let the breeze in to cool her heated face as they headed down the Overseas Highway to a popular eatery. "Fine. He made me dinner. We sat upstairs afterward. He put a move on me and I told him 'no'."

"I figured you'd say 'no' the first time out, but why?"

"You've got to be kidding! The more obvious question would be, why did he put a move on me in the first place?"

"Dora Lee! If you haven't figured out by now that . . . Hi, Melissa." Jo Jo greeted the waitress.

"Hey, you two. Grab a table anywhere. Specials are fish dip, blackened mahi sandwich, or a Cobb salad. Be with you in a minute. Drinks before you decide?"

"Iced tea for me, please," said Dora.

"Make it two."

They'd barely settled at the table before Jo Jo launched in again. "Why on earth wouldn't you expect him to put a move on you? He's been hot for you since he was in high school."

"That was a million years ago. And thirty or forty pounds." That Cobb salad special sounded like just the thing. Dressing on the side, and no bread or crackers.

"Your weight?" In the midst of unfolding a paper napkin, her friend's jaw dropped. "Are you telling me *that's* your worry?"

Dora drew patterns in the condensation on her glass. "Well, actually, the age thing gets to me, too."

Jo Jo snorted. "That's plain crazy."

"You sound like your brother."

"That's because we both have more than our share of common sense." Her friend fixed a stern look on her over the rim of her iced tea. "Maybe you oughta listen."

"Maybe this time one of you ought to listen to me instead!" Exasperated, she ripped into a plastic packet of crackers from the bowl on the table. So much for no carbs. "God knows I tried hard enough to make him understand last night."

"Understand what? That you're too fat or too old? No wonder he didn't pay you any mind. That's nonsense."

"It isn't just those things. It's . . ."

Her voice cracked and, just like that, Jo Jo's face lost its fierce expression and she covered Dora's hand with her own. "Okay, sweetie. Take it easy. Explain to me what's really got you so upset."

"Are you going to bark at me again?"

"No. I promise. I'll pinky swear it if you want."

That prompted a tiny smile. Dora swallowed more tea and began again, this time more calmly. "After going through J. Walter dumping me for another woman, believe me, your brother's doing and saying all the right things, but they aren't easy for me to hear."

"Why? He's not saying anything he doesn't mean. Wait a minute. You don't think he's pushing you because you're vulnerable and he wants to take advantage? Bobby wouldn't do that. Not to any woman, and especially not to you."

"No! Of course he wouldn't. Trust me, he might be all-guy, but I know he wouldn't use me. It's the other way around. I *am* vulnerable and that's why if I go through with anything more than friendship, I'll be the one taking advantage."

"Oh, for Chrissake. I can imagine how that logic went over last night. You told him this, right? What did he say?"

Dora related the entire conversation. Half way through,

Jo Jo shook her head and rolled her eyes so hard they almost did a three-sixty in their sockets.

"Well, my brother might not always be right, but he is in this case and I gotta tell you, girlfriend, I'm glad he's not backing down."

Terrific. "Even though it's for his own good?"

Jo Jo's lips quirked. "According to him, it isn't good and he's a grown man, so he ought to know."

The waitress served their lunch. Dora stabbed at her salad with a plastic fork, dipped the lettuce in salad dressing, and stuffed it into her mouth. Chewing thoroughly was one way to avoid responding.

They ate for awhile without talking. Jo Jo attacked her fish sandwich with the gusto of a girl who had great metabolism. Dora's salad was delicious with its smoked turkey, crisp bacon, and crumbled bleu cheese, but it was huge. If she packed it all in, she'd bloat like a puffer fish. So she stopped halfway and put down her fork. "You probably think that it's stupid for me to feel so insecure."

"Do not. There's nothing stupid about you, first of all. Secondly, everybody's insecure about some thing or another." She twirled a French fry in ketchup and popped it in her mouth. "I do, however, think it's silly to let the insecurity run your life and make your decisions."

"What if I can't help it?"

"Bull crap again. Sweetie, you never had an insecure cell in your entire body until now. That alone ought to tell you it's a temporary abnormality, brought on by that yahoo ex. It isn't a permanent condition, so the next time it rears its ugly little head, tell it to get lost. You are a beautiful, accomplished woman who is about to embark on her own wonderful new career as an entrepreneur. Any time you feel unsure, you tell yourself that over and over until you believe it."

Her eyes lit with wicked glee. "Or, you can cut to the chase and call my brother. He'll be more than happy to remind you."

Dora pursed her lips and drew down her brows. "Can't I just call you instead?" she groused.

"My gate doesn't swing your way, if you know what I mean. Now, we could have an old fashioned girl primp party — do each other's hair and nails — but honestly . . ." She leaned forward and winked. "Wouldn't sweating up the sheets with Bobby be a helluva lot more fun?"

Dora scrubbed her face with her hands. "You're incorrigible."

"And proud of it, but that doesn't answer the question." Smiling, she pinned Dora's hands to the table. "Tell you what. I'll leave you alone about my brother if you can look me in the eye and swear on our friendship that he's the lousiest kisser in the world. Tell me that he's got a mouth like a grouper and that the whole time he had you in a lip lock, you felt nothing but revulsion and were counting the seconds until he let you go."

"Jo Jo, I . . . That's not . . ."

"Nuh uh. Look me right in the eyes and say it."

"Damn it all. Fine! Okay. I can't. Bobby's a terrific

kisser." She yanked her hands free and gulped down the rest of her tea. "My brain spins remembering it. He makes my hands shake and my cottage cheese thighs sweat. Are you happy?"

Her friend hooted, a deep throaty, completely infectious laugh. "Thigh sweat and all? It's a wonder you didn't jump him where he stood." Heedless of the other customers in the restaurant, she slapped the table and laughed so hard that, finally, Dora couldn't help but join in.

"He didn't give me a chance. He was too busy trying to jump me."

"Well, the next time, don't fight him off. It'll be good for you. Good for both of you."

Dora sucked in some air, grabbed a paper napkin and swiped under her eyes. "I don't know if an affair is such a good idea right now."

"If you ask me, I'd say it's exactly what you need. Nothing like multiple orgasms to knock that insecurity right out of you."

CHAPTER 12

THAT THOUGHT OF sex with Bobby stayed with her the rest of the afternoon. "Thanks a lot, Jo Jo," Dora grumbled to herself as she parked at the marina complex. Like she needed multiple orgasms and Bobby on the brain when she presented her idea to her grandfather. At least she didn't have to worry about running into the object of her lustful thoughts for the time being. He was out on the ocean with clients. No sign of any disapproving, scowling shop owners either, she realized as she walked past the strip of stores. They were all still inside seeing to customers.

If thinking positive, no, she amended that to *when* Gramps gave her his go-ahead, she'd be committed to living and working at the complex. That meant frequent sunset gatherings with a group of near-strangers who hadn't exactly warmed her with their welcome. She had some work to do there as well, she realized. Since her plan would affect them, too, she needed them to buy into the project. Particularly since they'd have to make some changes. Improvements, actually. The class of clientele she aimed to attract to the guest cottages would turn up their noses at these stores in their current condition. Quaint was one thing. People loved quaint. Ramshackle was another thing all together.

She cringed at the thought of her guests strolling out to their cars and catching sight of Leo scratching his hairy belly on the porch. Well, repainting and renovating the façades of all the shops would help. Maybe instead of being scared off by the tattoo artist, the guests would chalk him up as "local color". Local color paired nicely with quaint.

Rosa's products, on the other hand, might actually be an asset. Again, local color was more easily embraced by vacationers who might like knowing that the bath amenities in the cottages were produced locally. She made a mental note to add that to her growing pile of ideas and continued on her way to find her grandfather.

He was lowering the engine cover on a boat when she spotted him and called hello. A grin split his face as he wiped oil off his hands and stepped off the vessel. "Hey, baby girl. No, don't hug me. I'm filthy and sweaty."

"You still look good to me, Gramps." She laughed and kissed his cheek.

"Me, too." Ruby came out of the office with a couple cans of soda in her hands. "Something about a hard-working man, ain't there, Dora Lee?"

"All right, you two. That's enough." Willie chuckled. "Where you been all day?" he asked. "And what the heck have you been up to? We dropped by your cottage earlier so Ruby could freshen up those flowers."

"You've been busy, that's for sure. That new paint looks real pretty."

"Thanks." They were giving her the perfect lead-in and her heart tripped. Suddenly, she realized how important it was to her that Gramps agree to her project. His approval was the first step to the bigger validation. "The place needed sprucing up and since I'm not busy with anything else, I figured, why not go on and do it." She glanced at Gramps. "You don't mind, do you?"

Silver eyebrows drew together and creased his weathered forehead. "Why the heck would I mind? This is your home, darlin'. That's your place. It always has been."

She smiled. "I was hoping you'd say that." Her eyes went from one dear old face to the other. "While I was working, I sort of had this idea that I want to run by you, Gramps. It'll take a little time to explain."

"I promised Joe Owens I'd get his tune-up finished today, so I got a couple of hours more work ahead of me. How about we talk after sunset?"

"Sounds good," she agreed. "Do you two have plans for dinner? My treat."

"Baby girl, you do not have to treat us."

"How about if I make a meal instead?" When it looked like he would protest again, she playfully pleaded. "Aww, c'mon, Gramps. I'll cook your steak the way you like it. Please."

"All right, all right." He swept his forearm across his brow. "Stop with those puppy-dog eyes."

She laughed and, swamped by love for the man who'd always been her rock, kissed him on the cheek again.

"Dang, Willie, you are the world's biggest pushover." Ruby hooted. "Your granddaughter's been using that look on you all of her life." She fake-batted her eyes at him. "Maybe I oughta try it more often."

He joined in their laughter. "Woman, you'd never use a look. You just bulldoze me until I get tired of saying 'no'."

"Whatever works."

Gramps grinned and swatted both of them affectionately on their butts. "Speaking of work, let me get back to mine. I'll see you both at sunset."

🦀 🦀 🦀

BOBBY DUG THE pole into the ocean bottom, smoothly propelling his boat forward. His eyes were on the water, scanning for fish, but his mind was on Dora Lee. Dang, she'd gotten to him last night with her beautiful golden eyes and her shaky confidence. All her talk about taking advantage of him and not using him as a Band-Aid had warmed his heart. Her kisses, tentative at first before turning hot, had juiced his libido.

Every time he got close, he wanted to cuddle her and soothe away her nerves. Strip her bare, lay her on his bed, and rock her world. A fierce ache shot through him and his knuckles whitened on the pole. He shook his head and blew out a breath. If he kept on like this, he'd have the devil of a time explaining to his client why he needed to take a quick plunge to cool off.

The water rippled ten feet ahead. "Fish off the starboard bow," he alerted the client. An Army Ranger on well-deserved leave, he had good hands on a cast, sailing the lure right on target. *Snap! Zing!* A bonefish snagged the line and took off running. The man played it well, fighting the fish with the rod and then reeling in fast. The battle between man and bonefish continued with Bobby steering the boat to his client's advantage.

"That's the way. Raise the tip. Keep him out of those rocks." He kept up a stream of encouragement. "He's a tough one. Reel him. Reel him! That's it." Bobby yanked the net free of its hooks. When the man had maneuvered his quarry to the side of the boat, he swooped in and netted the fish, bringing it aboard.

"Hoo-ah!" crowed the Ranger. An American citizen of Irish descent, the traditional victory yell was flavored with a hint of a brogue.

Bobby slapped him on the back and both of them grinned like fools, admiring the fish.

"Aye, he's a good one."

"Damn straight, Irish." He slapped the man on the shoulder. "Good job."

At this point, many of his clients wanted to hoist the catch up high while he took a picture, but he'd fished with Irish often enough to know he wasn't into souvenirs. Bobby carefully removed the hook from the bonefish's gaping mouth and the client gently lifted its wriggling body over the side and let him go.

Bobby wiped his hands on a rag then grabbed a couple of bottles of water from the cooler, handing one over before draining his in a couple long draughts. "You ready to go after another?"

"For sure I am," he answered, a twinkle in his blue eyes. "I'm thinking he must have a brother or two waiting to meet the lure."

It was one of those days when a fish struck on almost every cast. It was the Ranger's last full day of leave, so Bobby stayed out later than usual, determined to deliver as much sport as possible for his hard working client. The sun hung low in the darkening sky when they'd put in to shore, the speedy little boat skimming over the ocean.

Then the man insisted that they go for dinner and a beer after they'd both washed up. This kind of camaraderie counted with clients and Irish was good for a couple of trips a year. So, as much as Bobby would have liked checking in for the sunset gathering and, more to the point, seeing Dora Lee, his work day wouldn't be over until after the meal. He'd have to wait until later on to circle around to her cottage and tempt her out for a walk — or something more interesting.

🌺 🌺 🌺

"WELL, THE COTTAGES sure could use fixing up if you've a mind to do it, Dora Lee, but I'm not so sure about making them, what'd you call it, 'exclusive'." Willie ran his finger down the columns on the spreadsheet. His leg jerked beneath the table when Ruby kicked him. He shot her a glance, wondering what the hell she was trying to signal. She narrowed her blue eyes and quickly tilted her head toward Dora Lee. His granddaughter looked worried, like a prisoner waiting for a judge to declare a sentence. *Gotcha.*

"But you sure look like you've thought out the idea pretty good," he amended.

Her expression immediately relaxed. *Thank you, Ruby.*

"You really think so, Gramps?"

"Sure he does, darlin'. We both do. Look at all this work and these fancy spreadsheets. I swear you're as thorough as Victoria when it comes to laying down a plan." With a toothy grin, she patted Dora Lee on the arm with approval. "Now, tell me how you knew that you'd have to make the rooms a mite bigger?"

"Well, I've stayed in enough good hotels to know current preferences." Dora Lee launched into her explanation while Ruby nodded so hard that her blond top-knot swayed.

Ruby had jumped on this idea like it was a parade float and she a cheerleader. Willie wished he was as certain. Sure, Dora Lee was smart and she knew how to go after things she wanted. Hell, she'd left home determined to be a model and, while he hadn't been crazy about her marching her body around in those skimpy underclothes, she'd succeeded until that husband of hers swept her off her feet.

Thinking of J. Walter soured his stomach, dang near

ruining the fine meal they'd enjoyed. He'd never taken to
the man, not that the man had gone out of his way to be
friendly. Still, that didn't make it okay for him to dog around
and throw out his baby girl like she was trash.

At least she was finally home where she belonged. If he
gave her the go-ahead for her fancy idea, she'd have to stick
around. From the look on her face, right now she was running high on enthusiasm, but what about a few months down
the line?

"Gramps? You're frowning. What's troubling you?"

Hell. Well, best he put his concerns out on the table.
"Dora Lee. I don't want to spoil your mood, but I've got a
question that needs asking."

"We've always been up front with each other." She met
his eyes, but her hands twisted in her lap. "Go ahead."

He shot Ruby a quit-kicking-me look and turned back to
his granddaughter. "Baby girl, you're looking at a big undertaking and a huge investment. This project isn't something
you can start and then walk away from mid-way."

"I won't, I . . ."

He raised his hand, halting her protest. "Let me finish.
It's never been a secret that the Keys aren't your favorite place
in the world." As much as he believed in letting people live
their lives, that point still gigged his gut. "I know the divorce
turned your life upside down, but what's to say you won't
turn it right side up in a couple of months and get bored?"

She sat back, pressed her lips together, and nodded.
"That's a fair concern, Gramps. I don't know how to assure

you, other than to say that I finish what I start. I always have, haven't I?"

"True enough."

Fiddling with papers, she was quiet for a moment before looking at him again. In her eyes sparked the determination she'd had since she was a girl out to get her own way, mixed with a desperation that made him want to cuss out the ex-husband all over again.

"Gramps, if you give your blessing for Key of Sea Cottages, you won't be sorry. I'm going to make that area shine and have it running in the black within the year. I know that I'm committing myself to the Keys and, as strange as that might seem, I'm comfortable with the decision." Her laugh was shaky. "It took a lot of years and a divorce, but I finally got the message that I don't belong anywhere else."

Dang, her woebegone expression tore at his heart. He reached across the table and squeezed her hand. "Dora Lee, you've always belonged here, even when you didn't think so." For the sake of her happiness, he'd agree to stage a three-ring circus. Renovating cottages that weren't doing anybody any good in their current condition was an easy sell by comparison. Her hopeful expression clinched his decision. "If you want to go about making home a little more interesting and a lot prettier, I'm for it."

"Really, Gramps?" Her sudden smile was so bright, it outshone the lights in the kitchen.

"Really. Now, of course, before you get started we have to ask . . ."

Ruby cut him off, jumping out of her chair like she'd been bit by a snake. "Jesus, Mary and all the Saints in Heaven, what a fantastic night!" She squeezed Dora Lee first. "You just count on me for whatever help you might need, you hear?"

She ran around the table and dang near strangled him with her hug, whispering low in his ear. "Don't say anything about Bobby."

"Wh . . ."

A lip-smacking kiss cut off the rest of his sentence. What in the hell had gotten into the woman?

Dora Lee didn't give him a chance to find out. As soon as Ruby released him, she hugged him from behind, kissing him on the cheek. "Thanks, Gramps." *Kiss.* "Thank you so much. I'm going to make it a success, you just wait and see! Oh! I have to call Jo Jo. Thanks again. I'll let you know how I make out with the phone calls tomorrow."

Gathering up her papers, she shoved them into folders and practically danced out the door.

Ruby dropped back into her chair and swigged some tea. "Whew. That is one happy girl."

"Because she thinks she's got all the approval she needs. Why did you shush me about Bobby?"

"Dora Lee doesn't know he's your business partner, does she?"

"I don't think so. So what?"

"You have to talk to him first and make sure that he agrees."

"If everything turns out the way she plans, we'll all make money." He furrowed his brow. "What difference does it make if she knows she has to pitch the idea to him first?"

"You don't want her catching him off guard. He could blow his whole chance without meaning to."

"Ruby, what are you talking about?"

"I'm talking about how your business partner and your granddaughter were cozying up to each other with dinner for two last night on his boat."

"Woman, are you on that track again? I swear you're making something out of nothing."

"Ain't making up anything. I heard all about it from Rosa earlier. They came from Dora Lee's cottage for sunset and headed over to his boat afterward."

"That doesn't mean . . . aww hell. No sense wasting the breath to argue." Willie rubbed his chin. "You're always right about this sort of thing. I still ain't forgot about losing that bet to you about Jack and Victoria."

"Wanna go double or nothing, hon?" she cackled.

"I'll keep my ten spot this time around." He got up from his chair and walked to the window, watching his girl hurry across the parking lot, fretting over her happiness. "She ain't been free of her husband for all that long. Well, looky here." Damned if Bobby wasn't coming across the property at the same time.

Ruby joined him, sliding her arm around his waist while he hugged her around her shoulders. As they watched, Bobby caught up to Dora Lee, spun her around and dipped her over his arm for an exuberant kiss. When he let her go, Dora Lee immediately brought her folders up against her chest. Even in the dim light, her glare was obvious.

"Don't look too cozy to me, darlin'."

"Ha. Mark my words, she's every bit as attracted to him as he is to her. She's just gotta straighten it out in her heart."

Willie blew out a breath. "I don't know how I feel about this."

"Ain't how you feel, hon. It's how *they* feel." She squeezed him tight and snuggled against his chest. "Tell you one thing. He'll treat her well and that's the most important thing. I'm betting they'll be good for each other."

🦀 🦀 🦀

"IF WINDING UP with an armful of woman isn't a great way to end the day, I don't know what is." Bobby looked down at Dora Lee bent back over his arm, her beautiful face all flustered, and swooped in for a kiss.

"Mmm. Mmm." He smacked his lips. "Sweeter than any dessert." Knowing she'd push him away if she had the chance, he took full advantage of the fact that her hands were full of file folders to keep her off balance and steal another kiss before setting her upright. "How you doing tonight, babe?"

She clutched those folders to her fine looking chest. Much to his satisfaction, her eyes needed a second or two to focus before she lifted her chin. "Lucky for you, I'm in too

good a mood to give you hell for kissing me when I specifically told you not to."

That snotty, raised nose look nearly killed him. He ran
his hand down her arm. "You mean last night when you
threw out your little challenge?"

She made some sort of throaty, frustrated sound.

Ohh, baby. "Growl all sexy like that again for me, Dora Lee."

"Bobby!"

The exasperated snort only made him laugh. Whether
she liked it or not, even she had to admit she wasn't indiffer-
ent. He raised his hands, signaling a momentary truce. "Tell
me about this good mood."

Her face lit up like a summer sky. "I really ought to
thank you for giving me a great idea."

"Oh, yeah?" Whatever it was, he'd work with it and
moved in, but she stopped him with a hand to his solar plexus.
He grabbed it and kissed her palm before she yanked free.

"Do you want to hear the idea or not?"

"Lay it on me." This ought to be good if it made her so
happy that she couldn't maintain her annoyance.

"Remember last night when . . ."

"Oh, yeah!"

"Not that. Stay with me, will you please?"

"That's an invitation I'd never refuse." He didn't bother
to hold back a wolfish smile that escalated into a full laugh
when she smacked him with the folders.

"Forget it, you libido on legs. You're impossible." She
spun away.

He grabbed her hand and reeled her back. "You give me an opening like that, Dora Lee, you better expect I'm gonna take it. Don't go. I promise to behave."

"All right, but no more suggestive comments." She eyed him warily then nodded as if satisfied. "Last night when we were talking about my cottage, you said . . ."

"Evening, Bobby!" Ruby's voice called to them from the steps of Willie's trailer. Aw, hell. Busted. He couldn't exactly seduce Dora Lee in front of an audience. He turned and flashed a smile. "Evening, gorgeous," he answered.

Ruby cackled. "Ain't nearly as gorgeous as you, scamp."

At least she was smiling. Willie, on the other hand, stood beside her with his arm draped over her shoulders and his face like a thundercloud.

Uh oh. There was bound to be trouble if his partner and friend didn't approve of him courting his granddaughter. Damned if his neck didn't twitch like he was a teenager caught kissing a girl after bringing her home from a date. "Evening, Willie."

"Bobby. You got a minute?" Willie looked like he'd stepped on a sea urchin. Best they got this out of the way now. He and Dora Lee were both too old to need guardian approval.

Speaking of which, did she have to look so darned pleased that they were no longer alone? She jumped on the interruption as a reason to split.

"See you all tomorrow," she called to the older couple, and then looked at Bobby. "I have more work to finish tonight, but Gramps can fill you in on my project." Waving cheerfully, she hurried away. He ogled the swing in her backside for a minute before tearing away his attention. It wouldn't do to talk to Willie with a hard-on the size of the Florida panhandle. He turned to his partner.

"What's up?"

"Come inside, son. We have to talk."

"Sure thing." No matter what Willie said, he'd make him understand that he wasn't fooling around with Dora Lee. Well, yeah, he wanted to fool around in one meaning of the phrase, but that wasn't a topic of conversation to have with the woman's sole remaining family member. What he meant was that he was darned serious about his intentions. Crap. If he had it this twisted up in his mind and the talking hadn't even started, he was in trouble.

He entered the trailer with the couple and took the easy chair Willie indicated.

"You want some coffee, darlin'?"

"No thanks, Ruby." What he wanted was the reason for his partner's serious expression.

The other man sat across from him, forearms on his knees and a worried frown on his face. "Bobby, we gotta talk about my granddaughter."

"Look, I know I put on a show a couple of minutes ago but . . ."

"Pretty smooth move, scamp. Like something out of a movie," Ruby chimed in.

Willie waved them both off. "Yeah, well, I don't know about that yet, but like Ruby says, you're both adults. What you do with that isn't up to me. We've got other problems."

Bobby straightened. "If that asshole ex of hers is starting trouble, I promise I'll finish it."

"Nah. It's nothing with J. Walter. This problem started all with Dora Lee."

"I don't get it."

"You will."

Five minutes later, he'd heard the whole story. Right down to the last expanded idea. How in the hell had a woman gone from repainting some walls to knocking them down to make bigger rooms?

"And you agreed?" He stretched his jaw from side to side.

"I didn't mean to. I was only going to tell her that we had to talk to you first, but Ruby here cut me off."

"That's right. I did and you can thank me for it now," she said.

"You're *that* sure this scheme's gonna work?"

"I'm at least half sure."

"Terrific." Bobby groaned.

"Hear me out, scamp. Whether we think it will or won't work isn't the main thing. I just didn't want Dora Lee coming to you without warning. If you gave her this kind of reaction, what do you think that would have done to her?"

"Crap. You're right." He thought over the last few days and all the different times she'd run herself down, or he'd seen that unfamiliar insecurity shadowing her eyes. "The most important thing of all is that she *needs* to make it a success. Since we all love her, we gotta help it happen."

He looked Willie full in the eyes. "Yeah, you heard me. I love her, too, and the happier she is living back here in the Keys, the better for us both." His lips quirked in a half-smile. "Even if she doesn't see it my way just yet, she will."

"So, you'll go along with it?" This from Willie, who appraised him with gold eyes. No doubt who'd passed them down to the granddaughter.

"Hell, yeah and I'll like doing it, but I'm not the one that needs to be convinced." He grimaced and ran his hand through his hair. Getting him on board was a smooth sail on a sunny day. The store owners were going to bitch and moan about this until the next full moon.

"Mack's no problem, but Leo, Tilda, Vince, and the others . . ."

"I thought about that, too." Willie's glum expression said it all. "They're already upset about that big resort going up practically next door. Every time someone mentions it, one of them complains that the high priced places make the Keys more expensive for the rest of us."

"You'll have to convince them that this is a good plan for everybody," Ruby said. "That Osprey Cove place won't bring you all customers, but Dora Lee's idea will. Having a steady flow of tourists staying on the property means more business."

"Tourists, fishermen, and locals are fine. The class of people Dora Lee wants to attract make Leo's skin crawl. He thinks they're looking down on him and it puts a chip on his shoulder the size of a hundred-year-old Buttonwood tree."

"He already doesn't like her," Bobby added.

"He doesn't?" Ruby's voice squealed like a tea kettle.

Willie's face darkened. "What do you mean?"

"You know how he gets. Half the time, I don't think he likes his customers."

"Maybe it's some of that artistic temperament," Ruby suggested.

Both men snorted.

"Okay, so customer relations ain't his strong suit," she agreed, "but Willie, you've got the trump card. She's your granddaughter. He has to accept her."

"Bitchin' and moanin' the whole time — and how good is that gonna be for her guests when they visit the shops?" Willie stood and fetched a beer from the fridge, gesturing at Bobby with the bottle. "Want one?"

"I could use it." He also stood, taking the offered bottle. "Whether they like it or not, we're giving our go-ahead. The more time the store owners have to get used to the idea, the better." He twisted off the cap, took a long swallow. "I'll talk to Leo in the morning. Better that he hear it from me *because* she's your granddaughter."

"Bobby, don't tell him."

"Why not, Ruby? He's gotta know. We spring this, he'll have three kinds of fits."

She shook her head, adamant. "Don't tell him *first*. Talk to Rosa. That woman's a born entrepreneur and she's the most likely to see the advantages. Then she'll talk about it to Bitsy and Vince."

"That's plain smart." Willie saluted her with his beer.

"Thanks, darlin'. Get all of them on board and they'll bring Leo."

Yeah, right. A raised brow indicated Bobby's skepticism.

She rolled her eyes. "All right, so at least their approval will drown out his complaints."

Willie agreed. "Once you talk to them, you gonna see to Dora Lee, Bobby?"

"I intend to see your granddaughter a lot, but off the bat, she doesn't need to know that you and I are partners."

"Lying to her isn't smart."

"Hey. Hey! I'm not lying."

They double-teamed him with disapproval. "You're withholding information," Willie said.

"Bobby, I went through this with Victoria and Jack. It almost ruined them before they even had a chance."

"They worked out just fine, didn't they? I know what I'm doing and, believe me, it doesn't include hurting Dora Lee." The opposite was true and he needed to make them understand. He leaned against the door, crossing his arms while he laid his heart and his future out on the line.

"Willie, I'm in love with your granddaughter. She's not ready for me to be, but I'm going to change her mind." His smile was wry. "I'm navigating woman territory here, talking about feelings and such, but I've noticed that she isn't as tough and spunky as she used to be. That ex of hers . . ."

Twin pairs of narrowed eyes told him they shared his low opinion of that smug snake.

"Anyway, from what you say, this project is the thing she

needs to get her spunk back. I'm working on a plan of my own with her and I don't want her to know that I have any say over her project. If she thinks I have veto power. . ." It would piss her off no end for starters. "The last thing I want is for her to compare me with her husband and his control over what she could and couldn't do."

"Plus, you don't want her confusing your courtship with pressure. The boy makes a lot of sense, Willie."

The other man wasn't convinced. "But if you don't tell her, I can't either, and that don't set right with me."

Bobby thought fast. He could handle Dora Lee's changes in mood, confident that eventually he'd win her over, but he didn't want to cause trouble in the family. "How's this? I promise to tell her, but not right away. Let's give her a chance to make some progress. If it turns sour, I'll take the heat."

"I dunno, Bob." Willie glanced at Ruby.

"It could come back to bite you on the ass," she warned.

He nodded. "I'll handle it."

Willie blew out a breath. "All right, for now, but don't string her along."

"I won't."

The older man's face set like stone. He wouldn't stand for his partner hurting his granddaughter. Bobby knew it and was in full agreement. He himself would rip the guts out of anyone who hurt his woman.

She was his, even if she didn't acknowledge it yet, but at least he was going to have time to work on her. A wide grin broke over his face.

"What's that smile for, scamp?"

"Dora Lee's staying in town. That's the best news of the night."

"Amen to that, Bobby." Now, even Willie smiled. "Surprised the hell out of me, that's the truth, but I'm glad she's home."

Ruby looked at them both, speculation lighting up her sharp blue eyes. "Family. A new career. Those are great reasons to latch back onto your roots. A new love gives her even more reason to stay, no matter what happens with her cottages."

"Yeah?"

Bobby winked. "Oh, yeah."

"What are you getting at, Ruby?" Willie put down his empty bottle and braced his arms against the counter.

"Romance, darlin'." She poked Bobby in the abdomen on her way to hug her man. "This boy's set his mind on romancing your granddaughter. I think we need to help him with that project as much as he needs to help Dora Lee."

"Ruby . . ." Bobby envisioned a parade of people pushing Dora Lee toward him and her running away fast in the other direction.

"Don't get your lines tangled, Bobby. We're not gonna mess up your action."

Willie gathered her into his arms, rubbing his chin over her top-knot. "You're scarin' him, woman. I've seen that look on your face before and sometimes it even scares me. Better tell us what's on your mind."

"Positive reinforcement. Operant conditioning. Like

with the dolphins."

"Huh?"

"Bobby, you said that Dora Lee doesn't see things your way just yet. What do you think's holding her back?"

"Stupid stuff. She says she's too old for me. That she's gotten fat and unattractive."

"And you don't agree."

"Hell, no! Seven years is a spit on the ocean and she's always been beautiful."

"Exactly. So you keep showing her how you feel and what you think of her. Gradually, she'll start believing you."

"That's what you mean by operant conditioning."

"Yep. While she's getting used to the idea, we'll reinforce that you're a great guy."

"Positively." His lips quirked.

"Absolutely."

"Don't know how Dora Lee will take to you comparing her to dolphins," Willie cautioned.

"Why not? In a lot of ways dolphins are smarter than people. Flippers down. You won't catch my Marian or Scarlett fretting about their ages or weights. They know they're gorgeous."

"I guess she's got a point, son." Willie chuckled. "Even if we don't get it, there'll be no moving her off it now."

Ruby elbowed him lightly in the gut, making him laugh harder. "You'll see I'm right."

The whole thing made sense in a convoluted Ruby sort of way. "All right, you two. I'll handle the romance part, you take care of the positive reinforcement."

He pushed off the door and returned his empty beer to the kitchen. "Between us, we'll convince her to see it my way."

Leaving the trailer, he fought the urge to jog right down that pea rock path to Dora Lee. As much as his heart and body pointed him in that direction, his head said he needed to take care of the other business first. He had a half-day charter the following day. The Ranger had decided to get in one last good morning before flying back to join the rest of his team on duty. As soon as possible afterward, Bobby would drop in on Rosa's little aromatherapy shop and talk to her about the new changes coming down the road.

CHAPTER 13

ARCHITECTS, BUILDERS, DESIGNERS. Oh, my, there were a lot of people Dora Lee had to talk with and it was a lot of work merely setting up appointments. First thing in the morning, she'd called the architect Jo Jo recommended and another name gleaned from Ruby. Receptionists for both of them assured her they would be delighted to speak with her about a project, but neither could give her a definite time or date. One had to confer with her boss when he returned from a job site. Maybe next week, suggested the other, before remembering that the architect she worked for was going on vacation and already had a full schedule the week of his return. The week after, however, was a definite maybe.

She'd forgotten the *mañana* attitude of the Keys. Sure, you could find good people to work for you, but getting things done quickly was a foreign concept. Gramps was one of the exceptions and even he wasn't immune to an unscheduled break when the wind lay down and the day promised good fishing. The locals even had a name for it. *Keys disease.*

There were only two choices — accept that she'd get her

appointments in good time, or stroke out over the delay. At least there were plenty of other things she could do in the meantime.

Like web surf on her brand new computer, bought just this morning from the office supply store up the road — one of the few national chains to infiltrate the Keys. The cottage only had one phone line, so she'd left her cell phone number with the architect firms for call backs. Yes, the cable company would be happy to come out and wire her for a high speed modem — two weeks in the future. While she waited, she googled up five-star resorts from Aruba to the Bahamas and up and down both Florida coasts. Most of the websites showed pictures of guest rooms which she printed out for design ideas.

"Ohh, how pretty," she drooled over fine silk netting, hanging from the ceiling in long, graceful sweeps to frame the bed in one room. The duvet was a rich emerald jacquard and she counted no fewer than five plump pillows. "Wonder what the thread count is on those sheets?" On the legal pad beside the computer, she scrawled another note. *Minimum 500 ct, Egyptian cotton — all rooms.*

So many choices. What did she want her little places to look like? Ultra-formal would never do for such a cute little area. When guests first walked into their rooms, she wanted them to smile, exclaim over the prettiness and then instantly sink into relaxation mode. The "ooh-ahhh" factor, she called it in her head. Now, how to achieve it? Cool tile floors were more modern and durable, but wide-plank polished wood floors provided a warmer look. Satiny, rich fabrics, or the simple elegance of matelassé coverlets? Antique reproduction furniture like something out of British Colonial times, or airy wicker and rattan?

Maybe both, but in different buildings. She could decorate the cottages in different styles to appeal to the various tastes of her guests. Each one with its own name based on . . . flowers, tropical islands, famous authors? Jo Jo could help her decide. Down the road, maybe repeat guests would request their favorite cottage by name when booking their reservations. Tilting back her head, she floated the concept in her imagination.

Yes, Mrs. Harrington, we'd be happy to reserve the Hemingway cottage for you and Mr. Harrington for the week of February 21ˢᵗ. The Jasmine Cottage, Mrs. Wagner? Yes, it's available. Welcome back, Mr. and Mrs. Flagler. The Eleuthera Cottage is all ready for you.

It ought to be strange that she so totally envisioned herself in the role of gracious hostess and hotelier when a couple of weeks ago she didn't have a clue what to do with the rest of her life. Then again, it wasn't all that different than her teenage dreams of imagining herself as a model or, once she began dating J. Walter, picturing herself as his glamorous wife.

Dream it. Do it.

The more she worked, the higher the stack of printed pictures grew as design themes, colors and amenities overstuffed her brain. Neither architect had called back by the time she took a break. Her fingers itched with the urge to call their offices again, but she refrained. As anxious as she was to move forward, she remembered that these were Keys professionals in their own habitat, not the faster-moving, more aggressive counterparts she was used to on the mainland. Before she skipped over the line into being a pain in the ass, she promised to give them until the following day to at least return her phone call before she pestered.

Instead, she busied herself with a late lunch of soup and crackers. Eating at the far side of her kitchenette counter away from her precious papers, she studied her own surroundings. Painting finished, she'd removed the messy drop cloths and cleaned out the area. The walls glowed with their fresh new color. Now, she needed to hire someone to strip and re-polish the wood floors.

Gramps would surely know of someone, as would Ruby. Bobby would probably volunteer, too, but that meant she'd have to seek him out and ask. Then when he agreed, he'd be in her space, filling it up with all those rugged muscles and that sexy glitter in his green eyes.

She licked her lips, remembering the spicy taste of his kiss. Too much time in his company and she'd want him to strip her instead. Once that happened, she could imagine in vivid, pulse-jolting detail how they'd set about polishing her floors.

Before she dwelled on an even worse innuendo involving Bobby's wood, she gulped down a glass of ice cold water. No, calling him definitely was *not* an option.

That brought her back to asking Gramps, but he'd insist

on doing the work himself and he was busy enough with the marina. Well, she'd just have to insist more emphatically that he give her the name of a floor refinisher, unless . . .

She walked the floor, scuffing her sneaks across the surface. "How hard can it be?"

Returning to her computer, she logged back online. A quick search took her to the website of the home improvement store chain. A couple of more clicks brought up pictures of orbital floor sanders. Although she'd proved herself capable of wielding a paint roller, she admitted that an enormous electric sander intimidated the hell out of her. Still . . .

The choices were clear. Fall back on the old standby and hire someone then wait around for days until they were available, or tackle the floors on her own. A little more searching uncovered an overview on necessary supplies, equipment, and technique. After reading the guidelines, the job didn't seem so difficult. Using a nail punch was pretty self-explanatory. Face masks, a matter of common sense. The sander wasn't that much larger than an upright vacuum cleaner — and she'd be sure to rent one with a bag attached. Every sentence she read increased her confidence.

So what if her previous experience with power tools involved an ultra-fancy mixer and super-deluxe food processor? If she could follow a recipe and create a perfect chocolate soufflé, she could re-finish her own damn floors. Decision made, she grabbed her handbag and keys and ran out the door before she changed her mind.

An hour later, she wrestled the machine out of her car's

back seat. Of course, it was too heavy for her to carry, so she tilted it back on its wheels and dragged it across the parking lot, leaving little furrows in the pea rock. The tattoo king was taking a break on the porch, but instead of offering any help, he scowled at her like she was smuggling contraband.

"Damn fool woman," she heard him mutter. Resisting an uncharacteristic urge to flip him off, she flashed him a syrupy smile instead and continued on her way.

Reaching the cottage, she shoved the sofa out onto the lawn. With her computer equipment taking up the kitchenette counter, she was quickly running out of storage space for the prized tarpon, so she dragged it on a sheet into her bedroom and balanced it across the arms of the wicker rocker. After drawing on the knee pads that the store clerk insisted she needed, she took out her brand new nail punch and crawled across the floor, painstakingly hammering all the nail heads beneath the wood surface.

Only hit her finger once. *So far, so good.* She wheeled the sander into the center of the room. Donning her protective goggles and face mask made her feel like a race car driver at the starting line.

"Dora, start your engine!"

A flick of the switch and she was off and running. The powerful beast zoomed across the floor. "Whoa!" She grabbed the handle before the sander careened into the wall, and muscled it in the opposite direction. *It's always better to sand with the grain,* she'd read in the directions. Even better to avoid sanding her sneaker-clad feet.

Running the sander was like trying to waltz with a gorilla that didn't know the steps but insisted on leading. Her hands and arms ached from keeping it under control and she had to set her jaw to keep her teeth from clattering. Her entire body vibrated — and that was only on the lowest speed setting. If she kicked it up to high gear, she might never need sex again.

But she didn't dare. At top speed, the sander would run amok while she whirled around with her feet straight out behind her like a cartoon character.

Thank God the room and hallway were small. By the time she'd completed two passes over the floor with first the coarse sandpaper and then the medium grit, her body complained like she'd sanded an acre. Stubbornly ignoring her protesting muscles, she fit the fine grit sandpaper over the roller and fired up the machine. When she'd gone over the entire space again, she shut off the beast, removed her protective gear, and admired the results.

Slumping against the wall for support, she crouched and ran her hand over the wood. Other than the expected dust, the results astonished. "Smooth as glass." she whispered. "I did it."

Proud of her accomplishment, she struggled to her feet. The job wasn't finished. According to the directions she needed to vacuum thoroughly, wait a few hours and vacuum again to remove every last particle of dust. She dragged the cleaner out of the hall closet and maneuvered it in precise lines across the entire space. Once that chore was complete, she drank an entire tall glass of water, staggered outside and flopped onto the ancient sofa. Toeing off her sneakers, she lifted up her legs and stretched out.

Feathery clouds drifted overhead, tempering the late afternoon sun to a mellow warmth. Lumps and bumps made it obvious that more than a few springs had sprung in the couch cushions, but she was too tired to care. With the vacuuming timetable, she couldn't apply the floor finish until tomorrow morning. Since she'd need to vacate the cottage while it dried, she'd use the time to browse some of the furniture stores. After she called the architects again and nailed down an appointment.

Yawning hugely, she shifted onto her side, resting her head on the crook of her arm. There were more plans to make. More notes to take. She could surf some more websites. Maybe later. After dinner, or . . .

The rest of the thought evaporated as her eyelids fluttered closed.

🦀 🦀 🦀

SHE LOOKED LIKE an angel curled up on her couch, Bobby thought when he found her napping not long before sunset. He'd had his talk with Rosa, encountering less resistance than he'd expected. *Chalk up a point for Ruby's intuition.*

"*Sí*, more tourists create more business," she'd agreed. "But some of the others. They will need time to get used to the idea."

They'd have plenty of time. If she didn't know it already, Dora Lee would soon discover that even the permit process often took forever. He and Willie were fairly sure the property's land-use zoning had never changed, so at least that shouldn't be an obstacle, except that in the Keys, it paid to expect the unexpected.

That Dora Lee had decided to plant herself back in the Keys for the long run was the most unexpected thing of all. He had his doubts about the overall scheme. Not that she wasn't smart and capable, but she'd never actually run a business. Sure, she'd helped out back when Willie and her grandmother operated the place, but that was a far cry from creating and operating these so-called "exclusive" guest cottages. Still, she had her heart set on it and, since his heart was set on her, he dry-docked his misgivings and committed his support.

He'd left Rosa and gone on to talk with Mack and the deli owners, suggesting they discuss it with Rosa, too. Leo and Tilda had closed early for the day and gone off on their bike, lured, probably, by the mild weather and the call of the road.

All that remained was to chat with Dora Lee a little and let her know that he supported her project — hopefully having the discussion over dinner. He'd yet to take her out on a real date and had every intention of cajoling her into it tonight until he reached her cottage and discovered her sleeping.

Why the heck was her couch outside anyway? He quietly approached. From the depth of those breaths, this was no cat nap. Whatever she'd been doing all day, she'd worn herself out.

A look in the cottage cinched it. "Well, I'll be damned." He whistled long and low while he walked over the freshly sanded floor. "No wonder she's out for the count."

So much for dinner. No way would he disturb her sleep, but that posed a different problem.

The afternoon warmth would soon give way to a moist, cooler night. He couldn't just leave her outside where the dew would seep into her clothes. A peek into her bedroom showed him that her bed was clear of clutter, even if the rest of the room was jam packed with stuff.

Going back outdoors, he squatted by the couch and slipped his arms under her knees and shoulders. In one easy motion, he stood, cradling her against his chest.

"Shh, babe, it's me," he murmured when she stirred. "Go back to sleep."

So much for her worries about her weight. He carried her easily into her cottage and her bedroom. The tarpon gaping at them was on the creepy side, he thought when he gently placed her on the bed. Removing her clothes would wake her, and he doubted she'd appreciate the gesture. As much as he longed to share her bed, tonight wasn't the right time, so he contented himself with smoothing her rich, dark hair back from her face and tenderly kissing her lush mouth. Switching off the light, he left her to drift alone in her dreams.

🐚 🐚 🐚

A GOOD NIGHT'S sleep worked wonders for the human body. A hot shower eased the remaining aches from her sander tango. After a quick breakfast, Dora ran through the second vacuuming with a smile on her face and a cup of coffee in her free hand. Before nine o'clock, the entire floor was wiped down with spirits of ammonia and well on its way to drying. She refilled her mug and called the architects again. Neither was in, but each receptionist promised, swore, that her boss would definitely get in touch today.

Dora worked off that minor frustration by carefully applying the final finish. She stood at the doorway, roller in hand, and admired the floors like they were polyurethane works of art. Later on, she'd have to get Gramps over here to see them, too. Right now, she had no time to rest on this accomplishment. Her priority now was new furniture.

This couch had outlasted its usefulness. She shifted around for a spot on the cushions where springs didn't poke her butt. That she'd fallen asleep on it at all the night before was a testament to the power of exhaustion over the need for comfort. No wonder she'd crawled off it and found her way to her own bed at some point, although she didn't remember making the move.

Whatever, this piece of junk would be replaced as soon as possible, by the end of the day if she were lucky. Sipping her coffee, she leafed through one of the local weekly newspapers she'd picked up at the Marina Deli. Oddly enough, given that the Middle Keys weren't exactly a shopping Mecca, there was no shortage of furniture stores. Maybe not so odd, considering the number of people buying houses in the Keys. Surely she could find the right pieces once she decided on the appropriate style.

Since this was going to be both her living and working area, she wanted cool and comfortable. Casual, but not low-rent. The store ads showed everything from heavy wood designs by Tommy Bahama which would totally overwhelm her space, to painted rattan upholstered in gaudy tropical florals. Neither style appealed, so she flipped to the next store and the next. There she lit upon a rolled arm, high-backed micro-suede sofa in a rich creamy color with a matching club chair.

"That has possibilities," she murmured, dog-earing the page. Goodness, the thick cushions invited her to sink into their comfortable embrace. Some bright pillows and a chenille throw would work well on the neutral background. Oh, yes. Definite possibilities. The ad said that the store had most of their items in stock, so if she liked the couch as much in the store, perhaps she could borrow Willie's truck and bring it home. She would definitely need some help once she got back to the marina, but Gramps would round up his friends.

She ran her finger over the photograph, imagining the soft brush of the material. Underneath the softness, the couch looked solid. Handsome lines, but not fussy.

The crunch of footsteps on pea rock caught her attention. Speaking of solid, handsome, and not fussy, Bobby sauntered up the path.

"Morning, gorgeous."

That slashing dimple charmed her, even though she fought against it. "Morning, Bobby. No charter today?"

"Nope. Got a tournament starting tomorrow, so I took this morning to do some engine maintenance."

Before she could pull away, he cupped her cheek and dropped a light kiss on her mouth. The protest died in her throat when he presented her with a rose, woven from a palm frond. "Oh. That's so cute."

"Pop always told me I'd never go wrong bringing flowers to a lady."

"Thank you." She focused on the mug in her hand, swigging down the contents. Something told her she'd need a dozen cups of coffee to fortify herself against Bobby in full charm mode.

He dropped down beside her like he belonged and stretched his arm over the back of the couch. "You're up working early this morning. Get your floors finished?"

"Yes, I did. Want to see?" Hey, she was dying to show off to someone! Leaping up, she grabbed his hand. "C'mon." Two steps toward the cottage and she stopped, puzzled. "How do you know I redid the floors?"

"Saw the work for myself last night." He opened the door to the cottage. "Well, don't they look pretty." He squeezed her tight and kissed her again. "You did a great job."

"Thanks." For some reason, knowing he'd visited while she slept disquieted her. "You were here last night? I don't remember."

"You were sleeping so deeply, you wouldn't have remembered a parade marching by. I thought you might rouse when I carried you in, but you went right back to sleep."

"You carried me?"

"How else did you get from that couch to the bed? I could hardly leave you outside."

"You carried me." She backed up several steps and eyed him slowly up and down.

"Babe, we can't go inside until your floors dry, so if you keep looking at me like that we're gonna risk indecent exposure."

"Hush. I'm looking for the hernia."

"Cut that out." He nabbed her chin, glaring. "You aren't fat."

"I'm . . ."

She lost the rest of the sentence when he palmed her butt with both hands and lifted her off the ground. "Bobby, put me down!"

"Un uh. You keep spouting that nonsense and you force me to prove you wrong. Do I look like I'm suffering, holding you in my arms?"

Amazingly enough, he didn't.

"Do I?" he asked again.

She shook her head. "I, um, guess not."

"Good. Now we're getting somewhere." He nipped her lips, closing his mouth over hers for a short, searing kiss before sliding her down his body.

Unsteady, she clung to his thick, roped forearms. Her lips buzzed and she stared at his beautifully formed mouth. If she thought his charm was dangerous, then his kisses were lethal, slaying her objections and overpowering her better judgment.

From the gleam in his eyes, he knew he was getting to her and that would never do. If she had any hope of resisting him, she had to get them back on an even keel. The only way to do that was to outplay him at the game and somehow prove that he couldn't dismantle her objections with a single kiss.

Starting this minute, she'd demonstrate that she could spend time with him without caving — no matter how confident he was otherwise. "The only thing you proved is that you're strong." She let go of his arms and walked back to the couch, picking up her furniture ads.

"Uh huh."

Don't look at his grin, that dimple and the cleft in his chin where you're dying to dip your tongue. Don't think about that kiss shooting heat through your veins.

He slid his warm hand up and down her back. She refused to look at him, focusing her energy on controlling muscles that wanted to quiver under those slow, sensual strokes. His breath fanned her neck when he leaned in and whispered, "You know you want me, babe."

She wanted him to stop touching her. Okay, she didn't, but she believed that would be best. Unfortunately, as long as he knew the simple glide of his hand set off tremors in her synapses, he'd keep on proving his case, pulse point by aching pulse point.

Fight fire with fire, she told herself. *He won't accept it until you prove differently.*

She turned away from his hand, facing him with her fistful of store ads between them.

Lowering her voice to a throaty whisper, a bad combination of Mae West and Madeline Kahn in *Blazing Saddles*, she murmured, "Oh, yes, big boy. You definitely have something I want. Something I need."

If he wanted to be with her so much, he could damn well make himself useful. She gave him a smoldering look, licked her lips and slowly slid her hand into the front pocket of his cargo shorts. Pulling out his keys, she jangled them in front of his darkened eyes.

"Truck me."

CHAPTER 14

DAMNED IF SHE hadn't turned the tables on him with that "truck me" comment. He'd have made her pay for it, but she'd laughed uproariously at her own wit before picking up her things.

"C'mon, Bobby. Make yourself useful."

He'd done just that. First by toting the sander out to his truck, glaring at her when she tried to pick up one end. After they returned the equipment, he'd tagged along to this furniture store that was so crowded with merchandise, he had to suck in his breath to squeeze down the rows. For the life of him, he couldn't figure out what was wrong with the first ten examples they'd seen, but obviously Dora Lee was angling for the best. An hour later, he still struggled to cool his libido while she poked, caressed, and scooched her curvy ass on every single couch and chair in the place.

Do you think this one will look good, Bobby? What about that one? Like he gave a chum bag's worth of difference between duck cloth and micro-suede. Prints, stripes, or solids. As far as he was concerned, it only mattered that the furniture be big enough for the two of them to roll around on and that the materials feel good against their skin.

His fantasies tortured him the entire time that they were in the full company of a fawning salesman. At least the man was gay and only drooling over his anticipated sales commission. Otherwise, Bobby would be forced to clobber him right in the showroom.

"Come here. Try this one out." Having completed the entire circuit, Dora Lee beckoned him to the couch she'd first targeted.

"Babe, it's fine. Yeah, it'll look great in your room. It's comfortable." The way she wiggled her body from side to side, getting a feel, shot spikes of lust into his gut. He turned to the sales guy. "Before she falls in love with it, why don't you see if it's in stock?"

The guy looked between them. "Right away, Sir and Madam."

He swore the guy uttered a loud cat-like purr before he swished away.

"Check on the matching chair, too!" Dora Lee called before giggling. "I think he likes you, hot stuff."

"He likes that you're about to drop a thousand bucks in his store."

"It's worth it. I love this couch. It's so comfy. And this material." She stroked it like a lover's skin. "Mmm."

The hum of pleasure clinched it. She was killing him.

"*Truck me*" she'd dared to say, wrapping those luscious lips sinfully around the words.

The game was definitely on and before they were through, she'd finally realize that he was playing for keeps. That didn't mean he wouldn't make her eat those words — or at least the first two letters, before he had her substitute an "f" in their place.

A quick look around confirmed they were alone, so he slid his body up tight, wrapped his arm around her and nipped her ear. "Yeah, baby, this couch is gonna feel so good when I get you naked on it underneath me."

She stiffened and cut her eyes his way, but before she could volley back a comment, the salesman returned, confirming that both items were in stock and available for immediate pick up.

"Excellent." Dora Lee rose and swatted away his hand when he gave her butt a boost. "Before we complete the transaction, I'd like to see a few more end tables."

Bobby groaned, rolling his eyes. How much time could one woman spend in a single store? "Room's not that big."

She beamed a mega-watt smile at the dazzled salesman. "Perhaps some lamps, too."

"Heartless witch," Bobby muttered.

"Hormonal wretch," she countered as she followed the salesman down the crowded aisle.

Two tables and a couple of lamps later, he helped the stock guys load his truck and drove out of the parking lot with her belted in by his side. They cruised down the Overseas Highway. While they'd waited for her purchases, he'd demanded lunch as payment for his help.

"I can't wait to see how everything looks in the space." She hugged a large, colorful pillow to her middle. Its partner was wedged on the seat between them, blocking his hand from roaming over to her side of the truck.

"It'll look fine, but if you hate it, don't ask me to haul it back. I'd rather ground my boat on a sand bar than spend another five minutes in that store."

"Ohh, such shopping torture." She laughed, her shiny, thick hair swinging when she shook her head. "Like you couldn't spend twice that time in the tackle shop checking out rods and reels." She pantomimed casting and reeling and deepened her voice. "Check out the smooth action on this baby. Huh huhh."

He cracked up as they reached the restaurant. "Tools of my trade, babe."

After helping her out of the truck, he settled his hand at the small of her back. She'd tucked in her blouse so he had to settle for rubbing his palm against cotton fabric instead of the soft skin underneath while he guided her to an outdoor table.

"Going with your logic," she continued, "shopping for furniture *is* now part of my job."

"God help me if I have to watch you go through that process again."

"It wasn't *that* bad!" She picked up the plastic covered menu.

"Nah, babe. It was that good. Your gorgeous body wriggling all over those cushions makes me . . ."

Beethoven's Fifth chimed.

Dropping the menu, she yanked the phone off her purse strap. "Hello? Yes, it is. Thank you for calling me back, Mr. Thomas. Let me describe my proj . . . That's right. I'm Willie Hanson's granddaughter. I agree nobody can touch Gramps for boat repair in the entire Keys. Now, I contacted you about a . . . Jenna Lynne? Yes. She and I went to school together. Oh, you're married? Please give her my best."

She tapped her nails on the wooden picnic table. Bobby hid a smirk behind his menu. *Welcome to doing business in a small town. Get used to it.* Keys natives loved figuring out connections before getting down to the matter at hand. Finally, Dora Lee took control of the conversation, launching into an explanation of her cottage project.

He knew A.J. Thomas. The man liked to hear himself talk a lot, which explained why he auditioned for all of his sister's productions, but he was a good architect. Idly listening to the conversation, Bobby scanned the menu. They made a fine fish sandwich at this restaurant. Truth be told, it was near impossible to find a bad meal in the Keys.

"Yes, there are eleven cottages in all. About half are two-bedroom. All have a kitchenette and a living room area."

On the other hand, he'd eaten grilled mahi last night for dinner. Maybe a hamburger.

"All of the bedrooms need to be expanded, although that might mean we have to lose the kitchen space."

Ouch, that was going to kick up the cost projections. Willie either didn't know the full amount of Dora Lee's divorce settlement, or he'd kept it quiet, but it must have been adequate or Willie wouldn't have given the green light. He sneaked a look over the top of the menu. Whoo, she was a beautiful sight, focused on her phone call. The breeze from the Gulf stirred her hair and the afternoon sun illuminated her smooth, lightly browned skin. Sure, here and there he spotted a little fan of lines, a minor crease, but nothing that any woman should freak over. Why she worried over her age was beyond him.

That mouth, slicked a deep rose shade, could fuel his fantasies for nights on end. Her body, with her soft curves, long legs, spectacular breasts . . . *Down, boy.* He chugged some ice tea and ducked back behind the menu. If a fraction of what he felt showed in his expression and she noticed, he'd either flat-out piss her off or blow her concentration — which would then piss her off. Either way, he'd gain nothing.

What besides a good taste of Dora Lee stimulated his appetite this afternoon? Salads? No way. He wasn't in the mood for ribs, which brought him back to the hamburger.

"Mr. Thomas, okay, AJ. In addition to the building renovation, I want a conceptual design for the entire area, including the pool and hot tub."

Pool and hot tub? Holy hell! Abandoning the menu, he turned his full attention to the phone call.

"No, I realize they don't exist there now, but I want to add them," she continued. "Of course I realize that will increase the overall cost, but they are a necessary expenditure."

Willie hadn't mentioned this part of the plan. Bobby

was sure he wouldn't have missed so big an addition to their property. This had to be a brand new development bursting out of her brain. Where did she think she was going to put that pool?

"When you come out, I'll show you some possible locations. There's a jungle of uncleared land that might suit."

Visions of backhoes and cement mixers chugging through the complex past the horrified storeowners filled his head. Every time her scheme increased in scope, so would the opposition from Leo and the others.

Bobby *wanted* her to succeed and be happy so she'd stay in the Keys, but he also owed it to the storeowners to keep things on an even keel. They'd been with the marina for awhile, decades in the case of Vince, Bitsy, and Mack. They liked their lives the way they were, and dug in their heels about changes — particularly from outsiders. Conch roots and family connection regardless, to that crew Dora Lee was definitely an outsider.

Maybe land use zoning and laws about protected areas would foul this particular line and she'd content herself with sprucing up the buildings and the landscaping. The powers-that-be were mighty stingy with permits about clearing land. With any luck, he wouldn't have to be the bad guy that put his foot down and squashed her enthusiasm.

"Not until the end of next week? There isn't any way you can see me sooner, A.J.? We are talking about a substantial project. No, no. I understand that you have other clients already lined up. It's only that . . ." Like a cloud passing over the sun, disappointment dimmed the eager expression on her face. "Well, I'm just eager to begin."

The setback put a sad little hitch in her breath that old A.J. couldn't hear. Between the wistful look on her face and that sigh, Bobby wanted to cuddle her on his lap, tease away the sadness and put the sunlight back into her smile.

From alarm about her pool project to wanting to champion her effort in 5.2 seconds. Yeah, he had it bad. He tapped her arm to get her attention.

Let me talk to him, he mouthed the words.

She shot him a doubtful frown that he answered with a grin and a nod. "I can help," he whispered.

With a skeptical look she returned to the conversation. "A.J.? Bobby Daulton's here with me. He'd like to speak to you." She handed over the phone.

"Hey, old buddy, how's it going? Jen and the kids are doing well? Great. Jo Jo says you're gonna rock the house, you dog." He leaned back in his chair. "Yeah, the action's good in all waters, A.J. I swear it's like we get a strike on every cast. I hear you. Sounds like between the play production and all your clients, you don't have a free afternoon."

The man ran on about his business responsibilities, reminding Bobby for the millionth time in his life how glad he was that *his* office was the open ocean. "Hey, man, are you fishing in the locals' tournament next week? You didn't hear of it yet? First part of the week before the celebrity tarpon tourney. It's a benefit for Charlie Sawyer to help with his medical bills."

Dora Lee never took her eyes off of him, obviously wondering where he was going with this little chat. He winked.

"Anyway, with the action we're seeing on the water, it's sure gonna be a good day. I didn't think I was gonna be able to join in, but I had a charter cancel." That was a flat-out lie. He'd planned on fishing with buddies. "I guess if you're so busy that you can't even see Dora Lee's property plans until the end of the week, there's no way you can squeeze out a day for fishing. I'd offer to guide for you, but that could push off your appointment with her even longer and none of us want that."

Throw the cast, strip the line. "What's that? Sure. I can wait while you check your calendar."

Feel the strike. "You think you can reshuffle a few appointments? That would be real fine, A.J. I know how important this project is to her. That makes it important to me."

Play the fish. "This Friday? Hang on." He looked at Dora Lee, raising a brow in question. At her eager nod, he smiled and winked again. "She says that will be fine." He guided his catch to the boat. "Hey, that's great. Yeah. The tournament launches Monday from the city marina. Bright and early. See you then." *Catch and release.* "Thanks, man. Later."

He shut her phone and handed it back, surprised when she pressed her hands to his cheeks for a smacking kiss.

"You're brilliant. That was awesome. Thank you!" She picked up the menu. "What's good here?"

You. You look good enough to eat and then some, he wanted to say. "Fish sandwiches. The conch chowder's great."

"Fried or made with cream." She pressed her hand against her middle, regretfully. "I'll have the grilled tuna."

After giving their order to the waitress, he drank some more tea, rattling the ice in his glass. "You're all set with A.J. He'll do right by you."

"Jo Jo told me he's good. Thanks again. I can't believe how difficult it is to hire someone in this town." She shook her head. "You would think I was asking them to abet me in a crime."

He laughed. "There are a lot of folks who think work *is* a crime or a necessary evil that interrupts their Jimmy Buffet wasting away again 'tude, but that isn't A.J."

"Good to know."

Bobby rested his forearms on the table and opened up a packet of crackers. "So, tell me more about your project."

Damned if her face didn't light up like a streetlight at dusk. "I can almost see the entire complex, completely re-done in my mind's eye." While they waited for their food, she told him everything. Some of it he'd heard the evening before, but listening to her talk, she'd been busy with more than floor refinishing.

Now, instead of transforming all the cottages for people to stay in, she wanted to convert one to a little gym and work-out room and use another for massages, facials and . . .

"Dora Lee, are you telling me people pay to have some-one cover them up with rocks?"

"Hot stone therapy is very popular," she stated as if it made perfect sense.

That cinched it. There was no limit to the foolish ways that some people found to spend their money. At least those changes wouldn't trigger May Day alerts from the marina complex's store owners. Big construction projects were another matter all together.

He leaned back so the waitress could set down his basket and then squirted ketchup on his fries. Popping one in his mouth, he watched Dora Lee delicately unwrap her utensils and smooth a paper napkin on her lap. He waited while she sampled her tuna and felt his throat tighten when she forked the first delicate bite into her mouth, moaning with pleasure at the taste.

You've got it bad, he told himself, *if watching her eat revs your engines.*

Pulling himself together, he returned to the subject at hand. "Did I hear you right? You're thinking of putting in a pool and a hot tub?"

She nodded. "Everybody expects the place where they stay to have a pool. That's a given."

"What about that little beach right outside their doors?"

"Doesn't matter." She smiled and wagged her fork at him. "When people are looking for accommodations, they check for a pool, even if they never dip a toe in the water. I don't want them to find us lacking and cross us off the list of possibilities."

He rubbed the back of his neck. "Sounds like a lot of work and disruption, babe. That's if you even get the permits from the city and clear environmental restrictions."

"I thought about that." Her gorgeous mouth twisted. "The sooner we get started the better. I don't want to do anything that harms the environment." She flashed a smile. "Your sister would kick my butt."

"She'd give you a hard time about it, that's for sure." In addition to her commitment to the theater and various productions, Jo Jo was an active environmentalist. She volunteered for turtle watches, was trained to assess manatees, and several times a year corralled everyone she knew to participate in beach cleanups.

"Does she still pick up snarled fishing line when she walks on the Seven Mile Bridge?"

"Heck, yeah. And chews the ass off of anybody she sees littering or breaking off that line when they're fishing. Did you see the monofilament recycling bin at the marina? That's her doing, too."

"Good for her! Your sister has never been slow to act on her convictions."

"That's for sure."

"Well, even if she wasn't my best friend, I would still be careful about the property."

That gave him a good opening. "You know, I think it's great that you figured all this out so quickly and are ready to jump right in and get started, but can I give you a suggestion?"

She glanced up from her lunch. "Sure. What is it?"

"Just remember that Keys people aren't used to fast changes."

"What do you mean?"

"Some folks might need a little time to adjust to your ideas."

"Like who?" She put down her fork, studied his face. A beat later, distress filled her golden eyes and she reached for his arm. "Bobby, is it Gramps? Has he said something to you? Last night he told me he was all for my idea, but. . ."

She swallowed hard and he felt like a jerk for upsetting her.

"If Gramps doesn't really want me to do this, then there's no point to any of it."

He brought her hand to his lips, nuzzled her knuckles and squeezed. "No. Willie's fine with it all," he reassured her. "I'm talking more about the store owners."

Relief gave way to puzzlement. "Why would they care? It isn't their place."

"Technically, you're right. They don't own the complex, but they've got a stake in the property just the same."

"How so?"

"It accounts for their livelihood. You know how your Gramps has always managed things. They pay rent and take care of their places."

"As well they should. They lease their space and tenants are supposed to maintain, at least the insides. Gramps is responsible for the roof, plumbing and such, as well as the surrounding grounds. Whatever else he does with the complex is his business, not his tenants'."

The storeowners thought differently. Since everything else at the complex could affect their commerce, they figured that gave them a say in all matters. Telling her that flat-out would only put her back up, so he eased her into it. "They aren't just tenants. It's more like a family."

"I'm family." Her voice grew small.

Ah, shit. He hadn't meant to upset her. "Babe, you're absolutely Willie's family and he'd take the moon out of the sky to make you happy." *So would I,* he thought.

"Then what exactly are you getting at?"

He caressed her hand, smoothing his thumb over her skin. "All I'm suggesting is that you deal carefully with everybody. Understand that they're used to things the way they are. Some of them are old — think how long Bitsy, Vince and Mack have been around. Change can be kind of scary at first." He held her gaze and continued. "I'm sure they'll grow to like the whole thing and see the plusses, but it might take a little time. With someone like Leo, even longer."

"Isn't that the truth!" She rolled her eyes. "Does that man even know how to have a civil conversation? I said hello to him this morning when I went to the Marina Mart and he growled. What's *that* about?"

"Leo isn't real comfortable with strangers."

"What about customers? Does he scowl at them while he's sticking needles and ink into their skin? It's a wonder he gets any work at all."

"He's an artist. Just a temperamental one."

She snorted. "Sure. The Van Gogh of tattoos. I'll buy it." Picking up her fork again, she fiddled with the tuna before spearing another bite.

"Just keep it in mind, that's all I'm saying."

"Okay, Bobby, I hear you, and it's a smart idea to get them all to buy in to the project and, hopefully, get excited. After all, guests will surely patronize their businesses. Well, most of them anyway." She smiled and the sun broke out again over her face. "I'm in a hurry to get things rolling, but I promise I won't roll over anyone."

Satisfied that he'd made his point, he flashed a cocky grin and gave her a long smoldering look. "I won't mind it a bit when you roll over me."

CHAPTER 15

GIVE THE MAN an opening and he'd bulldoze through.
Respond to his *entendre* and he'd double it. Dora settled for
a withering glance and concentrated on her excellent lunch.
Rather than let the silence grow heavy, she filled it with more
information about her redecorating plans. Judging from his
reaction in the store, endless details about bath amenities,
furniture styles, flooring choices, and stationery ought to
make his eyes glaze over like a donut.

She continued for the entire ride home and he not only
stayed with the conversation, he actually sounded interested.
What's more, he gave her excellent suggestions.

"That's a great point about using Bahaman shutters, Bobby."

"You'll need the hurricane protection. By upgrading
to code, you'll save some money on your windstorm insur-
ance, too."

"Without sacrificing the look I want. They'll be a great
enhancement to the whole cottage atmosphere."

He shot her a look and a crooked smile. "You don't have
to sound so surprised. I know a thing or two about this stuff.

My boat, remember?"

"True." His cruiser was beautifully restored, down to the last cleat. She'd noticed all the details the other night before he kissed her blind.

Her skin warmed and, from the gleam that entered his eyes, he guessed the cause. He reached over and rubbed his knuckles across her cheek.

"Both hands on the wheel, sailor." She jerked her face away, her mouth set into a tight line when he chuckled.

He complied, but her skin pulsed from the light stroke. She dragged herself back to her project. "So, who do you recommend for the contract work, once the design plans are set?"

They discussed various names, their pros and cons, and Dora busied herself taking notes while he talked. He pulled into the marina complex and parked as close to the cottage path as possible. With mouth-watering ease, he hoisted the arm chair over his head while she followed with an end table.

"I'll get one of the guys to help me carry that sofa"

"I can help," she protested, for all the good it did.

"Sure you can. Grab a lamp. I'll be back in a sec." Before she could pull away, he smooched her cheek and walked off.

She'd made two breathless trips, toting not only the couch pillows and a lamp, but also the other end table — so there, macho man — before he and Mack brought in her sofa.

"Howdy, Dora Lee."

"Hi, Mack."

"Where do you want it, babe?"

"Against the wall, please." Its creamy color looked terrific against the walls. The pillows would really make the colors pop. "Perfect." She smiled at the older man. "Thanks for helping."

"No problem. Hear you got plans for shining up the old places."

"You bet. This area's going to be gorgeous when completed." She bumped him playfully with her shoulder. "I should have figured Gramps would share the news with you right off." It made her feel proud that her grandfather had told his best friend right away.

"Heard the news from . . ."

"Babe, you're positive this is where you want the couch?"

"Why? You don't think it looks good?" What was with the look Bobby gave Mack? The bait and tackle store owner was one of the most easy-going men alive. Surely, Bobby didn't include him in the group of people who might resist her ideas.

"Looks fine to me, but I know Mack's gotta get back to work, so I wanted to be sure before we lose the extra muscle."

The older man looked as puzzled as she felt, his eyes darting between the two of them. Eventually, he shrugged. "Got a new shipment of reels to inventory. Dora Lee, good luck with your project."

"I'll walk back with you and get the rest," Bobby said, and the two departed.

Hurrying Mack out of there was about as subtle as a college kid kicking out his roommate when he had a girl

stashed in the room. Did he think she was going to welcome him back so they could christen the couch with wild
monkey sex?

Although . . .

Stop it, Dora. Right this minute. Appalled at the flood
of heat that swamped her system, she shoved an end table
into place. Even putting his name in the same sentence as
the word sex was dangerous. Her libido mamboed at the
thought of making love with Bobby, until she pictured stripping down to reveal her overly fleshy self. Then the libido
cowered and hid. It didn't matter what he'd said so far about
his attraction. "What does <u>he</u> know about body image?" she
grumbled. Him with his skin stretched over all those honed
muscles, sculpted abs, and three percent body fat.

"Where do you want it, babe?" he asked, walking into
the cottage.

She whirled. "We are not getting naked on this couch!"

The devil's own smirk broke out on his face. "I meant
the lamp, but you've obviously got something else in mind."

Mentally kicking herself for opening the door to the very
topic she wanted to squelch, she bit back a curse. The room
shrank around them, such was his pure physical presence.
Even in a ballroom of five-hundred people, Bobby would
never have to call attention with a blustery voice or broad
gestures. He sauntered into a room and everybody naturally
took notice.

Breathe! She forced a smile as if her lungs weren't oxygen-
deprived, and pointed. "On that table, please."

He complied then moved over, standing way too close and rubbing her back while he studied the arrangement. "Looks real nice."

"Thanks." Her skin tingled under the circular strokes; she stepped out of range and picked up her decorative pillows.

Bobby followed. She blocked him with a pillow back-handed into that rock hard stomach. "Here. Hold this."

Ignoring his cocky grin, she fussed with the arrangement, nestling the other pillow in the corner of the couch. "No. That's not right." She aligned it perfectly in the middle, frowned and returned it to the corner, angling it this time. "That's better." Surveying the placement, she reached back for its mate. "Next."

Instead of soft chenille, her fingers touched his work-rough palm. She yanked back her hand like she'd fondled a scorpion. Over his laugh, she grabbed the pillow and took two steps to the other end of the couch.

This cottage *really* wasn't big enough. She could only re-arrange accessories for so long, especially when he refused to keep his distance. The warmth of his body registered against her back before he slid his hands around her middle. She jolted, knocking her head against his chin.

"Oww."

"Geezus." His jaw cracked when he flexed it and she winced at whatever damage she'd caused.

He didn't sound too pained, more like amused. "Jumpy all of a sudden."

"I'm working here, you might remember." She pried his

hands from her stomach, but instead of releasing her, he spun her around.

"I'm making you nervous."

"Not in this lifetime." She snorted, her eyes focused on his chest. "You know, maybe the couch might look better facing the opposite direction. It will better define this area apart from the kitchenette." Struggling did her no good. She'd have better luck dislodging an octopus. "Make yourself useful. Let go of me and grab hold of the couch and help me move it.

"In a minute. If you aren't nervous, why won't you look at me?"

"That's ridiculous. I'm looking at you. Where else *can* I look since you're squeezing me like a sponge?"

"Good try." He nabbed her chin. "C'mon, babe."

"Quit it. I told you that I wasn't going to bed with you."

"Mmm hmm. And I said I'd change your mind." Devilment lit his green eyes. "That's what's happening here, Dora Lee. I'm getting to you."

"Like a rash."

"Got an itch that needs scratchin', babe, that's what I'm here for. Among other things."

She jerked away. "I am *not* interested in those 'other things'."

"Sure you aren't." He stroked his fingers across her cheek, under her jaw, caressing her pulse point. "And your heart's not pounding either." He pressed lightly, first with his fingers, then with his lips. When he lifted his gaze to her again, his eyes had darkened to the emerald of the ocean at dusk. "Admit it and we can both have what we want."

A woman of her age and experience ought to be able to control her responses more effectively, but with far less effort than she'd dreamed, he steadily eroded her defenses. Like a beach washing out with the tide, those objections she'd shored up began to crumble. A soft kiss here, a nuzzle there. The slide of his palm over her back, pressing her closer, and she trembled. Desire mixed with nerves. Need with apprehension.

"Bobby," she whispered. "I can't."

"Sure you can."

He brushed his mouth down the side of her neck and her breath stuttered. God, yes, she wanted him — hot and craving her touch. His broad chest glistening with sweat, rising and falling when she made his heart pound fiercely. She wanted to make him so blind with passion that it wouldn't matter that her ass was broad and her breasts more like old pillows than firm melons.

He nipped her bottom lip and she broke. Spearing her fingers into his gold-tipped, thick hair, she lifted herself up on her toes and nailed him with a kiss. Her mouth moved against his while her thumbs stroked his cheekbones and she kissed him for all she was worth. Her tongue darted at the corners of his mouth before she licked inside his bottom lip. His hands slipped down to her bottom, squeezed and snugged her tight to his body while she fused their mouths together.

His erection was piston-hard and she wriggled up and

down, side to side, concentrating their attention on that area so he wouldn't register the sponginess of her ass cheeks in his palms.

"Babe, you're killing me," he growled.

"Good." She evaded another kiss and dipped her tongue into the small dent in his chin. Busying herself dragging his shirt out of the waistband of his shorts, she hooked her leg around his calf and rubbed against him even harder, her breasts to his chest, belly to his erection and everywhere in between.

His skin was warm, firm beneath the palms that she snaked under his shirt as she pushed it up his chest. He let go of her long enough to grab the collar behind his head and yank off the shirt the rest of the way.

She took advantage of his actions, quickly drawing her thumbs up the center of his torso, fanning out over his pecs, brushing his flat nubs. His hiss of pleasure inspired her to lean in and flick them with her tongue.

He massaged her nape, drew her close for another tongue-dueling kiss, and reached for her breasts. She grabbed that wayward hand, scraped his palm with her fingernail and, after breaking the kiss, bit the pad of his thumb before sucking his forefinger into her mouth, rewarded when he sharply inhaled.

"Dora Lee, slow down a little," he half-groaned, half-laughed. "Bet you never thought you'd hear me say that." He reached for her again. She pulled away, nipped him again, and swiftly palmed his groin.

She felt him throb and attacked his waistband, freeing

the button on the first try, and aimed for the zipper — definitely a two-handed job to avoid damaging the sizeable shaft that strained underneath.

"Damn, woman." He fought her off, bracketing her wrists in one hand, while he nabbed her chin. "Let me have a little fun here, too." He held her steady for a long, deep kiss that made her nipples peak and shot fire to her core. Her head swam and her muscles went soft with the heat, like gold under a jeweler's flame.

Taking advantage of her dizziness, he rapidly undid her buttons, yanking her blouse off her shoulders. With his other hand, he dipped inside the back of her shorts. The tender-rough caress on her bare skin shocked her back to reality. She pulled her hands free of his grip, slid them up to his shoulders, and pushed. He grabbed her by the waist, tumbling them both onto her new couch. Before he could roll her underneath and take control, she planted her knees on either side of his hips, leaned forward and plunged her tongue into his mouth. He targeted her breasts again, so she flattened against his chest, loving the tingling scrape of his chest hair against her tender nipples and feeding on his rough groan.

He pulled the scrunchie down her ponytail, buried his hands in her hair and feasted on the kiss. She slid herself up and down over his body, feeling him rock hard and twitching against her crotch. It took all her concentration to keep her eyes from crossing and remain focused on her mission.

Especially when he got his hands up under her loose-fitting shorts and worked his fingers inside her panties. One stroke and her back arched, giving him access to the front clasp of her bra. Oh, he moved quickly, releasing it with a flick and her breasts spilled free. She straightened up, grabbing them underneath, desperately afraid that they'd sag — and so would his erection.

"Oh, yeah. Hold those beauties for me."

Okay, good idea. Great camouflage. With her help, maybe he wouldn't notice that they'd lost their perkiness.

Bad idea. He nudged her closer, lifted his head from the cushions, closed his mouth around her nipple, suckled and she almost lost her mind. She shifted back.

"Little tease." But he smiled through the heat.

Inspiration. Let him think it was all part of her game. God knows J. Walter had liked it enough when she played the part of a vixen. He encouraged it, especially in the early years, and kept her well stocked in sexy lingerie long after she'd stopped modeling it for a living.

She dipped forward, letting Bobby suck some more, feeling the pull spear through her body, before backing away and wriggling her hips. He groaned, so she twisted some more, tilting her head and licking her lips when he looked at her through lowered-lids.

The next time she bent toward him, she shook her hair so that it brushed against his naked skin, dipped her head and nipped under his jaw . . . to his throat . . . and down over his chest.

She pressed her breasts against him and shifted her hands to the crooks of his elbows, gently holding down his arms. She drew her mouth down the center of his chest, scraped lightly with the edge of her teeth, and felt his big body shudder.

She shuddered, too, so turned on by the feel of him between her thighs, that it was all she could do not to rip open his pants and impale her body on him.

His stomach muscles contracted when she licked her way over his abs and his chest heaved.

"Dora Lee, babe, I . . ."

"Shhhh." She blew a soft breath over heated skin. "Let me."

His head fell back against her new multi-colored pillow and she scooted back on his thighs.

He exhaled like a racehorse. "Woman, what are you doing to me?" he asked, his voice hoarse.

"If you can still ask, I'm doing it wrong," she answered as she slipped her hand inside his unzipped shorts and wrapped her fingers around him.

An incoherent groan was his only comment as she stroked and fondled, pulling him free of his briefs. Her own throatiness wasn't faked when she took the full measure of him into her hands. "Ohh, yesss."

His eyes narrowed to slits of glittering green. He ran his hands up her arms and she backed away, shaking her head. She kept that coquettish half-smile on her face while she studied him. He was almost to the point of no return, but not quite, still trying to take control.

Difficult to do when a woman with experience plays with your penis. He tried to sit up, so she countered with an artful slide of her forefinger. A dangerous gleam entered his eyes, the look of a riled tiger coiling his muscles to pounce.

She dipped her head, brushed her hair against his stomach, and took him into her mouth.

From that point on, she won the battle. He fell back against the cushions and gave himself up to her licks and sucks, clenching the cushions until his knuckles went white and moans poured out of his throat. She knew the exact second his body tightened and delivered one long, last hard suck, then freed him from her mouth while he climaxed.

Some women thought it demeaning to give head, but from the first time she'd done it, with J. Walter, she'd reveled in the power of pleasuring him to his maximum limit with her sexual ability. Usually, it turned her on so strongly, that she nearly came just from the feel of her husband's body bucking under her while she brought him to orgasm.

Usually.

While Bobby sucked air back into his lungs and shuddered on the couch, she clambered off and went to the kitchenette, her stomach heaving not with desire, but with an empty, horrified nausea. She soaked a dishtowel with water, wrung out the excess and brought it to him, then busied her shaking hands by stuffing her boobs back into her bra, hooking it and buttoning her blouse up to her neck.

"Dora Lee."

He got his breath back sooner than J. Walter, and her husband had never once sounded furious after oral sex.

"Yes?" Facing away, she snared her scrunchie off of the floor.

"Come. Here."

Nerves ricocheted against her insides. She risked a glance, wished she hadn't, and then concentrated on pulling her hair together, securing it with the scrunchie. "What's the problem?"

He came off the couch in one fluid motion, grabbed her by the elbows and twirled her around, locking his thick arms around her back. His face muscles were taut, his nostrils flared and his eyes glittered. "You tell me."

"I don't know what you mean. I don't have a problem." Breaking his hold was like trying to bust through steel. "You can let go of me now."

"Not until you talk to me about what just happened here."

His chest rose and fell and his throat artery pulsed, not from sexual energy, she knew, but from the effort of holding his temper in check.

"You know, Bobby. Great sex is supposed to release tension, not create it."

"You think that's what just happened here. Great sex?"

"You came, didn't you?" she fired back. If she made him mad enough, maybe he wouldn't force the issue. "That's what you wanted. That's what you got."

His jaw clenched so tight he could shatter rocks with his teeth. It was a full minute before he could force out words. "I wanted to make love, not have you slut yourself for me."

"Slut?" she whispered, appalled. The accusation knifed through her — not because he'd said it, but because it was true. She'd serviced him like a street-walker. For what? To save herself the embarrassment of his rejection? This was twenty times worse.

She wrenched free — he'd have had to hurt her to maintain his grip — and twisted away, grasping the kitchenette counter to stop the sudden trembling of her limbs. At this point, she prayed he'd go away angry rather than stay and watch her fall apart.

No such luck. His hands settled on her shoulders. She flinched, but he didn't let go, massaging them instead. She could only guess at the effort it took for him to soften his tone along with his touch. "This doesn't track. Tell me why you went from resisting me to this."

No way could she explain it, not when she was so mortified at her own behavior that she couldn't even bear to look him in the face. The best she could manage was a weak head shake.

He made an exasperated rumble. "If you won't, then I'll have to guess." He tugged. "I'm having this conversation with the back of your head. Turn around." When she begrudgingly complied, he squeezed her shoulder. "That's better. I thought at first it was the challenge thing. That you weren't going to let me get the better of you. You can tease and play with the best of them, and it was damned hot."

"Right. I teased. I played. You had fun. Enough said."

"Not by a long shot." He shook her, gently, but got the point across. "Then, every time I tried to touch you, you pulled away. Why?"

She shrugged.

"Are you afraid of me? Did your husband hurt you?"

"He dumped me. Of course that hurt!"

"I mean physically."

"No! Never."

"Then what?"

When it came to interrogation, he could give lessons to a detective. The more he dug, the more she backpedaled. Maybe he'd handed her the reason she needed. "It was the challenge. Like you said. You were too sure of yourself. Too sure of me."

"I'd buy that except that it still doesn't track. If that were the case then you'd have bent over backwards proving that I don't turn you on. Instead, you didn't want me to touch you at all. So, if you weren't afraid of being hurt physically . . ."

He was anything but dumb. A glance told her he was carefully observing her reactions while working it all out in his mind.

"The only reason I can think of that you wouldn't want me to touch you is . . . damn." He cupped the back of her head, tilting her face so that she had to look at him. "It's that body image thing again. Geezus, woman, you've spent way too much time not paying attention if you honestly believe there's a single thing wrong with your body. What did you expect? I'd take one look at your body, and lose the hard-on?"

"No!" It was, but what woman wanted to admit that to a man?

"Liar." His mouth quirked. "If that's not your fear, then

you'll have no problem with me doing this."

Deliberately, he reached out for her breast. Her soft, squishy breast. She cringed and protectively folded her arms over her chest.

Trying once more to steer him off the topic, she snorted. "Most men don't complain about getting great head."

"Most men aren't in love with you."

She'd wondered what it felt like when people said the blood drained out of their heads. Now she knew. A buzz filled her brain. Her mouth fell open and breath expelled from her lungs on a *whoosh*.

She blinked.

He smiled, crookedly. "Yeah, this isn't how I planned to tell you. I thought I'd give you some more time."

"You can't be."

"If I wasn't, I'd have been out the door right after I zipped up my pants. That's probably what you expected. Bet you thought everything I've said and done was just to get in your pants and when I did, I'd be long gone. If you weren't so upset right now, I'd be seriously pissed at your lack of faith. If all I needed was to get off, I've got two hands and a good imagination."

He smoothed his fingers across her cheek. "I'm in love with you. Among other things, that means that I don't care if your boobs sag to your knees and your ass migrates south like a snowbird."

"That's flattering."

"It's okay for you to say it about yourself, but not for

anybody else? For the record, your boobs and ass are great, no matter what you think. And since I'm the only other one that's gonna see them naked, I ought to know."

"You aren't in love with me, Bobby."

He sighed and lightly shook her again. "Dora Lee, you can tell me anything else, even 'go to hell' if that's what's on your mind, but don't tell me what I feel for you."

His voice was so deep and warm, the words so sincere, that her heart hurt. She dropped her chin to her chest, suddenly exhausted. Tears threatened to spill over and she squeezed her eyes shut, but not enough to prevent tiny drops from leaking out the sides.

"I know you're not in love with me yet. But I also know that I get to you and that's a good enough start." He hugged her, refusing to let go when she struggled weakly. Lightly, comfortingly, he stroked her back. "Even if you don't love me, trust me," he whispered low in her ear. "You're the most beautiful woman in the world to me. The next time we're together, I want to spend hours proving it to you."

His heart thudded, strong and warm against her chest. "When you're ready, you'll come find me," he said before releasing her. Combing back stray strands of hair from her face, he thumbed away the wetness and kissed her lightly.

"When you do, we'll get rid of those insecurities together."

CHAPTER 16

THE NIGHT OUTSIDE didn't come close to the darkness inside Dora's heart as she numbly leafed through catalogs. Robbed of sleep, she curled up in the new armchair, unable to stretch out on that beautiful couch without thinking of what she'd done. A mug of what had once been hot, sweet tea cooled on the end table. She'd brewed it to settle her stomach, shortly after she threw up in the bathroom.

Of all the things she could have done, her stunt with Bobby took the prize for idiocy. Dumb, deprived and, worst of all, desperate. She'd let her fears run rampant over her common sense. Instead of saving her pride, she'd abandoned it and turned what should have been an intimate experience into a wretched, tawdry act that had no more meaning than a hooker's transaction.

What was wrong with her? After vowing that she wouldn't use him to make herself feel better, she'd had no intention of using him to make herself feel *worse*. Even in the last days of her marriage, she'd never used oral sex to hold on to her husband.

Bobby should have smacked her on the ass and sauntered off with a, "Thanks for the blow-job, babe." She'd all but asked for that kind of treatment and that's what she deserved.

Instead, she got a declaration of love.

A few hours ago, the quick look she'd taken of herself in the mirror after bowing to the bowl revealed an ashen-faced hag with puffy eyes, a red snuffling nose and swollen lips in a rumpled, mis-buttoned blouse. Real pretty.

She'd never felt less loveable, or more lonely.

Two a.m. in a half-redone cottage with a dead fish in her bedroom and a land crab as her only neighbor. "Heck of a night," she mocked. Thanks to her earlier sexcapade, there wasn't a single person she could talk to or a shoulder on which to cry. Sex was definitely not on the list of things to discuss with Gramps and for the first time ever, she couldn't even call her best friend. As much as Jo Jo might root for her and Bobby to hook up, Dora knew this wasn't what she'd had in mind. A quick, "Hey Jo, I blew your brother and feel like shit about it" was not going to earn her a hug and congratulations.

Disgusted, she forced herself from the chair and paced. She picked up a stack of paperwork from an end table. Since she wasn't sleeping, maybe she could get some work done. At least that was one area of her life where she'd made positive progress. The photographs and design notes blurred before her tired eyes and her head hurt when she tried to focus. *So much for work.* She slapped the papers down onto the counter.

So that left her talking to herself again, but she wasn't

the best of company and she had a lot of hours to fill. When she tired of speaking to an empty room, she supposed she could always go lie on her bed and talk to the tarpon. A one-sided conversation, at best, but at least it couldn't condemn her for her stupidity — not considering that its fatal mistake had landed it plasticized and nailed to a mounting board.

At least she was still alive.

Oh, good, Dora. You're playing imaginary one-upsmanship with a dead fish.

A stunning synopsis of the current state of her despair. Disgusted, she sank back into the chair. Clutching a pillow to her shaky stomach, she rested her chin on soft chenille and sobbed.

Bobby's clean, ocean breeze scent rose from the fabric, triggering a strong sensory memory of the strength of his arms wrapped around her and his warm, soothing breath on her neck. She squeezed her eyes as her muscles shivered, remembering his spectacular body beneath her on the couch, and then later, snuggled up tight after his anger waned and he told her he loved her. She'd wanted to sink into his embrace and never let go.

Trust me, he'd said. *When you're ready, you'll come find me.*

Did she dare? No, of course not. But, maybe . . .

She was no more ready for sex than she was to outrun a pack of flying monkeys, but deep inside, she knew that he offered more.

Again, not sex. Regardless of whether she believed his love declaration, she knew he was serious about not wanting a quick bang for the sake of getting off. She wasn't merely a challenge, either. He cared and, surprising as it was for a big, physical guy, he understood. Even if he thought her turmoil ridiculous, he got that, to her, the fears were real.

He said he loved her. That remained to be seen. He insisted that he wanted to make her feel better. God, she hoped that was true.

Trust me. A weak, watery laugh trickled from her throat. She slipped her feet into sandals and left the cottage. One whopping load of trust, coming up.

🦀 🦀 🦀

BOBBY STRETCHED OUT on his bed, arm crooked beneath his head, staring at the skylight. A dozen times since the afternoon, he'd fought the instinct to go back to Dora Lee's cottage, take her into her bedroom and show her how it should be when they made love.

A dozen times he'd stopped himself. He'd said what needed saying earlier when he told her he loved her. Clumsily maybe, not smooth and all poetic, not that he was the poetic type, but he'd gotten across the point.

Wondering what she'd do with the knowledge kept him awake long after he should have been logging zees before his early morning charter. He yanked the pillow from beneath his head, punched it up and stuck it back in place. Wondering, and a sizeable chunk of guilt.

He couldn't shake the gut-sickening feeling that he'd

driven her to that desperate act this afternoon. Maybe coming on to her every time they were together had made her think she had something to prove. Her self-esteem had gone the way of her wedding band. It killed him to think that this spectacular woman was so damned afraid of turning him off with her body that she'd sucked him off to distract him from touching her.

The timing couldn't be worse. Jazzed by her renovation project, she'd begun to reclaim her confidence. By the time he'd left that afternoon, she looked about as low as an anchor sunk down six fathoms.

Nice going, dumb ass.

I should have told her I loved her first. The night he first kissed her would have been a good time. Or today over lunch. Practically anytime *before* this afternoon would have been better.

He twisted on the bed. He hadn't said anything because he didn't want her to say that she didn't love him back. The truth stabbed him like a sea urchin spine. He'd opted to show her instead, but she never received the message, and now she probably didn't believe him.

Hell, if he'd needed any convincing himself, this afternoon's experience had cemented the idea with two simple truths. For a man in love, there was more to great sex than coming, and watching his woman cry had ripped his own heart in half.

He'd wanted to take her back onto the couch and cradle her in his arms, rid her of her anguish, but her body's rigid tension signaled that she wasn't ready yet for that kind of comfort. Leaving her alone was like leaving part of him behind, but he'd said all he could and she needed to come to terms with it on her own.

Trust me, he'd said, and left her there to work it out as if trust was the only thing keeping her from falling in love, too. There were as many holes in that strategy as there were drops of water in the ocean. Even a first time angler knew you didn't toss out your lure and walk away.

He swung his legs over the side of his bed and fumbled in the darkness for his shorts. He was up the steps, out of the main salon and ready to leap off the deck before the time registered. *Crap!* He could hardly charge into her place at this hour and hope she'd be in the mood to talk. She'd either refuse to answer the door or refuse to let him in or — holy hell!

The moon gilded her in silver as she carefully picked her footing up the dock to his gangway. She stopped each time the wood creaked under her feet, which was about every step. At that rate, she'd never make it. He stepped across the gap between boat and dock like it was no wider than a pencil.

Her head snapped up and she stared at him with haunted eyes. "Bobby, I'm sorry to wake you. I know it's ridiculously late."

"I was on my way to your place." Reaching her in a couple long strides, he hugged her tightly.

Her arms stuck like poles at her sides. Worry and pain choked her voice to a whisper. "I'm so sorry."

"For what?"

"For . . . you know."

He brushed kisses across her face, her hair. "I shouldn't have pushed you, babe."

"I could still have said no, but I . . . You were right. I wanted you, but then . . ." She burrowed her head, mumbling against his shoulder. "I don't know what I was thinking. What you must think of me."

The misery in her whisper tore at him like a gaff. He smoothed his hand up and down her back and rubbed his cheek against hers. "I told you what I think about you, how I feel about you, this afternoon. If you don't believe anything else, believe that."

She said nothing, but didn't pull away. Remaining in his arms, she trembled. "I know you said when I was ready to come find you, but I didn't come here for sex tonight."

He smiled, knowing she couldn't see. "Didn't expect that you had, babe."

"I couldn't sleep." Her body lost some of its stiffness and her hands came up, tentatively resting at his waist.

"Me either."

"I thought I'd feel better if I came over and apologized. No, don't tell me that I don't have to. Just accept it. Please."

"Okay. Apology accepted."

She nodded, breathed deep. "Thanks. Well then. I guess I should let you get back to bed."

He caught her hands before she could back away. "Dora Lee, don't go." Her eyes widened, silently questioning when he smoothed his hand down her cheek. He kissed her fore-head. "Stay with me for the rest of the night. Not for sex." He kissed the tip of her nose and then cuddled her close. "Let me hold you."

Her warm breath fanned his throat and she relaxed. "We'll hold each other."

"Even better." He crouched, slid his arm in back of her knees and lifted her.

She yelped and grabbed his shoulders. "What are you doing?"

"Proving a point."

Carrying her easily, he pulled his boat closer to the dock, stepped onto the deck and took her down to his bunk, leaving the night behind.

♔ ♔ ♔

WAKING UP WITH Bobby's arms around her and his chest warming her back rated as a high point of her return to the Keys. If his obnoxious alarm would stop buzzing the cabin like a World War II fighter plane so they could go back to sleep, the morning would be almost perfect. He groaned in her ear and reached across her head to slap the snooze alarm, smushing her face into the pillow in the process.

"Hey. Watch it, sailor." She giggled when he groaned again and snuggled even closer.

"Morning, sunshine."

"Sunshine. Ha," she grumbled. "It's pitch black. I can't

see a thing."

"Open your eyes. It's dawn." The T-shirt she'd slept in had bunched up around her waist. He playfully squeezed her butt, making her jump.

"Stop that!" She wriggled free and rolled to her back, pulling down the wayward shirt, but not before her behind brushed against prominent evidence that all of his body was awake and ready for the day. She giggled again.

"What's so funny, woman?" He propped himself up with an elbow.

"You have bed head." She stroked her hand through his sun-streaked blond waves.

God, he was so handsome. His face deeply tanned with that sexy dent in the chin and the slash of dimple in his cheek. Light fans of white lines radiating from the corners of his clear green eyes added maturity and character.

He grinned, making that dimple appear. "My ball cap will cover it up. You, on the other hand . . ."

"Oh, I know. I must look a wreck."

"Never." He slid his hand down the back of her head, gathering her hair together, tickling her nose with the ends. "On your worst day you'd never be anything less than gorgeous." He leaned over, kissed her tenderly and then rolled away and sat up.

His back was smooth, wide, and beautifully muscled. She couldn't keep from touching him, gliding her fingers down his spine. He jolted when she hit the dip at his waist.

"Watch it, woman."

"I am. Watching."

He rolled back, kissed her again, hungrily this time. Releasing her quickly, he boosted himself off the bed in a single motion and stood there, staring at her with an obvious tent in his briefs and dark heat in his eyes. She melted under the look and knew that if he came to her then, she wouldn't refuse.

Something on her face must have told him because he leaned over the bed, his eyes intense. "You make it damn hard to walk away."

Then don't, she thought, barely able to stop from speaking out loud.

"I have to go." His voice sounded strained. "I'm not rejecting you. If I didn't have a tournament charter, I'd climb back in with you and stay for the next three days. Do you understand?"

She nodded, but he searched her expression, maybe as much to reassure himself.

It looked like he almost weakened, swearing softly under his breath. "I have the damn sponsor dinner tonight. It's gonna run late and then we fish at first light tomorrow."

He looked so frustrated that she couldn't help but smile as she sat up. "I understand, Bobby. It's okay. We both have to work."

"If I get done early, I'll come by your place for awhile."

"The door will be open." She knelt in his bed, put her hands on his cheeks and softly kissed that firm sculpted mouth.

He groaned. "You do that again and there's going to be

one upset angler missing a fishing guide."

She laughed and scooted off the bed, grabbing up the rest of her clothes. "I don't want to be blamed for your client losing the tournament," she said, hurriedly pulling on her shorts. She stuffed her bra in her pocket. This early in the morning, she'd risk going without. Slipping her feet into her sandals, she smiled, happier than she'd been in days. "Go get 'em, sailor."

Blowing him a kiss, she scooted out of the cabin.

🦀 🦀 🦀

THE FEELING STAYED with her all morning through the grimiest jobs. The rest of the cottages hadn't been touched in years. Dora gleefully sacrificed a denim ensemble, pinned up her hair and got down to work. Even though Gramps had covered the furnishings in old sheets and plastic tarps, dirt was everywhere. Her sneakered feet left paths of footprints on the floors as she carried out the coverings from the second cottage and continued her mental inventory.

She'd have to arrange for a gargantuan Dumpster for the ancient beds, worn couches, and assorted junk. Gramps would know who to call. Speaking of which . . . She glanced at her watch. It was approaching lunch time, so hopefully she could corral him for a sandwich and talk over the idea of opening up a pool area.

Ugh. She needed to shower and change before going anywhere. *Wait a minute. I'm not heading for lunch at the club.* She laughed at herself. Gramps would no doubt have more than a few oil smears on his clothes. Dirt smudges wouldn't shock anybody. A thorough scrub of her hands in the sink, a quick swipe of lipstick and she was ready.

Lucky timing for her, she caught him as he came around the corner of the stores.

"Hey, baby girl." As she'd guessed, her less than pristine appearance didn't bother him a bit. He caught her up in a giant hug. "Somebody's been working hard this morning. Whatcha up to?"

"Cleaning and inventory. I started clearing out the cottages."

"Keeps you out of trouble," he joked. "Got time for lunch? Mack and I are grabbing sandwiches from the deli."

"That was my plan. There're a couple of things I need to discuss with you."

Mack joined them from the bait and tackle shop and the three of them ate out front on the porch while they talked.

"A pool?" Willie swigged tea and put the bottle back down on the porch. "Mighty big undertaking, darlin'." He and Mack exchanged a look.

Sweet of them to worry that she was taking on too much. She smiled reassuringly. "I'm pretty sure there's space in that area where you had those old shuffleboard courts and horse-shoe pitch. The architect will be able to tell me for sure."

"Ain't never been one there before, Dora Lee." Mack wiped away a dribble of mayonnaise from his whiskers.

"That's why it will be such a terrific enhancement."

"Enhancement. Right." He looked again at Gramps

who shrugged.

"We'll see what A.J. says." Willie nodded at them both. "As long as you're not ripping out any mangroves. They're protected, you know. Need all kinds of permits before you can even trim them."

"A pool." Mack shook his head, doubtful, and Dora reminded herself that, like Bobby had said, older people were often apprehensive about change. She smiled at him and patted his arm. "It's going to be great. You'll see."

Her Cuban pressed sandwich was delicious with its warm combination of pork, ham, and cheese. Hang the calories and carbs, she was starving and needed fuel for her labors. Speaking of which . . .

"Gramps, I need a Dumpster. Do we call the city garbage or a private supplier?"

"City. I got the number in my shop, baby girl. How big?"

"Huge. All that stuff's gotta go."

"What kinda stuff?" Mack asked around an immense hunk of roast beef and cheese.

"Furniture mostly. Kitchen ware — plates, mugs, utensils. Lots of little bric-a-brac, too." She bit off more of her sandwich, chewed and swallowed.

"And you're just gonna toss it all?" Alarm shot Mack's gravelly voice up half an octave.

"It's only ju . . ."

Gramps squeezed her knee. Hard. She shot him a look.

He cleared his throat, his expression carefully neutral. "Baby girl, if that stuff doesn't fit in your plans, it might still be good for some folks."

"But it's ancient."

"It's old, but it ain't been used for years, so it ain't worn out," Mack reasoned.

Gramps leaned over and whispered in her ear. "Not everyone has money to buy new whenever they want."

She thought of the gleeful way she'd handed over her credit card to the salesperson the day before, thinking nothing of purchasing new furniture for her cottage. Then she remembered her early years growing up and the slipcovers her Nana sewed when old ones wore out.

"You know, my daughter's youngest is ready to move out of his crib." Mack chuckled. "Tells me he's ready for a big-boy bed. Before you junk everything, can I take a look? Might be something we could use."

"Of course."

That earned her a pat on the knee from Gramps. "You know, you could have yourself one heck of a yard sale. Let people take advantage of all those things."

The deli door opened behind them. "Yard sale?" Bitsy asked. "What kind of stuff you selling?" Dora told her and she nodded. "I remember some of the what-nots and such your grandma had in those places. Can we get a sneak peak?"

"Bitsy, everyone here is family," said Gramps. "Once Dora Lee's got it all arranged, you all get first look and if there's something you want, you take it free. Right, baby girl?"

"Of course," Dora automatically agreed while she contemplated how on earth one prepared for a yard sale. Surely they couldn't be that big a deal. Price tags. Some signs. Rolls of coins from the bank. It was Gramps's idea, so whether he realized it yet, that obligated him to help. Jo Jo would surely pitch in, too.

"Well, that's real fine of you." Mack dusted crumbs off his shorts and stood. "Bitsy, great sandwich."

"Thanks."

"I'd best get back to work myself. Baby girl, what are you up to this afternoon?"

She got to her feet, her brain focused on the new task ahead. "Apparently, I'm going to be busy getting ready for the yard sale."

"I'll tell the others that one's coming up," said Bitsy.

"I'll let you know the day." Out with the old to make room for the new — and there was going to be a lot of new in the coming weeks. Speaking of which, she remembered another idea she'd had earlier in the morning and gave the older woman a bright smile. "Bitsy, have you and Vince ever thought of putting out some tables and chairs?" Dora Lee waved her hand, indicating the gravel area outside the deli at the corner of the building.

Bitsy looked surprised and then wrinkled her brow, maybe wondering why she and her husband had never thought of the idea. "We've only ever done stuff to-go and our boxed lunches for those folks going fishing."

Sometimes all it took was a fresh look and an objective outside opinion. "Now you could offer a little outdoor café." Dora pictured picnic tables with white sailcloth umbrellas.

"Guests love that quaint, hometown appeal."

Gramps looked a little surprised, like he wasn't used to hearing her spout good business sense. She kissed him on the cheek. "Thanks for lunch. I'll see you at sunset."

"Right, baby girl."

She waved to Bitsy and Mack and headed off.

"Quaint?" she heard Bitsy ask as she walked away.

🌺 🌺 🌺

OVER THE NEXT few days, Dora discovered that there was a lot to holding a yard sale — most of it dirty grunt work. On day one, she'd made the ultimate sacrifice — a quick run to Super K before she ruined all of her good clothes. Now, in cheap shorts and tourist T-shirts, she ripped through the cottages, cleaning, pricing, and arranging everything in her path. At the end of each day, she fell into a hot bath to soak away muscle aches and wash off the twenty years of dust that clogged her skin pores.

While she worked, she dreamed. The cottages bloomed in her mind's eye, right down to the lights outside their front doors and the pretty plantings she'd install as landscaping. When the architect arrived on Friday, she walked him around the property for two hours, discussing the vision. By the time he left, he carried a three-inch-thick folder that she'd filled with copies of her ideas and research and promised to get to work right away.

Tackling such a massive undertaking helped her in ways

she couldn't quite verbalize, but recognized all the same. Gramps kidded that the hard work was building her muscles, but Dora realized it was restoring her outlook on life. *Do anything, but do something.* Like her Gramps with his reputation for being able to fix any engine or motor ever built, or Ruby's home for her beloved dolphins, Dora discovered that sweat equity in a project reaped great returns. Instead of waking up each morning despairing over the future, she bounced from her bed, ready to tackle the next task.

Everything was progressing so well that she couldn't help but be pleased and excited, and every day sparked even more ideas. She couldn't wait to discuss some of them with Gramps, particularly for upgrading the storefronts. That could wait until sunset one evening, she decided. Maybe tonight when everyone was gathered and she could share it with them all at once.

Maybe tonight, Bobby would get back in time to join them. He hadn't been kidding about his demanding tournament schedule. Since leaving his boat days before, she'd seen him only once, yesterday when he'd caught up to her in the parking lot. His client had won the tournament with a record number of tarpon. Bobby had only enough time to shower and change for the awards dinner. She might have been miffed or insecure about the total lack of attention he had given her had he not backed her up against the building to kiss her breathless and prove how much he missed her.

That she missed him, too, worried her sometimes in those long, quiet baths and her infrequent work breaks.

When she'd returned to the Keys, she hadn't planned on getting involved with anyone, least of all him. Then again, she laughed to herself, she hadn't planned on becoming a hospitality entrepreneur. Life could change in the time between heartbeats. She'd no more expected to find herself back in the Keys constructing a whole new existence than Dorothy had anticipated getting swept up by a tornado and deposited in the land of Oz.

But here she was and, she congratulated herself, she was making the most of it.

As daylight dimmed, she stepped out of the bath, toweled off and dressed. A few swipes of the makeup brush and mascara wand sufficed. She pulled her hair back with twin combs, slid into sandals and hurried off to sunset. If it weren't for her grandfather and Ruby, who Gramps had said at lunch was stopping by, she wouldn't have bothered. Although she made it a point to join the gathering when Gramps was going to be there, on the rare nights that he had other plans, she didn't go either. She was doing her best to get along with everyone — reconnect with the ones she knew and make friends with the newer tenants — but their acceptance of her was still a long way away. Still, she kept trying by sharing her plans so they'd see that she was totally invested in bringing more business to the complex. She'd given them little suggestions here and there on other improvements, but had for the most part been met with blank stares. Bobby was right. The old-timers were slow to embrace change, no matter how positive.

She waved to Gramps and Ruby as she came out of the cottage area. *Oh, yes!* There was Bobby, strolling around the corner. He hugged her tight and after an exaggerated wink at her grandfather, bent her back over his arm and kissed her soundly.

"Wooeee, now that's the way to greet a woman!" Ruby crowed. "How come you never do that to me?"

"Darlin', all you had to do was ask." Bobby faked a move to scoop her out of the rocker and sent her into raucous laughter.

"Not you, scamp!" She swatted his arm.

"Step aside, son." A twinkle in his eyes, Willie caught her up, twirled her around and dipped her like a ballroom dancer.

"Be still, my aging heart." Ruby fluttered her eyelids, patted her chest and then grabbed his ears and smooched.

The rest of them applauded. Even Leo cut back on his sourness and lifted his beer bottle in a small toast. Willie returned Ruby to her chair and Bobby drew Dora down beside him on the steps as everyone else continued their conversations.

"Have you missed me as much as I've missed you?" he whispered.

She tilted her head and sneaked a sideways glance. "Maybe." *Definitely.*

From the look in his eyes, he knew she faked the casualness. He leaned in so close that his breath fanned the sensitive skin of her neck and his lips brushed her ear. "Give me five minutes alone and I'll show you what you've been missing."

Oh, he was good. The sensual promise in his voice and words

wiped out a teasing retort like an eraser over a chalkboard.

"Ahem." Willie cleared his throat, exaggerating, and she felt like a teenager caught necking.

Bobby laughed. "Sorry, Willie," he said, while not looking the least repentant.

"Quit flirting with my baby girl and watch the sunset."

"Yes, sir!" The quick response and a snappy salute made them all laugh again.

He leaned against the railing, slipped his arm around her and snuggled her close. "So, are you making progress?"

"Getting there. The meeting with A.J. was terrific. He'll have plans in a couple of weeks."

"Great." He squeezed her, his arm strong and solid around her shoulders.

"When's your yard sale?" asked Bitsy.

"Next weekend."

Rosa joined the group. "It is true that we can have, what do you say, first 'dibs'?"

"Yes, absolutely."

"Oh. Really?" Timid Tilda spoke.

Underneath her almost constant expression of apprehension, the woman had such a sweet face. Dora smiled. "Really."

Tilda's eyes lit up. "It's just like your grampa said. Did you hear that, Leo?"

"I heard."

Could the man not say anything without grousing? Dora ignored him and focused on the rest of the group. "You come over any time. If there's something you want, take it."

"Well, that's right fine, Dora Lee," said Mack. "My daughter's gonna come with me and look at those beds. By the way, I told her what all else you're planning. She's got experience working at some of the hotels in town, so she said when you get around to hiring, she'd like to talk to you about some part-time work."

That was as close to a positive comment about her renovation project as she'd heard from any of the storeowners. It surprised her so that she paused before responding. "That's great, Mack. I'd be happy to interview her when it's time."

Encouraged, she decided to bring up her latest plan. She leaned forward and smiled at all of them, even Leo. "If any of the rest of you have family members or friends that might be interested, please let me know."

Gramps winked and Ruby smiled her approval. The rest of the group appeared interested. Some nodded. Vince murmured that he'd keep it in mind.

So far so good. "I want Key of Sea Cottages to be good for all of you — us. The guests will naturally find your businesses convenient."

"Sure, they'll be lining up for ink work," Leo mumbled into his beer. Tilda gave him a pleading look.

Dora continued as if he'd said nothing. "I think you all have a lot to offer. Gramps and I have already talked about putting in some boats to rent."

"Great idea, darlin'." Ruby slapped Willie's knee. "Easy enough to do and no sense having them go elsewhere."

"So, Mack, they'll obviously come to you for their bait.

The Deli and Marina Mart will supply their lunches and other foods they might want to keep in their cottages."

"They will love my products for themselves and as souvenirs or gifts." Rosa quickly spotted the advantages.

"Exactly!" That left the tattoo and piercing parlor. Dora forced a smile. "Leo and Tilda, you never know. Tattoos have become more, um, mainstream. You might get some business from them."

"I could maybe sell some jewelry. Pretty sparklies. I've been working with sea glass and stuff."

That might have been the longest sentence Tilda had spoken since Dora's first night in town. "I think jewelry is a terrific idea. Tourists love purchasing things made by local artisans."

Judging by the expressions and nods from most of the others, they saw the potential benefits of her cottage renovation to their businesses and were warm to the idea. Encouraged, she plunged in with her latest plan.

"The mall complex is so convenient. Your businesses are terrific. We're all going to benefit by making their stay here as enjoyable an experience as possible. There's nothing like down home personal service and know-how — and all of you supply that in excess." Noting that they all listened closely, she smiled broadly. "Where we need improvement is in the esthetics." She waved her hand, encompassing the surrounding porch with its peeling paint, warped floorboards, and rough railings. "So, here's my idea."

She launched into her plans for the upgrade. "We'll

shore up the floor boards and replace the railings, of course. Then when we've replaced this overhang, I think we need to erect a different shape of roof for a seashore Victorian motif like you see so much of in Key West and we'll install ginger-bread trim." Of course, the entire place needed to be scraped down and repainted. In her mind, the ramshackle row was transformed into a charming collection of businesses. On her feet now, she waved her hands, as if conjuring up the image. "I can so see a variety of tropical colors. Coral, turquoise, periwinkle, maybe a key lime yellow. Lavender. Carved and painted wood signs for each store. Gold letter-ing on the windows."

Finally done, she stopped, beaming at her audience. "Won't it be beautiful?"

Silence.

Okay. Maybe they needed time to absorb the idea. She surveyed their expressions. Even Gramps and Ruby appeared stunned. Her smile wobbled.

"I know it's a lot to take in, but . . .?"

"Sí! It is a lot, but I think it will be good." Rosa nodded. "I would like the yellow for my store."

"This more of that quaint stuff?" ventured Bitsy.

Mack snorted. "Pretty darned frou-frou for a bait and tackle shop. Willie, are you on board with this?"

Gramps looked like he'd swallowed a fish hook. Poor man. She should have warned him, but the timing and at-mosphere had seemed so perfect. Bless him, he rallied.

"I think it bears considering."

Bobby rose and joined her at the railing, physically tele-graphing his support. Sweet of him to add his agreement, even though the decision didn't directly affect his business. Her cottages might give his clients a more convenient place to stay, but he'd never be short for charters whether or not the stores were redone.

"I dunno. That gingerbread whatchamacallit might do for a lady store like Rosa's, but I sell live shrimp, frozen chum, and fishing gear."

Lord, he was a tough sell, not that anyone besides Rosa looked anywhere close to convinced. "Mack, your space is in the middle, so we can forego the trim. But a little fresh paint isn't frou-frou."

"I think it's a fine idea, Dora Lee." Ruby to the rescue. "The whole place is long overdue for some sprucing up."

Leo hauled himself to his feet. "Nobody's turning my place into a freakin' damned purple tattoo palace!"

"Now, Leo . . ."

"Now, nuthin."

His outburst kicked off a conversational free-for-all. Everyone had an opinion to express and no interest in listen-ing to anybody else. Rosa loved it. Mack worried. Bitsy wavered. Vince declared that he better not be expected to pay for any of the repairs. He paid rent. That was enough.

Leo roared that it was a damn fool idea and he wasn't changing squat. Ruby shot Bobby a look as if suggesting he should do something about the mess. *What could he do?* won-dered Dora. He had the least input. Poor Gramps frowned and she felt even worse.

She tried to calm everyone down. "Folks, listen. Please. Before you get all upset, let's talk this over."

No such luck. They were so caught up in the argument that the sun melted into the horizon and nobody noticed. From the way they ran on, you'd think she'd suggested tearing down the building instead of merely painting.

"We don't need no fancy-pants woman coming down here and telling us how to run our business."

Gramps shot out of his rocker. "Watch it there, Leo. That's my granddaughter you're talking about."

Oh, no! Thank goodness Ruby grabbed him before Gramps advanced on the burly biker.

Dora tried again. "Everyone, please, calm down and let me . . .

An ear-splitting whistle blasted the night. "Quiet!"

Amazingly, the combatants shut up.

"All right. Everybody chill out. That's better," Bobby said, and settled his hand at the small of Dora's back, rubbing it soothingly. "Now, look around. Is there anybody here who doesn't think that their place will look better with a fresh coat of paint?" He tromped on a floorboard, demonstrating the wobble. "You have a safety hazard here that needs fixing." The railing shook under his hand. "Here, too. Agreed?"

Most of them nodded. Leo crossed his arms over his barrel chest, still belligerent.

"Okay. On that much, Dora Lee's got the right idea. Willie, outside maintenance is part of their leases, right?"

Gramps nodded.

"Okay, Vince, that settles your question. You won't pay out a dollar. Any other problems?"

The deli owner shook his head.

"For me, there is no problem." Rosa looked around. "I think this makes more sense. Make our places prettier and more people will want to shop."

"Pretty for you is good, Rosa, like I said before, but fishermen don't care about pretty. They care about fresh supplies." Mack shrugged. "I cain't help it. I like plain."

Bobby turned to Dora Lee. "Babe, he's got a point. You married to so many colors?"

Yes! She wanted to wail. Cheerful, candy-box tints filled her imagination — not something boring or basic. "I don't understand why everyone objects so much to a few bright shades of paint instead of this dingy white."

"Don't understand why you think you can show up one day and change everything," shot back Leo.

Technically, since her grandfather was the landlord, if he agreed there wasn't anything the tenants could do. "Gramps?"

He raked a hand through his silver hair, darting his glance between her and the storeowners. "Baby girl, it makes good sense to fix up the place, but . . ." He gestured helplessly. "I dunno."

Terrific. She sighed.

Bobby squeezed her shoulder. "What about finding some middle ground? Can you all settle on one color with white trim? Would that at least be okay?"

They exchanged looks and mumbled vague sounds of agreement — except for Leo who glared his disapproval in stony silence. At that point Dora knew better than to expect a miracle. Fed up with the whole argument, she tossed up her hands. "I'll bring by the paint samples and all of you can decide which color." She hugged Gramps and Ruby, said a quiet good night and walked off.

Pea rock crunched behind her. "Hey, babe, wait up."

In a snit, she ignored him.

Bobby snagged her hand. She tugged, but he didn't let go and she refused to struggle while still in full view of the audience on the porch. As soon as they reached the parking lot, she yanked free.

"Take it easy, Dora Lee. Look, I know you're not happy about the gang vetoing your paint choices, but . . ."

"Not happy? I'm completely pissed off."

"I get it, but don't take it out on me." He took her by the arm, brought her around. "I helped you out back there."

She snorted. "You bailed faster than a sailor in a leaking boat."

"I stopped the argument before you had a full scale revolt and got them all to see reason."

"Got them all their way, you mean."

"We reached a solution everyone can live with."

"Only because I never had a chance to show them otherwise. If they'd just gone along, they'd have seen the idea pay off."

They reached her cottage and she opened the door.

"Thanks for nothing. Goodnight."

He slapped his hand against the door, stopping it in mid-shut and followed her inside. *The nerve.* "What do you think you're doing?"

"Finishing this discussion."

"It's finished."

He strolled in like she wasn't glaring and emitting "get lost" signals.

"Like hell. Only your part of it is, but I'm not walking away and letting you stew on how all of us are wrong and you're right." Leaning back against the counter, he braced his hands on either side of his tall, big body.

"Dora Lee, the porch will get fixed and the stores painted something other than white."

"That isn't enough." She paced the small room. "What nobody understands is that I'm creating a look here, a particular design concept to attract business."

"The people who own those businesses made it clear that they don't agree with that design."

"And thanks to you, they're getting their way."

"Jesus H. Christ. Will you listen to yourself?" Bobby came off the counter like he'd been stung. "Look at this from their side. You wanted a bunch of prissy colors that obviously would have made most of them miserable. This way, instead of a bunch of unhappy people, you're getting one color that you like and they can live with." He punched his fist into the palm of his other hand. The crack echoed in the small surroundings. "It's the deal you're going to have to accept."

Bobby got right up in her face, making his point. "Did you see Willie during that whole scene?" he continued. "I've seen happier tourists in rainstorms."

Dora crossed her arms over her chest. "Of course he was upset. I'm his granddaughter and he's supporting my idea."

"You're putting him in the middle of a fight with tenants and friends he's known for years. Stop thinking only of yourself and consider somebody else for a change."

"Quit speaking to me like I'm a child."

"Quit acting like one."

Stunned, she gaped.

Bobby snorted. "Dora Lee, you've got people who care about you here, and are willing to back you to the wall in most situations. But that doesn't mean we'll let you bulldoze over us with your grand ideas. Sometimes you're gonna have to consider what other people want, too." He turned on his heel and strode out the door.

Damn it all. She wanted to heave one of her brand new lamps at his head, but braining him wouldn't change the facts. He was right about Gramps. And, she begrudgingly conceded, probably right about the paint compromise. While she wasn't a hundred percent satisfied, at least she'd made some forward progress. In the long run, maybe reaching an agreement this time would ease the way with future plans instead of having the storeowners kick up a fuss every step of the way.

It was only fair that she tell him. Besides, in a short period of time, she'd come to appreciate his support and hated that they'd argued. She hurried out the door. "Bobby, wait."

He stopped and turned around, waiting for her to catch up. Dora laced her fingers together and twiddled them while she framed an apology.

"Yeah?" he prompted.

"Don't go."

"I'm not spending the night fighting. It's like trying to teach a cat to whistle." He scowled, his eyes completely free of their devilish glint. "A waste of time."

"I don't want to fight either." She took a deep breath. "I guess you were right."

"About?" His clipped words indicated his upset.

"About wanting my own way all the time. I need to stop and think about other people."

He raised his gaze skyward. "Hallelujah, we're getting somewhere."

"I'm sorry that I took it out on you."

"Apology accepted."

"Good." She let out that breath.

"So, that's it? Fight's over?" He raised his brows, quirked a smile. "I knew you could be reasonable."

"What?" She pointed toward the parking lot. "That's it. You can just keep going."

He laughed out loud, caught her outstretched hand. "Gotcha." He pulled her close. "C'mere, woman. I've missed you." His mouth was warm, beguiling.

She gave in to the kiss for a moment, then stopped and pulled back her head. "Wait a minute. I'm mad at you."

That devilish dimple flashed. "That didn't taste mad. Kiss me again and we'll make sure."

CHAPTER 17

THE MAN HAD charm enough for three people. It dissolved the rest of her anger and made her laugh, her forehead resting on his chest. The rise and fall of his breathing, his strong embrace, soothed her. She slipped her arms around his waist, content to be held.

Truth was she *had* missed him the last few days. Since that morning on his boat, she'd thought of him often. Even in the middle of her hard, grimy chores, there'd been times when she'd stopped, pressed her hands against her middle and remembered the warm comfort of waking up in his arms.

Last night, she'd lain in bed alone and thought of him, of his searing kisses and the rough caress of his fingers on her skin. She'd remembered his hard, muscled body lying beneath her on the couch and gotten so turned on that she'd grown wet, tingling between her legs, and groaned aloud with the frustration.

Now, finally, they were alone together again and her body reacted to him right down to the last sizzling nerve-ending. The sensual pull swelled up, made her breathless and so weak with pure desire that she trembled. She clenched her arms around his waist, anchoring herself to the steady mooring of his big body.

He must have felt it, the tremble and the clench. His arms tightened before he leaned back and studied her face. Did he know how handsome he was, with the contrast of that tan, rugged face and boyish dimple, the sun-streaked hair and sea-green eyes?

Desire bloomed in her belly and her breath caught in her chest.

His eyes gleamed and he swore softly under his breath. "You look at me that way, babe, and I can't keep from kissing you." His hand slid to the nape of her neck, holding her gently while he put words to action and covered her mouth with his. Her eyes closed, her lips softened, and she yielded.

The sinking of her body against his flared heat through him from head to toe. He teased the seam of her lips with his tongue, tasting, and when she opened her mouth, he swept inside. Exploring, tempting. His body tightened and he bit down tenderly inside her plump bottom lip, growling with hunger.

"Bobby, I . . ."

That was all the protest he allowed. He grabbed her gorgeous ass and yanked her flush against him, all the time relentlessly kissing. He slid his hands lower, grasped her by the backs of the thighs and lifted. She gasped, wiggled as if to break free, and he turned, setting her on the counter. He slid his hands up under the edge of her shorts and spread open her legs, stepping in between until the fly of his shorts rubbed against the juncture of her thighs.

"Bobby . . ."

The breathlessness satisfied him no end. He nuzzled her throat, nipped the soft spot where her neck and shoulder met and smiled when she shivered. She reached for him, but he took her hands, pinning them gently on either side of her legs. Trailing kisses up to her ear, he murmured, his voice rich with sensual promise. "Last time, we did things your way, sweetheart. It's my turn."

He licked in to her mouth, brought his hands to her waist and slid up under her shirt. Her skin was velvet soft and he scripted small circles up her sides, rubbed the bumps of her spine, relishing each soft tremor. "Put your legs around me," he ordered. She sucked in a breath then obeyed. Slipping his hands inside the back of her shorts, he cupped her cheeks and picked her up. She grabbed his shoulders for support and then, as he swung around for the bedroom, speared her fingers in his hair and plunged her tongue into his mouth.

His penis swelled, achingly hard inside his shorts, and he ground against her pelvis with every step. Both of them were groaning by the time they reached her room. With her still in his arms, he knelt on the mattress and brought them both down on the bed. Bracing himself on his forearm, he cupped her breast, loving the weight and fullness of it in his hand. He thumbed her nipple, feeling it peak beneath her clothes. She moaned again and he smiled, pressing his mouth at the hollow of her throat while he busied himself unbuttoning her blouse. He yanked it off her shoulders to mid-way down her back and trapped her arms above her elbows.

"Bobby!" she gasped again, the third time she'd managed no more than his name. He unsnapped the front clasp of her bra, cupped her in both hands and ruthlessly played and nuzzled, admiring the contrast of her cocoa-brown aureoles against the delicate paler skin of her breasts. Her body bowed and her head fell back against the pillows. Only then did he draw one of those tempting nipples into his mouth and suck.

Her whimper wasn't just music to his ears, it was the whole damn band, urging him on to deeper pulls against tender flesh while he fondled and caressed the other breast. Her body writhed and her soft moans escalated. He shifted position, straddling her to play with both of her plump gorgeous breasts. Doubling his caresses, he switched from one taut peak to the other and then brought her mounds together, sucking both nipples into his mouth.

"Oh, God, Bobby!"

He took his sweet time with the breast play while she gasped and panted with pleasure. Finally, he moved lower, branding a trail of hot kisses down the center of her torso. She squirmed underneath him, almost frantic, and fought to free her arms from the shirt.

"Let me . . . I want . . ."

"Not this time, sweetheart," he told her, smiling darkly.

"But you're making me crazy!"

"Damn straight." He *wanted* her crazy with desire,

wanted her only able to think about how he made her feel so that there'd be no room in that brain of hers for those fears. By the time he finished, she'd have no doubts left about her attractiveness. They'd be lucky to have energy left to think at all.

He worked the zipper of her shorts and she strained for his hand.

"Relax, babe."

"But . . ."

In her breathless voice he heard apprehension. He raised his head and looked, hating the uneasiness in her eyes. Leaning forward, he stroked the bottom lip she worried with her teeth and then kissed her, taking her deep while he unzipped her shorts and stripped them down her legs and off in a single move. He broke the kiss, murmured against her mouth. "You think I'm turned off by your body?" His hand swept over her breasts. "These are incredible, so soft the way they fill my hands. Your nipples get hard waiting for me to suck on them." He dipped his head in her cleavage, biting gently, leaving his mark.

He flattened his palm on her torso, slowly drawing it down the center of her body. She flinched, shut her eyes.

"No, Dora Lee. Watch me," he ordered, and waited for her to comply. The gold of her eyes had darkened, her breathing deepened. Her abdomen trembled under his hand as he stroked it in wide arcs, hip to hip. He'd hardened like granite, and bent forward so she'd feel his erection and know that he was as turned on as she — no matter what she feared otherwise.

His fingers spread over the softness of her belly, the dip of her waist. "I love the feel of you," he whispered, flexing into the lush curves of her hips. Lowering his gaze, he growled hotly with satisfaction at the dampness spotting her mocha-silk panties — proof that she was turned on, too, despite her worries. He bent and nuzzled her bellybutton. Nipping lightly when she squirmed, he eased his fingertips inside the elastic, worked forward and slowly drew a finger up the damp, warm folds.

Her body jerked, tightened around his finger and he felt her pulse. He held her gaze while he played, working his fingers inside where her muscles tightened around them, and circled her delicate nub, teasing it until it swelled and throbbed for his touch. Her pants grew shorter, more frantic, and she arched. He pressed down with the heel of his hand, giving her some of the pressure she sought while he stroked her inside and out, teasing, plucking her clitoris.

His erection was so hard that he ached fit to howling, but he continued, driving her up higher and hotter.

Her head tossed from side to side against the pillows and she cried out his name, pleading. "Please. I need . . . Bobby, please!"

His big hand crowded inside her panties. He set up a pace then increased it, feeling in her response what she needed, then giving it to her until her hips rocked and met the rhythm of his fingers stroking that hot little clit back and forth. Finally, she tensed and shoved herself up against his hand, locked muscles around his fingers like a vise grip, and shattered.

While her body shook, he rolled to the side and shucked his shorts, found a condom in his pocket and covered himself with the protection. Then he knelt between her trembling legs, and drew her up to a sitting position. He nabbed her chin. "Dora Lee, there is no part of you that doesn't make me hot," he declared, his voice fierce. "Nothing about you that I don't love." He branded her with a hard kiss. "Do you understand?"

She sucked in a breath, nodded, and he finally freed her arms from the shirt, tossing it to the side, and then stripped off her bra. He bore her back down onto the bed. Bracing himself on a forearm, he gazed into her slumberous eyes, spread her with his hand and slid deeply inside.

God, she was so wet and hot, she fit slickly around him, her muscles still pulsing. She slipped her arms around his waist and held on tight while he thrust, true and hard, making love to her body and soul. She arched, pushing herself up to meet each thrust, crying out in pleasure when he drove home again and again.

Together they rocked, their moans blending, friction sparking heat, and taking them higher, faster. Her felt her shudders, swallowed her cries in a kiss and sensed the trigger of her second orgasm from the wild reaction of her body. Her nails dug into his skin, she locked her long legs around his hips, screamed his name and convulsed. Hot liquid flooded him, the blood pounded through his brain. He grabbed her ass, thrust hard one more time, then his powerful body shook as his orgasm rushed up and exploded.

🦀 🦀 🦀

"BOBBY?" EXHAUSTED, EXHILARATED, Dora curled up next to him in her bed. Her head pillowed on his shoulder while her hand played lightly across his chest.

"Yeah, babe?" He tangled his fingers in her hair and snuggled her close. His big body was like a furnace of heat against her wherever they touched.

It felt wonderful. *She* felt wonderful, like he'd taken the baggage she carried and jettisoned it overboard. And that was just the emotional boost from their lovemaking. Physically, she couldn't help but shiver from the marrow-deep sexual satisfaction. She sighed and cuddled even closer.

"You okay?" There was just enough light to see him when he lifted his head to give her a questioning look.

She smiled at the concern in his eyes, fanned her fingers over his cheek. "Okay doesn't even come close."

Turning his head, he brushed a kiss over her lips. "Then what?"

"I just wanted to thank you."

"For?"

How could she possibly put it into words? For showing her in a dozen ways that she hadn't lost her attractiveness along with her wedding ring? For making love to her so thoroughly, giving her orgasms that nearly shook her cottage off its foundations? Most of all, for listening to her insecurities and dismantling them one by one.

"For rocking my world." Inadequate, but right on the money.

His chuckle rumbled under her cheek. "We rocked each other's worlds." He smoothed his hand up and down her back. "Give me some time to recover and we'll do it again."

Her body cheered while her mind reflected that she hadn't had sex multiple times in a night since the early years of her marriage. In the last year before separating, she and J. Walter had rarely made love more than twice a month.

"Don't sound so surprised, woman." His aggrieved tone made her snicker.

He rolled to his side, pressed her against him with his hand on her butt and held her there by swinging a massive thigh over her legs. "Laugh at me, will you? I'm gonna prove it." He didn't so much kiss her as inhale her until she was weak.

It had been so long since her husband had lavished her with so much passionate promise. Bobby said he loved her and showed it by his actions. Her heart jumped in her chest, as if in joy, and Dora was stunned to realize that, not only did she believe him, but she was also glad. The realization surprised and worried her at the same time. She laid her hand against his cheek, taking in his handsome features, his ocean-colored eyes. Even when he was a boy, a teen, she'd cared about him, but only as a woman did a younger brother, with all of the affection and none of the passion.

Now? Tenderness, affection, and a genuine liking ran deep, while desire rose as high as a full moon tide. But was it love? That she couldn't answer and the not-knowing scraped raw on her nerves.

"Hey." Bobby gazed intently at her, rubbed his fingers over her brow. "What's going on, sweetheart? Tell me."

She started to drop her gaze, but stopped herself. He'd given her everything of himself today. If the most she could give him in return was honesty, he was entitled to no less.

"I hope . . . I mean, I want you to know that I . . ." A hot blush infused her skin and she was grateful for the dim light in the room. This was difficult enough. Tears choked her throat and her breath shook. "Okay, here it is. I care about you, but . . ."

"But you don't know if you're in love with me. It's okay, babe. I know."

She gaped. "You do?"

"Sure." He brushed back hair from her face and smiled into her eyes. "Don't upset yourself, Dora Lee. I didn't have some big fantasy that I'd get you naked, show you how much *I* love *you*, make you come a couple of times and — bingo! — you'd wake up in love, too."

"You didn't?" His matter-of-fact acceptance surprised the hell out of her.

"Nope. It's gonna take some time. I'm cool with it."

Instead of reassuring her, the blatant confidence triggered panic in the pit of her stomach. She tried to roll out of his embrace, struggled when he didn't let her budge. "I don't know that I'm ready to be in love with anybody, or if I'll ever be."

"Not to get all philosophical, but I figure it doesn't much matter whether we're ready. It happens when it happens."

"Like a train wreck."

He hugged her and laughed. "Geezus, woman. If that's how you feel about falling in love, you definitely need me around to lighten your attitude."

She worked her hand up between their bodies and planted her fingers across his mouth before he could kiss her again. "Bobby, be serious for just a minute, okay? I don't want to hurt you down the road."

He nibbled her fingers. "You won't."

Exasperated, she pinched his chin. "If *I* don't have a clue what I want, how on earth can *you* be so positive?"

He smiled at her again and she saw his love for her glowing in his eyes. "Because I know I can make you happy. Give me time and I'll prove it to you." He turned serious. "So that's the deal. No running scared when we've come this far. Agreed?"

Her heart jumped a little once more, this time a leap of faith. "Agreed."

"Then we're golden." His hand switched from lazy soft sweeps to slow, deliberate strokes. He rubbed his hair-rough thigh over hers and she felt him swell between their bodies. "While you're figuring out how you feel about me, I'll concentrate on rocking your world at every opportunity."

The deliberate promise stole her breath. "Oh, yeah?"

"Oh, yeah." He rolled, drawing her beneath him. "Luckily, you scored a younger man with plenty of stamina."

※ ※ ※

OVER THE NEXT week, he proved it often. Bobby courted her, Keys style. One night, he took her on a thrilling zoom across the bay in his flats boat to watch the sunset. Another time, he whisked her off to a popular Upper Keys outdoor restaurant for a full moon party, complete with dinner and dancing. Remembering, Dora stopped sweeping the floor of the cottage where she was working and leaned on the broom. No matter how much she teased and needled him, he'd steadfastly refused to join the crowd gyrating on the sand to a fast song, but then drew her out for the hottest, sexiest slow dance of her life. He'd pressed her as close as possible, swayed in time to the music and murmured a string of naughty suggestions in her ear until she clung to his shirt and nearly whimpered.

They'd left soon after, barely able to keep their hands off each other in his truck. Totally out of character, she'd tried to seduce him right there on the front seat, but he'd held her off, ordering her to "Behave, damn it!" through gritted teeth. He then retaliated by reaching up under her skirt, ruthlessly stripping off her panties and torturing her with his fingers the entire ride home down the Overseas Highway.

Every night, either at her cottage or on his boat, he showed her time and again how much he desired her and, yes, how turned on he was by her body. Each time they were together, he stripped away more than her clothes. With his unabashed approval of her body — extra pounds, abundant curves, cellulite and all — he helped her recover her physical self-confidence. When not delivering yet another devastating orgasm, he cuddled and teased her and listened to her plans. At best, J. Walter had attended to her activities with half an ear. Once satisfied that whatever she was doing reflected well on him, he'd smiled approvingly and then tuned her out.

Not Bobby. He paid attention because he was interested and, shocker of shockers, applauded her ideas. At least most of them. A few times he told her if he thought she was going over the top, and he was quick to point out if he thought she was doing something that might infringe too much on the comfort level of the storeowners. Although, to his credit, he also understood that the storeowners needed to expand that comfort level a little.

It wasn't long before she discovered that the champion flats fishing guide had a solid head for business and a heart as wide and deep as the Gulf of Mexico. Every morning when they kissed goodbye, she realized that a little more of her heart went out the door with him. She gazed out the window at the little white beach and saw a great white egret make its way across a picturesque cropping of coral rocks. In turn it lifted its spindly feet, slowly lowering them one after the other onto the rocks. Dora knew that while she might not have fallen in love with Bobby yet, like that careful bird, she was apparently picking her way down that path.

On the rare days when he didn't have a charter or work that had to be done on his boats, Bobby pitched in and helped her sort through the cottages, preparing for the yard sale. He wanted to be there for the actual sale but was committed to another tournament. Although he'd offered to pass off the client to another guide, she'd refused. Jo Jo and Ruby had already agreed to help and she assured him that the three of them could handle the sale.

She looked around. This was the last cottage that she'd needed to go through and now, with the final sweeping, it too was ready before the sale tomorrow. They'd decided that the smaller individual items like bric-a-brac and kitchenware would all be displayed on tables at the beginning of the path. Right now, everything was priced and stored in boxes, but she and her helpers would unpack the items and arrange them on the tables first thing in the morning. The other cottages still held their furnishings and customers could browse the buildings at will, then get her attention when ready to purchase anything from a bed to a mini-fridge.

Ads had been placed in the weekly newsletters and flyers posted at Publix, Winn Dixie, and all of the marina stores. Sandwich board signs on the highway and in the marina complex would bring in more customers. Dora laughed. In all the charity fundraising she'd worked on, she'd never done anything more laborious than address invitations or create centerpieces, but the events had raised tens of thousands of dollars. Over the last few weeks, she'd lifted, sweated, cleaned, moved, and priced on a daily basis. Her back was sore, her nails devastated and at the end of every day, she swore it took forever to wash her body free of sweat and grime. If she was lucky, she'd earn a couple of thousand dollars, but somehow knew she'd gain a ton more of satisfaction.

Carrying the broom, she left the building and saw Tilda and Rosa hurrying toward her. Leo meandered along behind, wearing his leather vest and trademark scowl. Beat and ready for her shower, Dora forced a bright smile.

"Hi, folks. Back for some more?" At some point over the last week, almost everyone from the marina had dropped in, looked over the items and taken something home. Mack's daughter had gushed over the bed, thanking her so eagerly for the gift that Dora had almost been embarrassed.

"*Si!*" said Rosa, ever cheerful. "I decided that wicker magazine basket will be perfect for my window display."

"We moved it up front." Dora pointed to one of the cottages. "Try over there." She turned to the other woman. Although Tilda had accompanied Rosa and Bitsy a few days earlier, she'd not left with anything. Probably thought she needed her husband's approval first. That might explain why he was here today, although from his body language, he'd rather be home sticking hot tattoo needles in his eye.

His wife, however, was truly a sweetheart, so if she wanted something then Dora was glad he had acquiesced. "What can I help you with, Tilda?" she asked.

"Well, I was talking to Leo 'bout one of them little fridges and how it would be good to have it in the shop," she answered, casting shy looks between Dora and her grumpy-faced husband.

"Of course." Dora warmly smiled. "From Gramps's records, the one in cottage four is the newest. Let's take a look." She led them over to the building.

Leo entered behind them, opened the door to the refrigerator and peered inside. Dora had to force herself not to stare at the intricate spider web inked across his bald pate. A tattoo instead of Rogaine. Who'd have guessed, she wondered.

"What do you think?" asked his wife. "Won't it be right nice?"

"It's fine," he grumbled, then straightened and looked at Dora. "How much?"

"No charge. Just like we said the other night."

His eyes narrowed and he snarled, "We don't need no charity."

Terrific. Did he have to fight about everything? She should just name a price, even five dollars, and be done with it but, perversely, she wanted to come out the winner in one of their conflicts. She arranged a neutral expression on her face. "We agreed from the beginning that you were welcome to whatever you wanted."

"Charity." He said it like another said 'shit'.

"A gift."

"Leo, please . . ."

"Quiet, woman. I'm handling this."

No matter how big a stick the man had up his ass, he shouldn't take it out on his wife. Dora longed to fire off a scathing retort, say something that would nail him firmly in his place, but she wisely realized that doing so would only escalate the situation. Instead, she pressed her lips into a thin line, breathed in through her nose and slowly exhaled. Then she said the only thing she could think of that wouldn't set him off. "Leo, I know that you don't like me, but you respect my grandfather. He wants his friends to have whatever items they want or need."

"He's a good man."

"Yes, he is. So please don't insult his generosity."

He rumbled, almost a growl, while he thought about her comment. She maintained a cool look and waited. Finally, the big man shrugged. "Willie knows what it means to be neighborly."

By inference, she didn't.

"He knows that it's hard enough to make a good life down here without people coming in and changing things."

Yet another jab. An impatient sigh escaped. "Gramps also knows a good thing when he sees it." She resisted starting up the entire debate. "Will you please take the refrigerator?"

He gifted her with a short nod and squatted, wrapping his arms around the appliance. Surely, he didn't think he could carry it all the way to his store?

"Leo, stop!" she yelped, and he halted. "Not that you aren't strong enough, but you don't have to lug that thing alone."

"Don't need no help. Tilda and me can manage."

Nobody would ever accuse him of being Mr. Gracious. "We brought over a hand dolly for this purpose. Wait. Please." She jogged outside and returned quickly, pulling the dolly behind her. "There, that's the extent of my help." She couldn't resist a tiny dig. "Now you can wheel it out all by yourself."

She stepped back and he rolled past. His wife closely followed, but stopped long enough to place a soft hand on Dora's arm and whisper, "Thank you."

"You're welcome," she whispered back, and watched them make their way down the path. While she didn't fool herself by thinking that she'd won a major battle, at least she'd managed to diffuse the conflict. Hopefully, it would help in any future skirmishes. Maybe when he was drinking an ice cold drink from that refrigerator, he'd remember that she'd been helpful. Maybe he wouldn't freak out as much when she suggested to him and the other storeowners that it would certainly look better if their old, dented, run-down vehicles weren't parked out front of their newly painted building. There was plenty of room in back. Oh, and she really needed to talk to Bitsy and Vince again about the outdoor table service idea.

Dora hurried to her own cottage, eager to wash off the day's collection of dirt so she could join Bobby and the others for sunset followed by a quiet dinner on his boat and, hopefully, some not-so-quiet sex before settling in for a solid night's sleep. Ruby and Jo Jo were meeting her at six o'clock sharp in the morning to finalize preparations for the sale that started at eight. Compared to the challenge of Leo, handling her customers tomorrow should be a breeze!

CHAPTER 18

APPARENTLY A YARD sale's promise of bargains kicked the Keys people "laid-back" attitude square in the rump. The crowd didn't wait for eight a.m. before they swarmed the grounds. An after-Christmas clearance sale at Morrison's didn't generate this much traffic, Dora thought while she simultaneously made change for one woman and haggled with another over the price of a lamp.

"Jesus, Mary, and all the Saints in Heaven, it's like pelicans fighting over a fish!" Ruby exclaimed, watching two customers argue over possession of a matching pair of blue glass dolphin statuettes.

Dora laughed and wrapped newspaper around another customer's purchase. The description was right on the money. "May the stronger bird win and not break merchandise in the process."

The crowd maintained its numbers for the first two hours. She, Ruby, and Jo Jo sold, wrapped, made change, and chatted non-stop. Jo Jo, today conservatively dressed for her in shorts and a midriff hugging top, was in her element even though she complained good-naturedly that her little waitress-style apron covered up her bellybutton ring. Sometime in the last week, she'd colored her hair again, this time opting for a rich coppery color, streaked with dark-brown.

She and Ruby greeted a host of friends and acquaintances and Dora was surprised at how many of the customers she remembered. Although there were significantly more that remembered her right off the bat, rather than the other way around. Time and again either Ruby or Jo Jo saved her from embarrassment by re-introducing her before her non-recognition of one person or another grew into an awkward moment.

In mid-afternoon, even Victoria and Jack Benton stopped by, but Dora suspected it was more a gesture of support than out of any great need. Still, they left with a lamp and a mirror, protesting loudly when she refused to take any money for the items.

"Listen here, Dora Lee, from what Ruby's told us of your plans, this money can help." Jack planted his feet with hands on hips in a typical alpha-male stance, and fixed his tropical-blue eyes in a no-nonsense stare.

"Give it up." Dora smiled sweetly, not the least bit intimidated. "That look might work if we hadn't known each other since grade school."

"It really isn't necessary for you to be so generous," tried his sweet, brainiac wife.

"You're as much family as Ruby, and that's that," she told them. "Need any help carrying them to your truck, or can he-man handle it all on his own?"

Her wink made Victoria laugh. "She really does know you, Bubba," she teased, using his aunt's favorite nickname.

In response, he dipped his head, whispered in her ear. Whatever he said made his wife blush. He grinned at the rest of them, then hoisted the mirror under his arm and picked up the lamp. "Thanks for the goods, Dora Lee. Don't be a stranger, remember."

They left and since the crowd had dwindled to a few remaining shoppers, took Ruby home with them after she'd hugged the older woman, thanking her enthusiastically for all of her help.

"I'll be back with bells on first thing in the morning. Don't expect we'll get as many customers, but it's best to be prepared."

"If you're certain it won't take you away from your work, Ruby."

The older woman gave her a saucy wink. "On Sundays, the only thing it'll take me away from is your grampa, but he'll hold."

The trio was almost out of sight before Dora stopped laughing. Jo Jo joined her at the table. "Oh, to be that young at heart when we're her age," said her friend, a broad grin on her face.

"Oh, to be that young at heart *now*." Dora snagged a cardboard box from beneath the table.

They laughed some more and began packing up various goods to store inside one of the buildings overnight.

"Y'all had a spectacular sale day," Jo Jo said, carefully placing a bronze and ceramic ship's wheel ashtray in the box. "Can you believe how it stayed busy all day long?"

Dora stretched to the side and rubbed her back. "I've got the sore muscles to remind me. Not to mention a decade's worth of dirt and grime. But still . . ." She looked around, thinking of all the chairs, beds, and dressers that happy new owners had carted past and the countless smaller items. "The results are worth it. Most of the big stuff's gone. I don't think we've got much more than these tables to set up in the morning." Into the box went a ceramic mermaid snuggled next to a clock flanked by painted palm trees. Amazing the kitsch-level of the remaining things. "I can't imagine that there's too many items left that anyone would want." Not anyone with real decorating taste anyway, she privately thought.

Footsteps crunching on pea rock drew their attention. Dora's eyes widened. The stranger strolling up the path didn't strike her as someone in the market for a ceramic candy dish shaped like the state of Florida. Not in a linen sport coat, silk shirt, and perfectly tailored trousers. The jacket's creamy beige shade contrasted with his dark hair and deep skin tone. He'd been born with that tan. She was as positive of that as she was that his eyes were dark brown behind those expensive sunglasses. She shot a glance at his shoes. Italian-crafted leather. She'd bet her Mercedes on it.

From ten feet away, he looked at the two of them and removed his sunglasses. "Good afternoon, ladies."

Deep voice, lightly accented. Slow, spreading smile. Brown eyes as dark as the Cuban coffee of his obvious heritage. A charming combination. Who *was* this man? Dora shot a look at Jo Jo. *Whoa.* Normally a man this prime presented her friend with an instant incentive to flirt, but instead of a grin and "hey there, handsome" welcome in her eyes, her expression was closed. "Jo Jo?"

Her friend's voice was cool as she regarded the stranger. She folded her arms across her chest. "Watch yourself, Dora Lee. He's trouble."

Dora stifled a gasp at her reaction. "Who . . ."

He reached them before she could finish the question. She greeted him. "Good afternoon. May we help you?"

His smile could melt a statue. *Oh, my!* His eyes warmed appreciably as he held out a hand — manicured, but not baby smooth — and squeezed hers in a firm grip. "Rafe Escobar and you are, if I'm not mistaken, Mrs. Morrison."

"Not anymore," she answered. "Have we met, Mr. Escobar? If so, I'm sorry, but I don't remember." It definitely hadn't been down here in the Keys. Up home on the Treasure Coast was the only other possibility, but she'd trained herself to remember people when they were introduced to guard against possibly forgetting an important business associate of her husband's. Besides, what woman alive, married, single, or in a nunnery, would forget a man this handsome?

"No, it has not been my good fortune to know you personally." He paused, his eyes direct on hers. "Before today."

A natural flirt, but a sophisticated one; charming but

not unctuous. Smooth, but not oily. Obviously, he was accustomed to the sort of flattering conversation normally exchanged at dinner parties. Well, so was she. She acknowledged the compliment with a nod and nonchalantly returned his gaze. "Then, how do you know my name?"

Jo Jo jumped in before he could answer. "If something moves in this town, Escobar knows about it. If it's got four walls and a roof, he tries to buy it."

Instead of scowling at her harsh assessment, the man laughed and sketched a small bow. "*Señorita* Daulton. A refreshing pleasure, as always."

Uh oh. The exchange told Dora that these two had clashed before. That alone surprised her, since Jo Jo got along with almost everyone. That the man appeared impervious to, even amused by, her sarcasm was the real shocker. When Jo Jo scrabbled, her opponents rarely came away unscathed. She cut them to pieces with her sharp tongue and even sharper wit.

Not only was Escobar unaffected, he continued as if Jo Jo's eyes weren't shooting green lasers. "I regret that another commitment will keep me from your theater event."

Wow. If he'd faked that sincerity, this man was beyond dangerous.

"Yeah, what a shame." Jo Jo's expression turned triumphant. "You should see how successful we've become."

"I'd looked forward to it, but instead must settle for showing my support more . . . impersonally."

If the undercurrents got any deeper, Dora decided, an

innocent bystander could drown. Whatever truly lay behind his last sentence, it hit some sort of target.

Jo Jo pressed her lips together. "Yeah. I got your donation check." She paused, lifting her head. "Thank you." From her short words and terse tone, she might as well have said "Eff you" but the man acknowledged the thanks with a graceful nod.

Whatever reason her friend had for not liking this man, she'd find out later. For now, Dora only wanted to de-escalate the tension. Subtly angling her body between them, she gave him an encouraging look. "What can we do for you today?"

"Mrs. Morrison, it may very well be what I can do for you, instead."

"How so? And it's Hanson. I no longer use my ex-husband's name. In any event, please call me Dora."

If possible, his eyes warmed even more. "*Gracias*, Dora." His voice caressed her name. Lord, but he was smooth. Another time she might have enjoyed the subtle flirting, but a handsome, sexy fishing guide already had a lock hold on her interest. With that in mind, she could listen dispassionately.

"I've heard about your plans for this property," he continued. "An excellent idea. *Sí*. This is a perfect spot for luxury cottages." He gazed around, approval frank in his expression. It figured that the first person to not automatically question her plans was a total stranger. "You may have heard that I am developing the adjoining property into a much needed resort."

"Much needed for the bottom line of your company," Jo

Jo muttered.

He continued as if she hadn't spoken. "I would like to speak with you, Dora, about a business proposition."

Oh, really? That was doubly interesting. Whatever the man wanted, however, he'd have to wait. At the moment, he had her at a disadvantage, obviously knowing much more about her than she did him. Sophisticated charm might emanate from him in sexy waves, but she'd been exposed to more than her share in her dozen plus years as the wife of a business magnate. She hadn't the slightest idea what he wanted, but she'd wait to find out until she was at her best. Her best definitely wasn't now, after a long day of hard work when her muscles begged for relief and her body was covered in dirt.

She smiled self-deprecatingly and spread her hands to indicate her clothes and appearance. "I'm afraid now isn't convenient. We've put in a long day."

"It would be my pleasure to buy you dinner."

Dora laughed. "I'm a mess."

His appraisal indicated he thought she was anything but. "Gold shines, even though it rarely lies on the surface waiting to be picked up."

"She isn't looking to be picked up either," Jo Jo bristled.

"Of course not." He seemed amused by her friend's attitude. "A business meeting, if you wish. Nothing more," he said to Dora.

She shook her head. "Not tonight, *Señor* Escobar."

"Rafe."

"Rafe," she conceded. "I have plans and the second day of our sale tomorrow."

"Then lunch, perhaps. On Monday." He stopped shy of insisting, but his smooth confidence indicated that he expected to eventually win her agreement.

By Monday she could have additional information. She cut her glance to Jo Jo and bumped her friend's hip in a warning not to argue. From the look on her face, she'd get the full lowdown as soon as the man was out of earshot.

For now, she could end the scene before it became a confrontation. "Monday's fine." They agreed on a time and restaurant, after she refused his offer to pick her up. Having him fetch her from the cottages made it feel more like a lunch date than a business meeting. If she felt that way, she imagined Bobby would, too.

The developer took her decision with equanimity. "Until Monday then, Dora," he agreed with another warm smile. He gave Jo Jo a long look. "*Tigresita*. I will see you again, too, I'm sure." With another of those graceful nods, he turned and left.

🦀 🦀 🦀

"EASY, JO JO. You slam those figurines in that box any harder and we'll be left with ceramic splinters to sell tomorrow." Dora Lee watched her friend while she finished packing another box. "So, what's the scoop on the handsome *Señor* Escobar?

"Handsome?" Her sneer would have done Brando proud. "If you like snakes."

Snakes? Dora's jaw dropped. The Cuban developer reminded her of all the good qualities of Andy Garcia and Jimmy Smits combined. "He seemed perfectly nice to me. Obviously you don't share that opinion, so you might as well spill it." She hoisted the box in her arms. "Particularly since he mentioned a business opportunity, although what he has in mind, I can't imagine."

"I can. Did you count your fingers after he shook your hand? He's after whatever he can get, whether it's property or women."

"Wow, you *really* don't like this guy. Is that on principle? Do you know something specific, or is it just one of those things?"

Jo Jo picked up a two-foot-tall pelican statue and walked to the cottage they were using for storage. "He's snatching up property as fast as it comes available and making offers for everything else. If Rafe Escobar has his way, this whole stretch of the Middle Keys will be nothing but resorts and time-share hotels."

Surely she was exaggerating. Nobody could swoop in and completely alter the character of the entire area. Thousands of people lived and worked in this section of the Keys and couldn't be displaced. "Really, it can't be *that* bad!"

Jo Jo's tirade continued. "No, it will get even worse. Forget family hotels. Easy-to-afford rentals, even the RV parks are going." She dropped the carton of goods on the kitchenette counter. "Almighty Heaven, Dora Lee, he almost bought the theater out behind my back!"

That explained the uncharacteristic level of animosity in her usually light-hearted friend. "Your theater? What happened?"

"He set his sights on our little building, but I headed him off at the pass." She tossed back her hair.

Tigresita, he'd called her. Little tiger. With the two-toned streaked mane of hair, Dora thought the nickname was on target, but no doubt it irritated the hell out of her friend. "How'd you stop the sale?"

"I took out a mortgage on my house and donated it to the theater foundation. Then we, the foundation, struck our own deal with the building's owner Marv Shimmer."

In addition to the community theater, the structure housed a coffee house, art gallery, and a small gift shop.

Jo Jo slapped the counter. "That damn Escobar thinks all he has to do is wave around a wad of money and everyone will sell. The tough thing is that the amounts he offers are such good deals, that most of the residents end up doing just that. Lucky for me that Marv's a third-generation conch who doesn't want to move out of the Keys and up to cheaper areas in central Florida. We gave him a hefty down payment and wrote up a contract where he sold us the building but holds the mortgage. He continues to get a steady income without a boat load of capital gains."

Lucky indeed that the landlord had agreed to turn down what must have been a sure shot at a lump sum huge profit. Although Dora was sure that Jo Jo had done some pretty hard sell convincing. Her green eyes triumphantly glowed.

Dora smiled. "Good for you, protecting your turf. Still . . ." She paused, considering. "It looks like the man took his defeat in stride. He sent a donation to your fundraiser."

"Yeah. He couldn't beat me, so he joined us. It's probably a ruse so that he looks like a benefactor to the community instead of a robber baron."

"But you deposited the check?"

"Hell, yeah! I wouldn't have a mortgage payment on my own house now if not for him. So, I'll take every buck he wants to throw our way." She walked out the door to get more stuff. I may be proud, but I'm a business woman, Dora Lee."

Speaking of business . . . "I wonder what he wants to talk to me about?"

"Nothing good."

"C'mon. He can't be all bad."

"Depends on your perspective, but I guarantee he wasn't here to welcome your cottages to the neighborhood. You'll be competition."

Dora snorted. "My little cottages against a five star resort? Hardly anything for him to worry about. I'm targeting a different clientele."

"If it isn't your business he wants, it's your body — the one that you're currently sharing with my brother."

Days ago, she'd told her friend the news about her and Bobby. No explicit details were given, but Jo Jo hadn't needed any to understand that the relationship included regular love-making. Given her fierce loyalty, her friend would view the interest of any other man as a poaching attempt.

"No worries there, girlfriend. I didn't expect to be involved with any man so soon after my divorce, but things worked out differently with Bobby. Believe me, I'm not interested in adding anybody else into the mix."

"Just be aware, that's all. I saw how that Cuban wannabe Romeo ate you up with his eyes!"

Wasn't me he really wanted to snack on, Dora thought. Yes, he'd flirted, but she recognized it for simple flattery, not a blazing declaration of sensual intent. When he'd looked at Jo Jo, on the other hand, his eyes flared, but her friend had obviously missed or ignored that clue.

Dora wondered if she should point it out, but decided against it. Her friend was holding a heavy doorstop shaped like a conch shell. Given her reaction to the developer, any observation about his interest was sure to be unwelcome. All told, she'd rather sell that doorstop than pick up its shattered pieces. Instead, she packed up another box of knick-knacks and carried them indoors. "Whatever the case, don't worry," she called back over her shoulder. "I can handle a simple business lunch, regardless of his intent."

"Regardless of whose intent, babe?" Bobby spread his hands around her middle and stepped up close behind her body.

"Hi, sailor." She leaned back, reached up and slid her hand through his hair, pulling his head down for a kiss. Freshly showered, he smelled delicious, all male warmth and that crisp aftershave. "Mmm."

"Hello, yourself." He nuzzled her neck.

"Get a room, you two," Jo Jo groused.

They laughed and broke apart.

"Hey, Sis." Bobby dropped a kiss on her forehead. "What's got you in a lousy mood?"

"That developer snake was here sniffing around your woman."

"He wasn't sniffing!" Dora protested, letting the "your woman" comment go for the moment. "He said he has a business proposition to discuss."

"Funny business." Jo Jo set down the items in her hands and untied her apron.

"Good Lord, when you don't like someone, you *really* don't like them." She gestured with her hand. "It's no big deal. He dropped by a few minutes ago and we scheduled a business lunch," she explained to Bobby. "No, I don't know what it's about. Yes, your sister has already given me his back story. No, there isn't anything for you to worry about."

"Did I say I was worried? I'm curious, but there's nothing wrong with that." He shrugged. "After your lunch, I'm sure you'll fill all of us in." He looked pointedly at his sister. "We trust Dora Lee to take care of her own business, don't we?"

"Isn't her I don't trust."

"Well, this isn't the first slick customer she's run across, right, babe?"

"Exactly." She removed her apron and washed her hands in the sink.

"So everything's cool. Now, how about I take you both to dinner?" He grinned. "My charter today caught a tarpon that makes yours look like a minnow, Dora Lee. I got a tip that's burning to be spent on my two favorite ladies."

"Love to, Bro, but I need to scoot. Even though it's Saturday night, with the fund raiser next week, we have rehearsal." She hugged them both. "See you in the morning, Dora Lee. Have fun tonight." Flashing a cheeky grin, she winked. "I'd say not to do anything that I wouldn't do, but you probably ought to have tighter boundaries."

Dora laughed as they left the cottage together and Jo Jo hurried off. "She's something else."

"Always has been." Bobby tucked her against him and they walked in synch. "It's just you and me for dinner. I've already seen your grampa. He and Ruby are heading out with friends for steak at the Elks."

A cozy meal sounded fine to her after the long day. More and more, she looked forward to spending time with him, in and out of the bedroom. "I need a half an hour or so to shower and change."

"No problem." He stroked her cheek. "What do you say we dress up a little fancier tonight? We'll go the big time route at Water's Edge." The restaurant he suggested was one of the finest in the area.

"You really are anxious to spend that tip." She smiled. "Pretty fancy."

"Table cloths and everything," he laughed. "I'll even wear a sport coat and tie. I got a pretty fancy lady to impress."

"A tie? You're pulling out all the stops." What on earth had gotten into him? She snuggled close, resting her chin against him while she looked up. "There's no need to strangle yourself, sweetheart." For a moment, her heart swelled too big for her chest. "You impress me just the way that you are."

He framed her face with his hands, brought her closer for a sweet, tender kiss before releasing her. "Go get ready, or we won't get out of here tonight."

"Would that be so bad?" She walked her fingers up his chest. "There's always take-out."

"No. I want to take *you* out and show you off tonight. Get moving."

He was adamant, but she suddenly couldn't stand the thought of a night out on the town. Not when she could spend it cozied up to this man right here at home. She tilted her head. The man said he found her body irresistible. Now was a great time to put that to the test.

Turning her back on him, she walked toward the hall, pulling up her T-shirt along the way. She stopped and yanked the garment off over her head then faced him in her bra. His gaze dropped immediately to her chest.

"You sure you don't want to change your mind?" Reaching behind her, she unhooked her bra and let it slip off her arms to the floor.

His abdominal muscles tightened like someone had punched him. "Dora Lee . . ." he warned, his voice suddenly hoarse.

It only made her smile and conjure an overly innocent look. She unhooked the waistband of her shorts. "I've been on my feet all day. The thought of stretching out is really appealing." Down went the zipper and so did his focus. One shove and her shorts dropped to the floor. She kicked her feet free and leaned against the wall. "I worked up quite an appetite all day long." A deaf man couldn't miss that innuendo.

Neither did Bobby. In a heartbeat, he'd pinned her in place, cupping her bottom and yanking her against him. "Temptress," he growled. "Tell me again about that appetite."

Dora laughed, triumphant, and whispered a hot suggestion in his ear.

He hoisted her over his shoulder, swatted her lightly on the butt and headed down the hallway. "First course, coming up."

CHAPTER 19

It felt good to leave off the bargain brand clothes she'd been working in over the last few weeks and dress in one of her crisp tailored suits. Dora checked her reflection in the mirror, smoothing her hand down the side slit of the skirt. She loved this outfit with its vibrant turquoise linen. Little embroidered cut-outs embellished the hem and the jacket's French cuffs. Underneath the jacket, she wore a pearl-hued, drape-necked blouse made of silk so soft it whispered against her skin. She'd have to be careful walking on pea rock in her heeled sandals, but the impractical shoes did great things for her legs.

"Looking good," she told her reflection, swinging her head from right to left to make the pearl and diamond drop earrings dance. "Cool, professional. A woman in charge."

That was the exact image she wanted to project for this mysterious lunch date with *Señor* Escobar. Both Jo Jo and Bobby had provided some background on the man's history with the Middle Keys. Over the last few years, he'd already completed a number of development projects, from office buildings to time share properties to resorts, and was now in various stages with several more. Osprey Cove, the resort next door to her grandfather's complex, was one of the most ambitious ones yet. A five-star paradise in the heart of the Florida Keys with every known amenity.

For a woman who professed to loathe the developer, her friend sure knew him chapter and verse. In Dora's opinion, Jo Jo was more interested in Rafe Escobar than she admitted and not merely for the "know thy enemy" reasons that she cited.

At any other time, Dora would have teased her about it, but the more that she heard about his business successes, the higher her personal fret factor. From all accounts, he was a development Midas whose every project reaped profits for his company and investors. She was a newly-divorced, mature woman whose experience in the industry came from staying in hotels, not running them. Small wonder that she felt like a small fish that was about to be swooped down on by a fierce sea hawk.

Ugh. Imagining herself as a helpless fish made her scrunch up her carefully made-up face. The victim attitude wouldn't do, not for the new and improved Dora Hanson. No way. She practiced lifting a single brow. Once she managed to do it without looking like an idiot, she regarded her image coolly in the mirror. That was infinitely better. If at any time during lunch the man stepped out of line or actively tried to intimidate her, she'd give him "the look" and stop him cold.

Now was not the time to yield to self-doubt, which was another reason she'd dressed with such care. The color, style, and fit of her outfit jazzed her attitude. She didn't just look good, she decided after another study, she looked great! If she also felt more than a little sexy, so much the better — not for the handsome Cuban developer, but for herself.

She had every reason to feel sexy this morning after another night in Bobby's arms. Dora looked in the mirror again and her vision fogged over as her brain kicked back to the previous evening. Only then she hadn't been standing here alone, prepped to go out. Instead, Bobby had stood there with her, both of them wearing nothing but their skin and smiles.

"Watch me, babe," he'd growled in her ear. "See yourself like I do." He'd swept his big, tanned hand up and down her body, caressing every inch until her knees trembled and she shuddered in his arms. "See what you do to me."

Dora blinked, shook herself and blew out a breath. "Whoo." Another memory like that and she'd never be able to concentrate on today's business lunch. "Another flashback like that and I'll jump him on the dock when he gets home tonight."

When they were together, whether they made love or not, he showed her with words and physical expression how much she meant to him. How much he loved her. Every time he did, he eroded another layer of her insecurity. In a very short time, he'd proven himself almost too good to be true. Her life had changed so radically in the preceding weeks that she could barely catch her breath, let alone believe that she could actually have found love and happiness again — in her old hometown with the younger man she'd known most of her life.

For some reason, she'd not yet reached the point where she could dive in emotionally, although constant exposure — in every naked, bawdy sense of the word — to Bobby's lovemaking rid her of the body image fears. By turns tender and randy, his obvious delight in her body made it impossible for her to continue doubting her attractiveness.

At this point, she felt like she was bobbing in the open ocean on a floating light buoy, trying to work up the courage to take the plunge. A death grip on the buoy kept her locked to her past, to her fears about the obstacles in their relationship, both internal and external. Breathless, she pressed her hand against her chest as her heart increased its pace. All she needed to do was let go, dive in, and trust that Bobby wouldn't let her drown.

Maybe tonight, she'd find the courage. For the last couple of days he'd pressed her for a fancy dinner date. Before he'd left for his charter this morning, she'd agreed. Maybe tonight she'd finally put all the old fears to rest and return the love he gave her, not just with her body, but also with her heart. In the meantime, she needed to muster her "Dora Hanson businesswoman" persona and find out what lay behind the resort developer's lunch invitation.

🌿 🌿 🌿

DETERMINED TO ENTER this meeting on equal footing, Dora walked into the restaurant like she owned it. Rafe's brown eyes gleamed with appreciation while he enfolded her hand in both of his and welcomed her. He guided her through the restaurant and smoothly held out a chair to seat her at their window table overlooking the water. She certainly couldn't fault him for looks, manners, or style. In fact, on short acquaintance, the only truly outstanding shortcoming she could find was that Rafe simply wasn't Bobby.

She restrained her curiosity about his reason for the meeting until he'd sampled and approved a pinot grigio and the waiter poured the wine into their glasses. When the man left, she tasted the crisp wine and nodded her agreement of his choice. Then she sat back, glass in hand, smiled and got to the point.

"Rafe, you never told me how you learned of my idea for the cottage property."

He smiled, showing even white teeth in his naturally tanned face. "It is a small community, Dora, as I'm sure you know. People talk." He sipped his wine. "I make it a point to listen, particularly when it involves one of my projects."

"But how do my little cottages involve your projects?"

"No doubt your grandfather and friends have explained that I made an offer to buy the entire property, including the marina, yes?"

She nodded. Oh, yes, she'd gotten an earful on all the details.

"It would have been the perfect addition to my new resort. But, while I would have liked to obtain the complex, I respect the decision. Your grandfather and his friends, they are comfortable with things the way that they are." He shrugged. "So be it. But then I hear of the beautiful granddaughter that has returned home and launched plans to renovate the very cottages I'd hoped to own and turn them into the kind of accommodations I myself had envisioned. Naturally, my interest was aroused." He spread his hands. the gesture both graceful and eloquent. "So, I came to meet you, to see if, perhaps, there is another way that we can do business."

Dora leaned back to let the waiter serve their appetizers. She chewed and swallowed a small forkful of conch ceviche. Tangy citrus and spice flavors burst over her tongue. "Mmm. Delicious."

"Good."

"If my grandfather wouldn't sell you the property before, why do you think we can do business now?"

He smiled again. "Perhaps his motivations will be different."

"How so?" She gestured with her fork. "If anything, the opposite is true. I have his full support to redo the cottages and open for business."

Rafe tasted seared ahi tuna, sipped more wine and smiled. Dora quickly learned that his smile was a potent weapon. If it weren't for Bobby, she herself might melt under the man's charm, like a squishy marshmallow over an open flame.

What exactly did that expression mean this time? Give

him credit, he held very little back. "When I approached with my proposal, there was no interest in doing anything at all with that cottage area. Now, in so short a time, you are accomplishing much. It is obvious that he will do much to make you happy."

She nodded. "We're family."

"I know much of the bonds of family." He ate more tuna before continuing. "Since your grandfather wants you to be happy above all, how do you think he will react when your idea does not succeed the way you hope?"

Instantly, her temper simmered. How dare he discount her plan, infer so casually that she would fail. Time for the eyebrow! She arched it perfectly. "My grandfather will be overjoyed when my cottages are filled with guests and the reservations are sold out."

"Of that, I would have no doubt, Dora, were it not for the fact that your little venture will be competing with my resort. Think about it. Osprey Cove will offer our guests everything they could wish for, before they even make the wish. You do not have the size or the means to match us, let alone surpass us for luxurious comfort and amenities."

He leaned forward, his expression and composure perfectly calm, even matter-of-fact. She'd have been less intimidated if he blustered or bragged, but instead found herself rattled by his confidence. She refused to let him see that his words made an impact. Instead, she shrugged. "Continue."

"Do you want to invest everything you have, only to lose it all?" His rich baritone turned beguiling. "Instead, you can join in a venture with guaranteed success."

"What do you mean?"

He unveiled his proposition. Since her cottages could not compete with Osprey Cove on their own, it would be far better for her grandfather to sell him that part of the property which would let him incorporate their unique charm into his overall scheme. He agreed that the small, quiet location would appeal to certain guests, but believed those same guests would appreciate the ability to avail themselves of the parent resort's outstanding qualities such as the extensive day spa, multiple pools, restaurants, and shops.

Listening to him talk, it was clear why the man was so successful. His pitch and presentation were so beautifully done, so convincing, he nearly swayed her right then and there.

"So, you see, there is no reason for you to take such a financial risk," he said. "With the money I am willing to pay for that section of the entire property, your grandfather will be far better off financially."

The waiter returned to check on them and the slight break helped her re-gather her wits. Ignoring her meal, she put down her fork and narrowed her eyes. "It's a lovely thought, but this isn't just about the money. If my grandfather wouldn't sell to you before, then clearly he's content and comfortable. I'm willing to put my time and energy into the enterprise and expect to not only earn back my investment, but also supply my livelihood for years to come." That was the plan, anyway, and one that she'd felt so good about before this man began pointing out that everything he planned was bigger and better.

Instead of debating the point, he surprised her by sitting back, sipping his wine, all the while holding her with his steady regard. She returned the gaze, refusing to overstate her case. Let him make the next volley. It was tough to wait him out, but she managed.

He put down his wine. "You are a determined woman, Dora," he said, surprising her again. "A courageous one, as well, to risk your financial security on a dream." He ran his finger around the base of his glass, thoughtful, before raising his gaze to hers and leaning forward once more. "I have need of a beautiful, determined woman."

Holy hell! Bobby's favorite exclamation burst in her head as she stifled a gasp. Was the man so supremely confident to think that if he couldn't lure her with dollars and cents, she'd cave under a barely concealed innuendo? She blasted him with a look so icy, frost should have formed on the silverware. "Look here, Mr. Escobar . . ."

"Dora, please." He held up a hand, laughing softly. "You mistake me and are insulted, as would be expected had I meant that in the way that you think." He grinned with the devil's own charm and his eyes gleamed. "Make no mistake, I would find great pleasure if you and I formed a personal relationship, but at the moment I am still focused on business."

"How so?"

"Consider this proposal. Since you are so set on investing in your cottages, perhaps we can form a partnership. If your grandfather sells the area to both of us, together we can develop it the way you intend. You will not only see the return on your investment over time, but as a managing partner, draw a salary — the livelihood of which you spoke. The cottage area will still be part of the overall Osprey Cove resort. Whether you are prepared at this time to admit it, this increases their overall desirability. In short, we both obtain what we want."

🦀 🦀 🦀

HE'D ALL BUT handed her guaranteed success wrapped up with a high profile bow. Dora's brain spun with the advantages of Rafe Escobar's second proposal. Everything he'd said made incredible sense.

She slowed to make the turn into Hanson's parking lot. Key of Sea Cottages was her dream, from the conception to the last duvet cover. She'd meant to tell Rafe "thanks, but no thanks" in civil terms as they completed their lunch. Before she could, he'd given her another one of those heart-stopping smiles and suggested she join him for a personal tour of his resort-in-progress.

Even though their properties neighbored on one another, she declined, more out of self-preservation than lack of time. Rather than allow her to make it a permanent "no", he'd convinced her to meet him at the job site the following day.

"Before you can make an informed decision about my proposal," he'd said in that smooth baritone, "you owe it to yourself to absorb the entire picture."

True enough, she realized, even as she marveled at the man's talent for getting his way without exerting undue pressure. He'd left the door open in more ways than one. The lingering kiss on her cheek told her that, should she be interested in a partnership that didn't involve business, he was available.

Although she got the message he delivered in the kiss, it made as little impact on her as a polite brush of lips at a cocktail party. No fault of Rafe Escobar's — the man had sex appeal enough for two — but deep inside she knew that his true interest in her resided with the property. Besides, no other man's kisses compared to those from a certain ultra-hunky flats guide fisherman.

If only she could forget the business proposition as easily. Now that he'd planted it in her mind, it clung there like a barnacle. She'd bet good money that he knew it, too, which was why he'd dissuaded her from making a decision before they finished their lunch.

Dora parked and walked slowly toward her cottage, the meeting very much in her thoughts. Having already promised not to make a decision until after she'd toured Osprey Cove, she didn't want to keep thinking about the proposal. With nothing else to occupy her mind at the moment, she'd drive herself crazy in the hours before her dinner date with Bobby.

She needed a project. The warm sun shining on her cottage suggested one to her. The trees and shrubbery around the building were long overdue for pruning. She spread the branches of a hibiscus, scraping free dead blossoms and dried leaves. Purple blade-leaved oyster plants had separated and grown to the point where they overwhelmed the area and the beds themselves hadn't been raked or restored in countless years. Suddenly, the thought of spending a few hours outdoors shaping foliage and cleaning up the beds appealed to her far more than sitting alone inside, poring over paperwork.

The decision boosted the spring in her step and she hurried inside to change clothes. All of her grandfather's yard tools were stored in one of the other buildings and within minutes she'd armed herself with rake, hoe, and clippers and hauled over a couple empty trash barrels. Protecting her hands with canvas gloves, she got down to work.

BOBBY UNHOOKED HIS boat trailer at half past six and bolted to his cruiser to shower and change into what served for his dress clothes. The whole time on the water, he'd been in a fever for the evening to arrive and had barely managed to drive straight to his slip without a quick side trip to Dora Lee's cottage.

All day long, he'd thought about her lunch meeting with Escobar, his brain working on why the man had chosen now to appear on the scene again and what he wanted with Dora Lee. A year back, after cinching the deal for the resort property next door, the developer had offered a staggering amount of money for the entire marina complex.

Bobby and Willie had discussed it at length. The deal would have meant that neither one of them need work another day.

"I *like* working. What would I do all day — sit on my ass?" Willie had said.

"We could fish all day, every day," Bobby remembered replying. Then he'd grinned. "Hell, I do that now and get paid for it."

There had been other people to consider, too, like their long-time storeowners and the other tenants — the folks who docked their boats and lived at the marina. In the end, they'd turned down the developer's offer — a decision that the man had taken with darned smooth grace.

Bobby pulled on a pair of khaki slacks and exchanged his pullover for a long-sleeved white shirt. He left the top two buttons undone and added a navy sport jacket before slipping his feet into shoes.

So why had the man circled back around? Hearing that Escobar had been anywhere near Dora Lee bothered him more than he wanted to admit, let alone show. Not that he worried that the Cuban developer meant her any physical harm. He smirked. His sister would have torn the man apart with her teeth and bare hands if he'd made any kind of dangerous move. His gut instinct told him that the man's interest was rooted mostly in the property. Either he smelled an opportunity in favor of his own resort, or he'd wanted to check out a possible threat.

Except that now that he'd been there and seen Dora Lee, the stakes had changed, as far as Bobby was concerned. What man in his right mind wouldn't take one look at her and want to get to know her? What man wouldn't flat out want her — period?

He glanced in the mirror. Muttering a curse, he swiftly buttoned up the final two buttons and yanked one of his two ties off a hanger. Whipping it under the collar, he fumbled with the ends. Geezus, he could fasten delicate flies to thin fishing line with knots no bigger than pinheads, but a Windsor knot challenged him like major surgery. *Shit.* After two tries, he left the ends hanging. He'd ask Dora Lee for help. With her prominent husband and their active social life, maybe she'd had more practice.

From the way he leapt off the boat and rushed back to her cottage, you'd think he was afraid she'd disappear before he returned. *Admit it, man,* he told himself. It wasn't that Escobar posed a threat to Dora Lee that had him sweating inside his cotton shirt and jacket. *You're worried that he's a threat to you.*

Hell, yeah! The wealthy developer could offer her a million things that he couldn't. A few million bucks. A ten bedroom house and a ticket back to that familiar society life.

He broke the land speed record getting to her cottage. Propping his hand against the door jamb, he gathered his breath as well as his thoughts. Every day she plunged deeper into her plans, but until the construction began — or even until it was all finished — he couldn't be certain that she'd see the deal through. Given her life-long determination to live anywhere but in the Keys, there was no guarantee that, presented with a better offer, she wouldn't change her mind and leave town.

His chest contracted, blocking his lungs from sucking in adequate air. The more they were together, the more he affected her. Damn it all, he knew that as solidly as he knew how to read a tide chart. But she hadn't admitted that she loved him yet and until she actually said the words, he couldn't be sure.

The uncertainty beat at him, no matter how hard he worked to ignore it. He reminded himself all the time to be patient; convinced himself that he was definitely bringing her around. But every day that went by, each time he said, "I love you" without her replying, "I love you, too" wore at his guts like a slow-burning acid.

Get it together. He was supposed to calm *her* insecurities, not launch his own. This was insane. He wasn't an eighteen year-old kid anymore, as he'd reminded her a couple of dozen times. There wasn't another man on earth who was going to take away *his* woman. Whatever Escobar had on his agenda didn't matter. Bobby's plans remain unchanged — to convince Dora Lee that the key to her future happiness was right here with him in the Florida Keys.

He straightened, rapped on the door. While waiting for her to answer, he reached over and picked a scarlet hibiscus bloom off the bush by the door. She'd been busy, he noticed, stepping back from the door to observe the spruced up landscaping. Sometime this afternoon, she'd tamed a small jungle of native bushes, cleared out a mess of weeds and dead ground plants, and brought some order to the flower beds that lined the cottage walls.

The door swung open. Holy hell!

CHAPTER 20

ONE LOOK NEARLY stopped his heart. She'd interpreted fancy to mean *pull out all the stops*, beginning with a silky red dress that bared most of her chest and stopped just short of her knees. His breath stalled in his chest as he scanned her from her high-heeled sandals to her hair. That mass of waves swept up on her head looked like they'd tumble free the first time he tangled them with his fingers. She'd done something with her makeup to accentuate her eyes, and slicked her lips a deep red.

That sultry mouth parted in a smile. "Bobby? You okay?"

"You kill me." He slid his hands up her bare arms, drew her to him and kissed her hungrily.

"Wow," she said, slightly breathless when he let them come up for air. "I guess that means you approve of my outfit."

"Babe, half of me can't wait to show you off. Every man in the place is gonna take a look at you and wish like hell that he was me. The other half wants to lock us inside your cottage alone and not come out for a week." He whistled low.

"Hell, yeah, I approve."

He did his best to quell a spurt of jealousy. Gawdamighty, if he felt this protective when they were alone, let one other man ogle her in public and he'd likely rip the poor guy's nuts out of his pants. The last thing he wanted to do was act like a caveman. To the contrary, he needed to show her that he could be as classy as any mainland guy — whether department store CEO or resort developer.

She laughed and busied herself tying his knot. Just like he figured, she got the job done right the first time. Her hands smoothed the tie into place.

"You look pretty hot yourself, sailor." She gathered a light wrap around her shoulders. "Ready to go?"

He nodded and slipped his arm around her waist when she closed the door.

"Your gardening work looks great."

The comment prompted an immediate smile. "It's a start," she said. "I could probably use some new bushes, but tomorrow I'll pick up some flowers. I think vinca will do great with this exposure, and they're so colorful." She leaned against him while they made their way slowly down the path, mindful of her heels. "Then fresh mulch, of course, to finish everything."

"I'm only booked for a half day tomorrow. If you can wait that long, we'll go in my truck."

"Perfect." Her eyes crinkled at the corners and her smile lit up the night. "I was hoping that you could help. Thank you."

For a smile like that, he'd dig in the dirt for a week.

They'd agreed to take her car but he claimed the keys, and helped her in for the drive to the restaurant. Her perfume drifted to him and they held hands while he drove. As far as he was concerned, the evening was off to a fine start and he aimed to see it only improve as the night progressed.

🌸 🌸 🌸

BY THE TIME the waiter served their appetizers, he was ready to rip holes in the linen tablecloth. The woman of his dreams sat across from him, looking like a sex goddess and talking about another man. If Dora Lee uttered the words "Rafe said" one more time, he'd choke on a soused shrimp.

He'd intended to talk about her progress, wanted to hear all about what she'd done. Damnit, he cared about the plan and meant to support her in any way possible, except when that included a possible partnership with the richer-than-the devil developer.

Her eyes gleamed in the candlelight, but instead of excitement over the terrific time they were enjoying, she was glowing over the opportunity Escobar had suggested.

"He's so sharp, Bobby," she enthused. "Yet, not obnoxious about it. He just lays the idea out there smoothly and it's hard to find any objection."

The Cuban was smooth all right, like a hand-rolled cigar and, the way Bobby was feeling right now, he figured just as lethal.

The waiter removed the first course and set down their salads. Bobby picked up their bottle of wine, which cost pretty much half that tip he'd received over the weekend, and topped off their glasses. "Yeah, he's good at making the improbable seem like a gold mine." He forced a smile, feeling like his lips were about to slice open. "I know you're too smart to fall for an easy con."

She swallowed a forkful of salad before answering. "What makes you think it's a con? It sounds like a solid suggestion to me."

For lack of a real reason, other than all-purpose jealousy, he shrugged and damned his own gender. "He's a guy. When he sees something he wants, he'll work it to his advantage."

"But he has a valid point." She put down her fork.

Shit. The last thing he wanted to do was upset her. Bobby swallowed some wine like it was medicine. "From his perspective. The guy's an operator." He gestured with the glass. "Sweetheart, when you told him you wouldn't encourage an outright sale, look how quickly he came back with another proposal to sweeten the deal."

"True."

Finally some agreement instead of further singing of the developer's praises. Bobby sat back and dug into his salad. "I'm not saying he's crooked, just that you shouldn't take everything he says at face value, at least not right from the get-go."

Dora Lee picked up her fork and speared more lettuce. "You're right," she huffed. "But you know, just because a joint partnership works to his advantage doesn't mean that it won't work to ours."

"In general that's so, but don't forget that he holds most of the power. You don't want to lose your rights."

"Of course not." She finished her salad and looked across the table at him, her lips pursed. "I guess it would be impossible to expect an equal partnership since, obviously, he has a lot more money to invest."

Even more progress. Things were looking up.

"Just for the sake of discussion," she said, "do you think Willie would even consider sub-dividing the property and selling it to us?"

Then again, maybe not.

Not "me" but "us", she said as if she and Escobar were already a pair. Bobby chomped through a carrot strip like it was a ten penny nail, almost cracking a molar. Willie might, but he sure as hell wouldn't. Set up his true love in partnership with another guy — not in this lifetime.

"I dunno. Your gramps is pretty particular about his place." He needed to do some damage control, and fast. Somehow, he had to convince her that the partnership was undesirable, but painting Escobar's motives in a negative light hadn't worked. He needed a different strategy.

After the server removed their plates, Bobby grasped her hand across the table. "Why worry about going to Willie with this when you haven't decided that you can't succeed on your own?"

"But Rafe said . . ."

"Rafe *wants* you to believe that you can't make it without being part of his resort."

Her eyes widened. At least he had her full attention. He looked at her, doing his earnest best to project his support. "It's *your* dream, Dora Lee. You haven't even seen A.J.'s plans, so why give up now?"

"Give up? I wouldn't, it's just . . ." She latched onto his hand like it was a lifeline. "Bobby, do you really believe that I can do this all by myself?"

Oh, fuck. He was *so* screwed. Yeah, he thought she could put the enterprise together, but as much as he hated to admit it, Key of Sea Cottages probably had a better shot with the backing and expertise of the high powered developer. Since she'd dreamed up the idea, he'd gradually seen her confidence begin to rebuild until her spirit was more like he remembered from their youth. Damned if he'd crush those hopes.

"I think you can do whatever you set your mind on, babe." He squeezed her hand. "Besides, you aren't all by yourself."

Her smile brightened her face like a shooting star lit up the southern sky. "You're right. I have Gramps and Ruby, Jo Jo, and . . . you." Those great golden eyes warmed with emotion and his throat constricted. *That* was the look he'd been waiting to see! Now if she only said . . ."

"Rack of lamb for the lady?"

Damn! Bobby reluctantly let go of her hand and sat back so that the waiter could serve their entrees. Suddenly, as much as he'd looked forward to taking her out and showing her a great time, he now wanted the evening to be over so he could get her back to her place and show her again how much he loved her. Five minutes after he got her inside her door, she wouldn't be able to think of anything or anybody but him.

They ate their meals, mostly in silence, but their awareness of each other ran high. It was like every sappy chick flick he'd ever been dragged to where the characters said little with words while their eyes did the talking.

Bobby barely tasted his steak. It could have been tree bark. He consumed it automatically while he stared transfixed at his love.

Dora Lee nibbled her lamb, sneaking looks up at him through her eyelashes. A light flush warmed her skin and he didn't think it came from the wine. They finished their meal, declined dessert and coffee. While waiting for the check, he took her hand again, brushing his fingers across her knuckles while inscribing small circles on her palm with his thumb. A delicate shiver ran up her skin under his fingers. He gave her a slow, lazy smile, brought her hand to his lips and nibbled her palm.

She jerked her hand, but he held on and chuckled. "Problem, sweetheart?"

"Stop looking at me like that," she whispered through clenched teeth, "before my clothes melt off!"

Oh, yeah. Now he had her thinking his way. Why should he be the only one aching with desire? Lucky for her the waiter brought the bill, or he'd have pushed the issue for the pure devilish pleasure of wrecking her composure.

"C'mon." Standing, he held her chair out for her, settled his hand at her hip and guided her from the restaurant. "I want you naked, but not in public."

He teased her on the ride home, skimming his hand up and down her warm thigh, while she foiled him from further progress by pressing her legs tight together and grabbing his wrist.

"Both hands on the wheel, sailor," she laughed, breathless. "Remember, the Overseas is a dangerous highway."

"*You're* dangerous. Dynamite curves in that red dress," he growled, twisting his wrist to break her grip.

"Bobby, watch it!"

Ahead of them, a car's turn signal blinked and it slowed. He pressed the brakes and stopped right in front of — didn't it figure — the Osprey Cove job site. "What the hell's the hold up?"

"Patience," she admonished. "Look, that's Rafe."

The streetlight threw a white glow on a low-slung Jaguar, clearly illuminating the developer waiting to pull out onto the highway. The man turned his head and obviously spotted Dora Lee, because he made eye contact and smiled like she was the only one sitting in the Mercedes. His warm look and intimate nod threw up a haze in front of Bobby's eyes.

"What's he waiting for?" Impatiently, Bobby honked the horn and motioned the other man out onto the road. As soon as the Jag passed, he accelerated, eager to get them home as soon as humanly possible. Pea rock spurted underneath the tires in the marina complex parking lot. He jumped out and ran around to Dora Lee's side, helping her out of the car almost faster than she could unsnap her seat belt.

"Good Lord, take it easy!"

Her tone had cooled some from the heat he'd stoked. He blamed that on Escobar, too. The man had intruded on their evening from the beginning — first in conversation and then in person, even if from twenty feet away in a separate car. "Sorry, babe. Can't help that you make me crazy for you."

"Crazy's right." Her muscles were stiff under his hand as he guided her up the path. "There's something going on here."

"Not yet, but there will be as soon as I get you alone." He gave her his best smile, packed with heat, and raked her up and down with his gaze.

"This isn't about passion." She yanked her elbow out of his grip and stopped. "What's wrong?"

"Nothing."

There was just enough moonlight to reveal her expression, concern mixed with confusion.

"I don't understand what put you in this mood," she said. "We were having a great time and now, all of a sudden, you're tense." She smoothed her hand up and down his forearm and he had to force his taut muscles to relax. "Come on inside, sailor, we'll work off some of that stress."

That's what he had in mind. He wrapped his arm around her shoulders, drew her close and matched his steps to hers on the walkway.

She rested her head against his shoulder. "Bobby?"

"Yeah?" He brushed a kiss against her hair.

"I'm sorry for obsessing. It's such a big deal that I can't help worrying."

"Don't sweat it, Dora Lee. Everything's going to be fine."

"But Rafe said . . ."

"Enough about Rafe!" Please, Lord, no more tonight about what Rafe said or thought or suggested. "Geezus. You meet the man twice and all of a sudden he's the guy with all the answers."

She stiffened and when he tried to pull her back against his shoulder, she resisted. "Well, what do you expect? He's an expert and we aren't."

"He's an expert out for himself. I think you can do whatever you set your mind to, with or without Rafe Escobar. Is that clear?"

"Crystal."

"Good. So put his proposal out of your mind and stay on your own course."

"Aye, aye." She snapped off a mock salute.

"Tomorrow you can tell him you're not interested, case closed." They reached her cottage and while she unlocked and opened the door, he nibbled the soft spot where her neck met her shoulder, darkly pleased when she shivered.

"Yes. After I tour his resort."

Bobby lifted his head like an animal scenting danger. "What?"

She led him inside. "Well, I promised to spend time

tomorrow to let him show me around."

"Spend time with him."

"Right." She put her wrap and purse on the counter, turned and reached for his tie. "To see all of his plans for the resort."

He grasped her hands, keeping her from undoing the knot. "That's not a good idea."

"Sure it is. C'mon. Let's get you de-strangled."

Her smile faltered when he brought their hands down together.

"What's wrong now?"

"I don't think you should go over there."

"Bobby, even if we aren't going into business, I should see what he has planned."

Jealousy spurted through his veins. "I don't like it."

Anger flared in her eyes. "You don't *like* it?"

"No, I don't. Any more than I liked you having lunch with him and then hearing you go on about him all night on *our* date."

He'd run aground with this discussion, and if he didn't hit reverse, he could sink the whole ship. Knowing and doing were two different things. Frustration, impatience, and that vicious jealousy drove out his sensible side. Right now, he didn't care how he achieved his goal. He wanted her to keep her distance from everything having to do with Rafe Escobar.

"For once, tune out what he said and listen to me." *Trust me, Dora Lee, the man who loves you,* he wanted to add, but didn't. "I'm telling you not to go over there tomorrow."

"What?" Arms akimbo on her killer hips, she glared. "You're *telling* me? You have no right."

"We're involved. That gives me every right. If I say that I don't want you hanging out with some other guy, you should listen." He planted his feet, folded his arms over his chest and returned the glare.

"That's ridiculous. It's a *business* meeting." Her voice rose and her generous chest rose and fell. "Even if it wasn't, it's still my decision." She flung out her arm, dramatically. "You don't have any say over what I do just because we're sleeping together."

"I'm in love with you. What say does *that* give me?"

"None!"

The single word hit him like a sharp slap. Hurt so icy that it burned drove out the other emotions. It froze his chest so he could barely breathe. He waited, choking on the pain, hoping she'd tell him she hadn't meant it.

They stared at each other and the silence grew.

Pulling together his shredded pride, he nodded sharply. "That tells me where I stand."

"Bobby, I . . ." She reached toward him and he couldn't keep himself from blocking the move, not even caring that she flinched.

"Save it for someone who cares," he sneered. "Save it for *Rafe.*"

CHAPTER 21

WAS THERE ANYTHING worse than realizing you loved a man right after you'd shot a bolt to his heart in the middle of a fight? When the damning word flew out of her mouth, Bobby looked like he'd taken a knee in the groin. Realizing the pain she'd inflicted, Dora Lee's stomach heaved. All she wanted to do was take him in her arms and swear that she hadn't meant it.

She got as far as opening the door he'd slammed and lost her nerve, knowing that if she tried to explain she'd only make things worse, because she *did* mean it — just not in the way that he thought. Love gave him the right to say what was on his mind and what he thought about her activities, but not the right to dictate what she did and who she dealt with in business.

In the midst of the argument, that's what she'd heard, that he was trying to control her and enforce his will. Shades of J. Walter. Instead of explaining the difference, she'd mouthed off in anger.

A sleepless night brought no relief. Every time she

closed her eyes, she saw the look on his face before he'd left and the memory triggered fresh waves of tears, regret, and an ache in her heart that she couldn't make go away. She counted the hours until daylight, then quickly dressed and rushed out of the cottage to make it to his boat before he left for the day's charter.

His truck and boat trailer tore past her in the parking lot.

"Bobby, wait," she yelled, and waved like an airport worker signaling a jumbo jet. "I need to talk to you!"

He pulled out onto the Overseas Highway and took off without so much as a "Later, babe" or "Screw you."

Her spirits slumped along with her shoulders. She dragged butt toward the Marina Mart for coffee, resigned to spending the day miserable. How on earth could she apologize if Bobby wouldn't stand still long enough to listen?

Even though it was barely full morning, Dora needed something to occupy her time. Back at the cottage, she grabbed her purse and keys. She looked like hell, but couldn't muster the spirit to care as she got in her car and headed for the home improvement center for the plants and mulch needed to complete her landscape project.

🦀 🦀 🦀

A FEW HOURS later, she was watering her newly planted bright pink, lavende,r and white flowering plants and admiring her handiwork when her cell phone rang.

Bobby! she thought and her heart jumped. "Hello?"

"Dora Lee, it's A.J. here. How ya doing?"

Disappointment soaked her spirit, but she forced enthusiasm into her voice. "Just fine. Yourself?" He launched into a detailed response and she rolled her eyes while waiting patiently. "Uh huh. Really? That's great."

"So listen, I've got sketches to show you. Not everything's complete, but the concept's in good shape."

Finally, something she could get excited about. "That's terrific. When can I see them?"

"I'm coming down to your end of town in the next hour if you'll be there."

"Absolutely. I can't wait."

"Cool. Oh, listen, Dora Lee. While I was working I had one hell of a great idea, so I worked it into the plans. Wait until you see."

The architect sounded almost as excited as she — a welcome change. "I'll be here, A.J."

✿ ✿ ✿

HOURS LATER, SHE still pored over the colorful sketches, brushing her fingers over the images. The renderings, even in their preliminary state, brought her ideas out of her head and onto paper where they could be seen and enjoyed. When A.J. had first rolled out the sheets on her kitchenette counter, she'd barely restrained herself from throwing her arms around him and whooping with joy.

These drawings made the entire plan more real and

restored Dora's confidence. Maybe Bobby was right and she didn't need Rafe Escobar after all. Not everyone who traveled wanted the big resort experience. There was room on this island for Osprey Cove and her pretty, more intimate Key of Sea cottages.

She traced her finger to the spot of A.J.'s surprise. He'd suggested a special gathering area at the cove where guests could watch the sunset. According to his plans, they would smooth out the ground surface, add sand instead of pea rock and put in a number of tall palms. A small outdoor bar with a tiki roof would allow them to serve soft drinks, maybe even beer and wine, but she'd have to look into the liquor permits. Lounge chairs would invite people to relax and enjoy the spectacular view as the sun melted into the horizon.

On her way out to her car for her meeting with Rafe, Dora stopped by the cove. The idea was imprinted with such detail in her mind that she hardly needed to refer to the drawings. Like a colorful invitation, a gorgeous sunset drew people to stop whatever they were doing and celebrate the end of another day. Look how long the tradition had existed from the porch right here at the marina complex. Guests would love it. *She* loved it!

Tucking the drawings under her arm, she made a square of her hands, like a photographer framing a shot. Oh, yes! The entire concept was so perfect that even the marina storeowners would embrace the idea since the landscape design would improve their view, too. Right now that cove area was an unkempt tangle of overgrown foliage, weedy gravel, and rough rocks. By the time she was done, the little area would be transformed. She planted her hands on her hips, lifted her face to the sky and happily sighed. Stoked by this new enhancement, she waved to Leo and Mack who appeared deep in conversation on the porch as she drove by on her way to Osprey Cove. A.J.'s plans had lifted her mood high enough that for once it didn't bother her when Leo glared in response.

FOR OVER TWO hours, Rafe escorted her around the development like it was already a designer showplace and not a collection of half-finished buildings surrounded by construction vehicles, mounds of dirt, and surveyor's stakes. He first pointed out all the different components — from the time-share suites to the main hotel building — on the architect's detailed model. With that in her mind, it was easy to see his vision in progress.

"In this area will sit the smaller hotel that is better suited to families with young children." He pointed toward a giant backhoe. "About there, we will construct a mermaid's lagoon with pool and waterfall. Lots of color with things to climb on and slides into the water."

He was clever, creative and very, very smooth. Instead of pressuring her in any way, he simply pointed out all the qualities that would make Osprey Cove the equal of the finest resorts in Florida, or the world. Then, he guided the tour to the edge of the property that bordered her grandfather's and described so vividly that she could see the details, the winding, palm, and orchid-landscaped path that would lead to the cottages if they joined together.

"When will you open for business?" she asked, veering away from a discussion of *her* cottages.

"By year's end." He steadied her elbow as they stepped over a ditch. "We have much to do here and other necessary components to put in place off site."

"Such as?"

"Part of my deal with the city is that I must also develop a percentage of housing for employees, as well as low-to-moderate income housing for area residents."

She knew from her grandfather that lack of affordable housing was a huge problem up and down the entire island chain. "That's certainly necessary, Rafe, and won't having some on-site housing for your own staff be to your benefit?"

"*Sí.*" His mouth quirked, giving a rueful cast to his handsome face. "I would have done this anyway for Osprey Cove's people and I believe in supporting the communities in which I do business. But, the cities themselves need also to do more and find other ways to manage the housing needs for their working people."

In the time that she'd been back home, she'd been so busy that she hadn't had the opportunity to get up to speed on all of the issues that faced her town. Now that she planned to live and operate a business here, she'd have to become better informed. Rather than extend the discussion, she asked him about his planned spa facilities.

Not long after, they said goodbye and she drove off, a thousand details crowding her brain. The neighboring resort and its developer were impressive as hell. Comparing Osprey Cove to Key of Sea was like deciding between Oz and Kansas. Dora snorted. Even the initials sort of matched. But as the sun began its nightly descent and she pulled into the complex's parking lot, she knew she was not yet ready to abandon hope.

There was a full house for the sunset. Bobby was absent and Dora cringed through a pang of disappointment. It was probably better, she decided, since she preferred privacy when she delivered her apology. Gramps, Ruby, and all of the storeowners were already gathered on the porch and none of them looked happy.

"Hey, everybody, what's up?" she asked as she came up the stairs and hugged Gramps and Ruby.

"You tell us," Leo snarled.

"Yeah, you got some explaining to do, Dora Lee." Vince crossed his arms, his face scrunched like a fist.

Bitsy patted his arm and cast her disappointed looks. "Never in all my born days." She sadly shook her head.

Huh? "I don't understand."

"Me, I have tried to be pleasant and see the advantages, but this . . ." Rosa clicked her tongue against her teeth. "No. With this, I do not agree."

Their collective disapproval fogged the atmosphere.

Flummoxed, Dora stopped on the top step. What the

hell had happened in the hours that she'd been gone? She turned to the only two people who weren't glaring at her like she was a convicted criminal. "Gramps? Ruby?"

Her grandfather stood, trouble clouding his eyes. "Baby girl, we . . ." He swallowed and ran his hand back through his hair. From its mussed appearance, it wasn't the first time. "That is, some of the folks heard that . . . aw, hell." He appealed to Ruby.

The older woman's expression faltered. "Dora Lee, your grampa's trying to say that A.J. Thomas stopped by here and . . ."

"And told us that you're gonna block our view." Mack leaned against his window, arms crossed. "S'cuse me for interruptin', Ruby, but it's gotta be said and I know Willie and you don't want to." He shook his finger at Dora. "Since before you were barely out of diapers, we've sat out here every night enjoying the sunset and each other's company. It's a damned tradition. What you're planning now just ain't right."

Leo spit over the rail. "It ain't enough that you act like we're dirty — making us paint our stores and park our vehicles out of sight like they're junk. Naw, you just wanna take over everything."

"No, I don't. I'm not taking anything away, just making what's here more beautiful."

Wax statues would have been more yielding. Dora took a breath and continued. "Did A.J. explain how we're going to clear out the mess and put in new trees? We'll have smooth sand instead of all that pitted dirt and rocks. Seats to relax in. A tiki bar."

"All of which is going to block the view from the porch, baby girl."

"But everyone can come down to the cove instead."

That blew the cap off of everyone's tempers. Suddenly, they all talked at once.

"I don't even like hanging out with *your* fancy ass, what makes you think I wanna swap shit with strangers?" Leo's spider web tattoo pulsed from a throbbing vein in his head.

"We don't want to go down and mix with a bunch of strangers every night when we can sit right here with our friends," Vince agreed. "Ain't that right, Bitsy?"

They argued against the plans, railed that too many changes were coming at once and accused her of trying to drive them out. *As if!*

Gramps jumped to her defense. "My granddaughter doesn't want to make anyone leave." He glared at them all, even his oldest friend Mack.

"I swear, Willie, if you give her the go-ahead, Tilda and I are pulling out tomorrow." Leo slammed his hand on the railing. "Lease or no lease!"

That spurred the rest of them to turn on her grandfather, and that she couldn't stand. "Everybody, wait. Please. Listen to me for a minute."

She might as well have been whispering against the wind. "Mack, Bitsy, Rosa, please."

Their harangue continued as if she hadn't spoken. She felt like a firefighter battling a blaze with a water pistol. "Everyone, please listen. You have to believe me." If anything, the volume increased as they shouted her down. "Look, if you'll just hear me out. I would never . . ."

An air-compression boat horn blasted. It surprised her to silence and miraculously shut up the crowd.

"What the hell is going on?" Bobby roared.

"Thank God!" Finally, a voice of reason. One who had every right to be pissed at hell at her, but at this point, he was the only port in the storm.

He tossed the horn back in his boat and came around the trailer. "I could hear you a mile away. Everybody settle down." Sparing her a cold glance, he focused on the storeowners. "Now. One of you. Tell me what's happening."

A gaggle of voices began, but he threw up a hand and they stopped. "I said *one*." He pointed at Rosa. "You."

In her softly accented voice she explained while the rest grumbled under their breaths. Dora listened, trying to look at it from their perspective. Even so, for the life of her, she couldn't see why they were so upset over a couple of trees and a tiki hut.

They didn't want to agree to *anything* she suggested. It was that simple. She'd tried to be reasonable — case in point the painting issue — but as far as she could see, this was *not* a valid complaint. Thankfully, Bobby had a way of putting everything into clean, unemotional terms. He might be angry with her personally, but surely he knew that her intentions toward the storeowners weren't evil.

"Let me see if I have this straight." He finally concentrated on Dora, his eyes as green and hard as jade. "You decided to completely change the look and purpose of an entire area of the place for your own benefit and the hell with the rest of us."

The cold summation hurt like a punch to the stomach. "That is not my intention at all," she denied, stunned. "A.J. presented the idea. I realized how beautiful it would be for everyone, including all of you." She gestured toward the scowling group on the porch. "Unfortunately, nobody else sees it that way and apparently they aren't willing to even consider the fact that it's a great idea."

"For you and your cottages maybe," muttered Leo.

"For *everyone*," she insisted, sick to death of the tattoo king's attitude. The man obviously wasn't happy unless he was sticking ink needles into someone's skin. Well, he'd certainly gotten under hers and she'd had enough.

"Leo, I get that you don't like me and the thought of interacting with people makes your skin crawl. If you want, we'll stick a separate chair off to the side where you can glower in private." She stuck her hands on her hips and stared him down. "But just because *you* hate people doesn't mean that the plan should be scrapped."

"I don't hate people, only . . ."

"Leo, don't." Panic in her eyes, Tilda grabbed his arm and he subsided.

Good thing, too, because Gramps looked ready to clobber him. Even Ruby was worried, standing with her arms hugging Gramps's waist, gnawing on her bottom lip with fret clouding her blue eyes.

Dora studied the rest. "All of you seem to think that my ideas threaten you in some way and you're bound and determined to put up roadblocks. Are you doing so well that you don't want extra people coming around to spend money in your stores?"

"Nobody's arguing that part, Dora Lee. You wanna fancy up the cottages, more power to you," answered Mack. "Paint the stores? That's fine, too, since you gave up on those baby-room colors. But no, when it comes to blocking the view that we've been looking at all our lives, my vote is no."

Like they actually all were entitled to vote. The bottom line was that her grandfather owned this entire property so only his agreement really mattered. She turned to him. "Gramps? Is my idea so horrible that you can't agree?"

He wiped the sweat off his forehead with his arm and looked as miserable as someone undergoing surgery without anesthesia. *Please, Gramps, please. Back me on this.* She wouldn't beg him verbally, but knew from the way he flinched that he'd seen the plea on her face.

He pushed out of Ruby's hug, straightened and fixed a helpless gaze on his old friends and tenants. "Folks, maybe we're all too set in our ways. Maybe we ought to . . ."

"Hold on right there, Willie." Vince bristled and smacked his fist in his palm. "You can't tell me you like it anymore than the rest of us. You're only caving because she's your damned granddaughter."

"That's right, she's my family," Gramps shot back. "And I won't tell her no."

Like the starting gun at a race, that set off another
round of loud complaints, insults and threats of leaving.
Then Bobby's voice rose above them all. "You won't, Willie,
but I will."

Dora gaped at him.

"That's right. You tell her!" Leo pumped his fist in the air.

Bobby looked at her, the strangest expression on his face,
sort of a cross between resolution and reluctance. "You can't
do this. That's final."

Who the hell did he think he was? She scowled, eyes
narrowed while blood pounded in her temples. "I told you
before that our relationship doesn't give you a say over what
I do."

Leo crowed. "It don't matter if he's fucking you. He's
half owner of the whole damned place!"

If he'd dropped a boulder on her head it couldn't have
packed any bigger a wallop. Everything around her — the
buildings, the people, the colorful sky — receded except for
one tight sucker-punch of shock.

She shook her head to quiet the ringing echo of Leo's
words and tried to focus on Bobby. From his expression, he
wasn't pleased that this particular bomb had dropped.

"Dora Lee, I . . ."

"Save it," she sneered, mimicking his words of the previous night's fight. Suddenly, she didn't care if he was sorry
or upset or still madder than hell. He was a partner in the
marina complex and everyone else knew it. Except for her, of
course, because nobody had bothered to share that important

little tidbit.

Not even her grandfather, who came off the porch and put his hands on her shoulders. "I know this sounds bad . . ."

"*Sounds* bad, Gramps?" she croaked, pulling away. Betrayal stung like a two-ton wasp. "How could you not tell me?"

"It's not his fault." Bobby joined them. "I asked him not to."

"Like that makes it all okay." Defeated, she turned and left. She wanted to run, flee the whole ugly scene, but she held onto her pride and maintained a steady pace.

Bobby caught up to her when they were out of sight of the porch. "We need to talk."

"You've said more than enough. Later than was appropriate, but hey, I'm sure you all did what you thought was best."

She shook off the hand he placed on her arm. "Don't touch me."

"I want my say."

Her lip curled. "You already got it. The sunset viewing area is a no-go." Lifting her chin, she stared him straight on. "If you think I'll sleep with you again in hopes that you'll change your mind, you're wrong."

An angry flush spread over his tanned skin. "If you think I'd manipulate you with sex, you don't know me at all." His face tightened. "And you sure as hell don't love me. Looks like I was a fool for thinking you could." He turned on his heel and stalked off.

Her stomach heaved and she fought back a wave of nausea. "That's where you're wrong," she said, knowing he was too far away to hear. "If I didn't love you, this wouldn't hurt so much."

Head down, she hurried along the path, thoughts spinning like a cyclone in her brain. Suddenly, she couldn't wait to get to her little place. Too rushed to appreciate the new plantings with their cheerful blossoms, she jogged across the lawn into her building. Inside, she paced the small rooms, too riled to settle down.

How dare they keep his share in the marina a secret? Regardless of whether it was Bobby's idea, she couldn't understand why Gramps had gone along. Granted, it had pained him; she wasn't blind to the look on his face during that whole nasty scene. On top of that, while he'd stated that he wouldn't nix her plan, he obviously wasn't thrilled with the idea. So no matter what else happened, her sunset viewing area idea was dead in the water.

And Bobby. What was his excuse? Love and anger made horrible partners, and right now she was so steamed at him that she could power an engine. Sure, she loved him, but that didn't mean she'd let him roll right over her either. She'd given up that kind of acquiescent behavior along with her wedding ring. He'd won tonight's skirmish, but how did his status as partner affect the rest of her plans? Would she run the same risk any time she ticked him off, or proposed something that he didn't personally like?

She was half tempted to blast out of the cottage, storm over to his cruiser and demand answers. The only thing that stopped her was remembering the look on his face at the end of the argument. The angry words they'd flung like daggers had cut them both and she doubted he was in any more mood to be reasonable than she. *Settle down, Dora*, she told herself. There was more at stake than her plans for Key of Sea Cottages. Right at this moment, she wasn't sure that their fledgling relationship would survive this battle, but she knew at the core that it wouldn't stand a chance until the rest of the issues were settled.

First thing tomorrow, even if she had to flatten the tires on his vehicles to keep him from leaving, the two of them were going to have it out.

🐰 🐰 🐰

THE ONLY DIFFERENCE between a kick in the balls and a punch to the heart was location. At least if Dora Lee had racked him a good one in the groin, the hurt would have been temporary. The pain throbbing inside his chest felt like it would never end.

That he was at least half responsible for the fight sure as shit didn't help matters. Sure, she'd lit the fuse, but he'd let the whole thing explode. Beginning with the argument the evening before over her appointment with Escobar, he'd achieved the very thing he'd intended to avoid — making it look to Dora Lee like he wanted to control what she did. No wonder she'd come out swinging.

Never before had he understood how insecurity so totally screwed with behavior. As determined as he'd been to stay patient, when faced with the idea that someone else could deliver more of what Dora Lee wanted than he could, he'd freaked out and tried to force the issue of their involvement.

Bad decision. Bad timing. If he could, he'd roll back time to yesterday morning, when they'd woken up in her bed. The more time they'd spent together, the more he'd seen genuine caring grow in her eyes and her manner. She might not have been able to say the words, but he was positive she held feelings for him in her heart.

Now, he might have totally trashed that, too. The damage was done and he couldn't begin to guess if he'd pushed her too far. For all he knew, she'd think her best choice was Escobar. She'd still need Bobby and her grampa's approval before entering any partnership, and that would only make things even worse. Gawdamighty, rather than subject herself to his will and wants, she could decide to give up everything and leave.

One way or another, he had to find a way to prevent that from happening.

THE MISTY DAWN was as damp as Dora's spirits. In the long hours of night, the confidence that she worked so hard to build had wavered. Part of her wanted to barricade herself in the cottage and not see anyone, just avoid the whole mess all together. The stronger, more determined Dora knew that she had to fight for what she wanted. Holding on to that resolve, she sailed through the cottage door, hit the lawn, and shrieked.

"Ack!"

There in the middle of her beautifully landscaped new flower bed sat a land crab as big as a salad plate. The beast sat there, staring at her with its beady eyes. She stepped forward, but instead of scuttling away in fear, it rose up on its legs and advanced, clicking its claws like castanets.

Dora jumped back before it could attack and amputate one of her toes. After all her hard work, she'd be damned if she'd put up with crustacean impudence. She retreated two steps to plan strategy. Making a quick grab was out of the question. That big claw could sever her artery with a single swipe.

I need a weapon, she thought. But what? Looking around, she spotted the gardening tools from the afternoon and snatched up the rake and hoe. Duly armed, she advanced. Instead of retreating, the *Crabus humongous* raised its mammoth front claw.

En garde!

Brandishing her weapons, she aimed for a body grab, but the creature parried. She thrust again, snaring the claw and part of the massive body. "Yes!" she cried, and pulled.

The crab refused to yield. Its smaller claw squeezed a low-lying hibiscus branch like an anchor. Dora attacked again, and this time grasped the body between the rake and hoe. She tugged. It stayed put, riveted to the ground. She yanked and it hissed, threatening her with its deadly forward claw.

Heat flushed her face and she panted, exasperated, as the tug-of-war continued. The Trojans had needed less effort to haul a wooden horse filled with Greeks. Was there not one single fight she could win on this whole chain of islands?

"You're a *crab!* Give it up!"

Suddenly this was more than a battle between woman and crustacean. Left alone, this land crab would destroy her landscaping as surely as the marina storeowners were ruining her dream.

A red haze of anger infused her brain. No way would she cede her territory to a lower life form. Throwing her back into the battle, she gave a mighty wrench.

"URRRAHHHHHH!" she screamed like a warrior princess. Finally, the enemy gave way.

Triumphant, she raised her prisoner to the sky. It writhed, claws waving and clacking against the metal tools. "Take that, you destructive menace, you beast, you . . . crab."

Dora's shoulders slumped. She'd vanquished a crab. *Now what?*

CHAPTER 22

IT WAS A hollow victory at best. As accomplishments went, this ranked somewhere between pumping her own gas and rearranging her underwear drawer.

"Big damn deal." She transported her captive to the small beach and tossed it into the water. "Stay off my lawn," she warned, an empty threat. She was as powerless against the crab as she was against the marina residents. The lot of them were comrades-in-arms, united in their efforts to destroy her plans for the property.

Now what?

She entered her cottage, switched on a lamp and curled up in the new arm chair. The question applied as succinctly to the rest of her dreams. More than the sunset viewing area was a casualty in this latest skirmish. The on-going struggles jeopardized her entire lovely dream. Although she believed deep in her heart that the changes would benefit everyone in the long run, the fight had proved in stark black and white that she and the tenants would never share the same goals. If she continued, she risked destroying the relationships and ties her grandfather had built over the years.

It wasn't fair for her to bulldoze in and rip up Gramps's life. Regardless of what the others thought, she wasn't a selfish bitch who would sacrifice his happiness to achieve her own.

Anymore than she felt good about the accusations she'd leveled at Bobby. How she wished she could believe he'd put his foot down out of spite because she'd gone to see Rafe over his objections. She knew better. He was protecting the interests of his tenants.

He and Gramps were wrong to conceal their partnership. *That* she had a right to be angry about. Maybe over the years Gramps thought she didn't care about his business dealings. Dora would be the first to admit she'd taken little interest before but once she'd returned, or at the very least when she first advanced the idea of refurbishing the property, they should have come clean.

Drawing her legs up, she rested her chin on top of her knees and stared wistfully at the pretty little watercolors she'd added to the walls. Key of Sea Cottages had grown so precious to her in a relatively short amount of time. She loved the idea of revamping these old, rundown buildings into something new, beautiful, desirable.

It didn't take a therapist to recognize the correlation between her dreams for the cottages and her wish for herself. Nor did she need someone else to point out that she couldn't put her needs so high above those of others. She had a right to be happy, but not at everyone else's expense. Perhaps she should abandon her plans all together and let the marina complex continue the way it had for years.

Yes, that would be best. In her mind's eye, she watched her dreams drift away like a hot air balloon let loose from its moorings. "*Bon voyage*," she whispered. "Better luck next time."

As tempting as it was to sit and wallow, she made herself get up and put coffee on to brew. There were still things that she needed to take care of today, including mending some important fences. Regardless of what happened from here on out, family was forever, so she wanted to talk to Gramps as soon as possible. Before she braved the gauntlet of the shop keepers to seek him out, she needed a serious hit of caffeine.

Finding the right time and place to talk to Bobby was another matter. Dora flinched. In a few vicious sentences she'd belittled his love and impugned his honor. That double-shot might have destroyed things beyond her power to repair. At best, she hoped her decision to close down the cottage project would show him that she'd taken his words to heart and was sincerely sorry for her actions.

🦀 🦀 🦀

GRAMPS WASN'T AT home when Dora knocked on his trailer door and there was no sign of him yet at the repair shop. A call to Ruby's confirmed that he'd spent the night. Rather than discuss everything on the phone, he promised to meet her at her cottage for lunch.

"It's gonna be okay, baby girl," he said, his voice deep and comforting. "We'll work everything out."

"Yes, we will," she agreed without telling him yet what she'd decided. "I'll see you later."

Likewise, when she got to Bobby's cruiser his truck was gone. The flats boat and trailer were there, which meant he didn't have a charter. She scribbled a note that said, "Bobby, we need to talk. Please." She stuck it on a nail in the dock piling.

Somehow she passed the stores twice without seeing any of the tenants. Eventually, she needed to visit each of them, even Leo, and make amends. They'd all be thrilled, no doubt, that their way of life wouldn't change a bit, but they'd have to wait until after she told their landlords.

She wished she could talk it over with someone, but the one other person who knew him best was his sister. Jo Jo had called three times in the last twenty-four hours, but when her name appeared on the cell phone's caller id, Dora dodged the call.

What could she say? "Hey, old friend, I'm here to cry on your shoulder. I'm miserable because I'm in love with your brother, but I tore out his heart anyway last night." That would go over like the last flight of the Hindenburg. No, unfortunately, Jo Jo was the last person she could go to today. She'd have to avoid her awhile long . . .

Jo Jo's old convertible was parked next to Dora's Mercedes. So much for avoiding.

🌺 🌺 🌺

"YOU DON'T RETURN my phone calls, I gotta figure either your cell phone's dead or my brother's not letting you up for air." Jo Jo sat on the stoop of Dora's cottage, a teasing smile on her face and mischief alight in her eyes. "You just dragging your butt back home from his boat, or . . ."

The light died like a blown-out bulb. "What happened? Did you two fight?" She jumped to her feet. "Of course you did, or you wouldn't look like crap warmed over."

"That good?" Dora gave a small self-deprecating smile and opened her door. "Come on in, but I'm warning you that it's worse than you think."

Jo Jo swatted her playfully on the back. "Girlfriend, nothing could be better or worse than the flights of my imagination." She shook her index finger. "If that brother of mine hurt you, I'll shove him out to sea in a dinghy, steal the oars and make him paddle his way home with his hands."

Leave it to her friend to try and lighten the mood. Dora's laugh was strained at best. "When you hear what I have to say, you may want to put me in the dinghy and sink it." First, she poured them both fresh cups of coffee. Then, she poured out her heart.

Jo Jo quietly listened, but her expressive face revealed her reactions. She winced, frowned, sighed, shook her head and, finally, leveled her with a stern look. "I swear! For intelligent, supposedly mature people, the two of you screwed this up royally. All you need are matching crowns and thrones."

"I know, I know. I treated him horribly. He'll never want anything to do with me again."

Jo Jo slapped the coffee table. "Did you hear me when I said 'the *two* of you'? He's every bit as responsible for this mess. The question is, do you know how to fix it?"

"If it can be fixed." Thoroughly dejected, Dora swirled the remaining brew in her mug.

"Girlfriend, sackcloth doesn't come with a designer label."

"Huh?"

"Unpack your bags. This guilt trip's lasted long enough." Jo Jo took hold of her hands. "I expect that if we could slap it on a scale, we'd find that your hurt weighs just as heavy as his. You both made mistakes. Agreed?"

"Well, I guess . . ."

"No guessing. We're agreed. So, both of you own up to your screw ups, apologize, and make things right together. Preferably with plenty of make-up sex."

"Jo Jo!" Afraid to hope, she voiced more misgivings. "You don't get it. It isn't going to be so easy."

"Sure it will. He loves you. You love him. Right? You *do* love him, don't you?"

"Yes. Yes, I do."

"Then apologizing and forgiving are as easy as clicking your heels." She stood, bussed Dora with a smacking kiss. "I'm late for a tech review at the theater, but I expect a full report later on. Don't make me hunt you down for it, you hear?"

"I hear." Dora walked her to the door and squeezed her tight. "Thanks, sweetie. You are the absolute best!"

Jo Jo winked on her way out. "So they all say."

🦀 🦀 🦀

JO JO HAD A talent for painting rainbows on the most miserable weather days. Bolstered by her friend's visit, Dora got in her car and drove to the supermarket. She'd fix a nice lunch for Gramps to enjoy while they talked.

The route took her past Osprey Cove. At some point, she also needed to call Rafe Escobar and let him know that all proposals were off the table. He would probably make a last appeal, but if her grandfather and Bobby had turned him down before, there was no reason for them to change their minds.

The developer would have to scrap intimate luxury cottages off his plans for the entire resort, but from the little she'd learned of him, he'd take the defeat in stride and find some other solution. Despite everyone's overall suspicions of the man, that flexibility and ability to adjust were admirable qualities. Ones from which she could benefit.

That had been her downfall with the cottages — wanting her own way so much that she ignored other opinions. In doing so had she also overlooked other possibilities? She carried her groceries to her cottage, looking at all the little buildings as she passed. Even if they weren't destined to become luxury accommodations, it would be a shame to let them sit there unoccupied and useless.

"There's another connection to make a therapist proud," she said aloud as she leaned against her cottage door, looking around the property. Just because she was no longer a glossy, shiny trophy wife didn't mean that she'd lost her value as a human being. No way.

If they weren't turned into guest houses, was there another purpose they could serve? Inside, she mulled over the matter while unpacking her purchases. A fishing camp was an option, but there were plenty of Mom and Pop motels that catered to that market. Her intimate cottages had been a unique idea, which was why she'd been so confident that they'd succeed.

So, what else did the area need that it didn't have enough of? She paused in the middle of stowing cheese and bacon in the fridge and thought of Rafe's development. During the tour, there was something else he'd said he must do before he could complete his resort and open for business later in the year.

"Holy hell," she whispered, borrowing Bobby's favorite epithet as a brand new idea took shape in her brain. "This could work!" She shut the fridge and ran for paper and pen. By the time Gramps came over, she wanted to show him a plausible new solution and get his input before she presented it to anyone else.

✿ ✿ ✿

BOBBY READ DORA Lee's note again before slipping it into his pocket. *Bobby, we need to talk. Please.* He could only imagine what she planned to say. In fact, while he drove around and distracted himself with errands, he'd run through a shitload of scenarios. The best had her telling him that she loved him and hadn't meant to throw his feelings back in his face. The worst would be her meeting him at the door with her bags packed as she prepared to leave the Keys.

Whatever it took, he couldn't let that happen. Somehow, someway they could resolve their differences as long as she stayed in town. Once she left, she'd be out of his reach and out of his life for good. Overnight, he'd realized how Willie had felt during that entire cluster fuck. As much as he respected and liked the storeowners, Dora Lee had his heart. If it came down to giving her up or giving in, his choice was obvious. *No question.*

When he passed the boatyard, Willie was busy pointing out something on a boat engine to a customer, but stopped long enough to wave. Surprisingly, instead of worry and stress lines, the older man looked relaxed and happy.

Maybe not so surprising. No matter what happened, he'd expect Dora Lee to make up with her grandfather.

"Hey, Bob, you going over to see Dora Lee?" Willie called out.

"Yeah, on my way."

"Good luck!" He gestured thumb's up and went back to discussing things with his customer.

Bobby had a feeling he'd need all the luck in the world.

🐾 🐾 🐾

HE'S ANSWERED MY note was Dora's first thought when she

opened the door, followed immediately by, *He looks like hell.*

"Bobby, come in, please. Thank you for coming over." She stepped back to let him enter, although her instinct was to throw her arms around him, beg his forgiveness, and ease the tightness that etched deep furrows around his mouth.

"Yeah. You said you wanted to talk." Stiff-legged, he walked in, looking as comfortable as a shackled prisoner.

Oh, darling. Look what I've done. She bit her lip. Inside, worry mixed with hope in an uncomfortable stew. Although Gramps had embraced the new idea with full enthusiasm, she had no idea how Bobby would react.

This wasn't only about the property. That was secondary. Whether he approved or not, she could live with his decision. What she really wanted to know was if they'd done too much damage to each other, or if they had any possible chance as a couple.

Tempted to jump right in, she lost her nerve. "Would you like something to drink?"

"No, thanks."

Ouch. She drew in a deep, steadying breath. Okay, she had to make the first move. "Bobby, I . . ."

"Dora Lee, I'm sorry."

"Huh?" The last thing she'd expected was an instant apology. "But I'm the one who . . ."

Shaking his head, he talked right over her. "I should have told you right away that I was Willie's partner. I thought it would be better if you didn't know that I had any control over your plans. I didn't want to remind you of your ex." He rubbed his nose. "Maybe if I'd told you up front, we could have worked together better."

"Granted," she started, "But I never should have . . ."

"I wanted you to feel good about what you were doing and instead I went overboard and ended up making you miserable." He pulled off his cap, combed tense fingers through his wavy hair. "When you started talking to Escobar, I went kind of nuts."

The last thing she'd wanted was for him to beat himself up over a mess that she'd caused. "Hang on a second, would you let me . . ."

"I gotta get this all out now or I might never."

He twisted his cap in his hands. "I'm not convinced that your viewing area is necessary and it's got the tenants stirred up worse than wasps, but if that's what you need, I'll find a way to work it out. *We'll* figure out something to settle down Leo and the others."

Oh, my God! He'd as much as said to hell with his principles — and all for her. "Bobby, we can't. It isn't . . ."

"Don't tell me it isn't possible." His heart shone at her from his eyes, pleading. "Don't say it's too late."

"I'm not!"

As if she hadn't spoken, he sucked in a breath and continued. "I'll do whatever it takes to make you happy."

"But you . . ."

"Please, don't leave . . ."

She clapped her hand over his mouth.

"Would you please let me finish a single sentence?"

He stared, then nodded.

"Finally!" She made a big show of fake exasperation, and then softened. "I'm not going anywhere."

His gorgeous green eyes lit up and his lips moved. If she had to guess, she'd say he'd mouthed *you aren't* against her palm.

"No. I'm staying right here. The only thing that's changed is that I'm not turning the property upside down to make luxury guest cottages."

He gently pulled back her wrist. "But, that's your dream."

"*Was* my dream. You made me see that it isn't the best thing. Since this is going to be my home, I want the people around me to be happy, too. I think I've come up with an alternative."

"Escobar." He grimaced and looked away.

She guided his face back to look him in the eyes. "Yes. But not in the way that you think."

"Then what?"

"When Rafe showed me around the development, he said something that today got me thinking." She described how they could convert the cottages into affordable housing. All of the buildings still needed to be refurbished, but overall the expenses would be less because they wouldn't need to add in the pool and hot tub.

"It goes without saying, no sunset viewing area at the cove," she added. "The marina stores will still benefit from year-round residents right next door. Gramps thinks that they'll all be able to live with the idea." She scraped her teeth over her lower lip. "What do you think?

"Damn straight they'll be able to live with it. Holy hell. It's a terrific plan."

Relieved beyond measure, she hugged him tight before remembering that they'd passed only the first hurdle. Suddenly apprehensive, she pushed back. "I'm glad you approve. You're so good with all the merchants. I know that when you present the idea, they'll see the good points."

"We'll present it together. Show a unified front."

"That's good. Really good." It gave her hope to continue, but before she could, he frowned.

Uh oh. "What is it?"

"However we go about this, once the renovations are done and people move in, you're not going to have as much to do. Will that suit you?"

"Oh, yes. I have a couple of ideas about that, too. I think I'm qualified for more jobs than I gave myself credit. I'm sure nobody expected to hear me say these words, but the Keys, and this place, feel like home again."

"That will be enough?"

She laughed nervously. "Well, not exactly."

"Then what will it take?"

You, she wanted to yell. *It will take you.* She swallowed hard. If there was ever a time to go for broke, here it was. "Bobby, now that we've cleared up the matter of the property, I want to say . . ." *I was a bitch. A jerk. Impossible.* This was easier in her head, but unless he'd developed a talent for mind-reading, she needed to say the words. After a deep breath, she tried again. "I'm sorry, too."

"For?"

Great, now when she wanted him to talk, to say he forgave her, he got monosyllabic.

Somehow she had to make him understand. "I treated you ugly. Said nasty things. You didn't deserve any of it."

"It wasn't a great moment for either one of us."

"I was horrible." She raised a hand, stopping his protest. "Even if you don't want anything more to do with me, do you think you can forgive me?"

He silently studied her for so long that she feared he didn't trust the apology. "Yes, absolutely."

"Thank you," she whispered, so relieved she felt weak.

"On one condition. That you forgive me, too."

"Absolutely," she echoed.

"Good, then we're on the same page." He cocked his head to the side. "Is that it? That's what it takes for you to be happy here?"

"Almost."

He gave her a sort of aggrieved *what else* groan, and she almost laughed.

"Okay, here's the deal. I'm pretty sure I can be happy living in the Keys. I love being with Gramps and Ruby. Your sister." She paused, looking at him solemnly. "But most of all, it comes down to you. I want to be with you, Bobby."

He put his forearms on her shoulders, pulling her close while holding her gaze locked to his. "I'm never going to be a rich man, Dora Lee. What you see is what you get. You sure this is going to be enough?"

"You make me happy." She placed her hand against his chest and felt the strong, steady thud of his heartbeat. "I love you, Bobby, and if you still care about me, that's all I need."

The hug he delivered fused her to him. Delighted, she laughed until he cut off the sound with a pulse-pounding kiss. When he came up for air, he held her tight, his whisper hoarse. "I love you. Always have and now that I know you love me, too, your heart will always have a home with me. What do you say to that?"

She pulled his head down to her and answered him first with a lingering kiss. "Lucky for me that there's no place like home."

❧ ❧ ❧

SIX MONTHS LATER

The prize tarpon hung over the office door, offering visitors a gap-mouthed welcome. Centered perfectly beneath it hung a wooden sign, painted in candy-box colors with lovely gold lettering.

> *Welcome to Key of Sea Cottages*
> *Established 2005*
> *Affordable Housing in the Florida Keys*
> *Dora Lee Daulton, Manager*

The End